Log Cabin Escape

"He leadeth me beside the still waters..."

A Christian based Novel

By Arnold Kropp

This is a work of fiction. Names, characters, businesses, places, events, locales, and incidents are either the products of the author's imagination or used in a fictitious manner. Any resemblance to actual persons, living or dead, or actual events is purely coincidental.

The use of the name of Jesus and all references to God are spiritually intended.

Scripture references taken from the AKJV.

Log Cabin Escape

Author : Kropp, Arnold
ISBN : 978-1-7923-5320-8

Yes, I dedicate this to all my grandsons, the blood born, the adopted, and those inherited by marriage.

And, to those faithful ones of the novel idea and the critical link group: Mary, Renee, Rita, Mike, and Yvonne, and the others who've suggested changes, and corrected my grammatical mishaps. Thank you. Thank you.

Previous books by the author.

Montesquieu, New World Island
A Novel November 2012

Montesquieu, New World Island Sequel
A Novel December 2013

Story Time: An incredible story of faith into the unknown.
A Novel December 2014

Rummaging's
A collection of the authors' comments on the political-cultural
scene of 2005 - 2007. January 2017

School Bus Then and Now: Short history of Public Education
When did it start, how it evolved and why it was necessary.
November 2017

Just A Matter Of time: Until the End of Time.
A Novel December 2019

"Then God said, "Let the waters abound with an abundance of living creatures, and let birds fly above the earth across the face of the [6]firmament of the heavens." So God created great sea creatures and every living thing that moves, with which the waters abounded, according to their kind, and every winged bird according to its kind. And God saw that *it was* good. And God blessed them, saying, "Be fruitful and multiply, and fill the waters in the seas, and let birds multiply on the earth." **And God said, "Let the earth bring forth living creatures according to their kinds—livestock and creeping things and beasts of the earth according to their kinds." And it was so. And God made the beasts of the earth according to their kinds and the livestock according to their kinds, and everything that creeps on the ground according to its kind. And God saw that it was good."**

Genesis 1:20-25 NKJV.

"Be still, and know that I am God:" Psalms 46:10

One.

Samuel rushes up the six steps between the four columns supporting the arched entrance to the office of his architectural firm established twenty-seven years ago. His excitement radiates from the ball cap down to his freshly polished black shoes, his all and all six-foot-one-inch firm 190-pound frame. He turns the golden handle of the oak framed six-paneled door, leading him into the office lounge.

"Oh my, Mr. Guardyall!" Wanda, the secretary, excitedly exclaims, seeing him enter the first set of doors, "It's so good to see you." She trots around the desk to embrace the boss she hasn't seen in months.

He whispers in her ear, "Thank you. I'm back."

"I'm so sorry."

"Thank you," Samuel says. "You're looking good as always."

"I've been praying for you," Wanda says, then turning toward the stairs leading to the upstairs drafting room, she hollers, "Dennis, we got company!"

"How's everything. We still in business?" Samuel asks.

"Dennis has been doing great. No problem," Wanda replies.

Seeing the architectural company owner from the balcony stairs, Dennis, along with Kacky, runs down to greet him.

"Sam, welcome back," Dennis greets his boss. "Sorry about your loss."

"Thanks, Dennis," Samuel says and then shakes the hand of the young Chinese apprentice, telling him, "Kacky, you're still with us. Good."

"Yep, hanging in there. We've missed you," Kacky says. "We finished the Monarch project and submitted it for approval."

"Kacky has been great, Sam. He's done some fantastic work."

"We've tried calling you every day, Sam," Wanda says.

"Well, the condition I was in, sorry, forgive me."

Wanda briefly tells Sam of how Dennis stepped up, handled all the calls, and kept us focused on the work of completing the Monarch.

"There are some new items on the docket, too. You'll be excited when you see it." Wanda adds.

"When you got time this morning. Right up your alley, you gotta see it," Dennis says.

"Dennis, thanks for covering for me. It's been a tough two months. But I'm back and ready to get with it again. But first, I want all of us out of here for a long lunch, a big steak, and that'd be it for the day. I'm ready to celebrate my rescue. That despair is over. Thanks to each of you for covering for me. I appreciate it, and I thank you for coming. The cards and all you guys did to encourage me was over the top. Thanks. Today's a new beginning. So, we are going to celebrate. Wanda, can we do that? Can you clear the schedule for today?"

"Sure, a few calls."

"While you're at it, let everyone know I'm back."

"Come on up and look at the new one," Dennis suggests.

"I will, Dennis. But first, I've got to make some calls." Samuel pauses some, looking at his three employees who've favorably helped him develop the Guardyall Architectural Design company.

He raises his voice, "Well, what are you looking at? Why are we standing around here? Get with it!"

"The boss is back. Go!" Wanda tells them as a coach would instruct the team, waiting for instructions. "Now!"

"Yep, he's back. Kacky, we got work to do," Dennis says.

Sam heads to his main floor office. Wanda returns to her desk to make calls as Dennis and Kacky head up the stairs.

Samuel designed homes and office buildings for the architectural firm he apprenticed with after graduation. Five years later, he broke away and inaugurated his own business. Looking around for a suitable office, he liked this brownstone style, two-story, 1920-ish original residence in a suburb of Indianapolis. He refurbished the insides and installed the columns out front to segregate it from similar old buildings on the brick-paved street.

Early in life, Sam was fascinated with Greece's culture, their observations of their surroundings, and how it all worked together. Form and function of architectural design started with the Greeks.

For his new venture, he wanted to impress. He desired to make a statement, and it worked well.

Any visitor opening the door would first stop, being smitten with the theme, wondering if they'd entered a museum. There are large photos of Greek castles and coliseums throughout the room, with numerous columns surrounding the magnificent ancient edifices. Samuel installed an eighteen-inch diameter floor to ceiling column at each corner of the room. He placed paintings of Greek gods on the walls, a sculpture of two naked men wrestling in one corner of the room, and a painted picture of a coliseum seating area filled with spectators. He intermixed his various designs with those Greek paintings and photographs.

Wanda's desk is hand-crafted, oak trimmed and sculptured triangular area framed by golden columns rising to chest-height hiding the file cabinets. Sitting behind the triangular desk's point, the secretary has an open view of every square inch of the entrance hall.

In his office, Samuel makes some calls and spends most of the morning catching up on the firm's progress during his absence. An hour later, he makes it upstairs to the design room of seven large drafting tables along the walls.

"They're great," Samuel exclaims. "Dennis, you've done an excellent job. Kacky, you too. Now, let's get out of here and enjoy ourselves." The three men descend the wide oak quarter-circle staircase to the entrance hall.

"Wanda, ready? Let's close the place down and go. You all deserve it."

Comfortably seated at a round table of the local steak house, Sam initiates the conversation. "I've shared with you what my response has been over the past two months, how bitter I was, how I desired to stand before God and kick the daylights out of him for allowing such a thing to happen. I got drunk instead, drowning the sorrow.

"I got delivered from that dread forever. I will not ever allow myself to come under the influence of alcohol, not ever again. But it's not the alcohol, as it only has a physical identity. No, it's the weakness of our fleshly desires allowing ourselves to enjoy the removal of sadness with a fake joy that quickly ends, so more is needed.

"That's over. I have control, and to celebrate, I will allow myself one glass of wine as a spit in the face of its temptation. You're my guests today. We've closed the shop for this. Now, let's all show our united strength by doing just that, a literal spit in the wine. I have with me special cups, which we will each pour a bit out of our glass of wine and then literally spit into it. You can then take it home as a reminder, as I intend to do. You with me? Wanda?"

Wanda says, "I love it. Yes, let's do it."

During the dinner, they bring Samuel up to date on how the Monarch project progressed. Who did what, who suggested what, who contacted who?

"So, you don't need me, is that it?" Sam says.

Dennis shares about his year-old walking grandson. "I suggested getting him a tricycle when my daughter-in-law abruptly told me to stay out of it. "No," she said. "I'll train him my way, not yours, as you had your chance. Now it's my turn to foul things up."

Wanda shares about her Sunday school class of middle school kids, who text selfies of the changes in their bodies. She ended her dialogue: "Bible studies, hah, they think that's old-time stuff. They rode camels."

Kacky tells of his recent family reunion of sixteen adults, and numerous children gathered together at his parents' home, where speaking Chinese was the custom.

On this Thursday morning, Sam is at the site of the newest project. He meets with Jack Johnson, the building contractor, and Norman Smithan, the real estate company owner. Standing under the canopy of the trees, they discuss the plans of the new high-rise apartment-entertainment complex on this hill-side acreage on the edge of town.

"Sam, I'm sorry about your loss," Norman says. "I don't know what I would've done, probably get drunk to forget it."

"That's what I did. But I'm ready to take on the physical part of this project. It's going to draw thousands into the area."

"The city has finally agreed to let us proceed. How's everything on your end?" Norman asks.

"Great. All we need is the go-ahead," Samuel says.

"Okay, then," Norman replies. "Start bringing the equipment in for a Monday morning start. You okay with that, Jack?"

"We're ready," he answers. "Sam, can you get your portable office here before the weekend?"

"Yeah, sure."

"Good," Norman says. "Jack, if there's anything you'll need, anything, let me know."

"Thanks."

Jack excuses himself, leaving Norman and Sam standing at the edge of the woods that will soon be changed into brick and mortar. "Sam, you and I have worked closely on many projects over the years. I think I know when something isn't right with you. I sense it. You're still grieving."

"Well, yes, but I'll be fine," Sam answers.

"Dennis can handle this if you need more time. You've been through hell and came back, but you don't just carry on as if nothing happened. Take it slow and easy, one day at a time."

"Thanks, Norm. I've got to get back to the office for a bit, and then, yes, I'll make time for a ball-game."

Upon returning to the office, Wanda informs him that a special delivery folder came in for him. "It's on your desk."

Sam slides the letter opener into the manila folder, pulling out a stapled six-page legal document. He opens an enclosed envelope, scans a half-dozen pictures, and starts to read the letter. He periodically scratches his head. He reads it again and again. All he hears coming off his lips is, "Huh. What? Huh? No way."

He picks up the phone, pushes a button to call Wanda. "Please cancel the afternoon for me. No calls. Nothing."

"Are you okay?" Wanda asks.

"I'll be in the closet."

Samuel picks up the phone to dial the number at the top of each page. He carefully listens to the voice on the other end, answering his questions. He softly lays the phone down to fully comprehend the six-page document, the pictures, and the letter. Leaning back in the chair, he looks to the ceiling and starts to pray.

"Why, Lord?" He breathes deeply.

Several minutes, Samuel calls out, "Wanda!"

Wanda knocks on the office door and enters. "What's up?"

"Sit down and read this."

"Good news?" Wanda asks.

"Just read it, and then you tell me."

Sam watches the facial expressions of his long-time sixtyish secretary as she slowly reads the letter. Her emotions change from a smile to biting lips, to raised eyebrows, back to a warm smile. She looks at the pictures, periodically pausing to look at Sam.

"Now read this," Sam says, as he hands her the legal document.

She slowly reads it, page after page, coming to the part requiring signatures and legal stamp. She pauses and peers into the eyes of Samuel. "Go for it!"

"But . . ."

"No buts about it. I've worked with you for what, twenty-seven years now. So, I think I know, perhaps more about you than you do yourself. Yes, do it. Now. Start on it today, right now."

Wanda pauses again, waiting for a response as Samuel sits there in a stupor.

"At our luncheon, you told us you wanted to vacation away somewhere for a bit. To get into a different atmosphere for a week or two and let the healing process work some more. This is your answer." She pauses again, seeking some sign from her boss that he was getting the message. "Sam, just as you envision a building before you start making marks on paper, do that now with this. Lean back, look up, close your eyes, and visualize yourself there in those surroundings and how you'd handle it day by day. The pictures are beautiful. I'd jump at the chance."

"Now, get out of here." Wanda tells her boss as she gets up from the comfortable winged cushioned chair and leaves his office with one last word, "Good luck, and I'll be praying for you all the way."

Ten minutes later, Samuel exits the office, his eyes looking over the Greek decorated room, the scene he had imagined.

"Wanda, I'm on the way to see my lawyer. Thanks."

Two

"Sam, this is it, the road you're looking for," Jimmy says as he curves off the blacktop into the gravel-dirt entrance framed by tall evergreens and cedars. "Follow the road. It's down there about one-hundred yards. Beautiful setting."

"Thank you, Jimmy. I'd love to meet the rest of your family. Bring them out someday, Okay? You're sure you can't come in now?"

"No. Sorry, I've got to get to work. The sheriff has been checking on this cabin now and then, so let him know you're here whenever you get the chance. If you don't, he might send in the troops, thinking you're trespassing."

"Thanks again. Yeah, bring Susan and the kids out, possibly this weekend. They could go swimming, and we'd roast marshmallows."

"We'll talk about it, but first, you'll probably need some time to adjust. It's just like those pictures you showed me. Good luck."

Samuel shakes Jimmy's hand and opens the door to the silver pickup as King, his German Shepherd, jumps off the truck-bed. Samuel removes his suitcase, backpack, duffle bag, brown paper wrapped framed picture, and sleeping bag from the pick-up bed. He waves to Jimmy, and the truck speeds off down the road.

Admiring the entrance road's attractiveness to the new beginning of his new life, he pauses in excited anticipation and wonderment. His eyes focus on the mailbox. Some twenty feet along the road is a small boarded-up rectangular log building with a canopy extending out front. A chain connected to two posts hangs across the entrance road. He takes a deep breath. Exhales and focuses on the narrow path of two tire tracks leading into the tall trees' creating a tunneled effect.

"King, come, let's go. Lead the way."

King sees a squirrel running across the more dirt than gravel path and quickly takes off in hot pursuit running between the tree trunks and out of sight. Carrying his luggage, Samuel slowly walks while admiring the various trees. He comes to a sharp left turn and a slight decline. "Wow," he mutters. Transfixed at the scenery before him, his German Shepherd approaches with its tail wagging back and forth. The large dog comes to a stop at Sam's feet, looking up and making eye contact, his tongue dripping saliva to the dirt.

"So, the squirrel beat you, eh?"

The trail starts a slow decline, opening to a broader view, and there it is. A lake surrounded by the same dense forest and rising rolling hills with snowcapped mountains far off in the distance. The water reflects the scattered, puffed white clouds. '*He leadeth me beside the still water'* crosses his mind. He sees his new home at his left, one of those log cabins built long ago by the original settlers.

"Oh, Angelia, I wish you were here."

To his right is a half-acre chain link fenced area with remains of some corn and wheat stalks. '*Hmm? I'm going to have to grow my own.*'

Reaching the cabin, he sets the luggage down on the porch. "Buddy, let's air this place out, get some light inside," he tells King. He selects the key, unlocks the Dutch door. He pulls on the latch of the black perpendicular handle, and the two sections swing-out. Samuel steps into his new home. He stops and looks it over.

King sniffs around the room, the floor, the base of the bookcase, the couch in front of the fireplace, and the edges of many logs. He turns left toward the bed. He jumps on it, turns circles, and jumps off, his nose pointed down, smelling everything.

"King, I know where I'm sleeping, but how about you?"

He brings the luggage into the bedroom area. "Hmm?" He slides a floor-to-ceiling curtain aside. "a closet, and yes! An Inside bathroom. Oh, thank you."

King is back circling and sniffing cushions of the couch in front of the fireplace. Samuel's eyes the small single drawer pedestal desk with two hinged shelves begging him to come over and try the typewriter. He reaches over the desk and opens the window.

Looking down at the typewriter, at the keys, the handle, and the paper roller, he muses, *'Well gotta start somewhere. This has been on my mind, so here goes.'*

 He inserts a sheet into the rear of the roller, repeatedly pushing the handle to his right, soon seeing the white paper emerging in front of the roller. Looking at King and back to the Remington, Sam tells his dog, "Okay," and he starts pressing the keys.

Menoirs of Samurl Guaedyall and pushes the handle and types some more. He pauses, his head bent, looking over the roller for a concentrated glance at the few lines of type. "Oh! Yuck! Why are my fingers pressing the wrong keys?" Samuel thinks out loud, "Why are the letters N and M, or E and R next to each other? Hmm? He thinks: *Who decided which letters should go where*? *But, it's the same layout on keyboards, just on different levels*."

Leaning back, the chair's front legs rise. He yanks the sheet out, crumbles it, and throws it in a basket. *'Got time for this later. Let's look over the kitchen area.'*

There's a deep silver sink in front of a window facing the incoming road. He reaches across it, making sure his right elbow stays clear of the manually operated water pump, and opens the window. He tests the water pump, pushing down on the handle several times, and then grayish water flows into the sink. He keeps pumping, and the water slowly turns clear.

He takes a couple of steps toward the back wall and pushes aside a full length deep red draped cloth covering an opening to a square closet. Four rows of shelving on the three sides hold many plastic containers and numerous glass canned items. He picks up one at random reading, Green beans.11-5. Next to it, Olives, 6-15. From a lower shelf, Corn, 9-18. King is sniffing away, poking his nose at one of the large plastic containers on the floor.

Returning into the main area, Sam blows the dust off some of the books on the eight-foot-wide bookcase. Blowing dust and intently looking at the titles again and again, he selects one off a shelf titled, *"Quick Greek and Latin."* Next to that is; *"Aramaic, the language of Jesus."* The next one, *"How to use New Testament Greek Study Aids."* Looking at the top shelf, he steps on a stool and blows more dust, reading the first that got his attention, *"The Spirit of Laws,"* by Montesquieu. Next to it is *"Essays of Voltaire,"* and a work by Isaac Newton and Einstein. There are books by Galileo, G.K. Chesterton, Francis Bacon, and Richard Dawkins, along with a series by C.S. Lewis and Dietrich Bonhoeffer. Blowing more dust, he wonders, *"Did Grandpa read all these? How did he have the time to read this stuff,* and then he answers, *there's nothing else to do, no TV to get caught up in.*

Stepping off the stool, he looks down, noticing a stack of *"National Geographic"* magazines, *"Smithsonian,"* and some old *"Time"* magazines. On the bottom shelf, he sees a complete set of *"Encyclopedia Britannica"* along with an 8-volume set, Will Durant, *"Story of Civilization."* Sam picks up the first one and blows the dust off *"Our Oriental Heritage."*

"Gads," Sam thinks of his grandparents he never got to know and wonders why he was left out of their life.

"King, what say we go for a walk? Come on, let's get some fresh air, and let this cabin air out."

Taking a few steps to the front door, he notices the key rack to the right. He pushes the door open and steps onto the deck to admire the view of the lake. He sits in one of the rocking chairs, rocking back and forth to test it. *Oh, I'll be sitting here for hours with a book and a cup of coffee.* King is at the edge of the pier barking at something, possibly a signal to the area his ownership of the pier. Sam sees a couple of boys in a canoe with fishing poles extending off the side across the lake. King looks back at Sam, back to the boys, and barks some more. As Sam approaches the pier, he waves at the boys, but there's no response.

"King, leave them alone; let's go see what else is nearby." Turning to his left, heading along the shore and into the woods, he comes upon a four-foot-wide shallow rock-filled creek feeding the bubbly water into the lake. It has a slow bend to the right about thirty yards into the woods. Samuel reasons that this is the southern property line. Turning around, Sam walks past the pier to see just how far this twenty-acre property extends to the north. He walks and walks as King stays at his side. He comes upon a fence extending about ten feet into the lake with a sign, **Maddison National Forest**. Peering into the dense forest, Sam mutters, "Good! Just woods. No neighbors."

He turns to walk back to the open area and up to his new home. Inside, Sam retrieves a key to the barn hanging on the key rack. King rushes past Sam into the closet off the kitchen, barking and sniffing at the container on the floor.

"Hey, what is it?" Sam asks as King continues his woofs. Sam reaches down to remove the cover and finds a few cat food bags and a sack of doggie biscuits. "Uh, huh, that's it. Eh." Samuel finds a bowl and fills it with samples and holds it shoulder high to tease his pet, barking and jumping at the dish.

"Outside, we go with this." Sam sets the bowl down on the porch and heads to check out the barn. He slides the key into the padlock, pulls the latch, and pushes the door to the right as far as it goes revealing the back end of a 1950s red Ford pick-up. *"Ah-ha, my truck."* To his left are two stalls, one of them with a few hay bales in the corner. In the next stall sits a rototiller, a snowblower, rakes, and shovels. Opening the hood, he checks the oil level, the radiator, brake fluid, the belts seeing all appear to be normal. The tires look worn but usable. Sitting behind the smooth black steering wheel, he turns the key one notch and notices the gas level is three-quarters-full. He pushes the red button, and the engine purrs. *'It's been two years since grandpa's death. The sheriff has been taking care of this too?'* He goes back to the cabin and sees King curled up on a cushioned rug next to one of the rocking chairs.

"Okay, buddy, you've had your food, so now it's time for me. Stay!" He instructs the dog and heads inside. Samuel places some kindling in the stove, lights it, watching for a good-sized flame, and then sticks two small logs inside and checks that the vent is at least partially open. *'That should be enough for a pot of coffee.'* He enters the closet looking for some lunch material. He selects a can of tuna and some saltine crackers seen through a plastic container. Finding a plate, he pulls out a drawer to the left of the sink for a fork and places some tuna between crackers and nibbles away. "Lunch." He pushes the handle down several times, seeing the well water a bit grey, and then it turns to clear water. He holds his forefinger under the flow bringing his finger up to smell and lick the finger dry. *'Tastes good.'*

On one of the shelf behind the red curtain, he grabs a decorative porcelain coffee pot with some foreign words on two sides. He removes the cover, the tin basket, and stem and holds the pot under the water to clean the insides of any dust or residue accumulated over the months. He fills it to basket level and puts it on the warming stove plate. He reaches in his backpack for a can of coffee and spoons grounds into the small tin basket. He carefully inserts the stem, the basket onto the stem and places the glass bubbled lid on the pot's rim. *'Okay, I figured that out.'*

He picks up the plate, pulls the door shut, and heads to the rocking chair to enjoy the view. *'This is wonderful, but Angie, we should have been able to enjoy this together.'*

Breaking into his relaxation and daze off into the distant mountains, he hears the pot boiling. *'Time for some coffee.'*

He takes a few sips and then moves to the bookcase looking for some interesting material to read. King follows him, licking his lips as Sam recognizes the sign as wanting some water. He finds a bowl, filling it to take outside to the porch. And then back to select a book. He returns with a hard-covered book, *"New Testament Greek Study Aids."*

Three

Driving the 1950's Ford pick-up into the small town in northern Colorado, Samuel finds his way to the sheriff's office at the rear of the county courthouse on the town square. He pulls into a parking slot, removes the key, rolls his window up half-way. "This won't be long," he tells his German Shepherd.

Inside he approaches the clerk sitting at a desk behind the counter, "I am here to check with the sheriff."

"He's out right now, but how can I help?"

"My name is Samuel Guardyall. I've just moved into the cabin up the road a bit, the one my grandfather had, Joshua Guardyall."

"All right, we heard you were coming. I'm James Anderson." He stands, extending his hand over the counter. "We're glad to have someone moving into that cabin and appreciate that you took time to come down and let us know. Your grandfather and the sheriff were friends."

"Friends?"

"Sheriffs have friends. They fished and hunted together, stuff like that."

"Nice to know. Anyway, have you had any trouble watching over the cabin?"

"Nah. All of that was from the direction of your grandfather. Ah! Excuse me," the clerk announces.

"Hey, just tell him about me moving in," Samuel says.

"Samuel, hold on a minute."

James announces on the radio, "Accident on 22 at the fifteen-mile mark. Northern lane. Two trucks."

"Samuel, you need to know that the EPA has been monitoring the lake closely. There are no power boats allowed on it. A canoe or rowboat is fine, but that's it."

"Thanks. Oh, ah, where can I get a block of ice?"

"Sure, on the outskirts of town heading north, there's an ice-making plant. Samuel, I'll see that the sheriff knows you're here and settling in. If there's anything else we can do, give us a call."

"Thank you."

Outside, he notices the library across the street. *I'll get a map of the area.* Sam walks along the passenger side of his truck and strokes the head of King, whose nose is out the half-open window.

Sam opens the door to the library, stops to scan the area, and turns his personal information over to the librarian, a sweet looking lady, black ponytails down below her shoulders. Possibly in her fifty's.

Recording the information from his driver's license, she asks, "You any relationship to Joshua Guardyall?"

"Yes, he was my grandfather," Sam answers.

"Are you moving into his cabin?"

"Yes."

"I miss that old man. He read stories to the kids. Parents loved it. We all miss him."

"I'm finding out bits and pieces about him."

"Your grandfather wrote some, but I don't know if anything ever got published."

"Hmm, I didn't know that. I was thinking of doing some myself to pass the time."

"Do you have a history of writing? Hey, there's a book here you may be able to use. Follow me." She brushes his arm with her shoulder, leads him down a few aisles, picks out a book, and hands it to Sam.

He notes the title, *"Let the imagination flow."*

"Sam, it was nice to meet you, and hope to see you often. Cup of coffee? I could tell you more about the area. Oh, my name is Mary Wontomimie." She hands him the scanned book and card. "I'm available this evening."

"No, that's all, Mary, and thank you for your help."

Sam heads toward the door with the book under his arm, then remembers and returns to the desk. "I almost forgot. I came in just wanting a map of the local area. I'm out of my normal element."

"You can use one of those computers over there. Google maps will do it for you," she indicates. "Follow me."

"Mary, I can do it."

"Sure, but first, you got to log in. Come on. No problem." She grabs Sam's elbow, looks up to meet his eyes, and leads him to one of the computers. Sitting, she relates what she is doing and points to the monitor. "That's your cabin right there, so would you like a printout of what, thirty miles?"

"No, better make it twice as far."

"I'll put a note right there on top of your cabin. The roads are marked. North is at the top of the page. Good enough?" She pushes a button, and out it comes from below.

"Thank you. Just what I wanted."

"Samuel, any time. I'm off every evening if you'd want some further help. Here's my card. Oh, and there's a golf course in Johnsonville. We could play sometime."

"I sold my clubs." Looking at the card seeing her name and phone number under bold type indicating, Head Librarian. "Mary, thanks again."

"Sure, and good luck in that cabin, and ah, I don't work evenings."

He turns and slowly opens the door as a mother and little girl approach from the outside.

"Thank you," the mother tells Sam as he holds the door. He looks both ways to get his bearings as to which way is north. He pushes King off his seat, turns the key, pushes the ignition button, backs out, and heads north to find the ice plant.

Parking in front of the door indicating office. Sam carefully avoids the raised areas of the broken apart sidewalk. He pushes the door open, seeing a desk with a young man ruffling some papers.

"Can I help you?"

"Yes, I need a block of ice."

"What size do you want? Ten, twenty? Regular? Dry?"

"Hey, I'm new at this. I've got one of those old oak three-door-ice-boxes."

"That would be a twenty-pounder. Do you want to take it with you, or shall we deliver it in the morning?"

"The morning would be great."

"The truck leaves here about seven. Where to, ah, the address?"

"I've moved into the Joshua Guardyall log cabin. Do you know where that is?"

"Yeah, of course. He was one of our best customers."

How could this teen know of my grandfather since he passed on two years ago? "I'm Samuel Guardyall, his grandson."

The teenager stands and reaches to shake Sam's hand. "Norman Whitecraft. The scouts would go out there for our summer campouts. I loved to sit at the campfire and listen to him relate history to today. Wow! Mind if some of us come out sometime?"

"No, of course not. I'd enjoy the company."

"That first block of ice will be on us, Mr. Guardyall. When the driver delivers it in the morning, he can brief you on everything. My father, he's teaching school now, but he'll want to meet you."

"Thanks, Norman."

Samuel heads back into town. He spots a sign indicating a diner of some sort next to the courthouse square. He selects a parking spot. Opening the door, he scans the area, seeing the only occupants are three men sitting at the counter to his left. One of them calls out, "Joanna! You got a customer."

To his right are three empty booths next to a window view of Main Street. Sam slides into the third booth.

Her jaws are moving up and down, the middle-aged petite lady, in a white apron with the straps tied around her waist with the two side pockets bulging out, heads directly to Sam.

"Afternoon, sir. What can I get you?" Joanna asks, and the gum-chewing resumes. She hands him a single page plastic menu. "Our dinner menu is not quite ready yet, sir. We usually start serving dinner at four-thirty but look at the rest of the menu. What can I get you to drink?"

"Coffee will be fine."

"Coming right up." She leaves the booth and looking at the three guys at the counter, "You guys need refills?" One of them raises his cup toward her. She grabs the coffee pot and pours the remains into his cup. Looking back toward Sam, she raises her voice, "Sir, I've got to make a fresh pot, so it'll be a bit."

Soon approaching Sam's table, she sets the cup down along with a spoon and napkin. "Have you decided on anything?"

"The double-grilled ham and cheese, and a side of those onion rings."

"You'll love it. I've not seen you in here before. Are you just passing through?"

One of the guys at the counter announces, "She has to know everything about everybody."

She looks at the men, "Hey, Jack, shut up." Turning back to Sam, "If you're heading south, you've got a beautiful ride, but there's been a truck accident blocking part of that road out of town a bit."

"Nope, I'm moving in," Sam says.

Looking intently at him, pausing a few seconds as the gum-chewing continues, Joanna asks, "Hey, are you the guy taking over that Guardyall cabin?"

"Yep, that's me, Samuel Guardyall."

"Well, I'll be. I'm Joanna Smithbennet. I've been serving here for 15 years. Your grandparents stopped often." Joanna turns toward the counter. "Hey guys, this is Joshua Guardyall's grandson. He's taking over the cabin."

"Did everyone know my grandfather?"

"Oh yeah. He was a legend around here."

"I'm his nearest offspring, so now it's mine. I think I'm ready, but oh …"

"Wow! I'm so glad you stopped," Joanna interrupts. "After his death, they put a portrait of him in the courthouse."

The three men come over to the booth. "You don't mind if we join you, do you?"

"No, have a seat. I'm Samuel Guardyall, and yes, I'm taking over the cabin."

Two sit opposite Sam and the other pulls up a chair from a nearby table. The one sitting in the chair introduces himself. "I'm Jack, this is Mallard, as in duck, and he's Ruddy, as in muddy. We work at the mill."

Sam reaches across the table to shake hands with each of them. "Nice to meet you. Jack, Mallard, Ruddy."

Ruddy asks, "So what plans do you have for the land and cabin?"

"Haven't been here long enough even to get used to the idea."

"You don't have any plans to sell, do you?" Jack asks.

"Nope, don't think so," Sam answers.

"Good, but watch out for those EPA and Fish and Wildlife guys," Jack says. "They've been after your acreage for some time now. Your cabin sits in the middle of the national forest."

"What do they want with the cabin?" Sam questions.

"It's the clean water zealots wanting control of that lake," Mallard says. "Until a few years ago, we could put our boats in there for water skiing. They shut that down, claiming the exhaust of the boats was harming the natural fish population. A small lake."

"It didn't look small to me," Sam states.

"They also say that your waste contaminates the lake along with the water that you use will decrease the level of the lake."

"Ha." Sam chuckles at the idea. "My drinking water comes from the lake?"

"Yep, that's what they insist. Idiots, but they got the power," Jack says.

Joanna approaches the booth, "Ain't it time you guys got back to work?"

Looking at his watch, Jack replies, "I guess," and then adds, "Samuel, if you need anything, let Joanna know, and the entire town will know in a few minutes. Take care."

"Go! Do something productive for once," Joanna replies.

"Thanks, guys. And, for the heads up." Sam replies, waving goodbye to the three of them. He watches them leave the diner and board a black 4x4 truck backing into the middle of the street.

"Thank you, Joanna. This is good. Very good. Thanks."

"You're welcome, and hope you get into town often. Any other questions about us, the town, or what we do here?" She asks as an older couple enters and sits in the first booth.

The gum-chewing pauses, "Tom, Mary. Be right with you."

Sam is finishing his sandwich and nibbling on the onion rings while noticing an increase in foot and vehicle traffic outside. *Good time to head home. Home?'* He gets up, leaves a five-dollar tip on the table, and asks Joanna for the bill.

"It's on me this time, Samuel. Welcome to Prairieville."

"Thanks. I'll be back."

"Welcome to Prairieville."

He pushes the door open and looks both ways for a sign indicating a hardware store. He notices Jimmy getting out of his truck two vehicles to his right. He watches a woman in tight jeans get out of the passenger side as a young girl of about five or six jumps out of the pickup bed.

Jimmy shouts, "Sam!"

"Hi, Jimmy, good to see you again. Is this your lovely wife, and what a darling little girl," Sam says.

"Yeah, my wife, Susan, and Amy. We're going in for a bite. Would you join us?"

"Thanks, but I just finished. Nice to meet you," Samuel says. "Your husband took me out to the cabin my first day here, or else I'd never found it."

"He told me about it," Susan answers. "How's it going? Amy, say something to this nice gentleman."

Meekly, she responds with a "hi."

"Hi, Amy." Looking up to Susan, Samuel says, "Hey! Yes! Why don't you come out for a cook-out and then a campfire? Saturday? The kids could go swimming."

Susan looks at Jimmy for approval. "Saturday sounds good. What time?"

"About two or three, I guess." Sam answers. "They could go swimming or do some fishing before we eat, and Amy looks like she could probably show the boys how to put worms on the hook."

With a frown creasing her forehead, Amy says, "No way."

"You'd enjoy playing with my dog then," Sam tells Amy. "Susan, it'll be nice to have the company, so see you, Saturday. Come early afternoon, okay."

Looking down at Amy, Sam bends over to put his open hand in front of Amy. "Give me five." Amy goes to slap his palm, but Samuel moves it to the side before her hand would have met his. He puts that hand out again, and she tries again and misses. Her face lights up, tries it once more, but misses. Seeing her delighted face at the game now turning disgusted, he leaves his hand in place, and she wallops him good.

"Oww! That hurt." Sam says, shaking his hand to her delight.

"Susan, Jimmy, I'm looking forward to it. See you guys, Saturday. Bye, Amy, I'll save the worms for someone else."

Four

Returning to the cabin, Sam stores the supplies in the draped closet, under the sink, and the drawers on both sides. He looks around. *Now what?* He looks at the crammed bookcase, then at the desk in front of the window. He looks again at the desk and that Remington. He lights two oil lamps, places one behind the typewriter, another on the table next to the couch in front of the gray-stone fireplace where King is circling and sniffing the cushions.

Looking down at the keys, the handle, and the roller, he muses, *Gotta start somewhere. This has been on my mind the entire trip, so here goes.* He inserts a sheet into the rear of the roller and repeatedly pushes the handle to his left, soon seeing the white paper emerging in front of the roller. Looking at King and back to the Remington, Sam tells his dog, "Take a nap," and he starts pressing the keys.

Why am I here? A brief account.

I've never done much writing as I'm now led to do, in this cabin willed to me by my grandfather. I'm using one of those old Remington's one only sees in antique shows.

Okay, here I am using my forefingers on this old typewriter to express the thoughts coming. Yes, occasionally a key will stick, or I press the wrong key, and the reach is for the jug of white-out. There's not the automatic spell checks and grammar checks. So, to anyone who might read these entries in the future, if you discover misspellings, incorrect use of punctuation, please consider the fact that a brush of white-out is my copy editor (usually in a rush) and I am not writing this to get an A in English composition. So, here it goes.

Yes, here I am embracing it all, adjusting. All I know is that this came along at just the right time. My wife of 35 years died several months ago in an awful car wreck. I'd been dealing with that grief and sudden disruption of everything cozy and enjoyable.

We'd gone through quite a bit in our marriage; one tragedy after another it seemed, and then her sudden death capped it all. How much worse can it get, I wondered. Our only son dying. He was born with epilepsy, and the seizures periodically continued regardless of any of the medicines recommended. It was hard on Angelia having to deal with it all the time while I could escape to the office. She was extremely gallant, putting her professional life aside. We, well, she managed it in sacrificial loving care for ten years, and then one day, a seizure was massive, and he died on the way to the hospital. At first, there was quite a bit of grief, but we soon went back to our pursuit of riches.

Why me? Everyone else seemed to be so happy. Nothing like what happened to me seemed to have occurred to any of my friends. I thought I had made good choices, and then this happened. To put it bluntly, I was questioning this God thing when our son was taken from us. If God is good, loving, and all-powerful, why would he let this happen to us? He could have healed my son, but no.

Angelia accepted it as God's will for us.

She went back to being a surgical nurse, and we did well. Periodically, we took time off, enjoyed exotic vacations, and lived the American dream. We were looking forward to and planning for retirement when we would travel the world, see the sights, and enjoy those golden years. During that period, we did go to church when it was convenient, and nothing else was foremost. I gave myself high-fives after completing that obligation.

And then she was taken. What did I do wrong? I considered myself a Christian, so why me? I had several months of sheer agony over it. I drank myself to sleep to put it out of my mind.

The turmoil between then and the time when I saw the blood exploding was pure bitterness itself, a time of my emotions gone wild, my mind in neutral.

Now, I am here in this lovely cabin gifted to me by my grandfather, whom I had never met.

I'm a new man, a new creature willing and able to adjust to this rugged lifestyle, so help me, God.

Yes, Lord, I will need your help.

Sam leans back in the chair to read it. He sighs deeply as those remembrances cruise across his consciousness.

Scanning the titles of the hundreds of books in that eight-foot-wide, floor to rafters five-shelf oak bookcase, he chooses one. Since he's always been fascinated with Greek architecture, Sam selects a modern Greek language handbook. He also picks the Greek study aids book and takes them both outside to sit in the custom-made rocker under the porch canopy. He lights a lantern.

"No! King! Sit! Stay!" Rubbing the ears of his German Shepherd, he wonders why his education never included any of the classical languages, having been taught the whole word method of learning English, memorizing words. Opening the book, Sam finds a note pasted inside the cover.

Samuel, my grandson, so glad you're reading this. The study of the classical languages has improved my understanding of the English language, its words, and its meaning. But read slowly, take your time, and understand that as you learn, you will become a better communicator, a better writer, and will have a more profound and thorough knowledge of history.

"Grandpa, why were you left out of my life?" Samuel wonders out loud. He reads further.

The founders of America were mostly tutored at home or by someone knowledgeable in the classics. Children as young as eight in that eighteenth century and before were expected to learn the classics and be able to translate Greek into English and English into Greek, or Latin. The Greeks of long ago held to the theory that the purpose of education is the cultivation of wisdom and virtue, and thus to happiness.

Sam pictures kids growing up in homes like this cabin having to walk from the farm to the one-room schoolhouse. *They couldn't go to*

Barnes and Noble to buy a book, nor a library down the block, nor be able to download it to a tablet.

He reads the last of the note.

So, Samuel, my grandson, you were meant to have all of this. It's my gift to you. Slow down and do it well.

Joshua

Hmm? What happened between my father and you?

The introduction tells him Greek was the language of the New Testament. He also reads that ancient Greek is the foundation of many English words. Remembering that our founding fathers were expected to know the classical languages even before they attended college entices him to delve further into the study.

Picking up the second book chosen off the shelf, *"Greek Study Aids,"* he opens to Chapter one, *"Light from the Rubbish Heaps."* He reads and re-reads some key points. Moving on to chapter two, he reads, "To pretend that any word that has proceeded from God is not worthy of our attention is to prove without question that such a one is a fool … The responsibility of a Christian . . ."

Am I, have I been a fool? He wonders as parts of his past streak across his mind.

Ah, Sam thinks. *It'd be so much easier if I learned of these essential advantages as a child. Now at my age, it's much more difficult.*

Looking up at the ceiling, he states, "Honey, we could have studied this together."

"King, come on, it's time to hit the sack."

Saturday morning has arrived, and now the visit of Jimmy and his family is approaching. *It's time to clean up this place a bit.*

Remembering something read from an article on survival, he starts a fire in the cast iron stove. He puts a big pot of water on top to boil, ensuring him that his guests will have safe water if needed, and he'll have extra water ready for his morning coffee. The thoughts of using that water to make coffee, brushing his teeth and such from the dirty ole' lake water, drinking that fish pooh, and whatever else gets mixed in. Swimmers, deer, and other creatures are stepping into the lake with dirty muddy hoofs. All those thoughts stream across his mind. "Yuck." *How was it that my grandfather was so healthy into his 90's without filtering that water? Hmm?*

Sam is back on the porch, rocking and reading his introduction to Greek, the alphabet, and pronunciation. He briefly recalls his college days of fraternities using Greek alphabet letters, as close to the language he got. While trying to grasp the subject, his mind wanders to the newness of his surroundings. He periodically reaches down to rub the dog's ears, neck, and down his side. *Did grandfather know enough Greek to have read the original classics?*

The book is resting in Sam's lap as his mind looks upon the tranquil view of the lake surrounded by evergreens rolling up to the snow-capped mountains off in the distance. He wakes himself out of his state of numbness, thinking he'll never finish anything if he allows himself to drift away like that. Then the remembrance of the legal notes he received detailing the cabin race across his mind. *The water comes from a well ninety-five-foot' deep underground.*

"Gads! Okay, repeat after me, the water comes from a well, not the lake."

He puts the book down and goes into the cabin for a coffee refill when he hears King barking like crazy. He looks out the window above the one-piece sink seeing a black 4-door sedan with a symbol on the door and lettering below. King follows it around the circle encompassing the gazebo. It stops in front of the porch. *Ah, it looks like the sheriff* as the grey-haired uniformed man exits the vehicle.

Sam goes out to greet and welcome the sheriff.

"Hell-O," the sheriff greets. "I assume you are Samuel Guardyall. That's quite a dog."

"Yes, sir. He's my companion. King, say hi to the sheriff."

King sits, and the sheriff shakes the raised paw, "Good doggie."

"Your agent told me you'd stop by," Sam says. "Yes, I'm Samuel. Thanks for coming."

"Bruce Olsen," the sheriff replies. "I've heard of your arrival all over town, so let's get acquainted."

"Sure. Can I get you something to drink? All I got is coffee or just plain water."

"Nah, I'm fine. Thanks. So, what plans do you have for this place?"

"Sheriff, I originally thought I'd use it as a periodic escape, but that changed to just moving lock stock and barrel and make it my home. I'm slowly adjusting."

"What'd you do back home? Where was it? Indiana?"

"I was an architect in one of those suburbs of Indianapolis. Did that for twenty-seven years, and then this came up. It was a complete surprise to me. But it came at just the right time." Sam pauses and sips his coffee.

"How, what?"

"It was a few months after my wife died in a car wreck, and now being away from that home we shared, and in this setting makes it easier to deal with that grief and loneliness. I think."

"You'll have solitude here for sure."

"What a difference it's been."

"Sam, for your information, we work at being visible to the public, patrolling the highways and back roads. We even walk the streets. We try to spend the bulk of our time as that agent of peace by being visible."

"The thought of the sheriff coming to visit me, I'd wonder what I did wrong. And, ah, any troubles with rioters, or just teens out having fun damaging areas. You know, like we did as teens throwing toilet rolls over trees at Halloween?"

"No, not really. Small town and county here. Our crime rate is low. Mostly guys getting drunk, and occasional accidents. My term as sheriff will be ending soon. Retire and relax. Your grandfather and I became good friends over the years. Before he died, he asked me to look after this cabin. It's as he left it."

"Thank you. You won't get any trouble out of me. I got one question, though."

"Sure."

"I've heard that the wildlife agency or the forest service wants to take over this property. Is there anything to that?"

"Ah, you've already met Joanna and the mill workers," the sheriff replies. "As long as the property is left as it is, as it was from the time they declared it as a national forest and wildlife park, they won't touch it."

"Thanks. I can't electrify this place then, can I? Oh, one more thing. If I need to contact you or need something, how do I notify you since I don't have the power to keep a cell-phone charged?"

"Originally, your grandparents hung a red cloth off the mailbox, then the last few years when he didn't get out much, he consented to a two-way radio. It's in there somewhere. Operates on double-A batteries. Sam, I just wanted to make contact with you, so if I see you around, I'll recognize you and won't get suspicious that an outsider may be doing something he shouldn't. I must go. I just wanted to stop to say hi."

"Thanks, sheriff. Glad you did. You're welcome to come for a cook-out or fishing anytime. Okay?"

"Sure. Take care of yourself now, and good luck." The sheriff shakes Sam's hand. He takes the few steps to his van, turns around, and says, "Don't get drunk driving that pick-up, or we'll meet again."

He heads out the dirt road with King chasing the van as it goes around the corner.

Sam goes into the cabin looking in cabinet drawers, the closet, around the bookcase, and other spots he had not fully explored. He finds the radio hanging from a hook near the front door. He turns it on and checks the batteries.

Back on the porch, slowly rocking and picking up the book again, he tries to get involved in the details of Greek grammar, but still, his mind wanders. He picks up the tennis ball and throws it over the deck railing. King takes off and hurriedly brings it back for another toss. The throw, catch, and return repeats. King's tongue is hanging and drooling, and Sam throws it as hard as he can. The ball bounces out into the water. King makes a jump five-feet out, finding the ball floating in the still waters. He swims back to shore, back to Sam, and drops the ball at his feet. King shakes his body, and the water twirls out onto Sam.

"Hey, you got water on my book. Okay, King, have you had enough?" Sam tells his dog. He reaches to pick up the book sitting on the table between him and King. He begins reading. Several minutes later. *Ugg. Enough of the Greek studies today.* He puts the book back on the table. He leans his head back against a small pillow tied onto the detail carved backrest of the rocker. He breathes in deeply and closes his eyes to everything.

His mind wanders to the upcoming visit of Jimmy and his family. *Susan looked nice. What kind of a mother is she? Does she work too? They go to church? The kids, Amy looked tired, kind of shy. The boys? Good students? Into sports? Respectful? In scouting or anything like that? What am I getting into? Entertaining this family, I just met. Whatever possessed me to do this? What'll we talk about? I'm still discovering this newness. I can keep asking questions about the area, the town, the happenings around, their connections, the schools, and outside activities.*

Five

King suddenly perks up, barking, standing tall and rigid with his tail straight back, his nose pointing directly into the woods, and then off he runs full throttle. Sam barely recognizes the swiftness of two whitetail deer turning and bouncing back into the woods. "King, stop. Stop!" Sam yells as King chases the deer. "Stop." The German Shepherd keeps on going in hot pursuit. *Oh boy. His new hobby.*

Sam hears the engine of a vehicle coming down the trail closer and closer. Jimmy's truck and King running alongside soon appears in the opening and comes to a stop in front of the porch. Sam gets up from his rocker. The two boys and girl, riding in the bed of the truck, jump over the side.

Jimmy yells, "Hi, Sam, ready or not, here we are."

"Good, just in time," Sam replies. "I'm glad to see you." Looking at the kids, Sam says, "let's see, this cute one is Amy."

King trots up with tongue hanging out, tail wagging. He sniffs the young girl who backs away to use her mother as a shield. Sam turns, looking at the boys. *The oldest one must be about thirteen or fourteen and the youngest, about ten.* Sam reaches his hand out to the tallest, "Hi, I'm Sam, and you are?"

"Peter." The boy responds without shaking hands.

"I'm thrilled to meet you, Peter," as the boy turns and runs to the pier.

Sam repeats to the other boy, "And you must be...."

The kid runs to catch up with Peter, who is nearing the pier with King running alongside. Getting there first, Peter has kicked off his sandals and pushes the rowboat out into the water as the smaller boy catches up to climb in the small boat. Peter has the oars pushing against the shore, slowly moving the boat. King is on the pier barking at them.

"He's Bill." Susan answers and then hollers out at the kids, "Hey boys, be careful out there. Peter! Sorry, Sam. Manners?"

Changing the focus, she states, "Sam, we weren't sure what to bring, so we just brought it all, hot dogs, hamburgers, buns, chips, and of course, Jimmy brought a six-pack."

"Hey, that's great," Sam replies.

"Jim, get the ice chest, please," Susan says to her husband.

 "Amy, want to help daddy?" Jimmy picks it out of the truck's bed and sets it down on the porch, and Amy drops a plastic bag next to the ice chest.

"That's fine, Jimmy," Sam says. "Sit down and relax."

Amy steps close to her mother, whispering something. "Sure, go ahead, honey. But be careful." Amy runs toward the pier.

Leaning her head against the small pillow and starting the rocking motion, Susan closes her eyes, sighs, and softly says, "It's so peaceful here."

"Yes, it is," Sam replies, reclining in a lawn chair placed between the couple, each on the rocking chairs.

 Jimmy sighs, relaxing in the shaded porch out of the direct sunlight. He opens a can of beer. They quietly watch the two boys enjoying themselves in the small boat, rocking with it as the oars are pulled, moving the boat out into the lake. Back and forth, they go as King is standing on the shore watching. Amy bends over, picks up a stone and throws it a few feet into the lake, then tosses one the size of a tennis ball, and King jumps in after it.

Sam says, "Peter looks old enough to be in the scouts. I've heard they liked to camp out here."

"A couple of years ago," Jimmy says.

"Sam, you're not married, right?" Susan says.

He replies. "Nope, but in here," pointing to his heart with palm open across his chest.

Susan, watching the kids getting rambunctious, turns toward Jimmy as the beer can is about to meet his lips. He recognizes the look, "All right!" Jimmy takes a few steps toward the lake while yelling out to his sons, "Get back in here, NOW!" he yells at them. "Mommy wants you to have those life jackets. So, come back here now!"

"Ah, bull. We never get to have any fun," Peter yells back.

"Get in here now!" Jimmy yells louder, watching them in their slow obedience.

Susan tells Sam, "I'm sorry you had to see this, but they just don't know how dangerous that could be."

"Susan, they appear to be healthy, well-fed, and taken care of," Sam says.

"Thank you," as she picks a cigarette out of the pack and lights up.

"Susan, watching all this," Sam says. "Reminds me of when I was a kid about the age of Peter. What is he now, fifteen?"

"He turned fourteen a month ago," she answers as she leans her head back against the pillow for a gentle movement of the rocker while taking a drag off the cigarette. "Sam, I know they're boys having fun, but still."

"As a kid Peter's age, I'd go water skiing, and nobody back then ever thought about life jackets when skiing behind a boat. And many times, I'd fall. I'd tread water until the boat could turn around and get back to me."

"What are you saying?" Susan asks.

Not wanting to forge into disagreements, Sam stalls, "What I'm saying, Susan, is that we learned to swim without taking swim classes."

"Yeah, I know, but still…"

Samuel interrupts, "I'm sure when you were coming of age, you did some things that would now be off-limits, but you lived through it. Back then, we knew our safety and security was our responsibility, and for the most part, we were careful."

Susan replies, "Yes, I guess I did, but I'm not telling." She pauses and takes another drag. "Oh, forgive me, I didn't ask if it was okay if I smoked out here."

"Susan, that's fine."

Jimmy and the boys approach and about to step onto the porch. "Come on in and look around, see where my grandfather lived for his ninety-four years," Sam states. He opens the Dutch door for Susan to enter first. She flicks her cigarette onto the gravel driveway.

Peter and Bill head toward the fireplace, sitting down on the stuffed chairs. Peter removes a cell phone from his shirt pocket and takes a picture of the logs placed on a metal rack. He changes positions and takes a few more.

At first, Amy is quietly standing beside her mother, and then she notices the boys looking over the fireplace. She silently looks around the big stone-faced fireplace. "Does this work?" She asks.

Jimmy meanders toward the bookcase while Susan turns toward the kitchen area looking at the sink, the water pump, and the antique stove. She runs her hands over the large butcher block table and lightly touches a few of the pots and pans hanging from the ceiling rack. She notices the drapery cloth hanging on the wall. "This is a pantry? Okay, if I check?" Susan asks.

"Yes, it is. Go ahead." Sam answers.

"Your grandmother was quite a cook, I heard, but I never had the inclination to get out here for her classes," Susan says. She pushes aside the drapery to enter the closet.

Jimmy scans the titles of the books along each shelf, then down a row, briefly looking at each when he speaks up, "Peter, have a look at these books over here." Peter has his concentration on his cell phone. "Sam. You've got a collection of books here that our library wishes they had. Have you read any yet?" he asks.

"I've made a start," Sam says.

Susan exits the closet. "Wow, amazing! Sam, you could survive for months on just what's inside those jars."

"Go ahead, pick something."

"Are you sure?"

"Yes, it amazed me when I first saw it. Hey, Jimmy, why don't you and the kids go swimming? You don't mind, Susan?"

"No. Where can they change?"

"Ah, Amy could use the pantry and the boys behind the curtain there. That's my bedroom." Sam points to the eight-foot-wide drapery hung from the fireplace edge to the bookcase.

"Be careful out there," Susan instructs as they appear ready to go.

"We'll call when it's time to eat," Sam instructs them.

"Are these okay?" Susan asks, holding two jars so Sam can see the labels of sliced pickles and one of pinto beans.

"Yeah, good. Now, let's sit on the porch and watch."

She starts the slow rocking looking at them, jumping off the end of the pier, and splashing each other. "Samuel, thank you for inviting us out. I needed it."

"You needed it?" Sam asks.

"Oh, nothing. Tell me something about you, Samuel," Susan asks. "You're a mystery around town."

"This is still a mystery to me too. I was an architect. I'm trying to embrace this life here. I don't know what I expected."

"You got any kids?"

"We had one boy born with epilepsy. He had a massive fit and died twelve years ago."

"I'm so sorry."

"What's happening with you, Jimmy, and your family? How did you two meet?"

"Oh, Jimmy and I were high school sweethearts from the tenth grade. We couldn't get enough of each other; both of us were born and raised here in Prairieville and got married right after graduating.

Jimmy went to work at the mill, and I waitressed for a while until Peter was born, and later I got into secretarial work at the mill, where I've been ever since."

"This seems like a nice town."

"Yes, it is, but it's changing. Jimmy doesn't know how much longer he'll have a job as one of the superintendents. They're regulating more and more as the demand for wood is decreasing. As the secretary, I see all the documents being sent our way by the feds," Susan states, and then adds, "I'm afraid Sam. I don't see a bright future for the area."

"I sensed that something negative was going on that second day I was here. How about the kids? Are they doing okay in school?"

"Not too bad. Peter is not involved in anything, except that stupid cell phone and computer stuff. And Bill spends more time waving a pointer at the TV in one of those games he plays for hours. It drives me up the wall as Jimmy plays with him. Amy is coming along okay, but I sense that she is beginning to change from loving her dolls and dressing up as Miss America to liking jeans and tee-shirts more . . . and, competing with Bill on those games."

"What does Jimmy say about the cell phone usage and the games?"

"He thinks it's just a stage the kids are going through. Says it'll pass."

"How about church?" Sam asks. "Have you or are you active in a church?"

"Eh, we go now and then and have lunch with some friends."

"The basic question I had to answer for myself, after all I went through, was do I sincerely believe that there is a God who created this universe and us too and that the Bible is the best explanation even though I don't understand it all. You believe, don't you?" Sam asks.

"Yes, sure, and yes," She pauses, takes a deep breath. "Sam, to be honest, sometimes I wonder."

"It was the same way with me until I met the Lord. Angelia and I never discussed our faith much. Church was just something to do on

Sunday. Get dressed up, enjoy the singing, and listen to the sermons telling me how much God loves me."

Susan interrupts, "Shouldn't we begin cooking?"

"Yeah, maybe so," Sam acknowledges. "I'll start the fire."

"Show me where you keep your utensils and a pot to use," Susan says.

"Follow me," Sam answers. "It's all in these two drawers," Pointing toward one of the shelves on the wall, he tells her the plates are in there. He then pulls out a few drawers searching for the lighter fluid to help ignite the wood. "There must be a can here somewhere." He speculates out loud, and then he finds a can on a shelf below the sink.

"Sam, here, use my lighter."

Sam slowly pours the fluid over some coals flicking the lighter near a sidepiece. In a few minutes, he adds more wood as Susan brings out the pot of pinto beans. She puts it down on one side of the grill, where it's the hottest.

"Now, I'll get those dogs and burgers ready," Susan states as she heads back into the cabin.

Enjoying their choice of burger and or a hot dog, the six of them are now roasting marshmallows over a campfire in front of the gazebo, adding chocolate to the crackers. The sun slips below the horizon; the sky is mostly clear, exposing the navy-blue look into the universe, as the three-quarter moon rises. When first settling around the campfire, there was a quietness as they gazed into the flames, reaching three to four feet into the night sky. Peter has taken pictures of the fire, close-ups of the yellow heat under and between the logs. He clicks and clicks and clicks from all different angles, pausing now and then, peering into the phone's face, and then he continues taking more and more photos.

Sam starts a conversation. "I always get somewhat transfixed on this view into the heavens on a night like tonight. What's out there? And, to think, that a man, just an ordinary person like us, had been standing on the surface of that moon up there."

Jimmy responds, "We took a vacation last year to Florida and visited Cape Canaveral, where we saw the movies of that space rocket ship blowing up."

"Yeah, to see it up close like that was unforgettable," Susan says.

"Yeah, that was tragic," Sam says. And then looking at Peter, who is still doing things with that cell phone, "Peter, what'd you think?" Sam asks, desiring to get Peter involved in the conversation.

No response, as Peter is still repeatedly pushing that button when Susan speaks up, "Peter, Samuel asked you a question."

"Ah, what?"

"He asked about, remember last summer at Cape Canaveral watching the rocket blowing up."

"What about it?" Peter answers.

Jimmy tells Peter, "Samuel asked what you remember about seeing that explode. He'd appreciate an answer."

"Ah, it was like fireworks on the fourth," Peter says.

"That's a great observation, Peter. Anything else," Sam asks.

"Nobody was cheering."

"Wow, what an observation. Peter, I've noticed you've been busy taking pictures. I assume you enjoy viewing them later." Sam says while wanting to get this kid engaged.

"Yeah." Peter softly answers.

"Do you share them with anyone?"

"A few with a friend."

"What does he say about them?"

"Nothing much."

Susan interjects, "He's continually on that phone. Seems like that's all he does."

"Peter, I didn't have a computer when I was growing up. All I ever had was a thirty-five-millimeter camera. Does that phone take as good a picture as the old cameras?" Sam asks, wanting to appear ignorant about the ability of cell phones.

"Much better."

"Why is that?"

"Megapixels." Peter answers.

"Can they be printed on photo paper?"

"Easy."

"With the old cameras, we had to choose between having a slide made or printed. It took three days for processing. If you print from your phone, is the picture then deleted?"

"No, it's still there," Peter answers.

"Peter, I'd love to see some of your pictures sometime." And then, looking at Susan and Jimmy, "You could drop him off someday."

"Sure, we could do that," Susan answers while looking at Peter for his facial expression.

"Yeah, Peter, I'd love it. Perhaps you could update me," Sam says.

Peter responds, "I guess."

"Good deal, I'll be waiting. This new-fangled technology of the last few years has lost me."

"Bill, I understand you want a dog. Am I right?" Sam asks.

"Yeah, sure. Dad promised me we'd get one."

"What kind?"

"I like King," Bill answers.

Amy responds, "No, I want a small dog, one that can sit on my lap."

"Yeah, King is too big for lap sitting, but he likes to lay his head on my lap," Sam responds while reaching down to rub King's ears, looking in his eyes and giving a signal. Sitting up, King raises his front paws upon Sam's thighs and lowers his head between those paws, getting the rubdown from Sam.

Watching King, Amy responds, "He's too big."

"No, come on, invite King over. He wants to have his ears and neck rubbed."

"No, he's too big."

Bill then welcomes King next to him, leaning in closer, rubbing his ears, neck, and down his back to the tail.

A period of silence envelops them all, and then Sam adds, "I'm so glad you came out today. It's been refreshing. Jim, how's the work at the mill?"

"We're hanging in there."

"The Forest service bugging you?"

"It's the monthly and sometimes weekly visits to our sites that keep us straddling the line. And, I've heard through the grapevine that they'll be watching you closely too," Jimmy says.

"Yeah, the sheriff told me that too. What's their motive?" Sam asks. "What do they want?"

"They say that cutting down trees for our building materials is devastating the forest and animal life, driving the native animals to find other nesting spots. When they see how we leave certain trees standing as a way of preserving the animal habitat, they agree we're doing good, but then it's never enough. They'll never be satisfied."

"I've read some of the major news, making it appear that loggers don't care and are just cutting down everything leaving the land bare. I had those same thoughts back home, but now getting a firsthand look up close and hearing your side, it changes my perspective," Sam adds.

Susan joins in, "We're concerned that our livelihood here may be jeopardized, and we may have to move. The entire town would become a piece of history."

"Sorry to hear that. I'll keep this in my prayers," Sam consoles. Looking at Bill and Peter, Sam asks, "How are you guys doing in school?"

Bill responds, "I hate it. The teachers are dumb."

"Huh?" Sam is astounded by the quick remark. "What?"

"Yeah, teachers don't know nothing."

Susan gives Bill an intimidating look for making that remark.

"Oh, come on, Bill. I'm sure the teachers are doing their best," Sam replies.

Jimmy adds, "What I think he means is that the teachers ask them to write essays and then take more time telling them what's wrong."

"She asked me to write what I thought," Bill says.

"Wow, Bill. You know that you just made an adult observation. I'm impressed," Sam tells him. "Jimmy and Susan, you've got a smart kid here. Bill, what do you want to be when you grow up?"

"I don't want to be a teacher."

"You might make an excellent teacher," Sam says.

Peter looks at Sam, "He's copying some other kid. He's only in the fifth grade."

"How about you, Peter. What do you want to do?"

"I don't know," Peter softly answers.

"How about photography? Taking pictures for National Geographic going around the world shooting the scenery and wildlife."

"I don't know."

Noticing that Amy is beginning to doze off, Jimmy looks over at Susan, who recognizes the expression and nodding in agreement. Jimmy announces,

"Sam, we should go," Susan says. "It's getting late."

"Well, I thank you. I've enjoyed the fellowship. The food was great. Thanks." Sam replies and starts to spread the logs out to diminish the fire. "Peter, I'll be looking forward to seeing those pictures."

"I hope you'll enjoy your time here, but we should get home. Soon time for bed. Right, Sue?"

"Yes, we've had a good time. Thank You."

"It's been a beautiful evening, and thank you for coming. I've enjoyed it all, and Susan, thanks for the food. It's been like ages since I last had a s'more." Sam tells them.

Jimmy picks up Amy and carries her to the truck setting her down on Susan's lap.

"See you all again, and thanks for coming." Sam waves to them as they head out the rugged road to the main drive back to town, watching King race alongside. He sits on one of the rockers admiring the clear dark blue sky sparkled with thousands of stars. *Why only one moon,* he questions. *It could be bigger. Hmm?*

"Oh Lord, I ask you to bless this family in all that they do, guide them in securing their needs and direct their paths, and Lord, protect this town from the advances of the enemy. If this town depends on my decision to maintain, then yes, Lord, help me to do that, help me to want to do that. Bless them, Lord, and rejuvenate their knowledge of You, Lord. And please, bring Peter back with the pictures. Let him know I truly am interested. Thank You, Lord, for the wonderful evening."

Time to turn in. Tomorrow, I must get back to town for more supplies. No, Monday.

Six

Inside the diner Monday morning, Sam is quietly scanning one of the library books when the Sheriff walks in—seeing Sam. He approaches the booth.

"Mind if I join you?" the sheriff asks.

"Of course, have a seat."

"I'm glad I caught you here as the forest agency is in the area surveying around the town. They got the instruments busy, and I wouldn't be surprised if they gave you a visit while here."

"I'm ready. Let 'em come," Sam replies.

"Be careful, Sam," The sheriff declares.

"Good morning, sheriff," Joanna greets. "Is everybody being good today?"

"Not bad. Are you?"

"Is it the usual, or will cold eggs be good enough?" she asks as the gum-chewing stops a bit.

"The usual, thanks."

"Sam, have you been over to Johnsonville yet?" the sheriff asks. "A thirty-minute drive directly north of here."

"No, I haven't. What's there?"

"Oh, go over and eat in the new restaurant called Home Town. Great food, and I'd like to know what you think."

"Tell me more."

"But you'd better be early for dinner, say about four, as it gets crowded at quitting time. One of the specialties is liver and onions."

"Wow, how long has it been since I had liver and onions?"

Sam relates a bit of his history about when his mother cooked meals. "About once a week, she'd fix liver and onions covered with thick brown gravy. I hated it. But I had to look like I enjoyed it and had to clean my plate too, or else. That was before mom divorced dad, and she had to go to work. So, retirement is approaching?" Samuel asks.

"Yes, it is. January."

"Then what?"

"Ah, traveling, fishing, relaxing. Going down to Arizona for the winter."

Gum-chewing Joanna sets the plate of scrambled eggs sprinkled with shredded cheese, with a side of biscuits and gravy in front of the sheriff, along with refilling their coffee. "Sheriff, what are those agents doing this morning?" she asks, resting the coffee pot on the table.

"Surveying. You scared them off. They go to Johnsonville to eat."

"I don't need them, and they feel better associating with other agents. Then they can talk about us,"

"Good morning, Tom, Mary," she greets an elderly couple and then turns toward the counter.

"Sheriff, come out and catch some trout with me. I'd enjoy the company. Sunday afternoon would be fine."

"Sure."

Approaching Johnsonville's town, Sam makes mental notes of the area; the homes along the tree-lined road leading into town were neat and beautiful. He sees a sign noting the population of 30,420. Slowing down, he takes note of a small hospital on the outskirts next to an independent motel and a sign pointing toward the high school. After passing through the downtown commercial area, there is a big parking lot along the street, a tall sign street side in bold flashing lights. **"Home Town. Free Desserts."**

"Here I am," Sam declares to his pet.

Lining up with the others patiently waiting for an opening, he observes the patrons as they patiently wait while talking, and some fingering cell phones.

Samuel whispers out loud, "When was the last time I waited outside to enter a restaurant?"

A young lady standing near hears his remark. "You came at the best time as an hour from now, and this line will extend around the block. Quitting time, you know. Are you from out of town?"

"I guess you can call it that. I just moved into Prairieville."

"Well then, welcome," the lady responds. "It's a beautiful area, but wait for the snowy season. I've been here all my life. People have different reactions to this restaurant, but I love it, and the food is fantastic, like home cooking. And the desserts are fantastic. No extra charge."

Sam responds, "We're paying for it in other ways then."

"It opened about three months ago."

One at a time, the people step through the latticework entrance. Eight feet high and about three feet wide, the vines creeping up the sides and over the top to merge with those from the other side.

"You'll be next, Mr. and Mrs. Wilson," A gentleman tells the elderly couple waiting in front.

"Welcome, Mr. Guardyall. You're next."

"Thank you, but ah, what? How did you know my name?" Sam asks.

Sam hears, "June Jefferson, come on in," as she steps through the trellis.

"How did he know my name? Did he recognize me someday while I was in the diner hearing Joanna? Huh?"

Sam pauses in the open-door entrance to the restaurant, watching a waiter retrieve a menu from a printer, who then greets him, "good afternoon Mr. Guardyall. Here's your menu."

"Hey," the lady asks. "Are you related to Joshua Guardyall?"

Sam looks at her, still pondering the information these people have. "Yes, I'm his grandson."

"Well, I'll be. I assume you're alone. My partner called and said she couldn't make it, so will you join me? I hate eating alone. My name is June Jefferson. I knew your grandfather."

Sam hesitates, as he wanted to relax and quietly enjoy the food, "Well, ah, sure, Ms. Jefferson, why not. I'm Samuel. I just moved into that cabin of his."

"Oh, this is unbelievable," June declares, and then tells the waiter that the two of them will be sitting together. "Wow, I'll be having dinner with the grandson of Joshua," she exclaims softly.

The waiter leads them to a booth on the rear wall placing their specific menu on the table. "Your waitress today is Andrea, and she'll be here shortly."

Sam looks down at his menu seeing his picture at the top of the page, his name, and hometown in Indiana below his photo.

"Mr. Guardyall, mind if I call you Samuel?" June asks.

"Yeah, sure," Sam agrees.

 He settles into the cushioned seat and back support, looking directly into the eyes of this stranger sitting opposite him. *Is this one of those acts of God bringing this woman suddenly into my life, in a restaurant in a strange town the sheriff told me to try. And He picked this day and this stranger, who said her friend couldn't make it at the last minute?*

Sam then asks, "how do they know all this personal stuff about me?"

"On the back page of the menu are the explanations," June answers.

"I don't believe this!" Sam tells June.' He looks around the restaurant for a clue as to how the rest of the customers receive the information. Looking at June, "this menu has my picture, name, and hometown. How did they get that? Don't you wonder why and how?"

"No, I guess I haven't given it a thought. It's just the way things are. What's the big deal, Sam? Read the explanation."

"I don't care." *Why does the sheriff recommend this place?* Sam wonders, as he looks at the others, acting as if in a typical restaurant. "I'm not sure I like this," he tells June. *No, I don't like it. And why would the sheriff recommend it? He must know and agree that this breaches the privacy issue. The sheriff of all people! God, why am I here?*

"At least read the explanation first," June responds.

"But," Sam responds. "what's happened to privacy?"

"You're here, Samuel. And look at the line of people. That says something about the food. This is amazing. I'm sitting across the table with Joshua's grandson. When did you move in?"

"A couple of weeks, now. The sheriff recommended this restaurant, and that's how I found out about it. So, I decided to give it a go, and here I am." His mind is running over the thoughts of this unexpected happening. *Was the sheriff pulling my leg? Did he want me to see for myself how far this thingy of individual privacy is like a kid kicks a can down the block to see where it ends up going?*

"Welcome, Mr. Guardyall and Ms. Jefferson, my name is Andrea, and I'll be serving you today." She carefully places covered glasses of ice water along with a wrapped straw in front of them. "We're pleased you joined us today. Can I get your drink first?"

Andrea's hair is tucked in a net, her hands in white plastic gloves. She's wearing a beautifully decorated apron hung around her neck with two straps tied around her waist, covering her from just below the neckline down to her knees. There's a blue cloth tied behind her head that covers her mouth and nose. The apron exhibits a peaceful scene of a lake in front of forested mountains with clear blue skies, sparkled with pure white clouds strategically placed between peaks.

"Coffee," Sam says.

"Hot tea for me," June orders.

Before she got a chance to turn away, Sam asks Andrea, "I'm a bit perplexed at the technology employed here. You've got my name, my picture, my hometown. How? And yes, Why? Why?"

"Mr. Guardyall, the explanations are pointed out on the back of the menu. Take some time to digest it all. Then if you have any further questions, I'll be glad to answer when I bring your drinks back. Okay?" She turns to walk away from the booth.

Sam briefly spans the menu seeing a listing of all the ingredients, the calories, and carbohydrates below each item, and then on the back of the menu, he slowly reads.

Public Announcement.

This restaurant has been chosen by the Department of Health and Human Services in conjunction with the Center for Disease Control and Prevention to participate in a public health sampling initiative to meet the needs of public safety and health concerns about America's restaurants. For certain agreed-upon conditions, additional health safety procedures have been instituted for citizen safety, well-being, and trust. You have been provided a specially printed and personal menu with items recommended for your own nutritional needs based on your personal index, age included.

You will note that our waiters are all wearing plastic gloves, hairnets, face masks, and select clothing to protect everyone from possible germs; those unseen microbes being transmitted from either direction, a simple human mistake, or intentional. You will also note that each meal will be covered when brought to the table. Again, to protect diseases from being spread through the air to your food as it's being transported to you.

You will also note the caloric notations, the specific ingredients below each menu item. That's for your nutritious information. You'll now have the necessary information to make the correct informed decision from your own printed menu of recommended items selected for you by experienced and knowledgeable health experts.

Behind the scenes, you can be assured that every health safety procedure, as proscribed by HHS and CDCP, has been implemented and is carefully scrutinized.

Thank you for coming, and we hope your visit will be satisfactory.

"I don't know what to make of this June. In one way, it's amazing, and then it reminds me of some of what's being said about the new world order. I had no idea anything like this was being done anywhere, especially out here. You say it's been open for three months."

"Yep. This restaurant has been a staple of the town for about 30 years, but four months ago, it closed for a few weeks making these changes, and actually, the business has increased dramatically since then."

"But, June, how did they get our personal information?"

"In the trellis, there's a camera, and when you walk through, you step on a scale."

"A camera and scales? Gads, now I got it. Oh, boy."

"What?"

"Through that computer, the picture links to my driver's license retrieving my personal information. Wow, we're on the verge of tomorrow land," Sam tells her.

"I like it, as I can compare today with the last time. It's like a history of my eating and how it affects me."

Pausing a bit, she then adds, "Sam, I want to get something straight right from the start, okay. I'm involved with another teacher, my partner that couldn't make it, so let's leave it at that, enjoy the company rather than trying to look as if we enjoy eating alone. Agreed?"

"The same thoughts came to me, June. I lost my wife Angelia not long ago, and the fact that my grandfather died and left his cabin to me came at this time may help me to get over that grief."

Sam then reaches across the table with an open palm, "Agree?" June shakes his hand. "Agreed."

"Let me tell you something about me," June says. "I was married for two years and then discovered he had been cheating on me. A jerk. A real jack—a Jack of all trades. I divorced him right away and now intend on staying that way, loose and fancy-free in love with my partner, which is suiting me just fine."

"Ah, June, there are still millions of men out there, and you're quite attractive. Don't give up. One of them will come along."

"Nope, I've lost that dream. It's gone. All they want is your body. So now I'm living with this other teacher. I'm a high school teacher of Geography and coach of the girl's golf team."

"A teacher, huh," Sam politely answers. He decides to tread lightly. Glancing at the choices offered in the menu, he impatiently responds, "I don't. . .. oops, there it is, Liver and Onions. Ah, do you recommend that? Have you had it?"

"No way," she responds.

"Ah, come on, the sheriff recommended it to me."

"No, not for me. Meatballs and spaghetti." She emphatically states as the waitress approaches the booth.

Andrea sets the coffee and tea on the table, each one wrapped in plastic, "What will it be?"

"I got a question first," Sam asks.

"Shoot."

"Okay, I've read the back page, but could you expand on it."

"Sure. I'll give you the quickie version. A year ago, the Department of Health and Human Services came to the owners asking if they'd like to participate in a new survey. It's a new study for food safety at privately owned restaurants in smaller communities. Several months later, the owners contracted with them, and here we are wearing gloves, hairnets, and this mouth and nose cover, which I've got to continually replace with a new set for each table and trip I make. We think it's a bit overboard, but It's one of their safety regulations. Ah, Can I have your orders?"

"All my personal information. Where does all this data go?"

"Go? What do you mean— where does it go?" She questions.

"Yes, is all this information then sent to the government?"

"I don't know. So?" Andrea answers. "Mr. Guardyall, have you decided what you want?"

"Sure, I'll take the liver and onions. Can you add some mushrooms?"

"Sure. Ms. Jefferson? What it'll be for you?"

June requests the smaller version of the meatloaf with spaghetti plus a small salad with ranch dressing. "Andrea, you were one of my students in geography a few years ago. If I remember right, you did well in the class. Have you considered college?"

"I thought I recognized you too. No college for me. I've got to help mom," Andrea answers while entering the selections into her tablet. She then leaves the booth.

Sam leans back, taking a sip of coffee while looking around the dining area seeing everyone relaxed and enjoying themselves as they would in any restaurant. He sips the coffee again.

"So, Sam, tell me something about yourself. How was your relationship with your grandfather, and did you ever get up here for a visit?"

Sam is still wondering, neglecting the question of June, so she asks again, "Sam, did you ever get up here to visit your grandfather?"

"Huh." Sam replies as the question asked the second time, wakes him back to the present, "Did I ever visit my grandfather here?"

"Yeah, Sam. Surely you did, right?"

"No, never got to. When I was dropped off at the entrance, that was the first time I set foot on the property. I learned that my dad had it out with his dad and left at sixteen and never returned. He later married mom, and a few years later, became an alcoholic. Mom left him, and I was raised mostly by her."

"Oh, I'm sorry."

"No, wait. I think mom did bring me out here once. I vaguely saw myself sitting on the porch and seeing a deer; I think it was. It's just one of those memories that we put away somewhere."

"What are your plans for the cabin?" June asks just as Andrea approaches the table, her right elbow extended out, the forearm and hand under the circular tray balanced at shoulder height. She slowly lowers the tray to the table. She sets the plastic-covered plates down in front of each of them and removes the hardcovers.

"Wow, now that's a plate of liver and onions," Sam tells the waitress, and glancing at June's plate, he says, "Your meatloaf and spaghetti looks terrific."

"I'll be right back to refill your coffee. Enjoy your dinner."

Sam stretches both arms out across the table, reaching for the hands of June, asking, "June, do you mind if I say grace over this food and our discussions?"

June timidly replies, "Ah."

His fingers firmly hold her hands, sensing at first a rigid-ness in her fingers, which she loses as his grip is relaxed. "Father God, I thank you for your blessings this day and now for this food. I thank you for this opportunity for my protection in this new adventure and now for this new acquaintance. Father, I ask for your grace and mercy to be upon June in all she does and lead each of us and everyone here into a life filled with righteousness. Thank You. Now, we accept this food as blessed for our physical health in that wonderful name of Jesus. Amen"

"Dig in," Sam states as he picks up the knife and fork, cutting a piece of the liver. Taking a bite of the dark brown medium-cut liver covered with gobs of fried onions, mushrooms, and gravy, Sam exclaims, "Wow, this is good."

"Now, June, it's your turn. Tell me more about yourself and your teaching experiences. I'm afraid I'm out of touch with teens. They seem to be lost in another world as technology takes over. How are your classes going?"

"Geography is one of those required classes for graduation, so it's a real challenge to keep them interested. They are there because they must be. They know they have geographic information available anytime through the web, so why go over it in class. It's become teach to the national testing program. It's frustrating. I wish the subject was not required, and I had a few students who wanted the knowledge. Then we could dig into things."

"So, how's the meatloaf?"

"Unbelievable. It's the kind my grandmother used to make."

She reaches into her purse, retrieving her cell phone. "Excuse me, Sam, It's my partner. She turns away from looking at Sam and says, "Yeah, I'm inside, and guess what. I'm sitting with Samuel Guardyall, the grandson of Joshua. We met outside while waiting." Another pause and June finalize the call speaking to the piece of plastic, "Honey, I'll be home in about an hour or so, and then we can watch a movie. See you then." She pushes a button placing the phone back in her purse, and again apologizes for the interruption.

"Moving out here, I can't have a phone." Then changing the subject, Sam adds, "This is undoubtedly the best liver and onions I've ever had. The liver is thicker too."

Samuel then says, "I've read some of the new educational standards, but hey, not that long-ago geography was memorizing where certain countries were on this earth, how rivers irrigated the lands along with mountains, deserts, and oceans keeping us apart. We had to memorize that, while now it's there on every cell phone."

June interjects, "Teaching is not as enjoyable as it used to be just a few years ago. Hopefully, this new school year may be better with the new principal, but I've already seen some additional paperwork. As the country grows, it's more necessary, I guess."

Sam adds, "it's going that way. Away from the old days."

"My biggest thrill has been coaching the girls' golf team, which has won the last two state championships. Two of those girls are very good and could end up on the pro circuit if they put their minds to it. A few colleges have already contacted them."

"That's fantastic. I used to play a lot of golf. A few years ago, it was two to three times a week. Is there a good course here in town?"

"The public course is okay. Samuel, tell me more about your plans. Your grandfather was a blessing to me as he was the one who got me interested in teaching. Sitting on the floor, listening to his storytelling while in the second and third grade excited me. Even in eighth grade, I loved going to hear him. When he read Nancy Drew, it was like I was there."

"He got you interested in teaching?"

"Yes, he did. Often, he would interrupt his reading and make comments. He'd ask us questions about the mystery, about the events in the story, and somehow, later on, in the eighth grade, I began to see that a teacher could do the same by suggesting and asking questions to get the students thinking on their own. I could see it wasn't just passing on knowledge but helping them develop thinking and reasoning skills. I had a teacher somewhat like that in high school, a civics class, Mr. Whitecraft. After that, I never wondered what I'd do with my life."

June further explains her early interest in golf and how she used those experiences to get the college scholarship.

"How about church? June, do you ever read the Bible?" Sam asks.

"Nope, that's not for me."

"Why not?"

"Ah, that's, well, I just don't."

"Not for you? Hmm, I never did see your name, or anyone else's name in the forward or introduction to the Bible saying, June Jefferson, this is not for you, you're exempt."

Sam adds, "Yeah, I never did much thinking about things either. But since I got healed and set free." Pausing a bit, Sam continues, "I think you might get a kick out of it. Can you imagine sitting around a campfire and having a chat with some of those biblical characters, Moses, Noah, or even Peter or John the Baptist? What was their daily life like? Finding food to eat. Living in a tent in the desert. Did they have sleeping bags? Any entertainment? And how did they learn to read and write? There's so much in there, and it's fascinating to me."

"Hmm. I never thought about it like that."

"June, there was a time when I never thought about it either. After my son died, I reasoned how a just and loving God let this happen, but no answers came. I gave up on it. Then my wife was taken away from me. That was it for me, until…"

Andrea comes by still wearing that protective clothing, asking if he wants a refill of the coffee or the tea, handing them each a bill. "Mr.

Guardyall, Ms. Peterson," pointing to the envelope placed in front of each. "Please complete the survey and send it back, and now the owners are offering you your choice of desserts. I could get one for you now, or you can take it home. You'll find the display case on your way out. You can pick anything. it's been a pleasure to serve you." Andrea removes her plastic gloves imprinted with the restaurant's name and places them on the table next to the envelopes.

"Sam, I've got to go. I've enjoyed meeting you, and I hope you enjoy that cabin life, but I must go. Here, let me pay for mine."

"It's on me, June, and thanks for inviting me. It was nice to have your company."

He is quietly looking around for a last look at the pleasurable time everyone is having. His credit card is swiped at the front desk and told again, "thank you for coming. Now choose a desert."

June reaches in the open refrigerated case picking a slice of coconut cream pie.

"Sam, pick something."

"No, thanks," as he walks past the case. A waiter thanks them for coming and reminds them to complete the survey and send it back in the postage-paid envelope.

"June, thanks for introducing yourself. God bless your classes, and perhaps we'll meet again sometime. Of course, you're welcome to visit me too. Just show up."

"Goodbye, Sam, I enjoyed it," as she opens the door to her car, slides into the seat. Looking back at Sam, she nods her head. "Thanks."

"God's blessings on you and the kids you teach. Our creator is always there. Another time then. See yah."

Back in the cabin, Sam unpacks the supplies, the long matches for lighting the fireplace, the notebook and pencils, a pack of typing paper, a flashlight and batteries, and is now relaxing on the porch with a fresh cup of coffee reminiscing the dinner with June. He opens the survey reading the questions with boxes to check. Enjoyed it very much, not so much, not at all. The food was excellent, average, disappointed. The service was quick and efficient, yes or no. On and on questions are asked, two pages of them. At the bottom of the page, he notices a seven-digit number.

"Nope," He surmises, *"that number is mine alone, and I will not send it back to some PO Box in Kansas City."*

Seven

Sam fixes himself a bowl of oatmeal, some raisins scattered on top and drenched in milk, along with a pot of coffee. He lets King out for his morning needs. King returns and is peacefully lying next to the desk. Periodically his head is raised, hearing some of the woodsy forest life. Sometimes it's enough to cause him to stand with two paws on the windowsill to peer outside and then to nudge Sam with that big nose to open the door.

Sitting at the desk, Samuel slowly and carefully uses his two forefingers to push the old typewriter's keys.

I'm going to label these ramblings as "My Cabin Life." This is the first of ... well ... whatever comes next.

My Cabin Life 1

I, Samuel F. Guardyall, sitting in this log cabin willed to me by my late Grandfather Joshua Guardyall, write this as best I perceive. Describing my life unfolding, hopefully, to bring light into my periods of darkness. I've discovered that putting my thoughts on paper is challenging to find the right expression to state the desires of, the needs of, and the state of my inner heart and soul. The keys I press on this typewriter forming words are permanently there in black on white, whereas when alone speaking, the words go into the air, never to be heard again. I can claim I never said that unless those spoken thoughts entered the ears of another.

In front of me and through this double window, I see the boundless beauty of nature, a clear water lakeside vista surrounded by a national park rising to snowcapped mountains, visible as the clouds pass. The forest surrounds me. The quietness engulfs me as only distant sounds of wild animals periodically break the stillness.

Yes, today is one of those days, no wind rustling the treetops, barely a ripple on the waters, a clear blue sky, the sun shining its brilliance, warming my soul. It's a day when I could choose to sit still, lean back, and rest in the thoughts that the Creator may want to get into my mind and into the depths of my soul.

Angelia and I were able to vacation away from the hustle and bustle of modern-day life to a remote camping site for just a few days a year. Those times of putting aside the highway traffic for a time of quiet, restful relaxation among the wonders of nature energized us. We did not recognize why we had this yearly desire to get away, of being drawn closer to the awesome majesties of this earth. To us, it was just a vacation. We did not connect that innate need to be still and know.

My grandparents lived that every day, every year, for their entire life. What a blessing! And now, here I am trying to adapt. Working on adapting to life in a cabin built hundreds of years ago: no electricity, none whatsoever, no light bulbs, no microwaves, no automatic thermostats changing from cold to warm, no computer, cell phone, and not even a telephone wire connecting me with the world. The cold water comes from a hundred feet below the grass. Pieces of wood must be set on fire for cooking, for warmth at night, and oil must be burned in a lamp to read by or find the way. And some of those bountiful trees must be sacrificed for my comfort.

At times, I've wanted to scrub it all and return to what I know, but I've made a vow that somehow, by the grace of God, I will do it. My grandparents did it as their parents did. As millions of our ancestors did before the age of industrialization produced those modern inventions of the simple light bulb, a means of talking through a wire, and other cables sending power to our homes from falling waters. The automobile replaced the horse and buggy, and flying machines imitate gliding eagles.

Returning to those olden days is not easy, as this nature of mine wants it all. My grandfather must have had a will of granite resisting the urge to electrify this cabin. Sometime in the past, he did add a space for the restroom with a sink, a commode, and a base for bathing, along with the closet for the storage of canned items.

This cabin, now surrounded by a designated federal forest, operated and maintained by the government, insists that this cabin must be left as it is. It was here first, and grandpa could have electrified it before, but now it's a demand, or else it will be apprehended. They now have the right since the surrounding land was declared a national namesake, and everything had to be left as it was.

I was told they'd use the cabin as a museum. My grandfather said no. They will not take away this homestead where he was born. It was here first. It's been in the family since my great grandfather built it in the 1800s.

Yes, my grandparents had wills of granite, enabling them to continue this life of survival of the fittest while watching the world embrace the conveniences of technology. Has he left notes for me in that footlocker in front of the bed? Where is the key to that footlocker? I must find it. Surely, he would not have buried it or thrown it away knowing that sooner or later, my curiosity would take over, and I'd break the lock damaging that precious antique. Or, have the trustees stored it away, forgetting to forward it to me?

Regardless of those desires to forgo this harder life, I again vow to my Lord that I will adjust and accept this fate granted to me. Do or die, I will make it.

There, I wrote it down in black on white for me to remember. These pages will not be set aflame.

That's it. No more, it's over, and I will not desire a microwave. Amen.

He sits back, reading the pages mumbling, "I'll keep it." And then the thought comes *I should put the layout of this cabin on paper. Yes. Do it. But I can't. No drafting tools.*

A half-hour later, he slides the completed sketch into the drawer. He leans back in the chair to peer out the window. His thoughts go to wondering how much time it took for the founders of America to write that declaration to send to England using a quill that required dips in ink. No typewriters, no keyboards.

Sam takes another sip of coffee while gazing out the window for another peaceful scene. He pulls the last sheet out and places it in a new folder he labels "My Cabin Life."

"Well, okay, here goes." Sam moves the typewriter to one side, places a blank paper on the desk, and starts drawing, periodically looking at a section of the cabin and stepping off the distance between points.

"King, yeah, let's go." Sam fills the cup. He relaxes on the porch a bit and then heads to the pier. He slowly walks out to the end while peering into the still waters. Small crappies break the surface, a frog near the shore, and a lone eagle circling the lake– as the only signs of life. He turns to take the narrow trail into the western woods to the end of his property, meeting the chain link fence. A sign lets him know the government forest starts here. The fence stops after ten paces, and from then on, just a post every so often with a red ribbon marking the forbidden territory. Leading the way, King periodically looks back at his master, stops, waiting for Sam to catch up, then off again, as if was King was saying, *Why is it taking you so long?*

Deeper in the woods, they go on the narrow path that previous walks kept the brush beat down and dead, possibly formed by his grandfather or even before. Scattered at the trees' base are numerous undisturbed tree limbs, new trees emerging, tall weeds, which King quickly jumps over on his many side excursions after a rabbit, a squirrel, or a whitetail deer. The path is wide enough for the two of them to walk together, but King leads. They continue along the curvy path, finally reaching a spot where he can see the road leading into town. They continue, but far enough into the woods that anybody, as they sped down the highway, would not see them walking amidst the trees.

Soon they are in the open spaces of his entrance leading back to the cabin. Finding the mailbox empty, Sam signals King to head to the cabin.

Sam sits in a rocker, leans back, takes a deep breath, gives thanks, and reaches to take a sip of the chilled coffee. The past week, Sam and the dog adapting to the solitude, the howl of a wolf at night, the sounds of owls, birds chirping, the annoying crickets or cicadas, and the sound of keys hitting the paper-covered roller.

"Why did Angelia have to go at that time? It'd be much easier if she was here for loving company and to share it all with."

Sam starts writing.

Angelia, this is for you.

Yes, I am slowly adjusting to this new lifestyle, loving it in a sense. Yet at times, I want to return to what I've done all my life, in and adapted to the world, living within the community, whereas now I'm outside the community and not a part of it.

Does that make sense?

My dear, we could have done this together a long time ago, and how blessed it would have been. Adam was alone at first, even though he had lots of company with the animals. He did not know loneliness as he had never seen another human before. Adam woke up one-day feeling fingers on his wrist and thought, "wo-man, what have I here?" Adam was gifted with a companion.

My life has been the reverse, having a companion, and then suddenly she is gone leaving me with the world of animals.

So, my dear Angelia, loneliness is part of the learning as the days pass.

Sam removes the paper and files it.

Putting together a quick sandwich, Sam takes to the porch to enjoy the beautiful sunny mid-seventies with his book of Greek. Opening to the book-marked page, he reviews the basics of the Greek alphabet. He finds himself more interested in the history of the Greek language, that goes back to possibly a thousand years BC. He reads, 'Your English language evolved from Europe finding its home in Britain less than a thousand years ago, a two-thousand-year difference."

His thoughts again go imaginative, and he inserts a fresh sheet of paper into the Remington.

My Cabin Life 2.

These are part of my rambling thoughts this day.

The Bible tells us that God confounded the universal language of the descendants of Noah at the tower of Babel and the peoples were dispersed across the globe. Were they divinely transported to the different continents across this earth? Hmm? God opened Adam's skin, removing a rib while he slept, so the Almighty could have moved the people without them feeling a thing. Instead of being in the Middle East, imagine that some families woke up in North Dakota, New Zealand, South Africa, China, Brazil, or Finland.

"Burr, it's cold here. Where are we?" Did they even know they were speaking differently than before and had to learn new means of communicating? Or were they able to talk with each other that first-day using different sounds for words? And now the world has thousands of different languages and dialects.

During this dispersion, was it the Great I Am that also changed some of their physical features, shades of skin, eyes, and hair? Now we have easily evident physical appearances that we use designating our different races. Or, was it the wonders of nature over the thousands of years that changed their physical features as they adapted to the new surroundings? What the scientists call evolution.

There is only one human race, not dozens, all of us descendants of Adam through Noah. But because we gravitated to disobedience, we've been dispersed into various shades of that one beginning. Shouldn't our physical differences be a sign to us, a reminder of that first disobedience? No, we don't think about it like that, do we? No, our thinking dominates toward the present circumstances. We don't call dark-skinned horses blacks; no, they're horses. They are one and all the same. It's that invisible enemy with continual suggestions dividing us.

Another point we don't think about was the age of those early humans. Adam is said to have lived 930 years, Methuselah for 969 years, and Noah 950. Wow! Did their hair turn grey at sixty years, or after their six-hundredth? Were they still producing children in their seven-hundredth year? Then after the tower fiasco, this physical life of humankind decreased dramatically and has been ever since.

Adam, you bum.

Sam returns to the porch, still pondering the historical differences humanity has gone through when suddenly King, knocking Sam out of his musings, runs toward the entrance road. His eyes focus on King, and then he sees Peter peddling his bicycle around the bend into plain view with King jumping alongside.

Laying his book down on the table, Sam steps to the edge of the porch watching Peter and King approach.

"Peter! Welcome! It's good to see you. Did you ride that bike from home?"

"No, dad, let me out at the entrance. He had something else to do."

"Mom coming?"

"Nope."

"It's just you and me then. Oh boy, you're in for it, buddy. Did you bring some pictures?"

"You wanted to see them."

"Yes, I did, and do. Come on up, sit in the rocker, lean back and rest."

Peter reaches down to rub the ears and down the neck of King, back and forth again and again, "How old is King?" He asks.

"Three years now. Can I get you something to drink? All I got is milk, tea, or coffee, or just plain ole well water."

Peter sets his backpack down next to the rocker to reach inside. "I got a Pcpsi."

Sam rocks while Peter fumbles around inside the camouflaged backpack looking as if it's packed full, the side pockets bulging out to capacity. "How much does that weigh?"

"Oh, I don't know." What looks like a scrapbook is pulled out of the sack and handed to Sam. "Here."

"Thanks, Peter."

Quietly looking at the first page of four-by-six pictures, Sam turns the page viewing each, turns the page again, and again coming to one enlarged to eight–by–ten. He turns the page to scan the photos, turns to the next, looking at each picture, without saying a word. A pleasant smile brings a smile to Peter. Sam chuckles, looking at one page, then turns to another. Having looked at each page, Sam turns back and starts over at the front. No comments are below any of the pictures, no dates except where the date and time were part of the photograph itself.

"These were all done with that cell phone of yours?" Sam asks.

"Yeah."

"They're amazingly clear, focused, and bright. How does it do that? But Peter, what I'm more impressed with is the subjects and the angle you used to capture it. You've got a talent for this," Sam pauses to look at the teen.

"This one of the fire. Look at it. The color, deep into the sticks of the chard pieces of wood, is that bright yellowish-orange sun color, the hottest part of the fire. Then the outward flame changes to shades of red with sparks rising into the air. The action of the fire that you captured at just the right time magnifies the beauty, the magnificence of the fire, even its terror. I see why you printed this full page. It's as if I'm staring into that fire. I can visualize myself standing in front of it as a large poster and not wanting to leave, being traumatized by the fire as we do sitting around the campfire.

"It's amazing to me that your cell phone can capture such vivid pictures. Gads, Peter, back in my youth, it was almost impossible to get pictures like this. And here's another one that should be on tomorrow's front page of a fish and wildlife brochure."

Peter turns to look at the picture.

"You captured the frog with a look of total satisfaction, resting but ready. It's head just above the surface of the water, the knees of those hind legs above the surface positioned and ready for a jump, as it pushed its tongue out sensing the area. Wow, I'm impressed. These are amazing. What do mom and dad say about these?"

"Nothing."

"What'd you mean nothing? They don't recognize this as a talent?"

"They haven't seen them."

"They haven't seen them?" Sam repeats. "Why not? Oh, don't tell me you've not shared them with your parents. How about your friends in school, or a teacher?"

"No, you're the first."

"Oh, my God!"

Sam then reflects. *Here is a kid, a mere youngster with a talent that's hidden from everybody. How can I help him? The boy himself thinks his pictures are good. He likes capturing the things around him and knows how to use a cell phone to do it. What will he be able to do with a real camera?*

Sam goes on to the next page, intently looking at each picture, page after page. He turns back a few pages. Sam chuckles, pauses, then chuckles again, about to release uncontrollable laughter. Peter leans over to see what's so funny.

"When did you take this? How did you get it?"

"About two months ago, I think. But what's so funny?"

The picture shows a policeman talking with a young lady in front of a Laundromat. It's at night, where the only lights are from the inside. The sign naming it as a Laundromat is centered directly above them. The woman with her back to the camera is topless and in laced panties, her left elbow brought in close to her body, her hand showing a cigarette not far from her mouth. Her right arm is raised shoulder high, the index finger pointing into the lighted Laundromat. A policeman is standing with his hands on his hips, his head slightly tilted back, his face and eyes centered away from her semi-nakedness.

Sam chuckles some more. "Now, Peter, tell me how you got this one."

"But what's so funny?"

"I don't know. It just struck a funny bone. It's the story that the picture tells. She got caught sneaking out for a smoke. Tell me, how did you get it?"

"Oh, I was riding the bike around town that evening and stopped to look in the window of the hardware store. Then I saw the reflection of the policeman. I snapped a few shots."

"Yeah, kind of late at night too. The clock inside tells me it was 10:45. I'll bet your friends got a kick of that one."

"No, nobody's seen it."

"How come? I think that you'd be eager to share these pictures."

"Ah, all they want to do is just hang out doing nothing or playing those stupid games."

"Ah, come on. You do have some friends you spend time with, right?"

"No."

Again, Sam is paging through the album, surveying for another one that grabs his attention. Sam closes the album, leans back in his rocker. Peter copies the action.

"Peter, let me show you one of my cameras, and also an old antique one." Sam stands, he opens the half door to the cabin, while Peter remains seated, snapping a few shots of King following Sam as that big hairy tail wags his hind end from side to side. Shortly, Sam comes out and throws a tennis ball into the yard, his left hand carrying two camera bags.

"Here, this Nikon is for you, Peter. It's just an instrument enabling you to capture what you see. Just as a doctor uses knives, it's a tool of the trade. It's digital and has done me well. Here, it's yours. The instruction booklet is in the bag."

"What, you're giving it to me. Why?"

"It's yours to keep and experiment with it. This other one here, I've had for a long time, back to when I was in Germany. It's an Exacta. It only takes thirty-five-millimeter pictures that must be processed either as slides or prints. I also have a 250 lens for close-ups. But that Nikon has that built-in telescopic ability. I'm keeping this antique just for old times' sake."

Peter handles his new camera looking at the controls, the on-off button, the zoom control, the flash, the lens. He removes the lens cover, pushes the power button, and investigates the three-inch screen to see the lake and forest, and then presses the menu button looking at the options. "It's beautiful. Thanks. But why?"

"Peter, I see a talent within you that you've been flirting with, and as you have, you're beginning to develop a skill for seeing objects and the things around you that others just pass by without taking notice. I see it. That's a God-given skill, and you need to develop it. When you look out around this area, what do you see? We all see things differently." Sam pauses to watch Peter fiddling the controls.

"Peter, when I sit here and look out across the lake, seeing the forest of trees surrounding the still waters, the rising hills, and finally the mountains behind it, all of it framing the waters of the lake. Do you know else what I see?"

"No," Peter says, looking up at the view before him.

"At first glance, I see just what I told you. But then my perception opens, and I see more. Yeah, we all notice the calm waters and its color. But then, I see the pure, colorless liquid we call water. From here, it looks as though we could walk on it. I've seen the fish, I've drunk and gone swimming in that body of water. It's the basics of life; that body of a clear fluid that draws every kind of animal to come and drink of it, the roots of the trees reaching out to feed on it. Without water, we'd be in a desert, and if unable to get water, we'd die just as the grasses, trees, and all animals would die. This earth would be like that moon up there, barren, nothing but rocks and sand."

He pauses and looks at Peter, concentrating on that new camera. "I'm boring you, Peter. I can see it on your face. Sorry about my ranting on like this."

"No, go on."

"That water does not burn like every other substance on this planet, it boils and makes steam, and that steam goes into the air. Water is the one thing we can count on to put out the fires that destroy life, a perpetual battle of good against evil." Sam pauses to look intently at this kid and then continues. "That's what I see, and Peter, you have the same ability to see beyond the surface, into depths that others take for granted. You saw into the fires.

"What are you? Fourteen now? Yet, you're catching on, and I believe you've found your passion for life already. It's not just aiming and pressing a button that makes taking pictures fun and satisfying, but in doing so, you freeze a bit of life. Don't hide them, Peter. Just as that one picture brought me to laughter, your ability to capture moments will bring joy, happiness, delight, and yes, even sadness to others. Show them to your teachers, oh, and especially your parents."

Waiting for a reaction from Peter fingering the controls of his new camera, Sam continues, "Every picture tells a story. Norman Rockwell was able to tell a story with just tools of brushes and mere paint by changing a blank into beauty. You've got a talent. Don't waste it, Peter. And that's why I'm giving you this camera. That camera is a mere tool, and you're the captain storyteller."

Still messing with his new toy as Sam was talking, Peter meekly says, "Thanks."

"I think the batteries are still good, so go ahead mess with it some, and then I guess, you'd better be heading home."

Peter stands and takes a few steps toward the lake, turns around, and points the lens at Sam. Then, at King, back to Sam with the lens extended out some. He shifts focus to the cabin and then takes a few steps toward the lake. He looks at the controls of his new tool, pushes a button, looks at the screen, pushes another button, aims it at King, and presses the button on top. Viewing all this from the porch pleases Sam as his thoughts go back to those days living in Germany as an exchange student, and the first time he held that heavy, bulky Exacta to focus on his view of the Alps. And now Sam is feeling that same kind of happiness by exciting a kid with a new toy.

Peter makes his way back to the porch announcing that the disk is full.

"Already?" Sam questions. "I must have had a bunch of pictures on it. We should delete all of those. Peter hands him the camera watching Sam press button after button while looking into the screen, and he finally tells Peter, "There, now it's clean except for those you took. There's another disk in the bag. I think I had three altogether."

Peter reaches into a side pocket of the camera bag pulling out a small black disk. He turns the camera upside down, then picks up the instruction booklet scanning the pages, looking at the diagrams, and proceeds to open the battery compartment finding batteries and the disk.

"Peter, I know you could spend more time taking pictures here, but I think perhaps mom and dad may be concerned. And, when I see them, I'll tell them that I gave you the camera and thank them for letting you come out. And dag gone it, come back again sometime. I enjoyed it."

"Thanks, Mr. Guardyall. I won't forget this."

Peter pulls the strap connected to the camera around his neck, cramming the empty camera bag into his backpack, pulling the straps over his shoulders. He picks up the bike, raises his right leg over the seat, and starts peddling off as King runs alongside around the bend and into the tree-lined road.

Watching him leave, Sam wonders if he got too preachy about the water, as Peter did not question nor make any remark. *Should I have been more outright about God and brought Jesus into the conversation? I think he enjoyed the time here, as Peter seemed pleased and proud of the pictures he shared.*

"Bless this young man Father. Guide him in all he does and nudge Peter, secure him into your blessed family. Father God, he's got your life inside, but does he know it? I can see it. Lead him the way you'd have him to go. And please, Lord, bring Peter back to me again."

Eight

Typing notes of the meeting with Peter, Sam labels the page, "Notes on Peter, first meeting." He records his thoughts, filling two pages of the details while they're fresh to put aside for some possible future reference. He removes the sheet, places the notes in a folder, and inserts a new page.

My Cabin Life 3

Again, I write about this transitional phase I'm experiencing. The fall months will be approaching, and I must not whine and must learn how to manage these daily needs. This meeting with Peter has been a blessing. I desire more of this. I discovered that connecting with this teen was fun and rewarding. Is this why I'm here?

Those thoughts of that more comfortable life keep returning when I'm confronted with the daily task of cleaning and feeding this body since my cooking skills were just about nil back in Indiana. The blessing of having all those canned vegetables in the closet and those recipes have been a gift from my grandmother, all that grinding work she and grandpa did day after day. I don't want to use them up so fast. So now I've got to learn if I'm going to make it. Cooking on that wood-fired stove has become a chore.

Why can't I have at least a camp stove connected to a source of gas? Will that be giving in?

One more thing I have discovered during this short period away from the hustle of society when a friend had enticed me to get a four-by-four off-road vehicle we could use for days of fun in the woods. Why not, I reasoned, as I had just received a bonus on a completed project. So yeah, it'd be fun. I had the cash. I could find the time, and Angelia would enjoy the rides too. So, I did. Sure, it was fun. We had a good time.

That desire later became a need, a need to maintain the thing, a need to keep it clean, a need to keep it working, a need to park it somewhere, as we needed the garage for the cars we used daily. I needed to take the time to use it, to have the fun and the excitement it afforded me. And yet, we only used the thing five times in the two years we had it.

That lust had enslaved me.

A camp stove can't enslave me, can it? No, it just makes it easier, so sure, I will get one. Why not? Is that giving an inch, and soon I'll want to go a mile?

That's all for now.

Back outside on the porch rubbing the ears of King after a few throws of the tennis ball, watching the slow setting of the sun, the clouds looking as though they're on fire, their shapes and colors changing and diminishing as the view of the sun fade below the horizon, his thoughts go a-wandering.

Back in earlier days, people thought of the sun circling this earth. We think the sun is moving because we don't feel the earth moving. What if this planet was a stationary object, and the sun and the moon moved around it? That would mean that the sun and the rest of the universe depended on the gravitational pull of the earth keeping the sun, being millions of miles away circling this tiny planet. How would our days be different? Would my legs be strong enough to move this body, as I might then weigh two or ten-thousand pounds? Couldn't the ancients have reasoned that out?

Yet those ancient astronomers and philosophers of the third century BC had calculated the circumference of the earth and its distance to the sun. They formulated that the earth revolved around the sun, that this earth was just another planet of many. Yeah, how did they do that way back then in the days of camels carrying the wood for fires to heat their coffee?

"Gads," he summarizes, "thoughts like this never crossed my mind back home, but now they're more frequent." *Why then did some people of Columbus's days, some 1700 hundred years later, think the earth was like a flat disk?*

"King, come on, let's go in, and I'll play you a game of chess."

Monday morning comes, and Sam decides to have a decent breakfast at the diner, a couple of pancakes covered with strawberries, crushed walnuts, and a dash of whipped cream along with that morning coffee.

Joanna greets him at the door, "Samuel. It must be going well with you. It's been a while since that first day. How're you doing?"

"Just fine. I got homesick for a good breakfast."

"I heard you took a drive to Johnsonville to try out that government restaurant."

"Yes, I did."

"Sheriff Olsen suggested it, right?"

"Yes, he did."

"He'll want your opinion of it sooner or later. That's what he's doing. I think he's preparing a survey as ammunition to give state legislators another proof of intrusive government regulations deeper into our lives."

"You think so?"

"Yeah, he's one of the few that still wants to do things the good old ways, making his inmates perform menial tasks as part of their sentence. No TV's in his jail."

"Joanna, I'll have that pancake special and a cup of coffee."

"I'll be right back, and it's good to see you again." Gum chewing, Joanna heads to another booth.

Scanning the twenty-some patrons seeing not one he recognizes, as he was hoping he could have the morning without the endless questions of how's things working out for you. Joanna was the exception, regarding her as refreshing in her directness and information. Finishing the meal and his third cup of coffee, Sam leaves a hefty tip on the table and goes to pay the bill at the counter.

 Joanna tells him, "beware of the bears as soon they will start migrating down from the high country before hibernating."

"Thanks, Joanna, I hadn't thought of that. Gotta go, got a few things to get."

"Good luck, Samuel, and don't stay away so long."

Standing in front of the magazine racks in the pharmacy, Sam is paging through a 'Living off the grid' magazine, noting the articles, mostly promoting solar and wind power and all kinds of ads for self-sufficient life products and services. Another magazine has advice on preparing meals over a fire, menus for healthy eating, learning to cook from scratch, growing your own in small plots, and staying warm, listing many websites one could go to for more information. Finally, he selects two magazines and moves over to scan the books available. Mostly novels. At the check-out counter, he asks the clerk about bookstores. She replies that there is one in Johnsonville.

Okay, to the library I go.

Walking through the library's sliding doors, he drops his borrowed books into the return slot and walks past the check-out desk. He notes each corridor of shelves' labels when he sees one labeled, 'Agriculture.' He scans the available books, noting there's only a couple that touches his interests, not enough to borrow and must bring it back.

At the desk, the clerk looks up from the book she was reading, "Hey, it's good to see you again, Samuel. How are you making out?"

"Mary, it is, right? Hi again. Mary, I was looking for a book on survival techniques."

"Sorry, but with what's available here, you won't find one strictly devoted to that one subject. You'd only get bits and pieces in some of the Agricultural books. Sorry."

"I've been told there's a book store in Johnsonville?"

"Ah, yes! It's a family-owned store that concentrates on used books. It surprises me whenever I go there what I might find. I could go with you sometime."

"Thanks, but I guess that can wait. But anyway, while I was in town, I thought I'd check. I'll see you again then."

"Hey, check our computer listing of books."

"Nah, forget it. I'd just have to bring it back."

"Good to see you again, Samuel. I'm here Monday through Friday, nine-to-five." Mary announces as he turned heading toward the exit.

He parks the pick-up near the grocery store, where two elderly gentlemen are seated at a table playing a game of checkers. He then remembers to get some dog food, which he forgot to write down. *"Lord,"* he ponders, *"you're always here. Thank you."*

He pushes the cart up and down the aisles to find his items and then checking them off. The cart is slowly filling up. *What a refreshing task this is here, compared with the shopping back home. Always a rush, a feeling that you've got to get it and get out as there's always something else to do, someplace to go, or a meeting to attend. Pressure. Continual pressure. This small-town rural life has its advantages seeing others in the store stop and chat with friends, neighbors, acquaintances.*

"Okay, time to pay, load this stuff in the back of the pick-up, and head to the ranch."

As Sam is transferring the bags to the bed of his truck when a fortyish man dressed in a dark suit and green tie with a string around his neck holding a name tag approaches. "Say, aren't you the Guardyall relative taking over the cabin?"

Sam turns to greet the stranger. "Yes, I am. Samuel Guardyall."

"Sir, my name is Frank Outmoure. I'm with the Fish and Wildlife Agency, and we need to sit down and chat."

Sam reaches out to shake the gentleman's hand, "Nice to meet you, Mr. Outmoure. But how did you recognize me?"

"It's that truck you're driving. Would you mind if I followed you home, and we could finish my business quickly?"

"Don't mind a bit. I'm heading that way."

Frank follows Sam to the cabin, and as Sam turns into his entrance road, he glances in the rear-view mirror, seeing Frank pulled off to the side. He's out of his car and taking pictures. Sam watches and then continues down the gravel entrance. He parks his truck and slowly walks to his porch carrying the sacks of groceries. *"Hmm? Should I let King out or keep him inside?"* Mr. Outmoure slowly pulls into the yard, snapping pictures as he drives in.

"Mr. Guardyall, let me review what this visit is all about." Mr. Outmoure tells Sam as he walks with a briefcase in hand toward Sam on the porch.

"The agency heard that you have moved into this cabin having inherited it from your grandfather, but we need to know what your intentions are. As you know, your acreage is surrounded by a National Forest, so our concerns are focused on protecting that land, the lakes, fish, and of course, the animal life. Your grandfather was gracious to keep his property the same as it was and has been. He did that. What are your intentions, Mr. Guardyall?"

Hearing the barks of King inside the cabin, he asks, "You have a dog?"

"Yes, a German Shepherd. He's my companion."

"Why don't you let it out?"

"Mr. Outmoure, I wasn't sure how you'd react to seeing a big dog running toward you when you got out of the car."

"He's friendly, right?"

"Yeah, as long as I'm around."

Sam opens the door, and King thrusts his front paws up onto Sam's waist, getting rubs around his neck from Sam. "King, say hello to Mr. Outmoure."

King rushes past the stranger toward the gazebo. They watch King as he goes from one shrub to another, sniffing each and then settles on one. King turns and runs back to the porch sniffing the legs of Frank. King sits at the side of Sam, barking a few times at the visitor. Frank snaps his fingers, makes a little welcoming sound with his lips, but King continues to stare at Frank.

Sam reaches over to rub his head and neck as King gives out a few woofs at the stranger. "I don't understand this. Normally he's quite friendly," Sam tells Frank.

King runs off again.

"Maybe it's my cologne," Frank suggests. "Anyway, again, ah, where were we? Oh yeah, your intentions."

"My intentions? Yes. I will do all I can to protect the property, and as you can see, it's just as it was when I first walked in several weeks ago. Well, except the boat may be on the other side of the pier."

"Are you having a tough time adjusting to the off the grid lifestyle? What would you change if you had the opportunity?"

"Not a thing."

"Ah, Samuel, that's hard to believe. Surely, you'd want to have electric power, right?"

"At times, yes, but no, I've made the decision that I would adjust to these primitive ways or die trying," Sam says. Looking at the briefcase positioned on the floor between them and then back to his guest. Sam continues, "I made that decision after reading some of my grandfather's notes about the previous attempts to get him to electrify."

"But, come on, it can't be comfortable, is it?"

"Who said anything about comfort? If my grandparents lived and survived into their nineties, why can't I?" Sam replies. Curious as to what his dog is doing, he calls out, "King, come." Looking up from his sniffing, King comes a–running, jumping up on the porch. King sniffs the briefcase, the back of the rocker, along the seating area and down Frank's leg.

Sensing the dogs' desire, Frank timidly reaches down to rub the ears and neck. "Ah, good doggie," Frank mutters, continuing to pet around the ears and neck. "My wife wanted a poodle. As a kid, I had a Labrador."

Focusing on Sam, Frank asks, "Surely you miss the conveniences of electrical power."

"Yes, there are times when I'd like to throw something into the microwave or throw my clothes into a machine instead of hanging them outside to dry. But as I said, I made the decision, and that's final. Final, like in . . . dead."

"What if we could arrange electrical power for you?"

"If I wanted some juice around here, I'd have already bought a generator, but I don't like the noise. And, deciding to live like grandpa means living the same way. They did, and so will I, with God's help."

"I understand where you're coming from, but the reality is that the winter months are coming, and with that, the snows, and you may not be able to get to town for weeks or more."

"Hmm? Do you think I haven't wondered about that? Previously you were concerned that the place must be as my grandfather had it. Now, you're offering me electricity. I don't get it. I would wish to change something though, ah, no . . . " Sam was thinking of his hopes of having the entrance road smoothed out and possibly finished with asphalt. "No, forget it, I can manage."

"What was that, Sam?"

"Nothing."

"What if we put up a wind turbine to supply your needs. Would you go for that? One put right about there." He points to a high spot near the garden. "It'd be tall enough to clear the trees."

"Nope."

"We could do that."

"But why? I understand that I was to leave everything as I found it. I'm doing that, and now you want to change something."

"We thought you would want the conveniences of electricity, so the department sent me to make that offer. We would not be favorable to having you hook up to the power grid, which is already overloaded, but there are some alternatives available that millions are taking advantage of. How about solar?"

"No, not solar, either. No wind turbines, no power grids, and no generators. Nada."

"Are you a gun owner?"

"Nope, don't have one. Back home, I was too busy to take time off to hunt. I never saw the need or the desire to acquire one, but I see the need more and more with what's been happening lately. I did have a bow and arrow as a teen."

"Your grandfather had quite a collection of guns. He hunted all through the area until . . . oh, about five or six years ago. Some people still do, as we okay hunting under certain circumstances. That season has begun, so be careful. Our goal is to preserve our natural heritage, animal life, and the forest. It's their land and their water. And when we think about it, the fish and animals were here long before we settled the land, so we're the invaders."

"I've got my fishing license, as you probably already know. But hunting has never been a priority for me living in the city. Not that I'm against it if that's what they want to do. Are you against me getting a gun?"

"Not as long as it's registered and licensed."

"How about changes to the insides? Could I hang a hammock from the rafters? I did hang a beautiful one of a kind picture above the fireplace. Want to see it?"

"Nothing permanent, like altering walls. You know, those kinds of interior changes." Fank answers.

Between comments, Sam has been thinking. *How to witness to this government agent? How to say it or what to say.* "Frank, whether you know or believe this, but our Creator put us here on this earth to live on those substances that He created for our needs: the plants, vegetables, fruits, water, and yes, the animal life too. The Creator placed that sun for heat and light, the moon, and the stars up there, declaring His glory. We're not the invaders as you called us, but in one way, you're right as the animals were here first, and then Adam and Eve disobeyed, and since then, we've been enjoying their delicious meats."

Sam pauses, looking for a reaction from Frank, and then adds, "In this modern society of ours, we've become so dependent on technology we no longer know how dependent we are. Sure, those imaginations of Thomas Edison provide us with electrical light, so we can easily read at night. That invention blessed the entire world. Now, the government has decided that the incandescent bulb is not efficient enough, and we've got to adapt to a newer version that is much more dangerous. I can live without it, and I will."

Interrupting, Frank speaks up, "I'll take what you've told me back to the department. You can continue, but if you change your mind, we'd be happy to talk again," Frank concludes. He reaches down to rub the dog's neck. "King, take good care of Mr. Guardyall."

"One other thing, Frank. The idea that using wind or solar power alone will save the planet is a fairy tale. You will not entice me. I recently saw the truth of our being. It transformed me, and since you're in my presence, I had to share some of that truth with you."

Frank slides a bit forward in the rocker, grabs his unopened briefcase, puts his cell phone in his shirt pocket, stands, and offers his hand. "I was pleased to have been selected to make contact with you. Take care, Mr. Guardyall, and good luck."

"You too, Frank. You may want to get a German Shepherd sometime. Yes, and Jesus is ready to receive you any time, a lot more welcoming than King."

King follows Frank driving into the tree-lined road and out of sight. Sam heads into the cabin for a cup of coffee. He rehashes the meeting when the thought comes. Gads, what's wrong with me? I never offered the guy a cup of coffee or tea or anything. He wonders about the initial actions of King, shunning the gentleman.

Back in the rocker sipping the coffee, he thinks back to when Frank carefully placed the briefcase between them, wondering if there was a microphone recording the conversation. At the time, he concluded that no, he wouldn't, as that would have been a direct violation of his privacy. Now he questions it again and then summarizes the meeting. *If they had imagined that I would update the cabin by modernizing it, I believe they now know that I intend to leave everything as it was in no uncertain terms. And, if the department heads hear the tape, they'll also hear my brief testimony.*

Sitting down in front of the typewriter, he makes his notes of the meeting titling the page, **"Meeting with FWA."** He files the single-page document in the desk drawer. Sam then retrieves records from the folder on which he was writing about this life in this cabin. He reads the last page to refresh his memory and starts a new section.

My Cabin Life 4

I've been haunted again by those thoughts of Angelia suddenly taken away from me. Why Lord? It tore me up. The two of us were as happy together as anyone could be after adjusting to our lone child dying. We were well on our way to the time of total acceptance. We were living the good life, productive employment, a beautiful home in a suburb of a nice city providing anything we could desire, and enjoying the company of the other. Loved it, and then the next day she is gone. A drunken driver, unable to comprehend things did it. Yeah, and I rejoiced that he also died, hoping he had suffered more.

Her death tore me up. Why Lord?

The church continually told me of a good God who always wants the best for his children, and yet how can something like that be a blessing? And then the ever-used phrase, 'God works in mysterious ways.' 'Have faith, my brother,' they'd tell me. Yeah, mysterious ways? If that's the way God works, forget it, a bottle of liquor made me feel better.

Remembering back to those days, weeks, and months, I felt abandoned. Those questions, the hurts I felt for some time. The guilt plagued me. The drunkenness I succumbed to after the funeral, trying to deal with that sudden loneliness. I took months away from the office drowning my sorrows. Getting drunk and putting me out of my mind was the only peace I could find to drown the thoughts that tormented me.

That's all today. The remembrances of it all are enough. Memories, what are they anyway? I've got to learn to apply those to the clarity of the present, using the light that has broken through my darkness, so now, I'm not blinded anymore. The past is gone, and now, today is what is alive. I see. I see.

Thank You, Lord, God Almighty.

"Hey King, let's go relax a bit in that gazebo and watch the sunset," Sam instructs his companion while reaching to rub-down along his neck. "Come." He stands, pushes the chair under the desk. He refreshes his coffee, then goes into the closet to grab a few treats for King, and out they go. King leads the way to the chairs, looking back, wanting the biscuits.

"No King, this way," as Sam grabs a camp chair, and steps off the porch to make his way to shore, then a left, following the path into the woods toward the creek. Coffee in one hand, the chair in the other, and the doggie treats in the pocket of his sweatshirt.

Sam places the chair in an open area next to the streaming waters to the lake. He watches the sun slowly approaching its decline behind the snow-capped mountains. The shades of orangey colors shine through the scattered clouds' edges, mingling and separate as the gray colors transition into darker blues.

"Ah, the heavens declare the majesty of this creation," Sam tells King, who's holding the piece of a bone-shaped treat upright as his teeth bite off a chunk. "You don't even think about it, do you? Nope, I was like you once. Give me a treat, and I'd be happy."

Looking back at the beautiful sight of changing colors, Sam asks the air, "God, how did you do it? Where did you get the idea?" The wondering continues. *I mean, as humans, you've given us imaginations, and we've used them in marvelous ways. But all this is beyond anything we could imagine. It took you all of the first day to make light to penetrate the blackness. Or, was it an instant snapping of fingers, and it was? Wow, the speed of it too. Even turning on a flashlight, we don't see the particles of light moving from the bulb to the object. No Lord, we can't comprehend how this all happened, and yet it's written that you did it in six days. Come on now, that's impossible, right?*

And then the thought comes to him where Peter says, "a day is as a thousand years." *Could it have taken you six thousand of our years to put it all together, and then you rested? That would be more reasonable, right?*

But no, no watches, no alarm clocks in the heavens. No dated calendars. God is yesterday and today and tomorrow at the same moment, which we have no concept of that whatsoever. God is similar to that light; too fast to see it moving, and we are too slow in our understandings.

Anyway, this human nature of ours has lots of harebrained thinking, which is just that, our hair doing the thinking.

"Come on, King. I'm ready to go in. Go find a tree."

Sam starts the fireplace warming the room, comfortably sitting on the couch in front of the fireplace, his legs on the footstool. He lights two oil lamps, one placed over his right shoulder. Sam picks up the book, opening to the paper-clipped page as King spreads out on the floor. A few days ago, he picked Volume one of *The Story of Civilization, Our Oriental Heritage* by Will Durant of the early 1900s to get him started in his quest for a deeper understanding of how the ancients thought and lived.

From page five of the text part, he reads,

"In one important sense the "savage" too, is civilized, for he carefully transmits to his children the heritage of the tribe-that complex of economic, political, mental, and moral habits and institutions which it has developed in its efforts to maintain and enjoy itself on the earth. It is impossible to be scientific here, for in calling other human beings "savage" or "barbarous," we may be expressing no objective fact, but only our fierce fondness for ourselves and our timid shyness in the presence of alien ways."

King, let's go out one more time before hitting the sack. Shall we?"

Nine

In the mornings, Sam has developed a routine. He lets King out and then sees to his own needs. He pushes down on the pump handle, watching the water turn clear, and then splashes the cold fresh well water on his face, dries it, and dresses accordingly. In the kitchen, he strikes a match to fire up the compressed gas camp stove, the one item he reneged on his promise to live precisely as his grandparents had done. He fills the coffee maker basket with his favorite grounds, grabs a banana to eat out on the porch while viewing and feeling the atmosphere, and keeping an eye on King.

Finishing the banana, he returns to the kitchen, opens the icebox to pour him a glass of orange juice. Having felt the chill outside, he grabs a thick sweatshirt, takes his coffee out to enjoy it all by the stream, to watch the sunrise make its way above the treetops. The weather is turning into fall. The leaves are changing colors and falling.

Sam watches King bite into a chunk of the biscuit, and for the first time, he notices that his pet's tail appears to be keeping time with his jaws munching the dry brown food. The jaws bite down, and his tail wags at the same rate. He takes longer, slower intense bites, and the tail slows, shorter, faster snacks, and the tail moves faster.

"King, how do you do that? All right, buddy, I'm going in and do some writing while the subject is fresh. Go chase something."

My Cabin Life 5.

Watching the sunrise in all its glorious color, hearing the musical bubbling waters of the stream meet the lake, where five ducks peacefully float, and quack echoes. When suddenly, as if telling each other, "we're being watched! Let's get out of here!" Their wings expand, and off they flew over the treetops and out of sight.

It was then that I seemed to have flown to a witness stand in the heavens, so I must transcribe what I was seeing.

The Triune Lord God has called the heavenly host together to hear the new idea. "Listen carefully, take note, as I'm about to create a physical realm that never existed before. This will be phenomenal, very majestic. It will be maintained by physical laws governing this nature, overseen, and regulated by us. To start, I will create a substance I will name light, which will illuminate this new world in a new concept of daytime and nighttime, morning, and evening. There will be a sun shedding this light, a moon ball reflecting the rays upon a rotating earth ball, having a clear fluid keeping it moist and full of life.

"On this earth, we'll make thousands of beautiful flowers growing from their own seeds, trees bearing fruit, and many different vegetables grown from seeds getting their nutrients from the dirt of this earth.

"It'll be a circular type of life according to the seasons.

"This spiritual realm of ours will be in this, below it and above it.

"Then, an animal world, able to move about under their specifically designed physical abilities. Finally, I'll put together another new element in our likeness; that of a male and from him, the female, each inhabiting physical bodies holding a spirit and soul that we can connect with, and it with us for additional fellowship. These two beings will join together as one making more humans operating under the rule of its soul, communicating, and making choices. They'll have jurisdiction over this earth, as it is populated. We will guide and be ever-present with them in this endeavor.

Michael and Gabriel, all those beautiful angelic tones together, "yes, do it. Praise be the Almighty Lord God."

The hosts of angels started singing.

Lucifer then shouts above the songs, 'That's crazy, I cannot agree, we've been doing fine, why?" Lucifer turns, going away from the host gathering.

"Lucifer, come back here!" the Lord God commands.

That one keeps going.

"Okay, Lucifer, have it your way. You do know that you're leaving your reality behind, so, from now on, there shall be no truth to be found in you, and you'll be limited to this new physical realm. Do any of you wish to join Lucifer?

Yes, it was like I was called as a witness.

Am I off my rocker for imagining such a scenario?

Sam stalls, leans back, blankly looking out the window, gathering his thoughts. Suddenly, King's woof, woof sounds with his paws on the outside windowsill, his nose pressed against the glass, breaks the concentration.

"Okay, buddy."

Sam gets up and opens the door letting King inside, thinking *he wants to be around me.* King stalls at the open door, barks and turns toward the lake barking more, looks up at Sam, barks, turns back, his nose pointing around the pier. King takes a few steps in that direction, then turns his head to Sam, barks some more, and turns looking at the dock again.

Catching on, Sam speaks, "Okay, I know the drill. What did you find? What's out there?"

King takes off running, barking, and then stopping at the beginning of the path leading into the pine woods along the shoreline, looking back to Sam walking at his usual pace. The dog starts a slow but deliberate pace into the trees, sniffing the ground as he goes. Slower and slower, the dog sniffs and looks back to his owner every so often. Catching on to the instructions his dog is giving him, Sam pays more attention to the trail, looking for signs of anything unusual. He looks in front of his dog, looks on each side of the path, and back to the grass-covered ground.

"What is it that King is sniffing."

Suddenly he is captured at what appears as dark red spots on the beaten-down tan grass.

Bending down to inspect the ground, he lightly touches the area with his forefinger, smells it, and recognizes it as blood. The drops of blood, separated by perhaps a foot or more, and then several steps farther on, the spots get closer and closer together, then again further apart.

"Hmm?" His curiosity now heightened as King continues his sniffing as the path turns sharply deeper into the woods away from the shoreline.

A bit further into the woods, he sees it several yards off the path into the trees, a white-tailed doe lying on its side. Kneeling beside it, Sam sees the wound. A gunshot into its lower stomach area. "King, it's dead as a doorknob.

"Now what?"

Here I go again, being faced with something else I'm not familiar with. The subject has not come up in conversations with any of the locals, nor did the agent say anything about it. Whoops, he did, remembering the comments Frank made about hunting season.

"What do I do with it? "King, we've got to leave it here for now, as ewe. I've never like venison." Following the trail back to the cabin, Sam finds the two-way radio to call the Sheriff's office.

"Yes, Mr. Guardyall, what can we do for you," Sam holds the button down, speaking into the mouthpiece to inform the officer of his find.

"What am I supposed to do?" Sam asks.

"I'll send an agent out there shortly. Sam, leave everything as it is until he gets there." The officer instructs.

"Where was I before this came up?" Then, recalling the session desiring to continue putting his thoughts and remembrances on paper while they're fresh, he sits at the desk, rereading the most previous notes.

Wanting to finish this segment, while waiting for someone to arrive, Sam continues writing about his distraught feelings while periodically looking up for the arrival of a sheriff's agent. Leaning back in the chair with his feet pushing against the floor, imitating the rocking effect, he re-reads the page and furiously rips it out of the typewriter, and crumbles the paper, and tosses it in the basket. He starts over.

My Cabin Life 6

I once was blind, but now I see, and those feelings about an angry God are gone. They were only feelings anyway, an emotion brought on by that personal tragedy. As so many of our scientists' claim, that if we cannot see it, hear it, taste it, smell it, or touch it, then 'it' cannot be. But that's irrational too. It's only sensible to those who wish to accept the notion that nothing whatsoever had a big bang all by itself, and now here we are.

The irrational thoughts and all that high minded scientific evolutionary hypotheses bunk is just that, bunk. It's the imaginations of a few so-called scientists for which they gained notoriety. Hypothesis? Of course. Since they can't see, hear, touch, taste, or smell the Creator, then there cannot be such.

Can we see, taste, smell, touch, or hear our emotions? Not really. They need expression. No one will know you're disgusted, mad, sad, or happy till they see it in your eyes, or that smile turns to a frown, or the fingers tighten before you're about to hit someone in the mouth. Those emotions I had were visible and heard by my actions. My voice changed to loud and crude. Yes, and one could smell it too. Oh, the days I went without a shower. Emotions have physical expressions, just as this universe is a physical manifestation of the glory and majesty of the Creator.

Those well-educated scientific bunch could not allow themselves time to rationalize the concept of creation versus evolution. Their use of the words, theory, hypothesis, probability, conjecture, proposition, is only guesswork that boils down to the fact that there is no written detailed scientific account of how the physical world came to be. There never will be. The process of creation cannot be put in a test tube, shaken, heated, and analyzed, so, therefore, they surmise, it cannot be.

Anyway, mankind, being deceived by the evil one, has been arguing along these lines since language manifested.

As their numerous books intone, they are scientifically educated men. They now know how a cell grows as they've seen it in microscopes, but their conclusions remain a theory. They're thrilled, exhibiting a fierce fondness for themselves because of their expertise. The common folk looks up to them as the professionals, who must know what they're talking about because they have letters after their names.

The scriptures inform us, "But the natural man receiveth not the things of the Spirit of God, for they are foolishness unto him, neither can he know them, because they are spiritually discerned."

It's been that way since Eve and Adam disobeyed getting kicked out of that paradise garden, and it'll be that way till God decides, sending the Lord back to set up that thousand-year reign. Science has been fantastic, but this physical creation is superbly marvelous.

Pushing the chair away from the desk, Sam looks out the window seeing King, sitting upright on the porch looking like he's waiting for the master to come home. Periodically, the tail waves slowly, then it stops, then another slow-wave and a pause, repeatedly repeating the sequence. King's head and eyes focused back and forth on the entrance area and the path leading into the woods.

"He's watching for me. Time to make more coffee and grab an apple."

Bending over to smooth the bumps of the area rug in front of the couch, he neatly places the decorative pillows at each end of the sofa and replaces the throw cover over the back-rest cushions. He checks the fireplace vent handle. He removes a partially filled cup left on the table and carries it to the kitchen sink, where he pumps some water for another pot of coffee. He turns on the camp stove, waiting for the steam. He takes the first bite into a golden delicious apple and sits down at the typewriter, ready to write new thoughts coming.

Sam starts to insert a piece of paper when he hears the barking, and through the window, he watches a sheriff's vehicle pull around the gazebo stopping at his front door. Opening the upper part of the cabin door, he sees the sheriff himself reaching down, stroking the head and neck of King.

"Good morning Sheriff Olsen. I didn't expect you to come out, but glad you did. Good to see you again."

"Good morning to you, Sam. How're you getting along? I heard you found something and didn't know what to do with it."

"That's right. Being a city kid, I never have had to deal with anything like this before, so I called for help."

"We'll take care of it for you, but we got to wait for that wildlife agent as he wants to see it also. You know, it's the governments' animals."

"Come on up and sit then. Coffee? I recently made a fresh pot."

"Thanks, don't mind if I do. It's been one of those days already."

Sam goes in to fetch a cup of brew for his friend and carefully carries the stone cup through the open door as King runs inside, causing him almost to spill the coffee.

"Gads King, take it easy."

Setting the cup next to the sheriff, Sam declares, "If we're going to have a treat, I guess King decided he would too. I should make a doggie door for him."

"How would it be without him?"

"Oh, he was the best decision I made pondering my coming out here. I never knew how much a dog could mean to me. To have a companion like that has been amazing, and he's such a smart fellow too."

"Yeah, they are. He found that deer, right?"

"Yeah, took me to it, sniffing and barking the entire way making sure I was right behind him."

"Sam, this time of year, he'll probably be scaring off the bears as they begin their thing, or they may be running after him. I tried to talk your grandfather into getting a German Shepherd, but the misses preferred not to have a dog. She liked cats."

"That's strange. In this short time that I've been here, I've found out how valuable a dog like King can be. So, what's been happening around the county? Any new uprisings?"

"It's been relatively quiet. Hey, did you make it to Johnsonville to visit that restaurant?"

"Sure did, and one time is enough for me."

"How come?"

"Sheriff, it's another one of those government knows best, and you better get on board for the ride. In a few years, the program will be everywhere."

"Hmm? What else? The food was good, right?"

"Oh yes, it was good, the service was good, the atmosphere was good, and the desserts looked good too."

"So, what's the problem?" the sheriff asks as King comes back onto the porch putting his nose in the lap of Sam. "Hmm, what's wrong then? Why won't you go back?"

"Sheriff, sure the food was good along with the service, but again, they think we're not smart enough to choose wisely, and well, some may not even care, so all of us must buckle down to that level. Seat belt laws are the same. I don't put anybody else in danger when I choose not to buckle-up. It's my choice, and I'm aware of the possible consequences too. It's the same with food. If I want to gorge myself, that's my choice. Now they've got statistics proving we don't make wise decisions, so they're going to help."

"I see where you're coming from, and come to think of it; retailers use the same tactics to get you in the stores."

"Sure, they do. The advertising on TV. They show you an actress, good looking of course, slim of course, usually seductively dressed and holding the product in her hand, or she just took a bite of something and having the time of her life, jumping and throwing her hands high as if she won the lottery."

"I assume that you keep up with the political side of life."

"I used to, but not anymore. Don't read the newspapers. I'm not here to cause trouble. I can take care of myself, and that's what I told that guy from the agency, leave me alone. It's that live and let live idea."

"Sam, can I use your thoughts in a survey I'm taking?"

"Sure, have at it. You can use my name too. When is that guy supposed to be here anyway?"

"He told my officer he was on the way as I pulled in." Sheriff Olsen answers, leaning forward in the rocker sipping some coffee.

"When he sees that doe out there, what should I expect?" Sam asks.

"All he's concerned with now that hunting season has opened is, What kind of gun? What caliber? He may even dig the slug out to have it examined."

"How about the body? What must be done with it?"

"If it's on your land, it's your responsibility. Inside the forest, it's theirs, and they won't do anything.

"Great. What should I do?"

"There are several options. Skin it and enjoy the meat, bury it, or bring it to a landfill and dump it for a fee, but then you'll need a permit to transport the carcass, or you can let the scavengers have at it."

"Great. Choose one out of four."

"Anyway, I must be going. Tell that agent I couldn't stay all day and had other things to do. I'm sure you can take care of him. And, thanks for the coffee."

"Anytime in the area, stop in. Please do and bring your family out too."

"I'll see you, Sam, and good luck. Oh, here, this is the survey. Fill it out for me. I'll get it later."

Ten

The sheriff said he expected the agent to arrive during his short stay. Will it be the same one, that Mr. Outmoure fellow, or another? The sheriff could not be specific, only saying they called the agency as required, providing information about who to contact.

Sam peers along the shelves of the bookcase for an exciting read while he waits. That thick volume one by Will Durant was put back in the collection several days ago as one that was too detailed for right now, maybe later. He decides on one by G. K. Chesterton titled *The Everlasting Man.* He nibbles on a sandwich while reading and waiting. The early afternoon slowly slips away when a different sound than leaves fluttering in the soft breeze breaks his attention away from the book.

"Isn't this a surprise!" Samuel greets Peter as he and another youngster stop in front of the porch to get off their bikes, leaving their backpacks hanging on the handlebars. "Good to see you again, Peter. How's that camera working for you? And this is . . .?"

"Jounger Brownstein, a classmate of mine."

Reaching out to shake the kid's hand, Samuel tells the teenager, "Jounger, greetings, and this is my friend, King," as King was busy sniffing his ankles, shoes, and pant legs. Jounger reaches down to pet the ears, neck, bending forward with his knees on the ground, continuing the gestures.

"We've got a Shepherd," Jounger replies, continuing to pet King head to tail.

Peter waves a Frisbee in front of King and throws it toward the gazebo. King breaks away from the light hold of Jounger and takes off after the toy.

"Guys, come on up and enjoy the view from the porch. Can I get you something to drink?"

"I've got one," Peter replies, and Jounger echoes.

They step up on the porch as King returns the Frisbee to Jounger, whose hand reaches out. King keeps a tight hold as Jounger tries to pull it away. Jounger releases his grip. King backs away, drops it on the porch, then picks it up, taking a step closer to the boy. Jounger grabs it and tosses it out over the roof of the six-sided gazebo. King rushes it back. Jounger throws the toy out again, then turns and sees the rocker. He intently looks at the rocker, at the curved rocking rails, the wide sculptured seat, while softly rubbing the spindles and armrest, his forefingers move up and down the oval-shaped back supports connecting to the five-inch curved and carefully carved headrest. He rubs his hand over the smooth oak headrest.

"Mr. Guardyall," Peter says. "I shared my visit, and I told him you were an architect, and that's what he's interested in."

"Really?" Sam replies, looking up at Jounger, who continues playing fetch with King.

"Interesting. Jounger, why do you want to be an architect?

"Mr. Guardyall, did you make this?" The teen asks.

"No. I didn't, and I don't know if my grandfather made it or not."

"It's beautiful."

"You've passed the first test, Jounger."

Sam turns toward Peter, who was snapping shots of King catching the Frisbee and returning it to his feet. King holds the top edge while it dangles in front of Sam with the round disk still hanging from the grip of his teeth. "King, sit!"

"Peter, how's that camera working out for you?"

"The camera is great, and thanks again," Peter answers.

Rocking forward and back in the chair, Jounger asks, "First test? What do you mean?"

"Well, Peter said you wanted to be an architect, and when I saw you examining the chair. That one simple act showed your level of interest in form and function." Sam also has a few inside doubts about his sincerity. *Could he be expecting something from me as I gave a camera to Peter?* The thoughts of his own wild teenage years being able to impress some adults to gain something comes back, cautions him to proceed carefully.

"Okay, now tell me why you want to be an architect."

"I don't know, except that I enjoy sketching and drawing, especially houses, and when I see a design that appears to be off-kilter, it strikes me right away that something is wrong."

"An example, please," Sam asks.

"There's a house I pass on the way to school that has three arched brick openings to, ah, a covered deck." He pauses.

"So, what's wrong with that?"

"Uh, through one of the openings is a solid brick wall. Behind the center arch, it's part brick and part window. The one closest to the garage shows the front door off-center with a partial view of a window."

"I think I see the picture, but so what?"

"Uh, there's no balance?"

"Hang onto that thought," Sam instructs. Sam goes into the cabin and returns with a pad of paper and pencil, "Here, draw me a picture."

As Jounger begins sketching the image, Sam watches Peter take shots of his friend with paper and pencil in hand, and then he throws the Frisbee for King.

"Here, something like this." Jounger hands Samuel the two sketches. One shows the way it is, and the other how he thinks it ought to be.

"Okay, I see what you mean. From the street view, that looks much better, but you'd have to change the inside design also, right?" comments Sam.

"Oh, sure."

Samuel looks at the kid wondering why he's come out here, as he surely knows he's got some talent for mixing form and function. *So, what's he want?*

"Jounger, why did you come out here? Were you seeking my approval that you've got the gift of seeing integrated form and be able to express it? You already know it. Why did you come out?"

"Yeah, I think I do."

"Oh, come on. You know you do, so say it. Don't be mealy-mouthed about it. Say it out loud and mean it."

"Thanks."

"Well, let us hear it."

The boy looks at Sam, pauses, and then says, "Yeah, I'm going to be an architect."

"That's better. Now sketch something else for me." Then turning to Peter, still playing with King and taking shots of the dog catching and bringing the Frisbee back, Sam asks, "Peter, did you have some pictures you wanted me to see?"

"Ah, I do, if you don't mind?"

"Come on, get up here, Peter, and . . ."

A vehicle pulls into the drive, bearing the FWL symbol on the door. It goes around the circle drive and stops by the porch. Frank Outmoure gets out, waving at Sam over the top of the black suburban, as King barks like mad, standing several paces away from the van.

"Oh boy, just what we needed now," Sam quietly tells the boys, and then shouts, "King, hush!" And then, "Good afternoon Mr. Outmoure. Glad you could make it." Lowering his head to look at the boys, Sam says, "Boys, this guy is here to inspect a dead deer King found this morning."

Frank opens the rear door and reaches in for a zippered leather case. He strings a camera over his shoulder, shuts the door, and steps around the car and closer to the cabin, greeting Sam while asking, "So, you found something this morning. I'm sorry for being so late, but anyway, let's go see, shall we?"

"Mr. Outmoure, these two boys are Peter and Jounger. They've been keeping me company and teaching me some things."

"Hi, boys! Why aren't you in school?"

"Look at your watch, Frank," Sam says.

"Okay, let's go see this deer. Lead me on," Frank says.

"King, let's go. You guys want to come along and watch?"

"Not me," Jounger replies first, as Peter is ready to go, standing alongside King with his camera strapped over his shoulder.

"Come on, Jounger," Sam calls to the kid, still hanging back.

King leads the way. Sam is trying to keep up with his pet, being followed by Mr. Outmoure, Peter, and then Jounger, catching up.

Mr. Outmoure does as the sheriff had said he would do. He takes several pictures of the opening wound, turning the deer over and capturing a few shots. Jounger watches. King barks a few from the far side of the deer. Peter snaps pictures from behind the agent as the wound was opened with a long-bladed knife deeply cutting the flesh, searching for the bullet. Peter moves to the side for different angles when the agent tells him, "stop it, no pictures."

"Mr. Outmoure, he's only a kid with a new toy," Samuel tells him. "He can take as many as he likes. Go ahead, Peter."

"No, he can't. Put it away."

"Hey, this is my land, and if I say this friend of mine can take pictures on my property, then he can."

Mr. Outmoure stands and shouts at Peter, "Stop it now, or I'll confiscate the camera,"

Peter shyly looks to Sam for direction, for support, not wanting the camera taken away.

"How does his picture-taking interfere?" Sam asks.

"Give it to me."

"You don't have to, Peter! Frank, I authorized Peter to take pictures of that deer on my land, and that's final."

"Peter, Now!"

"Don't do it!" Sam loudly states.

Turning squarely to Samuel, Frank says, "According to our rules, no agent can be captured on any media while performing duties as required, without his prior written and witnessed consent."

"Hmm. Hey, you did not inform us of that before. You even witnessed Peter carrying his camera and taking shots as we walked to this site, and you didn't say anything then. So, what's so special about the deer that he can't take pictures of it, and not of you?"

"Regardless of that, I want those pictures. Don't take this too far, Mr. Guardyall. You don't want to do this."

"Oooh, that sounds like a threat. Now, isn't there a way we can agreeably move on? Mr. Outmoure, you've examined the deer as required. You've told me of my responsibility for the removal of the carcass. He intends no harm by taking those pictures. Here Peter, let me have it for a moment." Sam reaches for the camera. Peter pulls the strap over his head, letting loose of the camera.

Sam pushes the button and shows it to Frank. "Here, these are the pictures on the disk starting with the most recent. Okay, so let's delete those you don't like." Turning to Peter, "Will that be all right with you?"

"Yeah, sure, I guess," Peter replies.

"Okay, you've both agreed. So, Frank, we'll delete those."

"I don't need your permission."

One by one, Frank deletes picture after picture as Sam carefully watches before the delete button is pushed and then a second request by the camera. Peter and Jounger watch the hassle.

Suddenly Sam exclaims, "Whoa, not that one. It's of the deer and me. I want that. And while I'm thinking about it, Frank, how about those pictures you took coming into my driveway on your first visit?

Huh? You took some of me too, right? Don't I have a say-so on those? My property and all."

"Samuel, you're getting close."

"Close? To what?"

"Sam, I suggest you step back and out of my way. Your grandfather had the right to live here, not you."

"Ooops. Sorry Frank, but . . ." Sam pauses, perceiving that he ought to keep a distance from this agent as he's heard so many stories, and now he's personally faced with one. "Frank, I didn't know what to do, so I called the sheriff, and he did as he's required. Remember, I'm new to the area and don't wish to cause you any trouble. Okay? I get irritated too. Sorry."

"Good, let's keep it that way." Frank replies and then adds, "Okay, I did as required, so lead me back to my vehicle, and I'll fill out my report. You'll need to sign it."

The boys are back on the porch chatting while Sam stands next to the black SUV, watching Frank entering the information into the laptop.

"Initial there on the line, Sam, and I've finished my investigation. We'll send you a copy. You understand your responsibilities if you find another animal, right?"

"Yes, I do now, and I'm sorry you had to get involved, but, ah, as I said, I'm learning something new every day. I don't like venison; otherwise, I'd skinned it. Thanks for coming, Mr. Outmoure, and God's blessing on you always."

"Whew! Glad that's over!" Sam exclaims to the air as he steps onto the porch to sit next to the boys. "Well, guys, what do you think of all this?"

Jounger is the first. "He's an idiot." Peter nods his head.

"Not quite an idiot, just a government employee with too much power. You noticed that he was telling me what to do. There was a time when the government listened to the citizens and did what the people wanted. Now, that concept is buried in thousands, if not millions, of regulations of what we must do. In one way, it's become necessary as our human nature is such that we want our freedom to do as we please, forgetting others. Then we deal with additional outside controls to keep that nature from harming others. Speaking of such, are you taking civics or American history in school?"

"History. World."

"So, how's the teacher?"

Peter responds, "It's about dates and names."

 "Who cares what they did two hundred years ago?" Jounger adds.

"Does the teacher raise questions?" Sam asks.

"No. Read the textbook and be ready for the test."

"Yeah," says Jounger.

Picking up on their attitude toward classes, Sam starts, "Guys, thinking back, I had the same attitude as you toward history. How people lived on a day-to-day basis was not even brought up. All I wanted was to spend more time drawing and sketching houses. How would knowing about some king a thousand years ago help me be a better architect or even a better person?"

"Exactly," Peter replies.

"It's stupid," Jounger says. "Why, then? I mean, they were just surviving. Caveman days. Why is it so important to teach us about them? We should be teaching them."

"Hmmm? Now, Jounger, that's an interesting subject."

"What?"

"Yeah, you said we should be teaching them. Imagine a time if our current technology and scientific knowledge had been known four thousand years ago. How would that have changed the course of history? Instead of men drawing on the walls of caves, what if they had iPads back then? What kind of information would they have posted?" Sam pauses, thinking more of the proposition. "How would that have changed the course of history? Noah could have YouTubed it all on his smartphone, and scientists wouldn't question it."

"There'd be something else," Jounger says.

"Yep," Peter adds.

Sam then continues. "Imagine fifty years from now. You guys may be chatting with your grandsons, telling them you had to hold a cell phone in your hand, while you're now talking to an implanted chip at the base of your thumb. Will the kids be transported to an academy school in a robotic bus? Will people fifty years from now call us backward for, well, ah, boarding an airplane along with 200 others taking six hours to get to Paris, France, when they can do it in twenty minutes in a tube tunnel."

Sam pauses to watch their reactions and facial expressions. He adds, "Is it stupid to ponder such ideas? So, what if the cavemen had computers and the pyramids were software designed and using current building methods to place the blocks?"

 Peter says, "If they had cameras like this, we'd have books full of photos of them building it."

Jounger adds, "And articles and TV reporters reporting on another worker falling off the scaffold."

"Imagine what they'd be posting on Facebook," Sam adds, as the two teens appear more interested in the conversation. "And, what if we were now the cavemen? Look around here. We're sitting on the porch of a home built over a hundred years ago, and this is all we know, thinking the earth is a flat disk, like that Frisbee."

Peter thinks about it. "That's what you're doing here, Mr. Guardyall."

"Hey, you're right, Peter. I guess I am."

"Why?" Jounger asks.

"Oh, that's a long story. I inherited this cabin from my grandfather, and I wanted to get away from memories."

Jounger recalls, "I remember him. My mother would bring me to the library to listen to him read stories."

Sam looks down at his watch and to the sun getting closer to the horizon. "Hey, guys, I don't want to rush you off as I've enjoyed having you here, but ah, your parents may be wondering."

The two boys look at their watches and then at each other, as Peter is the first to answer, "Yeah, I guess I should."

Jounger replies, "Moms, not home anyway."

"It's a bit after five, Jounger. When does mom or dad get home?" Sam asks.

"Ah, don't have a dad, and mom gets home whenever."

"I'm sorry, Jounger. What happened with your dad?"

"He just up and left."

"Why?" Sam asks, and quickly adds, "my dad was an alcoholic, always causing fights, and then mom kicked him out. I'm sorry, Jounger. That's hard on both of you. What does your mom do work-wise?"

"She's a nurse somewhere."

"I'm going. Joung, are you coming?" Peter moves toward the steps of the porch. "Mr. Guardyall, thank you. Mind if I come back?"

Sam stands and reaches out to shake his hand, "Peter, anytime. Thanks for dropping by, and oops, I didn't get to see any of your new photos. Sorry. That agent showed up. Next time then. Yes, Peter, come back, please do. Okay?" Turning back to Jounger, still comfortably on the rocker, Sam asks, "Shouldn't you be going too?"

"Nah, I can stay a bit."

Peter pulls the backpack over his shoulder, raises his right leg over the bike, and tells Jounger, "I'll see you in class tomorrow." Peter peddles away with King following.

Back in the rocker, Sam asks, "Can I get you something to snack on, a root beer?"

"A root beer."

King returns with the Frisbee hanging from its jaws, dropping it at the feet of Jounger, who reaches down to grab the toy and throws it out. "Go get it, boy!"

Sam comes out with a can of pop in one hand and a cup of coffee in the other. He gives the soda to the boy. He leans back in the rocker, sips his coffee, and watches King bring the toy back. Jounger throws it out again.

"You said your mother is a nurse. Where?"

"She's an on-call nurse. Could be working in town, at the hospital, or somewhere."

"Do you have brothers or sisters?"

"A sister, probably home making out with her boyfriend. Don't want me around when mom's gone."

"How old is she?"

"Seventeen."

"Does your mother know?"

"Yeah, they argue about it all the time."

Sensing the boy's changed attitude that this could be a sensitive subject for Jounger, Sam decides to pursue the kid's architectural desires. He asks, "How long have you been interested in architecture? That sketch is good, and it shows that you do have a talent for it. Don't give up on it."

"I won't."

"In high school," Sam relates, "I took four years of drafting getting all A's, but the teacher and counselor never emphasized my need to study math as much as drawing. The two subjects work together, so I flunked the college test and had to go back for another year of math and physics. I almost gave up on it."

"I like math, but it's confusing too."

"Confusing? Two plus two equals four. How is that confusing?"

"The teacher asks if four is a reasonable answer."

"Huh? Reasonable?" Sam holds up his index and the middle finger of his left hand and the same with his right hand, then moving each finger as he counts, 'one, two, three, four.' Duh, it's a fact that can't be changed. Any first-grade student can do that. Why does she ask that?"

"We're supposed to think about it."

Sam then says, "Oh, this is society's goal of making everything relative, evolving, wanting to eliminate absolute truth that doesn't evolve, so now you can claim what's right in your own eyes." Getting off his rant, Sam asks, "How does the teacher explain the reasonable answer?"

"Read the textbook."

"Jounger, you're a smart kid for recognizing some of that. I'd like to see that textbook sometime. Ah, I noticed you don't have a cell phone? I thought everyone had cell phones now."

"No, mom says she can't afford another one."

"Your mom and sister do, right?"

"Yeah."

"How's that make you feel?"

"It's okay. I don't care about all that stuff, playing games, posting selfies that are better than yours."

"Oh, wow, what an observation! I sense that you'll go far in this world. Keep it up. You'll reach your goal and far more."

"Thanks, Mr. Guardyall, Peter told me about his visit with you, and I begged him to bring me out here."

"I'm glad he did." Sam looks at his watch, "I've enjoyed your visit. I don't want to run you off, but it's getting late."

"I guess. Mind if I come back?"

"You better! There's one more question I've got, though. Church? Do you go and have you found the saving grace that Jesus provides us?"

"No, and yes, I have."

"You don't go to church, but you're redeemed, and that old nature is enlightened, right?"

"Yes, Mr. Guardyall, I have."

"Praise God. How did that happen for you?"

"It was through your grandfather, oh, four years ago. He had a bunch of us out for a campfire chat and asked if we wanted to know the God who created this. I wanted to know more, so I responded. He took me aside and shared more. I walked away a different person."

"Hallelujah, How about Peter? I sense he's not saved yet."

"I'm working on him."

"Your sister is not a Christian? How about your mom?"

"Yeah, mom says she is."

"Good. Well, Jounger, this has been a terrific day for me. Thank you. And well, I thought I was to teach you something, and here you are teaching me. But hey, when you come back. Bring some more drawings."

Eleven

"King! Get off me!" Sam shouts. He pushes the quilt and the nose of his pet away from his face.

"Woof! Woof!" King barks as Sam turns and covers up in the thick quilt. Then more woofs, and his paws pull on the covers.

"Okay, okay, you gotta go. What time is it anyway?" He peaks at the alarm clock on the table and observes one hand on the quarter-hour point. "Gads! King! It's only three!" He turns away from King's nose. King's front legs push and pounds on Sam's shoulder.

He looks again and sees seven-fifteen. "Okay! Okay!" Sam grabs his thick woolen robe off the bedpost and follows King to the front door, unlatches the bottom half, and King runs to his favorite spot.

"I'm going to fix you a doggie door."

He glances at the thermometer hanging waist level on the outside doorpost and notices the red line between thirty and forty. Sam walks toward the fireplace and reaches for pieces of split wood to place on the ash-covered embers. He blows on those to get a few sparks. He steps to the kitchen to light the Coleman stove and places the water-filled coffee pot over medium-high flames. Sam looks out the window, remembering the necessity of a trip into town.

"Monday morning, it is. Thank You, Lord," he tells the air. While the coffee perks, Sam goes to the bathroom and splashes cold water on his face. He pulls a pair of jean coveralls up to his waist, slips into a red sweatshirt, and pulls the coverall straps over his shoulders. He slides into wool socks and his boots. *"I'm ready! Bring on the day. It's time for coffee and donuts."*

He pulls the hood of the sweatshirt over his head and steps outside to relax. In the rocker, he sips his coffee and watches King sniff around the yard. *"Lord, what is in store for me today?" More food for his pet, batteries, lamp oil, along with some fresh veggies and other items to last him another week.*

"I've got a bunch of reading to do and hopefully add more about this cabin life." Having finished two cups of coffee, Sam freshens King's water bowl and empties the last of his chow in the other bowl. He grabs the truck keys and invites King onto the passenger seat. They leave for town.

He finds a spot in front of the diner.

Finding an empty booth, Joanna greets him as her jaw tightens, and the gum-chewing stops.

"Samuel, it's nice to see you again, but I got a bone to pick with you!"

"Good morning to you, too," Sam replies. "Not busy this morning. Where is everybody?"

"Monday morning, Sam. I'll get your coffee. Anything else?"

"I've been thinking of three blueberry pancakes with crisp bacon. But go ahead and pick my bone. Which one do you want?"

"I'll be right back with your coffee." Joanna turns.

What did I do? Something's up or out of kilter. Her happy demeanor is upside down.

"Coffee." Joanna briskly places the cup on the table and turns to leave.

Sam asks, "What's up? What did I do?"

"No, I'm okay. I'm okay, Sam," she responds as a couple enters the diner. The husband points to a booth on the window side and follows his wife there as Joanna greets them. She walks past Sam on the way to the counter.

"Joanna, let me have it," Sam says.

"You buried my deer!" Joanna replies.

"What? That was your deer?"

"Yeah, I saw you."

"You shot that deer?"

"Sam, let me get their drinks and order first."

She returns with the couple's coffee. She scribbles their order and gives it to the cook, and then brings Sam's breakfast over. She slides into the booth and explains how upset she was to see him burying the only deer she and her husband saw that morning.

"Sam, we had been looking for that deer for hours, covering every area nearby where it could have gone. Through the scope, I could see the wound as it stumbled, and then it ran off into the woods. We looked for hours but finally gave up and were heading home. Coming upon the lake and across from your cabin, I saw you digging. I looked into the binoculars and saw you rolling 'MY' deer into the ditch. I wanted to scream. That was my first hunt of the season, and it got away."

"I'm sorry, Joanna. I had no idea."

"My first one, and you buried it!"

"So, that's what this pouting was all about?"

"Gotcha. Why did you bury it, Sam? Don't you like venison?"

"Nooooo! Never have acquired a taste for it."

"Sam, you're going to have to if you want to live like a frontiersman."

"Oh, yea! Watch me! I've got lots of turtles and snakes out there."

"Your grandfather liked venison."

"Joanna, on another subject, these pancakes are getting cold. Would you leave me alone to enjoy my breakfast? Refill my coffee!"

"Touché," she replies. "Okay, I know when I'm not wanted." Her warming smile graces the gum-chewing with those middle-aged wrinkles curved upwards from her bright deep brown eyes.

Joanna hollers, "Good morning June, Betty. Grab a table! I'll be right with you."

June pauses at Sam's booth while the other lady continues, "You're Samuel, right?" she asks.

"Yes. Hey, it's good to see you, June." Sam stands to greet her. "Join me?"

Looking ahead to her friend and back to Sam, she replies, "I'm with my partner, and you've heard that three is a crowd."

"Let's have a crowded table then."

"Hey, Betty. Come and meet the grandson of Joshua Guardyall."

"Hi, Betty, join me. Please do." Sam shakes her hand. "June and I met and had dinner together."

"She told me about it, Samuel."

Joanna approaches the table with two menus saying. "Ah, my favorite lesbians."

"Joanna!" Sam exclaims.

Joanna replies, "Hey, these girls are proud of it."

June answers, "She calls everyone names. You ought to hear her with the southern hicks."

"So, what will you babes have?" Joanna asks.

"Hot tea. Would you run over to Starbucks and get umm . . . chocolate parfait?"

"I'll run over you first, Betty! Hot tea, and the same for you, June the mimic?"

June replies, "That'll be the day when you can outrun your forever moving lips."

"If you're looking for ridicule, this is the place," Betty tells Sam, "We have a professional day, so here we are getting berated. Why do we continue to come back?"

To change the atmosphere, Sam asks, "What's your subject, Betty? I remember June telling me she teaches English."

"American History. I've got one class here in Prairieville and two in Johnsonville. And no, June teaches Geometry."

"Hmm! Sorry. History was not one of my favorite subjects, except for Greece. I've always had an interest in Greece because of those great columned buildings they created." Sam replies, noticing June reaching under the tabletop, sensing that she is now holding Betty's hand. "Generally, are the students learning anything from history that benefits their growth as adults?" Sam asks.

"Nah. Old-time stuff relating to names and dates. It's required."

"In other words, Washington was the first president, and he wore a wig."

Betty chuckles. "Yeah, that's it. Teaching to the test. Now, June has it tougher with Geometry and coaching the golf team."

"Betty, how long have you been teaching?"

"This is my ninth year. June thinks this may be her last."

"You're going to quit?" Sam asks. "Why would you want to quit, especially after the success you've had with girls' golf?"

"That's the one thing that's holding me back. I don't see the same enthusiasm among any of the younger girls. They just want to play. It's a game to them, something to enjoy. That's all."

Sensing an opening to bring his Christian faith into the conversation, Sam states, "Having that burning desire from within is a God-given gift. Recognizing it and following it is difficult in today's world."

June's hand rises to the tabletop as Johanna sets down the hot tea and asks the ladies, "do you want a cold breakfast, or do we have to warm it up for you?"

Betty replies, "No, just the drinks. We stopped by to watch you chew. That's all today."

Johanna lays down the bills and picks up Sam's plate, and Sam slides to the edge of the booth.

"Sam, are you leaving?" June asks.

"Yeah, I need to go. Got a shopping list down to my toes."

"Sam, let me buy your breakfast," June offers.

"Thanks, but no, I got it," Sam replies. He picks up their bills to put with his and adds, "Hmm? Thinking about the girls playing golf, I can't imagine being a teen in today's mixed-up world with technology saturating everything. Now, kids push a button and see what's happening in Moscow. And they can play games with a student over there."

Betty answers, "We've learned a lot since those days, and It's better and fairer for all of us."

"Sorry, but I've got to go. Blessings to both of you. Good luck with the golf June." Sam states. "But don't forget our creator, the majesty of the heavens, and the wonders around us. And one day, each of us will stand before Jehovah to justify our lives."

"Oh, you're one of those," Betty says.

"Goodbye, Sam," June says.

"God bless you in your endeavors with the kids," he says and leaves.

Sam recalls a hymn he had been smitten with and starts to sing it on the way back to the cabin. "Take my life and let it be. Consecrated, Lord to thee…."

After putting the groceries away, Sam is at the typewriter.

My Cabin Life 7

After Angelia died so suddenly, I lost any faith I had. I rebelled and gave in to drinking too much, desiring nothing. There was nothing left but work. The house was silent. The beauty of every little thing she had done to make it a happy place to come home to, was as she left it, gathering dust. Instead of rushing home after a day in the office, I'd find myself at a bar devouring liquor, peanuts, and more booze. What's the sense of anything?

Life is senseless. There's no meaning. It all comes to nothing anyway, so why not. Yeah! I lost that desire to create something new, and I turned to drowning my sorrows.

And then one day at home watching a ball game while having a few beers and snacks, I looked up and saw the picture hanging on the wall. Back to the ball game and another gulp of beer, I looked at it again. I liked the beautiful oak frame while Angelia loved the picture. She proudly hung it above the entertainment center, where we couldn't neglect seeing it every day, as we relaxed watching a movie.

Back and forth, my eyes drifted between the picture and the game. Over and over again. The picture slowly became my focus.

My soul was seeing it as if for the first time. It, that artistic painting for some strange reason, yet now not strange appeared alive to me. I saw the blood pouring out of his sides, his arms, shoulders, feet, and wrists, the blood dropping to the ground. The blood coming out of those thorns around his forehead, dripping down his cheeks and jaw, mingling with the flow from the other side, gathering on his neck and down to his chest. I saw the lifeless eyes, eyebrows sticking out, and his head hanging low to one side as he is suspended from that wooden cross.

Inside each drop of blood, I began to see videos exploding within each droplet of the wrongs I had committed throughout my life. What I had done to a girl while in the third grade, what I had called schoolmates, my secret transgressions, the lies I told, the items I pocketed without paying, and thousands more including actions I would never have considered as having crossed the line. Still, motion pictures and movies of all my wrongdoings coming alive out of each drop of blood, and then disappearing back into the drops.

I fell to my knees and sobbed. I felt ashamed. I wept. I cried out.

All those wrongs were now wiped away, and I was forgiven. I was healed. I was starting over. A new person. I wept again, this time with joy running over.

Life had meaning again, and I have not felt sorry for myself since His light penetrated my darkness.

Leaning back in the chair, Sam rereads what he wrote, rethinking that event and what transpired over the next week. After a few sips of his coffee, looking out the window for signs of King, he starts writing again.

A few days after my deliverance, I informed my secretary what had happened, and she enthusiastically responded with a big "Hallelujah! I've been praying for you." I was back, the old but renewed me had returned. Then the next week, Sandy brought me a registered document indicating it was from a lawyer somewhere in Colorado. Upon reading the first page, I was stunned, and all I could say was, "Huh?"

The letter told me of my grandfather I had never known, leaving me his log cabin and acres of land surrounded by the forest in the foothills of the Rocky Mountains. There were a few pictures of the cabin and the view. It was now mine. All I had to do was sign the enclosed receipt and return to the sender, and the deed would be returned shortly.

I called the attorney to be sure this wasn't a joke or hoax by some huckster out of reach of our federal laws.

Yep, no up-front money was demanded of me. I was told I would get a cash bundle of $5,000 to cover moving expenses.

Also, inside the envelope was a letter from my grandfather explaining how he missed knowing me as I was growing up, and how he missed my dad. He then went on to explain what had happened between them. I wept again, for my father and my grandparents, who suffered from the breakup. The letter tells of them being at my father's funeral and hoping that he would get to meet my mother and me. He was disappointed that we had not come. His wish was that upon his death that I would respect his desire for me to take care of the cabin for the rest of my days and pass it along to my heirs as a family heirloom.

The letter relates to the magnificence of frontier life being alone with nature and nature's God, experiencing the most serene, beautiful, and refreshing relationship with this God of ours on a daily and hourly basis. I'm in. I'm going for it. I'm selling all. A backpack, a suitcase, and that picture will be it.

Thank you, Lord.

Then after letting it all sink in, my thoughts went up to Angelia, now watching from the heavens. I knew that she would have loved the idea, loved the entire concept as described by this letter and the pictures enclosed. She would have been packing immediately.

Oh, Angelia, I miss you, but one of these days I'll be in your company again and you in mine. In the meantime, I will be thinking of you while experiencing and learning a different way of living.

"King, where have you been?" Sam shouts as his pet, pulls the door open with his paws and jumps over to be petted and loved on by his owner. "You look worn out and a bit cold." Sam rubs his ears, his head, under his jaw, and down his sides. "Go, get by the fireplace," Sam commands, but King turns toward the bowl of food next to the front door.

Twelve

"Now, where's that recipe?" Sam finds his grandmother's cookbook of favorite cabin recipes. He goes to the paper clipped page labeled, "**My favorite Chili.**" He puts a frying pan on the iron plate along with a pot for the pinto beans, a jar of diced tomatoes, and then he empties the package of chili sauce. Frying the ground beef, green pepper, onion, and garlic, he muses, *So what's so hard about cooking? This will be good for a week.*

While the chili slowly blends, Samuel goes out to the porch with the Greek language book. He rehearses the pronunciations while rocking in one of the chairs and periodically watching King roaming the yard sniffing and pushing the volleyball with his nose.

It's a chilly, still sunlit day shimmering bright orange, showering upon him a comfortable feeling. The reddish leaves are dropping from the two trees by the gazebo. The lake waters shine the reflections of the green forest rising and merging into the snow's pale whiteness down the sides of the peaks.

Sam had scanned the Farmer's Almanac. This will be a pleasant winter it posted; some rain but not much snow nor ice is forecast, relatively mild with chilly mornings and warmer afternoons.

"Yes, winter is creeping up on me, but bring it on. I'm as ready as I believe I can be."

Breathing deeply, he sighs, "Ah, nature, the magnificence of it all. God, how did you do it?" Sam speaks out to the clear blue sky as King approaches, wanting some loving. "Okay, buddy, here, go get it!" He tosses the Frisbee toward the shore. Back and forth, King chases the disk with never-ending energy. "Had enough? I want to relax." King starts running hard toward the entrance.

Soon, King is running and jumping alongside a pick-up that's coming into view at the corner. It slowly moves around the circle. It stops and backs up to the barn. *Ah.* Sam reflects, *my wood has arrived.* He gets up from the rocker to greet the two strangers. "King!" He shouts. "Here!" The dog obediently backs from the passenger door to get a pet on the head and neck. "Sit!"

Seeing the dog sitting at Sam's side, a middle-aged man slowly gets out the driver's side, "Mr. Guardyall, good morning."

"Morning."

"I'm George Patacky, sir."

Shaking hands, Sam replies, "Nice to meet you, and thanks for bringing the wood." Sam looks down at King, "King! Greet the man." King raises his paw.

George extends his hand to the paw. "Nice dog. He's a beauty."

From the passenger side, a young man gets out and slowly approaches. "Mr. Guardyall, this is my son, Steven."

"Hi, Steven." Sam then moves alongside George to the rear of the truck. Steven lifts the double board gate out of the restraining holes and lowers it to the ground. He places one end of an eight-foot-long, two-foot-wide track of rollers on the truck bed, and the other end on a knee-high bench at the entrance to the barn.

Standing in the truck, Steven puts bundle after bundle of five to six firewood pieces on the track, letting them slide down to where George and Sam stack them inside the empty stall.

"Sam, besides delivering wood this time of the year, I'm also the Scoutmaster," George tells him. "We spent many days and evenings out here with your grandparents."

As they unload the wood, George tells Sam of the many campouts, canoeing, and fishing the scouts had been able to do. "The scouts loved to sit beside a campfire listening to your grandfather tell stories. He also demonstrated the methods of skinning a rabbit, a deer, and de-feathering a goose and then preparing those for cooking over a fire."

"Wow," Sam replies. "Sounds as if I'd enjoy that and could use it to aid my cooking skills."

"Sam, it's a pleasure to have you here. Your grandparents were wonderful, and we miss them both."

"Thanks, George. I've been hearing stories of them since moving in." Sam answers and turns toward the young man, "Steven, I assume you're a scout too."

"Not anymore. I graduated."

George speaks again, "Steven reached the Eagle rank before graduation, but you know how expensive college is nowadays. We can't afford it, so he's been helping us and saving to at least get a start somewhere. He's been doing some studying online in the meantime."

"What are you interested in, Steven?" Sam asks.

"Engineering, possibly chemical."

They finish stacking the firewood, "Hey, you guys don't have to rush off, do you? Come on over and relax a bit on the porch." Sam says.

Looking at Steven, George answers. "Sure, why not? We've only got one more quick delivery to make today."

"Good," Sam replies. "King, we've got a couple of new friends. Let's go." Reaching the porch, Sam says, "Hey, how about some lunch? I've got a pot of chili stewing. I was ready to get me some when you guys pulled in. There's more than enough. Come on in."

"Steven?"

"Sure, Dad. I've always enjoyed seeing this cabin."

"Good." Sam opens the door, and King runs for his bowl of food. Steven goes to the bookcase and starts scanning the titles.

"Pull a chair up to the table, George. Any other work besides this and the scouts?"

"I'm a tree cutter supervisor for the mill."

"How long have you been doing that?"

"Twenty-two years."

"I've heard stories around town expressing the anxieties of the logging industry here." He then raises his voice toward Steven, who's fingering books, "Steven, how did you get interested in chemical engineering?"

"Through your grandfather on one of our scout camps," Steven replies as he takes the few steps over to the table.

Sam reaches up and pulls the drapery aside to reach in for three bowls. He dons the glove, lifts the large pot's cover and scoops out enough for each bowl, and carefully places them in front of his guests.

"Thanks, Mr. Guardyall." George tells him and then adds, "It smells good."

Samuel pauses and bows his head. "Yes, Father God, thank you for this day, these new friends, and our many, many blessings. Amen."

George says, "Sam, what did you do before moving here?"

"I was an architect outside Indianapolis when I received the notification that my grandfather willed this to me."

"Married?"

"No, my wife died," Samuel replies, and then he relates how that affected him and how he got redeemed. Sam takes a breather, filling the spoon with his chili, watching the reaction to his testimony as he devours more chili. "So, here I am."

"How are you adjusting?" George asks.

"I don't know how I could manage the sometimes loneliness I feel, but with King around, it has taken the sting out of it. King has been a blessing," he pauses, looking down at King.

"Steven, tell me more about what you see in chemistry that fascinates you."

"Oh, I'm just intrigued by what's under the surface, this physical realm."

"Yes, scientists have been peering deeper and deeper into the unseen world. This morning before you guys showed up, I asked God how He did this. This earth could have been placed a bit closer to the sun, and possibly we wouldn't freeze in the winter. He could have done it a million different ways, right?"

"Yeah!" George asks, "What did He say?"

"Ah, the thought of Adam and Eve disobeying that one command came to my mind, and here we are today having to work hard for everything rather than enjoying the fruit of the abundant gardens."

"Wow, He did respond to your question."

They look at each other, "Hey, isn't that the way we humans are?" Sam adds. "I wanted an out loud reply calling me by my name. I was so physically focused that I couldn't hear that still small voice, but I did, and still didn't recognize it."

"Hmm?" George responds. "I think we all have that problem."

"Thanks, George. One of the benefits I'm discovering by moving here. I can be still and know that God is God. It's a blessing I never had before. Hey, but enough of me, it's your turn George to tell me more about you, your family, work, and more about the scouts."

Sam pauses and then asks, "Steven, you devoured the chili. Was it that good, or doesn't dad feed you enough?"

Steven answers, "Dad abuses me by making me do his dirty work on an empty stomach."

"Yeah, right. You get paid too." George replies.

Sam slides out of his chair, reaches to the pot to refill their bowls along with his own. He sits back down, "Okay, George, your turn."

George puts the spoon into the bowl. "Well, ah. I grew up in this town, knowing that the mill would be my work. College was not even considered an alternative: married Mary, my girlfriend from back in the tenth grade, right after high school. Steven came along a year later. The mill was prospering, and we were able to purchase some acreage out of town. We have a few cows and chickens and plant a garden each year, living as naturally as we can. I have not experienced any tragedy as you have. My parents are still living in the same house in town. My brother and I get together frequently. Mary has three brothers; two of them graduated from college and are now off in Denver working. You have already met the other, Jimmy. He brought you out here your first day."

"No, kidding. Jimmy is your brother-in-law?"

"Yep."

"What a small world. Jimmy and his family came out for an evening not long ago. So, Steven, you and Peter have known each other for a while."

Steven answers, "We're not that close because of our age differences, but we do chat when the families get together. He told me about his visit here and that you gave him a camera. Peter is different from most of the kids his age, if you know what I mean."

"He sure does like taking pictures. Steven, tell me more of what is so interesting about chemistry? What would you like to do with it?"

"Not quite sure yet, but there must be better ways of combining materials to make our roads smoother and longer-lasting. The asphalt and concrete always break apart from the traffic. Can't we add something that'll make it last longer?"

"Doesn't the subsurface have a lot to do with that?" Samuel asks.

"Then we ought to figure out how to make it more stable. The roads are terrible. Bumpety, bump, bump. That's it."

"As an architect, I had to deal with stability problems all the time, and it's not always an easy solution. Cost always plays into it. Anyway, Steven, you're asking the right questions. Every improvement starts with a question, a wondering of why not. Look how long it took Edison to develop that first light bulb. It began with a question, an idea followed, and then the developing process to put the pieces together."

Steven ponders those remarks and then, "I've got lots of questions."

"Sam," George says. "Steven has streamlined our unloading operations coming up with the idea of that roller track. Previously we had to hand each piece to someone on the ground."

"Good going Steven."

"Thanks." Steven answers. "I couldn't understand why dad hadn't done it before."

"Say, George," Samuel says. "Tell me more about your work with the scouts. Hey, yeah! Why not? Bring them out. I think I'd enjoy that."

"There'd be about 30 of us."

"Sounds good."

"And ah, don't be concerned about restroom privileges, as we have Porta Johns. We'd take care of providing everything. All that's required is your Okay."

"Ah, but don't we need a contract signed in front of three witnesses?" Sam adds, looking for a reaction.

"Get outta here," George answers. "Seriously, the weekend after this would work for us. It'd give me time to round everyone up. We'd pitch the tents, have canoe races, build a campfire. We'd bring all the food. And, it'd be terrific if you'd participate in some way, perhaps giving a speech or fireside chat."

"Hey, that's fine by me. I could read parts of a Hardy Boys book."

"Oh, That Hardy Boys series. I think I read every one of them, kept them in my library, and Steven has enjoyed them too, right son."

"They were quick reads," Steven says.

"Yes, they were," Sam replies. "I don't know why, but I never read them as a kid, so some twenty-years ago, I borrowed one and started reading."

Turning his wrist over to see his watch, George looks at his son and then back to Sam, "Sam, I've enjoyed it, and thanks for the chili. It was excellent! We've got more work to do. I'll get to abuse Steven some more." He then pushes his son almost out of the chair, "we've got to go. Clean your bowl or no dessert."

"Yeah, right. You see that, Mr. Guardyall? College can't come quick enough."

"Sam, it was a pleasure to meet you," George says. "I've enjoyed the fellowship, and God bless you on your transition. We'll see you next Saturday, about noonish."

Watching them drive off, Sam whistles to King, following the truck along the gravel path. King stops, sits down, looks back at Sam, and back to the truck pulling around the corner and out of sight.

Raising his voice, Sam calls out, "Come, King, let's go!" Sam walks toward the gazebo, brushes leaves off the cushions. King leads Sam on their somewhat ritual walk, to the shoreline, and then into the woods, following the path deeper and further into the forest. Their walks together last anywhere from a half-hour to two hours, depending on the turns, the exploration interests, and Sam's mood. They come upon the sign. **You are entering a national forest. Please obey all rules of sanitation.** Sam stops and turns to head back to the dock and beyond to the stream. Reaching the creek, Sam says, "King, what say we sit and relax a bit."

Sam reflects on the day as his hand rubs the head and neck of his pet. Thoughts of the upcoming visit of the scouts. *What will I say? Scouts? What are they truly interested in?*

Then, the thoughts come again about that beautiful antique carved top wood case at the foot of his bed. Everything else in the cabin was open and readily available, with all the necessary keys neatly placed on the handmade rack by the front door. *Why hide that key? What's so valuable in there?*

Thirteen

"King! Stop it!" Sam brushes his cheeks and then pushes King's head away and rolls toward the edge of his bed. "Ah, come here! You're my alarm clock."

Standing, he throws the robe across his shoulders as King runs to the front door. Sam opens the bottom half of the Dutch door, and King rushes out. Sam notices the thermometer reading at 45°F. He leaves the door partially open. "Burr! Chilly! Yuck!" He Walks to the fireplace and places a few thin branches on the ashes from last night. Striking a match to some crumbled paper, he watches the wood slowly ignite and then puts a few logs on top. *King got his turn, and now it's my turn.*

"Oh, where's that hot water?" he mutters as the water slides from the pump onto his hands.

"God," he mumbles. "I've asked that that longing for convenience and comfort be gone. Why? It'd be easier if this were all I knew. You've told us to ask anything in Your name, and You'd do it. I've asked, pleaded, and yet at times like this, I still get a desire to chuck it all."

The coffee brews. King pushes the half-door open. The soft cool breeze penetrates the insides. Sam takes the few steps to close the door and reaches down to rub the dog's ears and neck, "Whew, you're cold!"

Sitting at the butcher-block table, Sam devours a banana, a glass of orange juice, and nibbles on a piece of hardtack topped with orange marmalade. *Ah. The scouts are coming soon. What will I tell them?* He scribbles on a notepad: FIND KEY, and below that, "Forgive me, Lord. But my flesh is still lusting after that easy, comfortable life I remember so often. I'm sorry. Forgive me. You've put me here, and I thank you for it. You have led me beside these still waters, and I will. I will. I will embrace it. Thank You."

He leans back in the chair and looks around the bookcase, the fireplace, the kitchen drawers wondering where the key to the footlocker would be. *Now, why didn't I think of that?*

"But first, gotta do some laundry."

The old stove is warming. He places a large pot on top. He goes into his bedroom area, gathers up the dirty clothes, carries the basket, and puts it on the counter. He pours some detergent and then the heated water into the sink, repeating until the sink is half full. Removing the items from the basket, he places them one at a time into the warmed soapy water. Stirs the water and lets it sit. As the pot of cold water is warming on the stove, Sam takes an item out, squeezes and twists the soapy water out. He neatly untangles each item and slowly pours the freshly warmed water over the linen, twists, and squeezes the soapy water out until Sam sees just clearwater dripping. Each cleaned item is then flipped and hung on a string to dry. Two hours have passed.

Sam then walks out to the shed, picks up the ax, and runs his fingertip over the blade.

Good. Now, split a dozen pieces in half. He selects those that look the best for the stove and places them beside the wooden stump. He chooses the first piece and stands it on its end, and swings the ax.

"Good going, kiddo. Not bad for a city guy." He tells the air. Ten pieces have been split and cut to the appropriate size for the stove. Just a few more, and he'll have enough wood for several days. Sam aims at the twelve-inch-long trunk standing on its edge. "Ouch! Yowie!" as he falls to the ground. He sees blood soaking his jeans as his hands reach down to his calf.

The blood runs down the side of his leg and into his boot. He pulls the sweatshirt over his head to wrap around the leg, hoping to get it tight enough to stem the flow of blood. Feeling the rushing pain, he stands and slowly hobbles back to the cabin. He grabs a towel from the table to replace the sweatshirt. He finds the first aid kit and rips the cover off a roll of gauze, and it fumbles to the floor. Sitting on the footstool, he pulls the pants leg up over his calf to expose the slice of skin and sees blood seeping out. He pushes the towel over the wound and wraps the gauze around the leg, and tapes it together.

Sam limps to the pick-up musing, *Thirty miles to the hospital.*

"Help me, God!" he hollers to the rafters of the barn.

He guides the truck into the country road while trying to ignore the pain and the creeping numbness. Managing the clutch and the accelerator pedal with his left foot, he gets it into high gear. He quickly passes one car and then another, honking and ignoring the speed limit.

Reaching the hospital, he sees Emergency Entrance. He comes to a quick breaking stop under the canopy. Leaning forward in a sigh of relief, Sam pushes hard on the horn, again and again. He leans forward onto the steering wheel. "I'm in your hands now. I quit." He says out loud.

A nurse comes around asking what the problem is. Sam opens the door, pointing down to his lower leg, which he can't move. She speaks into her cell phone, hooked onto her shoulder.

The next thing Sam is aware of is feeling a warm hand stroking his wrist. Opening his eyes, he sees the knuckles and a forearm in white. He slowly blinks a few times, and his eyes focus on the wires of a scope hanging around her neck. He blinks again and focuses on the eyes below a shrub of hair.

"I'm Dr. Ingersall. What day of the week is this?" she asks.

"Umm, Thursday." Samuel softly mutters.

"What's your name?"

Looking at the lady and around the room, back to the lady standing alongside, the white blanket covering him, and back to the lady holding his wrist. He feels the tightness of something around his leg and then remembers the ax hitting his leg and the scary trip. He asks, "What time is it?"

"It's six-thirty. You've been under sedation. Can you tell me your name?"

"Samuel Guardyall."

"Good. What happened? How did you cut your leg open? What do you recall?"

Gaining more consciousness, he tells the lady what happened. "The blade saw my leg and thought that would be more fun."

"I see. Yes, it did a good job of it. You now have thirty-two stitches down the side of your leg."

"Great. I gotta get home."

"You better have a good talk with that ax of yours when you get home, and tell me, how did you get so much blood on your ear?"

"My ear?"

"Yes, it looked like it was cut."

"I don't know. Is it okay?"

"Yes, we cleaned it, and it's fine."

"When can I go? My dog."

"We have to monitor your vitals for a bit. You should be able to go in the morning, so rest up tonight. You lost a lot of blood, Mr. Guardyall. I want you to come back in ten days, and we'll check your leg."

"Thanks, doctor. What's your name again?"

"Francinea Ingersall. I was the lucky one who put your leg back together. Be more careful next time."

"Thanks, but you won't see me again."

"You will in ten days. Now rest up. Would you like some coffee? Dinner is on the way. Ten days, and I'll look at it, okay?" Sam watches her turn and leave.

Around noon the next day, Sam drives into his domain. King excitedly welcomes the truck as Sam parks it in front of the barn. Opening the door, King jumps on him. "Hi, buddy, whatcha been up to?" He runs his hands up and down the dog's back. Kings' long tongue slides in and out over the cheek and ear of his master. "Yeah, I missed you too."

Sam reaches in to get the crutches and slowly adjusts to walking with his right knee bent and the foot elevated. Looking into the eyes of his pet, Sam says, "Yeah, I know that look. Now everything is fine, I'm okay, you're okay, and I'm back." Sam opens the cabin door, and the dog runs to the food bowl.

I've got to write this down while it's fresh in my mind. He sits at the desk, resting his leg on one of the cushioned chairs. He starts pressing the keys.

My Cabin Life 8

On my recent visit to the hospital, fully awake after being ministered to, resting while waiting to be discharged, I caught myself intently looking at all the equipment. At the beds, the nurses' stations and their computers, the beds that transport patients, the elevators, the ceiling lights, the individual rooms, the hallways, the offices, and that warming signal above each wide door. On and on, I saw all this stuff, wires plugged into the walls connecting with the main cables inside the hard support systems. Along with the wires, the plumbing system bringing necessary water in, and other pipes discharging the waste.

As an architect, I was visualizing those wires gathering together with other wires from the inside walls to the outside walls, all heading toward fuse boxes, which are connected to a primary outside source of power.

If that power source is interrupted or cut, then everything suddenly grinds to a halt. It dies unless there is an alternative source of power taking its place. Otherwise, the entire system is dead; only a physical building, a body of inner parts immobilized, just there, unable to function as designed.

Then I visualized this body of ours. We each have a head office where records are kept, and decisions are made within this physical machine that enables us to move about and communicate with others.

Inside this chest cavity are the various organs connecting with others, designed to function together with the other organs by tubes carrying a red fluid substance throughout this physical being. Along with those vessels are electrons from all the physical parts connecting to this head telling me, "That hurts."

"Oh, King! Stop it! Can't you see I'm busy?" Looking down at the dog who has that look of, 'it's time, let me out, now!' Sam puts the crutch under his arm and proceeds to open the door as King barks a loud 'Thank you. Was that so much trouble?'

Sam refills the coffee cup, hobbles back to the desk, reads the previous notes, and then starts typing again.

In the hospital, there's a powerful pump pushing water throughout the hospital walls to the restrooms and coffee stations. In our bodies, there's the pulsating motion of our heart pushing the blood throughout our bodies to our toes, fingers, and tongue enabling us to taste the coffee. But even that needs the invisible phenomenon known as the air we breathe into the double organ of our lungs. Without that oxygen, everything stops. It's over, just a physical dead thingy ready to decay back to dust.

But what starts this heart beating before we enter this physical world, and what initiates the lungs breathing in and out when we exit our creative domain?

As a designer, I lay out those electrical wires to connect with other wires at a fuse box, with several or many of them connected to the main outside source. One can disable parts of that building by scraping the protective coating of the wire or by pulling one fuse. And one of those can burn out by putting an overload in one area, or it simply gets old and wears out.

Are we able to do that with this body of ours? Can we overload an organ? Yes, we can and do that easily in this modern culture of ours, more often than not. It's our inherited nature to want more than we need.

We don't have a physical wire connecting us to an outside power source as that hospital has, or do we? It's invisible to our naked eyes, but it's there just the same. The air we breathe is invisible providing this body with oxygen and nitrogen, and small amounts of carbon dioxide and others, which is then transmitted through our bloodstream to the heart muscle and the rest of this body. Then, as we exhale, portions of that intake are sent back into the air. Inhale and exhale.

Apart from that air we breathe, we can do nothing, Physically and emotionally dead. Yep, just plain dead, of no use whatsoever.

A couple of days ago I randomly picked up a weed, brushed off the dirt covering the roots, wondering as I held it in my hand how the creator envisioned this tiny part of nature. From our standpoint, it's just an unwanted weed, with roots extending down below the surface into the dirt. That seed met the nourishing dirt which causes the seed to open and send a root down, along with a stem growing up and out into the oxygen with branches of leaves flowing out the sides breathing the air. Without the moisture in the dirt and the oxygen in the air, the planted seed would still be lying there. Remove one part and its purpose will die.

So, it is with us.

"I am the vine, you are the branches to bring forth much fruit when abiding in God," the scriptures tell us adding, "apart from me you can do nothing." That invisible oxygen from our Lord God Almighty Designer to our lungs and physical heart provides life to this body of ours.

Can we sever this connection? Yes and no. Just as that hospital power source can be physically hindered or disabled intentionally or accidentally, our physical relationship can be severed by a bullet in the head. But also, no, it cannot, if the oxygen is here to breathe our creator never severs that spiritual connection. That boundless love is always present knocking at our door desiring each of us to seek and to know Him, to love and to worship the great I AM.

Amazing when thought upon. Yes, even when neglected, it's still wonderfully magnificent.

Oh, how I get carried away by these thoughts, perhaps sometimes redundant. But here I am having been led to these still waters, now visualizing spiritual concepts all new to me. I want to shout it all out to the world.

Never before have I understood these amazing truths that I'm now beginning to understand. The amazing width, breadth, depth, and height of this creation. God with us, God in us, God for us, God in the heavens. God sustaining it all. God surrounding us with that ever-present evidence of those first six days.

The great Architect is in this bountifully beautiful earth of ours, in the fouls of the air, in the wild animals and the depth of the seas. With this natural eye of ours, we can't see the nitrogen, oxygen, carbon, or vapors in this air that sustains us. We can't see our spiritual nature either, nor do we see the spiritual part of this vast universe, but it's there; continually supporting us and keeping us alive.

Yes, it is here every day, every millisecond.

Oh, the majesties of it all!

"Oh, I like that!" Sam tells the air after re-reading those last notes. "But one more thought entered this skull of mine," he utters out loud and begins typing again.

In the book of Leviticus, way back when the Lord was speaking to Moses to sanctify the tabernacle, Moses took the blood of the ram, putting some on Aaron's thumb of his right hand and the big toe of the right foot and his right ear. The blood of my cut leg covered my right foot. In the process of wrapping the leg, I got some on my right hand and why, but I scratched or rubbed my ear. Why those specific areas?

I now claim the blood of the Lamb protects this cabin, the entire area, myself included, and all that is done here. So, hear this, you devil you. All you hovering demonic spirits, this place is covered by that sacred blood. I am covered, so get, now and forever.

I am free.

Fourteen

"King!" Sam calls. "Come here! Where are you, boy? You've got a mission to do for me this morning." Sam stands, reaching for the crutches. He leads his dog to stand in front of the wooden footlocker. "Smell this," Sam says, pointing at the lock.

King sniffs the front of the lock, the sides, the top and bottom, and back to the opening where the key would fit.

"Good boy. Now go find the key!"

King sniffs the base of the footlocker, under the bed, the tables, the room's perimeter, the edges of the cabinet, the restroom, and the baseboards, to the corner to the bookcase. He's sniffing the bottom shelves of books. King comes to a spot in the bookcase. He raises his paw to the third shelf to sniff a section of books. He stops at the only unlabeled book. His tail straight out and stiff, his nose pressing into the cover.

Sam reaches over to remove that book from the shelf. He opens the hardcover and discovers just a tan paper cover. The real book is titled; *"On the Incarnation."* He sees a scribbled note taped to the inside cover.

C.S. Lewis has been noted as saying, "It is a good rule, after reading a new book, never to allow yourself another new one till you have read an old one in-between. If that is too much for you,

you should at least read one old one to every three new ones."

Sam flips through the pages and finds a white envelope taped onto the inside of the rear cover. As he holds the envelope, his finger feels the hardness of a key inside. "Yippee. King, you did it! Good boy!" Sam reaches down to love on his pet, and King chomps down on the new treat. "Now, let's go see what's inside that foot-locker."

Inserting the small key into the built-in lock, Sam turns the key, and the locked fork is released. He slowly raises the curved top revealing a bunch of scrapbooks, perhaps a dozen or so. Opening the first one, he sees a black and white photo of a young lady in a wedding gown snuggled next to a young man dressed in his navy blues. They're standing in front of the gazebo. *Our day 1942,* is neatly written below the picture. The next page shows Joshua boarding a bus, the penciled note, *on the way to the Pacific.*

Turning each page, he slowly looks at the four by six pictures of different times in his grandparents' lives. Sam settles in, sitting on the floor with his back leaning against the bed, his right leg straight out. He picks up the next album with a dated series on the front. *"Why was the key hidden away so carefully just to protect these scrapbooks."* He wonders. He removes them all. Sam pulls up on the pieces of ribbon and raises the false floor.

"Wow." He exclaims at seeing a six-shooter pistol, a bright shining silver handle, an eight-inch-long barrel, and a six bullet-revolving chamber.

Next to that, carefully fitted inside the foamed cushion are the disassembled parts of a double-barrel rifle, again similar to those of bygone days. Below the foamed cushion, Sam discovers another hardboard. His fingers find the slips of ribbon, pulls the cover-up revealing more antiques, a Polaroid camera, a Brownie, and a leather holster holding a bayonet.

Leaning the cardboard upright, Sam turns his attention to the curved top area of the case, and pulls on the fake cover. He finds an old leather-bound book with a raised script, **Novum Testamentum Graece**

"Wow." Sam exclaims, *"this looks like an original. It probably should be in the Smithsonian."* He carefully picks it up, opening the cover, and immediately sees a few loose typed pages. Leaning back against the bed, Sam starts reading.

To my grandson Samuel,

Welcome.

You have found these notes I leave you, along with the cherished keepsakes from my parents and their parents too. I have prepared these notes when I realized the end of this physical life was approaching. Soon I shall be joining Gloria. I have lived a wonderful life, with no regrets, except for the antagonizing confrontations of your father wanting above all things to embrace technology in its fullness. And of course, that my dearest Gloria joined the Lord first, leaving me alone for this last year. I would rather have had us go together, but our human desires are often selfish. There was more for me to do.

I pray that these notes are encouraging. They relate some of our life here in this cabin where I was birthed. You've seen the scrapbooks, which Gloria has carefully put together. Those pictures were precious to us, keeping the past from being dismissed by the present.

As Mr. Lewis was so fond of reminding us that the past is the clue to our present in so many ways, but the here and now easily neglects the past because of our pride.

These older books have stood the test of time, whereas many new ones will soon fade away, not standing that test time has for everything. The new being continually replaced by even newer books.

One's heritage, where we have come from, our forefathers and their forefathers, siblings, aunts, uncles, and cousins from the same heritage. The family unit, how they lived, how they survived, what they learned and read, and how they related to each other, shed light on our present conditions. Sure, each generation gains additional knowledge and discoveries which often tempt us to dismiss the previous times as being out of date and filled with useless old customs, ignorant ideas, and stupid habits. The next generation will be saying the same about you.

Yes, I was amazed when NASA put a man on the moon, but then so what? We still had problems getting along with our neighbor and our neighbors neighbor near and far. Alexander Bell brought us together by speaking over a wire, and now we've learned to talk around the globe through the air, and we still don't get along with our neighbors. The Wright brothers failed and failed again and again, and now we hear the sounds as hundreds look down upon the rest of us, as we forget the days of horses pulling a wagon.

Yet, the ones in the wagon survived and may have been happier and more contented day by day than us hurrying to some far-off destination to relax a few days enjoying the palm trees and ocean breezes.

Long before, the Romans learned that individual happiness was greater when they were provided with entertainment to watch, and now, well, enough is enough, as we don't get bored with boredom.

So, Samuel, relax, be still, know, and embrace the stillness meeting the Lord God as this magnificent creation is revealed. What good is it when one eats properly, so the blood vessels keep the body alive, but allow the spirit to fade?

Samuel, I also regret that we had never been able to embrace each other, and I will be waiting for that time when your days are complete and you join us.

God's blessings upon you.

Joshua.

Sam leans back against the bed, his head against the mattress, his eyes visualizing the heavens above. "Thank You, Father God," Sam mutters as he gently rubs the head, neck, and down the side of his pet.

Finding a three-ring binder in the case above the Greek New Testament, his curiousness is again roused as to what else had been left for him. Opening the notebook, he sees newspaper pages with dates on top, the first one faded and edge worn. **"August 10, 1941."** Under the date is a headline, **"Churchill meets with FDR"** Below that is a handwritten note in underlined letters just one sentence long, it says,

Soon America will be immersed in a war on two fronts, against two enemies of freedom.

Pondering the note against his recollection of history, Sam mutters, "Huh? The headline is four months before Pearl Harbor."

Barely visible at the bottom of the note, he sees the initials **_BG_**

"My great-grandpa," Sam mutters.

He thumbs through the book seeing page after page of typewritten sheets; some taking the full page, some partially filled, some spilling over to the next page. Returning to the beginning, he finds the next page blank. The following page has a date at the top and below that a prominent headline and more writings. Flipping the pages, he notices the dates were getting more recent. He stops at one dated January 20, 2009. No title, just a full page of type.

Starting to read, King starts barking, breaking his concentration. King runs toward the front door. Placing the binder on top of the scrapbooks, Sam slowly stands; he makes it to the door using the crutches. Opening the top section, he sees three deer feeding off the grass in front of the gazebo.

"Quiet King." He softly says, as King paws on the bottom section wanting out. "Come on, boy, quiet, let me watch them." The barking continues as King jumps up to see out over the closed bottom door's height, and the deer run off into the forest.

"Okay. Time to get some work done. I've got that list somewhere." Back in the bedroom, "I'll get back to these later, but now…I think I can do this. I've got to. It must be done and done now. It's been on the list for over a week now." He carefully pulls on a pair of jeans, grabs a hooded sweatshirt from the closet, a couple of gloves, and at the front door, he slides into his left boot, then loosens the strings of the right boot before sliding his foot inside. Sam walks to the barn without the crutches, limping quite a bit. He grabs a funnel and the five-gallon can of gasoline to fill the tank of the rototiller. He primes it a few times. He pulls the handle once, twice, three times, and the machine spits out a few billows of smoke and then settles down to a rumbling purr.

Sam tests the switches, lowering the blades, raising the blades, and increasing and slowing their speeds. He shifts the machine into drive. He tightly grips the handles and limps off toward the garden area. Slowly he maneuvers the tiller blades into the dirt and proceeds forward, slowly turning the soil over the decayed vegetation. Holding tight the handle to release the pressure on his leg, he tries to negate the thumping numbness. He continues straight toward the fence.

Agitated, he stops. "Wisdom Sam. Use it. Pretending will not help."

"King, where are you?" Sam takes out his whistle and blows a long blast, then two short ones. Soon King is seen coming out of the forest with a rabbit hanging from his jaws.

"Oh, boy. Another one." King drops his prize catch at the feet of Sam, sits back looking at his master, his tongue moving in and out with the tail waving.

Sam picks up the rabbit, rubs his pet. Using the crutch, he enters the cabin and sets the carcass on the butcher block. Finding grandma Gloria's recipe and food preparation book, Sam opens to the page headed **"Rabbits."** Refreshing his memories of what he must do, he finds a sharp knife to cut the skin along the belly. His fingers reach in to remove the guts, saving the heart, liver, and kidneys. Using both hands, he pulls the skin away from the meat. He cuts the head off, the paws of the feet, and then washes it all in cold water. He carefully cuts and removes the silver skin attached to the raw meat, and when finished dressing it out, he cleans the beef again in cold water and plentifully rubs it with rock salt. He sticks it in a bag and places it alongside the block of ice next to two other rabbits. Discarding the remains, Sam washes his hands and pours himself a fresh cup of coffee. He refreshes Kings' water bowl and dishes out more treats for his pet.

"Now, it's time to rest a bit."

Sitting and rocking on the front porch, his right leg resting on a bench with King at his side, Sam reflects on what he will discuss with the scouts. He reviews the scout oath and law and what they promise to do, and how they will govern their lives as scouts.

"Yes," he surmises, "that's the subject. That's it. And, Yes. Why not?"

Sam sits down at the desk, picks up the pencil, and starts drawing.

An hour later, he stands. "King, let's go for a walk. Eh? No, I better not do that, but let's climb in the boat and do some fishing."

Using a single crutch, he goes to the barn to get two rods, some bait and dons those rubber boots. "Come," Sam hobbles off with crutch and poles.

Grabbing the rope holding the boat on the shore, Sam uses the crutch to push the back end into the water pulling it alongside the pier to sit on the dock's edge. He lowers his good leg in first for support as he swings the hurt leg in. King jumps toward the front seat. Sam pushes the boat away from the pier giving him room to operate the oars and guiding it along the shore toward the stream feeding the lake. The slow, steady stream bubbles into the calm, deeper waters where he drops the anchor. He baits one hook, throws the hook, sinker, and a bobber off one side of the boat, and throws the other line out off the rear of the boat. As the boat sits still, King stands, looking over the area, into the forest in front of him, periodically looking down into the water, his weight shift rocking the boat. "King, my boy, one of these days, you're going to fall in for a swim."

Looking around the area, the natural beauty around him captures his attention. The stream comes into his focus, noticing the many rocks of numerous sizes under the steady stream of clear water rushing into the lake. He focuses on the larger rocks upstream, causing a little waterfall, which has a deeper pool receiving the flow.

He ponders on the shape of the boulders forcing the water more to the edges of the stream. "As an architect, I would have made the center of the stream to have the greater flow of water," he reasons. Then the thought comes, *Ah! Isn't that the way we humans are, mostly unhappy with it as it is, often thinking we could do it better. What do we call that?*

He then visualizes the roots of the trees and how they reach out under the banks toward the water. Then back to the water itself, he notes how clear it is, transparent enough to see a foot or two through the surface, a shimmer of silver among the light blues continually changing as the water moves.

A saying comes to mind, *"one can touch the water of a flowing creek only once as the water that just touched has already flowed away and new waters have surrounded your hand. The first is long gone, new waters on the way."*

Time is like that." Sam summarizes. *This morning is gone, never to return. Angelia is gone, never to return. Grandfather is gone, so what's coming next?* He then feels a pull and sees that one of the bobbers is gone too.

"I've got one."

Fifteen

"King, here they come." Sam states as King rushes off the porch toward the white four-door pick-up pulling a trailer with six canoes. The truck carefully maneuvers around the trail, stops, and backs up to the lake. Two other cars pull into view and stop near the gazebo. King is alongside the truck as the door opens. George Patacky bends down to pet the dog. The other three doors open, and three boys dressed in scouting uniforms cautiously look at the dog, except for Peter, who calls out, "here, King!"

"Afternoon. Sam. We're a little late, but here we are."

Using the crutch as a pole vault, Sam rushes out to greet them.

"Sorry, but we had a little trouble getting our equipment loaded, but ready or not, here we are."

"Been looking forward to it," Sam replies.

"What'd you do to your leg?" George asks

"Ah, stupid me, I chopped my leg instead of the wood."

"Hmm, it's going to be okay, though, right?"

"Yeah, it just needs some time."

"Sam, are you up for this now? We could come back another time."

"Hey, all I'll be doing is watching anyway."

"Okay, then. Only ten could make it this weekend. Short notice. Sam, you recognize Peter, right? And these other two are Harry and Jack, both eagle scouts now.

"Hi, Peter. Good to see you again." Sam shakes his hand while noticing the camera hanging in front of his scout scarf. "Jack, glad you could make it." And to the other one, "Greetings, Harry. My dog and companion here is King. Say hello to him."

Harry reaches down to King as the dog raises his paw to receive Harry's hand. He's a tall, muscular youngster with a broad chest, looking like he could pick King up with one hand. Jack, shorter and slender like a marathoner, follows suit as the tail of King waves back and forth.

"What happened to the rest?" Sam asks.

Peter responds, "Ah, they chickened out because of the weather tonight."

"Now, Peter." George rebukes. "Yes, we are expecting cooler weather tonight, but it was the short notice that made it impractical. Anyway, let's get these canoes to the shore. Sam, I'm sorry about your leg, so sit back and watch, and I do appreciate your hospitality. These guys are ready." Another truck with a trailer pulls into the drive pausing at the bend. George asks, "Sam, where would you want us to put the Porta-John?"

Looking around the area, Sam tells him, "Wherever you put it all in the past. Just do it. It'll be fine with me."

As they're spreading out the supplies, Sam takes the opportunity to individually greet each scout as they erect the tents and throw their knapsack, sleeping bag, and air mattresses inside. Two boys to a tent. Five pup tents in a line outside the gravel path facing the gazebo. George locates his cabin type tent off to the side facing the lake. The Porta-John, a special design of the scouts, twice the size of those plastic ones, has two side-by-side doors, each door having a quarter moon.

"All right. Guys, let's go," George states.

George leads the scouts to the lake, where the canoes are unloaded and lined up on shore. "Sam, you can row a boat, can't you?"

"Yeah, sure."

"I need you to row your boat to the middle, drop the anchor of the buoy, and then go to about twenty yards in front of the stream, where I want you to anchor your boat. You'll stay there and watch the races. It'll be somewhat of a triangular course. This is how the first race goes. When I blow the whistle, the teams will race to their canoes, get in and paddle around the buoy, around your boat, and then back to the shore, pulling them up on the beach as they were. Five canoes going at it."

Sam responds, "Okay! I'll make faces as they come at me."

Peter hands the camera to Sam, "Here, if you don't mind, just keep clicking."

"Sure, Peter, so when you get close to me, smile."

"The oldest is paired with the youngest," George explains. He looks at Sam for any further questions. Seeing Sam's expression, and states, "Ready, let's start this thing. So, go ahead, and now I'll have some time to talk with the scouts."

On the way out to the middle of the lake with King in the front, Sam notices that George has the scouts lined up facing him, and then he leads them in calisthenics. Jumping jacks and then down for push-ups. Jumping jacks again, and then squats, back to jumping jacks and running in place.

Admiring their warming up period, Sam reflects *these kids are learning that old code, no work, no food, no play.*

In position, Sam waves to George standing at the edge of the pier. The ten scouts lined up in pairs on a line near the gazebo. George blows the whistle, and the kids rush to shore. They push their canoes out, jump in, grab the paddles, and they're off pushing the water as hard and as fast as they can, heading to the buoy's red flag. One canoe takes a short lead, three close behind, appearing like they were pushing off another's sides, and one slowly falls a bit behind.

Looking through the camera lens, Sam focuses on all canoes, then zooms in to each one, back to all of them as they circle the flag. Soon, he's able to distinguish the canoe of Peter and Martin in second place.

Watching the effort these kids are putting into this simple race, Sam thinks. *No audience to cheer them on, no cheerleaders jumping and shouting, throwing pom-poms in the air, no bands playing. No, it's only a race. Why aren't there hundreds of boys, thousands of youngsters in every town, and parents encouraging their sons to learn these principles? These boys are blessed to have a dedicated scoutmaster, as George certainly appears to be.*

Sam reminisces back to his teenage years of working to help his mother make ends meet, throwing newspapers before school, rain or shine. There was no time for this.

The kids finish as Harry and John John win by two lengths. John-John, the youngest, and a tenderfoot, is high-fived by Harry.

George announces, "Great race, guys. The next will be by rank. The two Eagles against each other. Then the two Life scouts. The three Stars, and last, the first-class scout against the two tenderfoots."

"Ready, get set," He blows the whistle, and Harry and Jack take off.

Sam rows the boat closer to the straight line from pier to buoy flag, where he continues to take pictures of each scout stroking hard on one side and then to the other side to keep the canoe going on a straight path to the red flag. In the last race, Harold, a chubby tenderfoot, was kneeling on the canoe's bottom while the other two are in the rear seats pulling the oar hard against the waters. Watching them, Sam notices how each appeared to be putting their best physical efforts into beating the opponent.

"Sam, come on in." George hollers. "These guys are resting a bit, and then we'll get to the next phase. Sam, this will be a race between you and me. Ready? The scouts will be egging us on in their canoes. Just the two of us. Ready?"

"No, no, no, no! Not me!" Sam emphatically resists. "I've never paddled a canoe. Never sat in one."

"You've never been in a canoe?"

"Yep, not once."

"It looked as if you know how to row that boat of yours. Okay, it'll be me in a canoe against you in the boat. How about that, then? Scouts, what do you think?"

"Yes. Yes. Yah. Go for it," The scouts insist.

Looking at the scouts and George, Sam finally says, "Oh. There's something fishy here."

"Come on, Mr. Guardyall, go for it. You'll enjoy it." Harry states. "Yeah, you have the advantage. You have two oars, and they have more pushing power than the canoe paddle. Two oars versus one. Go for it."

Jack speaks, "And your boat rides higher in the water compared to the canoe with its rounded bottom, and Mr. Patacky in the rear makes a deeper draft. Come on, Mr. Guardyall, do it."

"Hmm. Well . . . Ah . . . Okay. I give."

Peter takes the camera. Sam is seated in the rowboat on one side of the pier, while George is on the shore, ready to push and jump into the canoe on the other side.

Harry blows the whistle. Sam starts pushing the oars against the water; as George pushes the canoe into the water with the paddle pulling it alongside the pier, he steps in and starts paddling. Sam immediately takes a short lead as George leans forward, his left hand on the top, the right hand down near the broad paddle, and pulls hard. His upper body moves forward as his right-hand pulls the oar. He repeats and then changes hands as the oar is shifted to the left side. He is soon pulling alongside the rowboat, smiling at Sam.

Looking at George pulling alongside, Sam, starting to enjoy the contest, digs in. He pulls hard against the water. The two of them head-to-head toward the buoy. The scouts now have their canoes out and are approaching the two adults. They keep a respectable distance away, yelling and encouraging Sam to beat George. Sam is in his competitive mood, pulling hard to beat that younger, physically fit scoutmaster and mill worker.

Sam gains a foot and another foot. He's beginning to feel his heart beat faster, his breathing becoming more profound. He digs in, wanting more than anything to beat this guy. He takes a glance at George, who is now kneeling closer to the center of his canoe.

Sam sees the scouts donning raincoats out of the corner of his eye and then begin splashing water at their master. Another one pushes an oar full of water at George. Sam feels a few drops of water on his bare head and hands, turning to see Peter nearby, and Sam lowers his head, deflecting the splash.

He yells at Peter, "Hey, stop it." But Peter and then Jack intensify the splashes as the scouts in the three other canoes have already ganged up on George. Sam notices that George starts splashing the scouts.

A water fight, eh. Sam throws a big oar full of water right at Peter, who ducks and returns the splash.

The water fight began centered on the two adults, and then it turns into a free-for-all splashing each other, every canoe against every other canoe. Yet, the focus for the scouts was on the two adults without raincoats. George aims one at Sam. Sam back at George. Sam, realizing the bandages on his leg were wet, holds up his hands, surrendering, and then pointing down to the leg bandages.

George surrenders, but the kids continue splashing each other.

A minute later, George blows the whistle.

"I win, you lose," George tells Sam.

Agitated but happy, Sam exclaims, "You bum, you had this all planned from the beginning."

The ten scouts lean back, resting and chuckling, as they remove their wet raincoats, wiping the water off their hair, forearms, and legs.

"Okay, guys, let's go in and dry off, and then, we'll talk about it."

"Sam, I see you've got company."

Looking toward shore, Sam recognizes the iceman's truck followed by King, "It's my ice delivery. He knows where to put it."

Next to George's canoe, Sam rips into him, "You dog, you. Do you plan something like this on every camp-out?"

"Hmm. Sorry, Sam, I just realized that your bandages might have gotten wet. Did they?"

"Yeah, but it'll be okay. Watch out for the payback. And I beat you too, don't forget it."

Onshore, George tells Sam. "These guys will remember this a lot longer than the races. So, let's give them a chance to explore the area for a while, then we'll start the fire and eat."

"Okay, scouts. Now go, explore the area, or take a relaxing ride, whatever. Be back about an hour before sunset." Two by two, they head for a canoe, and others go off into the forest. As they leave, George shouts, "Remember, if you're not back on time for dinner, it'll be right to bed without any."

King looks back and forth at the scouts walking in different directions. He runs after Harry and three other kids, who head toward the forest.

"George, I'm going in and dry off. And change."

George goes to his tent and comes out with a towel, padding his head, jeans, arms, and wraps it around his shoulders as he walks to the gazebo. He strikes a long match to light some crumbled paper and then places it under some dried grass clippings and watches it ignite some limbs and then pieces of wood. Assured the wood is burning, George removes the ice chest and bags of supplies out of the truck, placing them near the edge of the gazebo.

"How about a cup of coffee?" Sam hollers out from the porch.

"Sure, thanks."

"Sugar? Cream?"

"No. Black."

One hand on the crutch, the other carrying two cups, he carefully sets them on the bench and drops the crutch. Sam leans back, taking a deep breath. *Ah, what a day. Thank you, Lord.* "George, sometimes, I forget I can't do some things. This morning I thought I could till the garden."

"When did you hurt the leg?"

"Almost a week now. I go back in a few days for that check-up."

"So, are you now adjusting to this lifestyle?" George asks, lowering the cup from his lips.

"Slowly but surely, I am. It's been quite an adventure."

"I would think so. Knowing how much I enjoy getting out into the woods for a weekend, I can't imagine this being it. I'd miss too much of the sports. Right now, I look forward to watching the Broncos."

"Oh, that TV. That's one thing I don't even think about. Don't miss it at all. Yep, even if I had the cabin wired, I'd pass on the TV. But I did enjoy watching the Colts and the Cubs too."

"Colts? Come on, the Broncos are going to beat the tar out of them."

"I don't care anymore. My focus has shifted, and I love it. What I've learned out here has been enlightening."

"Like what?"

"Oh, I've begun some writing on that old typewriter. The different ways the light of God's marvelous creation have ripped the curtains off of any fog or doubt that had control of me in the past."

"Hmm. Like?"

"As the scripture says, 'then I saw through a glass darkly, but now it's face to face.' It's as when I behold the majesties of creation, the little things, the ants, or the roots of the grass, the trees bearing fruit and water sliding over rocks, the sun, and the shades of the moon. And, Oh, the animals and how they do their thing. I feel like I'm standing there looking into the eyes of God, and nothing else matters."

George replies. "Wow, Sam, you are following your grandfather's path. He was always sharing those same kinds of revelations you're having." George then relates some of the special times he had with the old man and Gloria. "They had fifty of us from church out for a special thanksgiving to share their bounty of turkeys and veggies from the garden. He related stories of his parents' first thanksgiving in America and the building of this cabin in these woods."

Sipping the nearly empty coffee cup and setting it down on the bench next to him, George stands, "Ah, I think it's about time to call these kids in and get on with the evening."

"If it's okay with you, I was going to talk about that scout oath they take?"

"Sounds good," George responds and puts the whistle to his mouth. He takes a deep breath and blows loud, again and again.

"I've got a pot of chili that's been warming on that stove of mine. It'll be ready now."

"A pot of chili?" George repeats.

"Yep, and I made some bread too."

"Bread? You are learning."

"No, just a guy who can read directions. I'll get it. I guess they'll be ready to eat, right?" Sam stands to make the short trek to the cabin putting his full weight on that hurt leg, and suddenly utters, "Oooh!" He stops, reaches back for the crutch, and tells George, "there I go again. Pain is always a reminder?"

"I'll send a few kids in to help."

"Thanks."

Two scouts catch up with Sam as he reaches the porch, "What can we help you with, Mr. Guardyall?"

"Thanks. Come on in."

"Okay, here, you two grab a handle of that pot off the stove. That's it. So, if you'll carry that down there, I can handle the bread. Thanks."

They're all comfortably relaxed sitting around the fire. "King, here you go, have some chili," as Sam puts a bowl of the mix on the ground, and King sniffs and starts licking it up. "Ah, this guy here loves rabbit meat," Sam loudly says, wanting to see if there's a reaction to his mention of rabbit.

George asks, "rabbit meat? It's delicious."

One of the scouts spits out a mouth full.

George stands to address the scouts, "Okay, guys, it's time, and I'll turn this meeting over to Mr. Guardyall as you finish eating. He's got a few things to tell us of this life without any of our modern-day electronics and gadgets. Sam, it's all yours."

Standing with the crutch, Sam looks at each scout, "Guys, it's been fun today, and I'm glad, thrilled that you came out. I've enjoyed it, except for the water fight." He pauses, hearing the scouts chuckle and make a few comments. "But then, that was fun too."

"This life here, at first, was boring without that TV to watch, the computer to read and play games on. But I've adjusted. I've learned that reading is more enjoyable and enlightening than watching a game with three guys telling me what's happening. Or seeing a beautifully made-up young lady telling me what's going on in St. Louis, New York, or Paris, or telling me a tornado hit Oklahoma and those in Arkansas should take cover.

"Reading history and learning what happened hundreds of years ago is more interesting, along with recording those revelations on paper. I've also started to study Greek.

"With that in mind and what I've learned over these past few months, I've been changed. I no longer desire the modern technologically driven life. From my studies into the Greek language, I've learned that the deep meaning of words is vastly important to our understandings." Sam pauses and looks around.

"So, let's get started. I want you all to stand and recite the Boy Scout pledge and law. George, please lead us in that."

Standing with their right elbows extended out, their forearms vertical, and their hands open, and their fingers together. George leads them in the oath, "On my honor I will do my best, to do my duty to God and my country and to obey the Scout Law; to help other people at all times; to keep myself physically strong, mentally awake, and morally straight."

"And now the Scout Law," George leads, "A scout is trustworthy, loyal, helpful, friendly, courteous, kind, obedient, cheerful, thrifty, brave, clean and reverent."

The scouts sit down in a semi-type circle on the grass on one side of the campfire while Sam stands, leaning on his crutch, his back to the gazebo. "Thank You, Okay, now let's delve into what you promised, shall we?

"On your honor, you pledged. What does that mean? What does honor mean? Have you thought about it? I mean deep thought as to what that word honor means. Let me put it this way. While you were anticipating a great time in those canoes and roasting marshmallows, Mr. Patacky, instead of turning into my entrance road, he kept going. He was heading to a dealer who was to buy those canoes, tents, and gear. And you were there to unload it all. What would you think of him then? He misled you. He deceived you. Would you trust him again? No, he would have lost his place of honor. You'd probably be madder than a hornet.

"That word honor describes the highest moral principles and the absence of deceit or fraud. You'd rather die than disrespect what you've honored to do. Your reputation depends on it. That's being an honorable person. No lies, no stretching the truth, not one once of deceit. That's honor. That's what you pledge to do. On my honor, I will … is how you start the pledge. Are you sure that you're up to it? You won't give in, will you? You won't dishonor your pledge?"

"You pledged that you will . . . do your best.

"What does doing your best mean? How is it measured? I watched you doing your calisthenics as I rowed the boat out in the lake. It looked like you were doing your best, but were you? How do you know when you've done your best? Do you compare it with someone else, maybe a kid who tries hard but is not as physically fit as you are? No one will notice you're slacking off. Or, you do your best compared to what you're capable of doing and try to do it better than the last time you did something just because it's you. It's who you are. You made a pledge, and you will honor that pledge to do your best, not only when on a scout outing, but in every area of your life, your homework and studies, and on and on, you are pledging to do your best.

"You pledge that you will … do your duty to God. What duty do you have to God? Duty is a word that means you are expected or required to do something as an obligation. You are obligated to someone for something, perhaps because something was done to or for you, and you owe that one something in return. Now, it's expected of you. You are required to do something—no second-guessing. No questions asked. You've been informed as to what is required, so you do it as a duty.

"But what did God do for you that you owe the Almighty something in return? You're living. You've got life inside your body. God gave you the ability to choose, to reason, to imagine. You have a body to navigate around this world. God has done it all for You. He created this marvelous universe and put you here in this particular spot where you can breathe and learn to live abundantly, enjoying the benefits of a sun rising every day, with animals to enjoy and feed on, water to drink. And in these waters, fish to catch and eat. You have others to talk and fellowship with, and on and on.

"God has done this for you, so what do you have to give as a . . . as a duty in return for this life you've been given? God has also sacrificed His only Son for you. So how do you repay Him for that? You choose to live the way God wants you to live; no lying, no stealing, no cheating, none of that wanting what your neighbor has. And, yes, there's usually something more. And you want to tell others about this gift.

"On your honor, you will do that, right? It is your duty to God to live that way.

"And now here's a tricky one, you also pledge to do your duty to your country. Why do you have a duty to this country? What has this country done for you? So, what do you owe this country of ours? You've been blessed to be born and live in this country that's been a blessing to the rest of the nations. The wisdom of those brilliant men who desired to live free or die and were willing to sacrifice their lives, their fortunes, and their sacred honor to preserve and protect our freedoms began the process of making America. There's that word honor again.

"Think of the thousands of young men and boys about your age, willing to fight the British in our war of Independence. They volunteered, knowing that they may never return home again. There they were standing next to others in a straight line, rifles over their shoulders, marching toward the enemy a hundred yards away. At the sound of the whistle, they hit the ground and fired that one-shot rifle. Then, they possibly saw a friend was shot, who is now lying on his back, moaning and groaning. They reloaded, adding powder, aiming, and pulling the trigger as the rifle pushes back hard against their shoulder.

"Because of their sacrifices, we are blessed with freedoms to enjoy; the right to life, liberty, and the pursuit of happiness.

"Our founders established a contract that our government is obligated to follow. Read that document, and you will not see where it restricts the people, but it emphasizes the government's restrictions.

"Is it not then our duty to defend this country and that document we stand upon against all enemies, foreign or domestic? Is it also our duty to obey the country's laws and those of the individual states, the counties, and cities? That's your duty to this country.

"Sorry, guys, if I'm rattling on too much. But to me, it's exciting to think and reason along these lines, so I keep on going."

"No, it's good, Sam," George says. "I wish I had a recorder."

"Well then, okay. I'll continue into that law you pledged to obey. Have you counted the items in that law? Can you name each one separately and define what each of those twelve means? Why are those character traits called the scout law?

"You pledge to help others at all times. How far would you go to help others? Do you want to help your fellow scouts or the kid who has trouble with his homework, or the kid with one leg? Help others at all times? Hmm? Are you ready to stand in the gap against that bully when other kids have circled and cheered for the bully to beat the crap out of the four-eyed mentally challenged nobody, or the one who is continually picked on because he won't fight back? Will you help? Would you subject yourself, despite that bit of fear, you may have? Hmm? Help others at all times? Yes, because of your honor, you have pledged to do that.

"You pledge to keep yourself physically strong. Those calisthenics help. And the races. But what else can you do? How do you get physically stronger? How do you maintain that strength? Is it by eating happy meals, by snacking on cookies and donuts, and playing games on the computer? No, inside, you know that's not the answer. Have you ever known someone who wants to qualify for the Olympics?

"How about the mentally awake part? How is that done? Are you mentally awake sitting there in front of the TV? You say you're mentally awake playing games on the computer and the tube but are you? Do you desire to know more, desire to know why and how a problem became a problem? Are you always mentally awake sitting in the classroom? Are you now mentally awake, or has the desire to crawl in the sleeping bag crept into your consciousness?

"And last but not least, is the morally straight part. You pledge to keep yourself straight morally. Doing what is the right and proper thing to do, not taking any curves in the road, to see what's out there. You pledge not to bend that straight line. Why is that line straight? Are there dangers waiting in the brush for the adventurous one, for the one seeking a thrill, for the one following along behind the fool who is a follower of many others? We've been told that it's straight and narrow. Why? What's off the path? Where does that trail of dirt lead you? Save yourself a ton of grief by sticking to the morally straight path. It's been tested. It's been proven over centuries of time. It leads to righteousness. It leads to confidence. There is God's way, and then there is man's way of bending the morally straight path to satisfy our lust, our envy, and our pride.

"What are morals? The word moral comes from a Latin term meaning 'manner, character, proper behavior.' Hmm? What then is proper behavior? Who determines what is proper or improper? What are those established rules? It's summed up as the Bible says, "do unto others as you would have them do unto you." You don't want someone stealing your cell phone, right? So, you don't attempt to take theirs. Easy to understand, right? Over the years, has that been turned around to mean, do to others . . . as they have done to you? You understand the difference, right?

"Now, let's look at it in a different way. Do unto God what you'd like Him to do to you. Do you want His blessings, mercy, and forgiveness? Yes, of course, you do. So, you bless God by being merciful and forgiving to all others."

Sam pauses, reflecting on the words just spoken. "Hmm, I just learned something hearing those words coming out of my mouth."

"Scouts, that's about it for me, except, ah, can you tell me what element in this speech was common throughout? Anyone?"

"They all look at each other thinking of the request. Silence. Nothing. Then Harry raises his hand and says, "You kept asking questions."

"You're right, Harry, and thank you."

"Scouts, don't ever be afraid of asking questions. Ask. Even if you know the answer, ask why and how? We wouldn't have electricity if Edison did not ask questions. We wouldn't have the computer if that college dropout didn't ponder and ask questions. It's been said that there are no dumb questions, and whoever said that was right. So, ask; ask your teacher, your scoutmaster, your parents, and your friends too. Ask why, or who said so and what for."

"So, do you have a question for me?" Sam pauses, looking at the ten scouts sitting around the campfire with the flames reaching knee-high.

Looking at each other and back to Sam, there's a short pause, and then Jack raises his hand.

"Yes, Jack, what is it?"

"Ah, during the water fight, were you doing your best splashing water back on us when you yelled that's enough? Was that the best you could do?"

The rest of the scouts snicker, and then one repeats. "Yeah, you quit. So was that doing your best?".

"Good question. Ah, let me put it this way. Yes and No. Yes, at first. I was splashing that water as hard and as fast as I could. I wanted to drench you, and I was working hard on doing that. You guys with your raincoats while my sweatshirt got soaked, along with the bandages on my leg. That was not fair and equal. So that's why I quit. Now, if you did not have the raincoats, would you have even started it?"

"Another question?"

"What do you do in your spare time?" Another student asks.

"Spare time. Ha. One of the things I enjoy most is my rocking back and forth, letting my mind wander and ponder the majesty of this creation we live in, imagining and questioning how and why our creator made a sparrow, an eagle, and then snakes and possums. We'd be fine without snakes, right? So, why are poisonous snakes here?

"Another?"

"Yeah. Why?" Harry asks.

"Don't know. Or, could it be to remind us of Adam's and Eve's mistake?"

"Well then, my time is up. But, please feel free to ask anything anytime. I will always welcome any of you to come for a visit; whatever I'm doing can wait. I enjoy those visits. It'd be educational for me too. So, to end this chapter, I'll ask your eagle scout to lead us again in the scout oath. Harry."

Harry proudly stands in front of the others, raising his arm, his elbow bent and hand open. "On my honor…"

Finishing the pledge with a bit more emphasis on the words, they relax, sit, and place some marshmallows on rods while quietly watching the flames.

Harold moves close to Sam, and in a quiet voice, he stutters, "Ah, Mr. Guardyall, some…. ah, times I want… to…ah quit, but Mom… Dad… won't… let me…. I want to…. I don't… but . . ."

"Harold, that's your name, right? Sam asks the youngster, along with other questions finding out that the boy is twelve years old and joined the scout two months ago.

"I'm fat…. I …can't… what… others…can."

Sam's questions find that the other scouts have not been making fun of him. He has one sister who he considers not fat, but he is.

"You're a brave boy. You know that?" Sam says. "You showed courage when you came over to talk. I'm proud of you for doing that. You know that back in history, people did not eat three meals a day and snack in between. Nor did they have soda pops and potato chips, nor happy meals. Some were only able to eat once a day."

Samuel pauses to look around at what the other scouts are doing.

"Then Harold, starting during the industrial revolution, the idea that we must eat three meals a day slowly became the accepted norm for everybody. It started as a way to give the factory workers a break. Then as the huge grocery stores opened and drive-in restaurants developed, frozen food took the place of mom cooking from scratch. Food was no longer a work for necessity. Nope, it was now easily available, and so here we are being told that eating is fun." Sam pauses, looking for a reaction of some sort.

"What do you think you ought to do?" Sam asks.

"Lose some… weight."

"How?"

"I guess… ah… quit… eating so much."

"Anything else?"

"Exercise?"

"Harold, you've known the answers all along. You didn't need to ask me. That's known as the spirit of God instructing you. Obey it, and you'll be fine. And don't give up. It possibly took several years for you to put on that excess weight, and it'll take many moons to take it off. Keep on keeping on. And, that inner voice is worth following.

"Yes, it took a lot of courage to come over and ask, so again, I'm proud of you. Hmm? I don't think I would have done this when I was your age."

Sixteen

"Ah, warm this place up," Sam tells the air. He strikes a match to ignite a crumbled typewritten page he had put under several pieces of kindling.

Inside the closet, he retrieves some sourdough starter mix, sugar, a bit of salt, baking soda, to be mixed with some cold water, and two eggs for a few pancakes to start the day, along with that never-ending cup of coffee. *Not too bad for a city guy.* Sam contemplates while forking the first taste.

Now that hot coffee and food have hit his belly, Sam grabs the Greek book and gets warm and fuzzy in front of the fireplace for an hour or more study before typewriter time and venturing out with King.

After some diligent study, Sam looks down at King curled up on his pillow. "King, if you could speak Greek, this would be more interesting and easier."

Some thoughts are running through this skull of mine, so I'd better transfer them to paper. So here goes.

My Cabin Life 9

On that recent outing of the boy scouts, George, the scoutmaster, and I had a good discussion while the scouts were out exploring the area.

Think George, I said, how much time is spent sitting there in front of that tube. It's about 30 hours a week, around five hours a day for adults, and then for kids, it's more. One goes to work for eight hours, getting an hour off for lunch, and perhaps an hour's travel time. Add an hour in the morning preparing for work, a quick breakfast of some sort after, say seven to eight hours of sleep. Twenty-four hours are gone.

If there's laundry or home maintenance responsibilities, or activities for the children, where does it fit? We squeeze it in on those days off work. During the week, is there time for exercise, devotion, reading, conversational family dinnertime? No time for that, grab your plate, and let's watch American Idol, the NFL, MLB, or a movie. Oh, CNN has a special update on political shenanigans. Ah, record that, and we'll watch it later. A new hilarious movie has been released.

Commercials? Ha, we think we don't pay any attention to them, but the next time you drive by the sizzling burger joint, it comes to you that they've added a new item people are excitedly talking about. On the way home, stop and get that new improved sensational dietetic juice on sale before they're sold out.

On and on it goes, so who has time to sit, relax, and be captured by the majesties of creation and those heavenly revelations surrounding us?

I was like that until this phenomenal encounter.

I'd get fanatical about the chances of the Colts going all the way. Having season tickets, I'd spend my Sundays preparing for the game, donning the latest Colt jersey and jacket, and making certain to get a good parking spot and in my seat before the kick-off. And to watch the pre-game entertainment while enjoying snacks and beers in a huge coliseum packed to the rafters yelling, cheering, waving hankies, and booing the refs.

Going way back in history, the Romans started it all, and now we've built huge million-dollar facilities, so seventy thousand can gather for a few hours of watching grown men bumping heads over a pigskin ball.

What's the difference between the Roman idea and ours? We call it sports. They called it Gladiator contests.

Now I love sports and think it's great for the kids to learn to play together as a team while increasing their physical conditioning. Much is learned through competition. It's a game, it's a physical contest, and the best team wins. But then our human nature gets carried away.

The Romans were part of history, ancients, and here we are. We have the unbelievable, traveling at seventy miles per hour enjoying freedoms the rest of the world envies. We don't call our sport facilities coliseums, no, they're stadiums. But how many relate it to history repeating itself.

That TV has demoralized us too. Hollywood? People call it acting, deem it an art, and young kids dream about becoming a famous star. Those professionals use their talents to imitate another, and yes, they do it well. We're mesmerized for a couple of hours.

Down to basics, actors will do and say anything for a buck, and its big bucks too. They've mastered the skills of pretending to be someone else, so it's excused, not even imagined that they've abandoned any basic personal morality they may have had. Now it's make-believe, so it doesn't count.

Don't they look fantastic on red carpets gathering to applaud themselves? Like everything else we gravitate to, just pure simple entertainment, pleasing ourselves. It's our nature. It's that double-sided nature we are born with. We want what we don't have. We want what others have. We desire to live in the garden of plenty, never having to work for anything or sacrifice anything, because, well, that's what Adam and Eve were given, and now the Lord will soon return taking us out of here.

Do we even think about why that anticipated return is necessary?

We hear or read about it from so many of our preachers now. Books after books have been written about those last of days, so be of good cheer they say, the rapture is coming and we'll be delivered, . . . but, maybe God will wait until the super bowl is over, as I got a bet on the Colts.

Yet throughout history, the same old prophecies have been made of the soon coming finality being right around the corner, so relax people and be ready to hear the trumpets at midnight of next Saturday, or perhaps next month, the next new moon.

Nothing has changed; we're the same human as our great, great, great, great grandparents were. Only technology has changed, bringing us closer together even though we're still thousands of miles apart. But we're no different in our make up as were the cave dwellers. We just do more, faster, easier, and more comfortably. I often wish I could have it out with Adam, but I'd probably do the same as the temptation dangled before me.

And now these ever-present conveniences have affected the youth of today as a beep, not a spoken word, a frown or a smile from mommy or daddy letting the kiddies know they're wanted, loved, or needed. Nope, now it's Beep, "hi". Beep, "wats u do?" Beep, "nada."

Are we not concerned, as these will be the future leaders of our country and the teachers in our schools? Oooooh, what a thought that is. Beep. "ok, students." Beep. "recite the alphabet." Beep. "huh?"

But the questions keep coming back to me, and it's not time yet. These times are warnings for us to heed, to wake us up out of our stupor, to humble ourselves turning from our wicked ways. If we see the warnings, what do we do about it? Or, do we keep on keeping on forgetting?

It looked like I put George to sleep with those ramblings.

Is this my purpose here? To share these revelations with teens.

Whew, that's enough for today, and I'm going to need more white-out soon. Ah, for the days of computer typing and automatic corrections. Ah, there I go complaining again. "Sorry, Lord. Forgive me."

It's a cloudy day and cold, no sun shining through the treetops, so Sam resigns to spend the rest of the morning reading. Relaxed in front of the rising flames, a cup of coffee nearby and King at his feet. Sam's eyes get distracted to the window. *It's snowing, it's snowing.*

"King, let's go enjoy this first snow." Clothed in the hooded sweatshirt and jacket, he slides into his boots and opens the door for King to bolt out. Sam takes a few steps into the open-air. He raises his outstretched arms and hands to catch the big flakes.

"Come on. King, let's go for a walk."

Sam grabs the crutch and follows King to the lake, where he stops to admire the wide-open view of the waters absorbing the flakes. They tread inside the forest, shortly coming upon the bend of the creek bubbling into the lake. "We can do this," Sam tells the crutch. He meanders alongside the stream, going deeper into the woods and up toward the road while watching the snow resting on the higher branches, some filtering down to settle on his hood and shoulders. Reaching the road, Sam sees the roadside food stand. A few cars whiz pass as he reaches the mailbox, finding a few letters and a bundle of advertisements. *Yep, if it weren't for these businesses sending all this enticing stuff, our postage would be double or triple the cost, but I'm one they can forget. What would the newspapers have said during the days of Jesus performing miracles? Would there have been ads selling carefully collected bits of discarded bread and fish? Advertisements for vitamins enabling one to walk on water?*

"Anyway, King, let's go," Sam announces to his pet as he sees another car fast approaching from Johnsonville. Sam turns to start the walk down the dirt road to the cabin when he hears the long honk of a car as it passes, then stops, makes a U-turn, and turns into the dirt path behind Sam. The driver honks again.

Looking through the windshield, Sam recognizes the Eagle Scout as he opens the door waving and greeting Sam. "Hello, Mr. Guardyall. I'm Harry, remember me?"

"Yes, of course, Harry. It's good to see you again. How are you?"

"Good."

"Where you headed?"

"Ah, going for a ride, seeing some sights, and watching the snow."

"Beautiful, isn't it? Hey, why don't you come on in, and we can watch it hit the lake and the hillside."

"Ah, I got a friend with me."

"Yes, I see that."

Harry opens the passenger door. Sam sees a trim auburn-haired attractive young lady with expressive catchy eyes, showing a warm smile as Harry's friend steps out. She is donned in a fur-collared tan coat down below her knees, her lower legs covered by high-rise tan boots. "Mr. Guardyall, this is Meredith Ingersall. How's that leg doing?"

"It's healing fine, and I'll be off this crutch soon."

"Meredith is relatively new to the area, so I was taking her on a tour."

"Hi, Meredith." Sam removes his gloves to shake her hand.

King approaches, sniffing her jacket. Unhesitatingly she reaches down to pet the dog behind his ears and rubs his neck. "Nice dog, you sure are fuzzy." Continuing to pet the dog, she says, "Mr. Guardyall, Harry has told me about this cabin of yours. I'd enjoy seeing it sometime if you don't mind."

"Sure. Why not now?"

Meredith turns back to Harry to tell him she's going to walk along with Mr. Guardyall and the dog. "I'll meet you there." She hollers. Harry gets back into the car and slowly passes them.

"Meredith, Harry indicated you're new to the area, sometime earlier this year. Where from?"

"Indianapolis, Indiana."

"No, kidding. I moved up here from Shelbyville. Wow. What brought you here, Meredith?"

"My mother's work. She wanted to get out of the house and start over somewhere else, slow down, and get away from the big city rush. And memories. She found someone here she could partner with."

"Your father?" Sam softly asks.

"He was killed while filming some kind of military operation in Afghanistan."

"Oooh, I'm sorry. How long ago?" Sam states. "I'm sorry."

"Two years now," Meredith responds.

"My wife was killed in a car wreck. I had a difficult time coming to terms with it. I'm sure you and your mother had a hard time too, right?"

"Yeah, we did."

"You said he was filming a military operation in Afghanistan?"

"He was a photojournalist."

"A brave man. Wow."

"Yes, thank you. It was an operation where our men were providing food and shelter to displaced children when the terrorists captured him. Were you in the military?" She asks.

"Nope. Never was."

"Most of his work was travel type shots. He's been all over Africa, the Middle East, and to Easter Island."

"Wow, the comments you made indicate your pride to be a part of him. Exciting life for him, but how did your mother adjust to those absences?"

"Keeping busy while waiting for the daily calls."

He asks, "You're now okay with the move?" Sam reasons: *In one way, she has come to grips with her loss but is she still seeking answers to why these things happen?* "You're still in school, right?"

'Yeah, I'm a senior. And, yes, I resisted at first, didn't want to come, but then, this small-town experience is overwhelmingly better than those imaginative thoughts I had."

"Meredith, you're a very bright girl, as I sense you've been a Christian for some time now. Am I right?"

"Yes, I am. I got saved on one of my fathers' vacations when we took a trip to Yellowstone."

"Fantastic."

"This is a beautiful walk through these woods. I want to slow down and enjoy this. Wow!" She stops, catching a few snowflakes on her glove, bringing her hand up to eye level intently looking at the flakes hitting her mitten and slowly melting. "I wish I had my microscope."

"Oh, I would love to view each flake too. The heavens declare the works of God."

As they round the corner seeing the view of the still water lake, she stops. Admiring the scenery and the first sight of the cabin, she exclaims, "Wow. Now that's a cabin."

Sam notices the look of amazement on her. He pauses at the sight as he did the first time he had turned the corner with those thoughts of viewing a cover of a Nature magazine. Their stupor ends as Harry approaches with King alongside.

"Eh, Meredith, was I right?" Harry asks.

"Oh, seeing this in person is better than anything anyone could describe in words. Mr. Guardyall, my mother will want to see this too, and I want to send some pictures home to my friends so they can envy me."

"Sure. Come, look inside."

Sam opens the Dutch door for Meredith, followed by Harry, as King rushes by to tongue in some water and chew some food.

Sam goes to add a few logs to the fire seeing the inside thermometer reading 52^0.

"Have you read all these books?" Meredith asks.

"No, I'm just beginning. That may take a lifetime."

As the two teens scan the hardcover books' titles, Sam offers them a cup of hot tea or chocolate. Meredith chooses hot chocolate, and Harry asked about coffee. Harry sits down at the typewriter desk, watching Meredith's curiosity over the hundreds of books; every so often, she remarks on a specific one.

Interrupting Meredith's intense look at the bookcase, Sam hands her the hot chocolate and sets a cup of coffee down on the typewriter table. He asks Harry, "How did you two meet?"

"We met at church several months ago. She's a marathon runner." After a sip of the coffee, Harry adds, "Mr. Guardyall. I recently read a book about a guy who went into Alaska's deep woods and built a log cabin using only hand tools, an ax, a handsaw, hammer, and chisel. It was on a lakeside setting such as this."

"He built the cabin from scratch?"

"Yeah, it took a year."

"I'd want to read that. Does the library have a copy?" Sam asks.

"Could be. You could read mine when Meredith finishes."

Meredith responds from her glance at the books, "I'm about halfway through now. Who built this cabin? It's got to be a hundred years old. I'm always amazed at how the frontiersmen managed life." And then she adds, "And now we get upset if our Wi-Fi cuts off."

"Ha, I no longer miss that stuff anymore. I did the first week or so, but now with all these books to read, who needs it."

"Who built this cabin and when?" Meredith asks again.

"My great grandfather did somewhere in the 1800s. My grandfather was born in this cabin, probably right here in front of the fireplace. He lived here his entire life of 94 years."

"Now Meredith," Sam continues, "can you imagine giving birth to your first child, possibly right there on the floor. No nurses, doctors, and all the specialized equipment in use now, perhaps not even a midwife as it could happen unexpectedly."

"Oooh, I'm glad we progressed past that."

"Yet, somehow the pioneers survived, sometimes the mother cleaning the baby as her husband may have been out hunting for the day's food. He got the surprise when he walked through the door with a couple of rabbits to cook. Kind of revolting to think about it according to our standards, isn't it? Yet, that part of historical history is neglected. How did they manage? What was their daily life like? Was personal happiness a goal as it seems to be now?"

Harry adds, "I asked my history teacher about that, and she changed the subject back to the rulers and what they did."

"Did you, Harry? Asking questions, are you? That can be dangerous?" Sam jokingly tells him, and then he asks, "Meredith, have you an interest in a special career?"

"I want to be a doctor of some sort, like my mother. That's been with me since I was six, putting band-aids on my dolls. Possibly a missionary outreach."

"That's wonderful. How about you, Harry?"

"Not sure yet. Right now, I'm focused on getting a football scholarship. Have had two schools scouting our games."

"I understand you are good at it."

Meredith agrees, "He'll get that scholarship. I'm sure of it."

"But you'll still need a major course of study."

"Yeah, but a scholarship is the only way I'll get to college."

"If you don't get it, then what'll you do?"

"Mechanics. Work on cars or carpentry. If I do, then I'd choose a major in business or accounting."

"See, you do have a plan."

"You ought to see his birdhouses, and he made a podium for the youth director." Meredith proudly informs Sam as she moves away from the bookcase, carefully holding the half-full cup of chocolate to sit on the couch. Harry then joins her, taking her hand in his and pulling her closer.

Watching them, Sam's eyes move from Harry to Meredith and back again. Sam reclines in the cushioned chair next to the couch, wondering *just how intimate are these two teens*. "Can I ask you two a loaded question?" Sam asks and then notices the sudden change in the expressions on their faces as they turn to look at each other.

"Observing you too, your affection for each other is obvious. So, where are you two headed? Not that long ago in history, kids your age would have already started a family. Harry would be helping dad manage the farm, and Meredith would be getting a chicken ready for dinner while also keeping watch over the little one. That's the way it used to be. Were people back then happy as a lark?"

Pausing some, Sam takes a sip of coffee while wondering about these two who have suddenly come into his life. *They seem to be interested in history as well as each other.*

Sam starts the dialog again. "Maybe you got ideas. What does happiness mean? They put that into our declaration of independence next to the rights of life and liberty. What did our founders mean when they inserted the "pursuit of happiness" as one of our fundamental rights declared as being unalienable, a gift of God? Have any of your teachers broached the subject?"

A silence envelops the three of them as Sam looks out the window at the snow getting heavier and heavier. *It may be time for them to get on the road before the accumulation makes the road difficult.*

Meredith is the first to respond, "Oh my. It's an emotional thing. I've become happier by moving here and meeting Harry." Her eyes are shining, her smile broadening as she turns, leaning her shoulder into Harry.

"You're right on the money; it is an emotion. But it's something else too. Now, how does the dictionary define happiness?"

Harry asks, "How do you define happiness?"

"Never thought about it in the past as I was more interested in sketching and drawing houses than thinking about what happiness meant. Is that the fault of teachers? No, I think it goes back even before my generation." Sam pauses. *These two high school kids seem to desire more.* "The dictionary defines it as associated with pleasure or joy, which is closely related to big smiles, full tummy, and no frowns."

Meredith adds, "The game shows. Winning the lottery."

"Okay, back to definitions. What did the founders mean? It couldn't mean just the freedom, the right to find and pursue pleasure. What are they teaching now?"

"Ah, I don't recall the subject ever coming up except as a quote," Harry tells him.

Sam continues. "All I recall reading about it is that they argued over inserting the right to property into that declaration but decided against it as so many people did not have the means to acquire a slice of land. That was more of an economic issue, not an inalienable God-given right as Life and Liberty are."

Continuing, he adds, "The life and liberty part is easily understood as we all want life and to live as freely as we are able." He pauses, waiting for an acknowledgment to continue or quit. Seeing their somewhat interested looks, he continues.

"Nowadays, the idea of happiness has been systematically messed with by our culture of consumerism and secular ideology. You hear the phrase everyone is entitled to happiness, right? But the document says, 'the pursuit of happiness.' So then, we've got the right to pursue pleasure, and we sure have. We're happy when our football team wins. We're happy when we can get out to see a movie. The commercials tell us we'd be happy when getting a happy meal, and you won't have to cook. That's how we pursue happiness. That's life in this age.

"But, what did the likes of Jefferson mean when they declared that in the declaration of Independence? What did they mean? That phrase about happiness has intrigued me more and more.

"I suppose we'd have to go back and get inside the heads of that specially selected group of five originators of the declaration. We'd have to go back to live alongside them and be immersed in their society to know what they were thinking, but we can't do that. But this, we do know. They were Christians or deists holding to those basic morality and righteousness concepts, as written in the scriptures. They had studied the bible. The culture was such that Biblical moral principles dominated their lives. They considered those precepts as the foundation of knowledge and wisdom.

"Yes, the Bible was held in high esteem throughout society in America's beginnings, so much so that the first universities established were based on Christian principles evident even today as the Princeton Crest translated from Latin reads, 'Under God, she flourishes.' Yes, it was Christian ministers who initiated Harvard and Yale."

Pausing a bit, Sam reasons *they still appear interested in the subject and desire more*, so Sam continues.

"In these 200 plus years, culture has dramatically changed, as has the meaning of many of our words. The founders looked to the scriptures for wisdom, knowing Solomon's words, 'Happy are the people whose God is the Lord.' And in Psalms, 'Delight yourself in the Lord, and He will give you the desires of your heart.' Yes, delight yourself. Delight is related to happiness, right?

"Another one from Proverbs, 'Happy is the man that findeth wisdom, and the man that getteth understanding.' And, 'She is a tree of life to them that lay hold upon her, and happy is every one that retaineth her.'"

"Is this what those men had in mind when they included the pursuit of happiness in that declaration? Happiness comes as we pursue wisdom and understanding because we've learned something critical to our lives.

Sam pauses, breathes in deeply, followed by a long sigh, which Harry takes as an opening saying, "Mr. Guardyall, you should be a teacher."

"Oh no, but thank you. I'm, but a man who lives alone in the woods with nothing else to do but read and meditate on the majesties displayed here for me, and then it excites me to share it. Eh gads, I did not intend to rabble on like that. Sorry, but I got lost as those words seemed to flow like a river. Forgive me. I must have bored you guys."

Meredith says, "Yes, a teacher. You got my attention. No, it was not boring in the least. It was wonderful, and I wish I had it taped so I could listen to it over and over again."

"Yes, thank you," says Harry. "You've given me something to think about. I may bring it up in class."

"Meredith, I didn't get your last name."

"Ingersall."

"No!" Sam responds. "Francinea, right? Then it was your mother who treated my leg."

"No, kidding."

"Yeah, I'm supposed to see her tomorrow."

"That's mom. Wow, I got to call her." Meredith responds while reaches to get her cell phone out of the pocket of the coat. She pushes a button and soon is heard saying, "Mom, guess what? You know that shuttered fruit stand with the mailbox we pass, and we've wondered who or if anybody lives down there. Harry and I are here with a patient of yours." A pause as Meredith listens. "Yes, Samuel Guardyall. And you ought to see this cabin and the view." Another pause, and then she turns to look at Sam, "When are you scheduled to have the stitches out?"

"Tomorrow is the tenth day," Sam answers.

Turning back to Sam, Meredith tells him, "Mom says instead of driving all that way to the hospital that she'd look at it in the office. Anytime. She'd squeeze you in somehow."

"Tell her thanks. I'll be there, say about ten."

"Bye, mom, I'll be home shortly."

"Thanks, Meredith. Now, where is her office?" Sam questions. Then he adds, "Thank You, Lord."

Meredith describes where the office is located and the quickest way to get there.

"Thank your mother again for me," Sam tells her.

Looking out the window, Sam sees the snow becoming a thick blanket. He then suggests, "I don't mean to rush you off, but it may be better if you did leave. I'm sorry for my rambling on and on like that. I sit here alone, enjoying these wonders of nature, many times wishing I could share it all with another. Harry, thank you for stopping. Wow, the morning has gone fast. Thanks, I have enjoyed the visit."

Again, the teens tell him that he should consider teaching a class in history, come to church and talk with the youth group.

Moving closer to Harry, Meredith softly says, "Yeah, we'd better go. Thank You, Mr. Guardyall."

Harry thanks him and adds, "I'm going to talk with my civics teacher about this, and the youth director at church."

Sam watches them from the porch as the car turns around the corner with King following close behind. King stops and then chases flakes of snow falling in front of his nose. Sam sits quietly on the porch watching the snow softly drop in front of him. He starts humming the tune raising his voice, "so I'll cherish the old rugged cross . . . till my trophies, at last, I lay down.. . ."

"Yes, I did. *I did lay my trophies down by moving out here. Left them all. No more of those things being my Shepherd.*

"Father God, Bless these two teens in all they do. Guide them and bring them back. I enjoyed the visit. Thanks again, Lord, for the healing of this leg."

Seventeen

Shortly back inside the cabin, after he waves a good-bye, Sam moves to his typewriter. He inserts a sheet of paper and begins pushing the keys watching them make their marks on the paper.

My Cabin Life 10

This morning I was surprised by a visit from Harry, the eagle scout and football player, along with an attractive girl forced to have recently moved here from Indianapolis by her mother wanting to slow down her life and move away from memories. Her father had been killed by Islamic radicals. We had a delightful time chatting, and I got to know a bit more about today's teens, although these two, I sense, are the exception rather than the norm I hear so much about.

No doubt, their Christian upbringing has contributed much to their exceptionalism as they already have their sights set, recognizing and wanting to use their inspired gifts and talents in assuming adulthood. And these two are on a romantic journey too.

But one event has now penetrated this head of mine, a lightning rod opening my mind to the limitless majesties of this world of ours: not the physical world this time, but the unseen spiritual world. I had shared with Harry and Meredith some thoughts about why the pursuit of happiness was inserted into our declaration to the British Empire, when I glanced out the window seeing the snow dropping from the heavens.

These thoughts had their beginnings when Meredith brought up the beauty of each snowflake, wishing she had a microscope to view the flakes. In my mind, I was seeing each human intricately designed like individual snowflakes. Our unique design so different than the other millions and billions of people on this earth. Our DNA and fingerprints so unique they're used to identify us from others. Our physical being and outward appearance unique, the tone of our skin, our facial makeup so unique that our picture is used as an identifying tool.

As the snow falls and blends in with the trillion other unique flakes, so we humans blend in with the thousands gathered to watch a game in a stadium. And if we could view us sitting there from high above, we'd see a blanket of people, a mass, not individuals, just a bunch of flakes to be shoveled out of the way.

Isn't this the way rulers, kings, tyrants, and politicians see us, one big mass of people to be herded and led somewhere, to be guided, to be taught what they see as best, hoping that like sheep, we'd follow along.

Ah, we can look at the complete snowflake or get in close to view the intricate design. This human brain has been viewed by science, and so they inform us that these 100 billion neurons have somehow binded together to form this brain of ours. Trillions of combinations of a 1 and a 0; eight of which form a bite were organized and designed to create that smartphone. It didn't just evolve together over billions of years. No, designers were working on that.

Mega-trillions of those bytes put together to make the computer do marvelous things as we stare into that piece of plastic. We play games, connect through social media, read the latest news, and store all that information within a finger size disk. All, designed by human intelligence.

No, it was not just a random happening in a lab somewhere. Our human intelligence created that masterpiece.

A Divine intelligence designed and created this brain and body of ours.

I also imagined the insides of this body of flesh when viewed through a high-powered microscope is like outer space, a bunch of pieces (molecules our scientists call them) independent of each other but yet, part of and connected to the rest.

Just as this fingernail I'm now looking at is dependent upon the skin below and around it and connected to some sort of tissue at the base enabling it to grow longer and stronger. Without that hard surface at the end of our fingers, how different would our abilities be affected? How different our universe would be if our sun and those gobs of stars flung around like a tossed Frisbee. Something out there is holding them in place. We can't see that something, yet it's there. They say the gravity of this earth holds the moon in its orbit. That's quite a force and a precise amount too. A little bit more, and the moon would be pulled to the earth. A little less and that moon would be out further, and we might be skipping over treetops.

Yet, we're bombarded on all sides that over billions of years our brain, our physical body was being assembled by random mutations. Why do we even ponder such thoughts?

Praise God from whom all blessings flow.

As I quit writing today, I am already getting thoughts for the next segment, "Cease striving and know that I am God."

Again, I wonder, Is this why I'm here to share all this with teens?

Back on the porch peering into the falling snow, Sam musses, *in the morning, I will get these bandages off, the stitches removed, and I'll be back to normal again. I learned my lesson. As a city kid, I've got to remember that I'm learning new things. Be careful.*

"King, what shall we do? Hey boy, are you hungry?" Sam reaches down to rub behind his ears as King revels in the attention, slightly moving his head, showing Sam the places he'd like to have petted. *I'd better let this leg rest, so it's time to read and study, but first, a good cup of coffee.*

Leaning on the crutch, he reaches over to open the door as King rushes to that perpetual bowl of food, tonguing it in as if he'd not eaten in a week.

Coffee cup in one hand, the crutch under the other arm, Sam takes a dozen steps to the couch where he left the study of Greek on the side table. He carefully places three pieces of wood on the dwindling fire and then sits back with his leg elevated on the footrest. Picking up the book reviewing the previous segment, Sam scratches his head, thinking, *'why am I doing this? I've got no good reason, no goal of becoming a Greek scholar or reading the New Testament in the original Greek. Then why am I doing it? It'd be different if I were in a college class with other students, a teacher forging the way for us because the course was one of many required to graduate with a major in Biblical Studies.*

So, good-bye, Greek.

"King, come join me in a nap."

Sam wakes from his one-hour nap. He notices the clock at 2:35. He throws off the quilt, dons the sweatshirt, grabs the nearby crutch, and places more sticks of wood on top of those slowly turning into ashes. He looks out the window and sees the snow gracefully falling, "Wow!" he exclaims, peering out the window behind the desk. The thoughts come, *how will I get to town in the morning?*

Stumbling to the kitchen, Sam lights the camp stove to make a pot of coffee, when he discovers the coffee grounds are about gone, just enough for this one pot. *That's it—no coffee in the morning.* Sam rebukes himself for letting that happen. He turns off the stove. "Okay, time to go to town." He dons the outerwear, puts on the boots, his gloves, grabs the keys to the pick-up, the crutch, and he's out the door. "King, come on, buddy."

He opens the passenger door for King, who excitedly jumps in, licking his chops and sitting on the seat. Sam backs the truck out of the barn and slowly drives out to the road, where he notices he's been using both feet to drive. "Good, I'm over that hurdle. *Will the doctor see me this afternoon*?

Sam decides he'll go to her office first and check. He drives through the town square area. A gentleman is outside the hardware store shoveling snow off the sidewalk. Customers brush the newly falling flakes off the windows of the cars.

"Okay," Sam states, "there it is." He turns into the small parking lot next to the storefront type office, stops, lowers the window a bit for King. "Stay." Grabbing the crutch, he opens the door and sees five adults sitting in the waiting room. He goes to the front desk, telling the lady who he is and about the appointment set for tomorrow and why he's here today.

"Sorry, but we're filled up today."

"Yeah, I know it's unscheduled, but I may not be able to get here tomorrow because of the snow."

"I know it doesn't look good."

The phone buzzes. "Excuse me, Mr. Guardyall." She listens. She puts the phone down and calls out a name, and a lady stands, taking the few steps to the examining room's door. Sam turns away, looking at the pictures and sheets with instructions to patients about this and that. Dr. Ingersall greets her patient while scanning the room. "Go on in, I'll be there in a moment," she tells the lady, and then approaches the side of Sam, "aren't you Samuel Guardyall?" Sam turns to face the voice, recognizing her features he was captivated by in the hospital.

"Ah, yes. Yes, I'm Samuel. You stitched my leg a while back."

"Yeah, I remember. My daughter Meredith called and told me she and Harry were visiting you. Have a seat Mr. Guardyall, and I'll check that leg of yours as soon as I can."

"Thank you. I know I'm a day early, but this snow. The morning may be unsafe driving, so I chanced it," Sam tells her perpetual wrinkled smile.

"That's okay."

Sam closely watches as the Doctor leans over to tell the clerk that she'll see him later.

The clerk hands him a clipboard and numerous pages. "Mr. Guardyall, while you're waiting, I need you to fill out these papers, and I need to see your insurance card."

Sam settles in a chair, reading and filling in the blanks placing his signature where indicated, and returns it to the clerk. She returns his insurance card and driver's license. Returning to the seat, he picks up one of the magazines on the side table. *The Smithsonian*. Sam pages through the contents finding an article about Frank Lloyd Wright. His interest peaked. He starts reading.

One after another, the waiting room is slowly emptying as a male doctor takes some and Dr. Ingersall some, getting Sam's attention each time she greets a patient. Sam reads the article and periodically looks out the window at the continuing snow. The male Doctor opens the door to greet the last one waiting.

The clerk closes the window to the small office and leaves through the back door, and then the entrance to the secure area opens, and Dr. Ingersall appears. "Come on in, Mr. Guardyall."

"Ah, thank you. I took a chance coming here this afternoon, and thank you for seeing me."

"You're welcome. Not a problem."

She points to a room on the left. "Have a seat on the table and take your boot off, please." She pulls a rolling stool over to the table, pulls out a leg rest, and then gently rolls up the loose coverall to the knee. She starts the process of unwrapping the bandages from the calf down to the heel and around the ankle. "Hmm. Looks good. Yep, I can take those stitches out, and soon you'll have your leg back."

"Doctor, it was a privilege to have your daughter and Harry visit with me. Meredith is a beautiful, talented, and smart young lady."

"Thank You. You like to read history?"

"Yes, now, I do. I'm discovering just how fascinating our human history is."

"This may sting a bit." She tells Sam as she pulls and cuts, pulls and cuts one stitch after another. Sam is focused on the doctor, watching her delicate hands handle the fine instruments. His eyes focus on the smooth movements of the doctor and her physical attributes; auburn hair shining in brilliance down to her shoulders, a tint of gray emerging in spots, her small earrings with a round centerpiece of reflective cut glass, the unwrinkled forehead shadowing sun-rise smiling eyes, and the firmness of her shoulders, the straight backbone leading to a slim narrow waist.

"There you are," she informs, straightening and looking up into his melted eyes.

Smiling back, Sam tells her, "Thanks, Doc." Mesmerized by her facial expressions, bright shining blue eye wrinkles smiling back.

"You'll still need a bandage for a few days just in case any of those stitched areas bleed a bit. You can look after it yourself and remove the bandage when you desire. You won't need my services anymore."

"Thank you. I learned my lesson. Don't be stupid."

"Ah, I've seen worse from those guys working at the mill, and they're professionals. Mr. Guardyall, my daughter, was impressed by that cabin of yours, and by you."

"I was impressed by her, and Harry indicated that your daughter runs marathons. That's fantastic."

"I've run several with her, but that age difference. I can't keep up."

"She also shared with me about your husband and what happened to him. I'm sorry."

"Thank You. The move here is helping."

"That must have been a tremendous shock. My wife was killed in a car wreck."

"Oh, I'm sorry. That must have been horrible to get that kind of a call." The doctor responds.

"Say, why don't you and Meredith come out sometime? She indicated you'd love the setting. Huh? How about it?"

"Thanks, I'll consider it and talk it over with Meredith. But now it's time to close the office. It was a pleasure to treat you, Mr. Guardyall."

"I won't need this crutch anymore. Give it to someone who may need it more."

"No, you take it as your leg is still weak, and you may need it for a few days. To be safe."

She escorts Sam into the waiting room; he turns and watches her as the door closes behind her. He goes out the front door and around the corner to the truck as King barks loudly out the window. Sam drops the crutch into the bed of the truck. King moves onto the drivers' seat; his head right into Sam's face, and the tail wagging behind.

"Move over."

"I don't know about you, but I'm hungry." *The heck with fixing something.*" Sam heads down a couple of blocks to the diner noticing the parking spaces are full. He turns the corner and finds an empty slot. "Sorry, King, it's me first. Stay."

Sam enters the diner as Joanna walks by with the coffee pot.

"Hi, Mr. Guardyall, I see you're off the crutch. You expecting anyone?"

"Nope, alone. I'll sit at the counter today."

"Yep, you can watch them play games on their tablets. Coffee is it?"

Sam chooses one of the empty stools at the counter next to an elderly gray mustached man with a grayish-white long beard and an un-cut head of hair. He notices the man's plate of a double cheese, double burger along with a bowl of French fries. Sam picks up the menu from the rack looking at the list. The man seems unaware that someone has occupied the seat next to him, as he's intently focused on the hand-held tablet while taking a bite out of the burger.

Joanna slides the coffee cup down. "How's that cabin life treating you? The weatherman is calling for possibly two feet or more."

"No, kidding. I'll take the grilled ham and cheese with onion rings."

"I thought so. Okay, be right up."

While waiting for the food to arrive, Sam desires to start a conversation but is hesitant to break the guys' concentration on the screen.

Joanna sets the plate in front of Sam. "Well, are you adjusted to the rigors of frontier life?"

"Just about."

He bows his head and softly whispers, "Thank you, Lord, for this food, bless it for my health and provide me a safe trip back to the cabin. Amen." He bites into the sandwich, then an onion ring, and sipping coffee between bites.

The old guy has taking several quick back and forth glances toward Sam, finally speaks, "I heard Joanna mention cabin. You wouldn't be the guy who has taken over the Guardyall place, are you?"

"Yes, I am. I'm his grandson Samuel. And you are?"

"Jack Ripper."

"Did you say Jack Ripper?" Sam astonishingly asks and then apologizes, "I'm sorry."

"Yep, I'm Jack the Ripper." He chuckles. "I'm used to it. My dad thought it'd be neat or something. How's it going in the cabin? I've had many conversations with your grandfather as I was one of the forest service rangers until a few years ago when they let me go."

"You were fired?"

"Not according to them, rascals. They said they couldn't use me anymore. Yes, I was fired."

"Why."

The guy tells Sam that he couldn't go along with the radical environmental ideologies they were pushing. "I resisted and refused to adhere to some of the new rules they were importing. I told them it didn't make any sense and it'll shut this town down. They're wackos. You better watch it and don't make any of them mad, or you'll be closed up."

"I was visited by one not long ago offering me a windmill or solar panels. Frank Outmoure." Sam picks the last of the onion rings, followed by a fast gulp of coffee.

"Oh-oh. That kid's a nut bomb."

"I've been told that they'd take over if I connected to the grid."

"Yep, leave it as it is."

"Yeah, I've been informed of that. Mr. Ripper, I'd sure like to hear more, but I've got to go. We could possibly get two-feet, and I've got to stop for a few groceries. Hey, come on in some time. I'd love to hear more. Anytime."

"I would like to, but the misses and I are heading south for the winter."

"Have a good time then, and don't forget to come out when you get back. Mr. Ripper. I'd like to hear more."

"Good luck Mr. Guardyall."

"God bless you on that trip, Jack. Relax and enjoy it."

Sam pays for his dinner and turns to pull open the door when suddenly a girl lunges forward from the outside.

"Eh gads, what timing. Meredith?" Right behind Meredith is her mother, Francinea.

"Hi, Mr. Guardyall." Meredith cheerfully greets.

"Hi Meredith, and doctor, thanks again for squeezing me in today."

"My pleasure, and it saved us both a trip to Johnsonville."

Meredith asks, "Could you stay a bit and have a cup of coffee with us?"

"I'm sure Mr. Guardyall has plans," the doctor exclaims.

"Yes, I've got a few groceries to get before heading home, but thanks anyway."

"Ah, come on. Ten minutes." Meredith responds. "Mom?" the teen turns to look into the eyes of her mother, wanting approval.

Looking at them, Sam hesitates. "No. It'd be my pleasure, but that road of mine could be forbidden territory as these snows accumulate, and I've got a couple of errands first."

"Good luck, Mr. Guardyall," the doctor tells him, and then to Meredith, "Yes, we need to grab a quick bite and then get home ourselves." And turning back to Sam, "Take care, that leg needs encouragement, but not too much work for the next couple weeks, so take it easy."

"Thanks again. You saved me a trip to the hospital. The invitation is open to come to see the area for yourself. I wish you would."

Sam carefully makes his way to the store. He fills the cart paying the cashier, and places the paper sacks in the truck's bed. He stops at the gas station to fill the truck and his five-gallon gas can. He is back on the road toward the cabin, slowly following along in the tire tracks of previous drivers. Turning into his road, that's smoothly covered with snow close to a foot deep, he slows and downshifts into 2nd and then to $1^{st.}$ He's gently paving the way around one curve coming upon the slight downward slope to another curve and into the open area next to the garden, he turns left and into the barn. He turns off the ignition and reaches over to open the door for King, who jumps into the snow and runs toward the first pine tree.

Walking around the corner to the porch and into the cabin using both hands to carry the sacks of groceries, Sam puts them away. *Do I start shoveling or wait a bit?* King runs in to find the water bowl and then tongues in a few bits of the crunchy morsels and back for more water.

I guess I'll just touch up the porch a bit, and then It's inside for the evening. As the porch is swept clean, he muses, *Grandpa, thanks for the provisions you left. You did allow a few breaks into modern-day life, allowing yourself the easiness of the rototiller as being better than a mule pulling a plow. The snowblower is better than a shovel. The truck is better than riding a horse or walking. Where did you draw the line? Have I broken your rules when I got the camp stove to quicker and easier coffee, among other cooking aids?*

"Remind me, Lord, when I'm trending away from the wishes of my grandfather. I do desire to honor the honor he's given me, so help me, Lord."

He adds additional wood to the fireplace, opens the curtain to the bedroom, and puts his coffee cup next to the typewriter. He lights the oil lamp and then inserts a fresh sheet of paper and starts to type.

My Cabin Life 11

I've been asked if I don't feel lonely in this solitude I've embraced. Well, yes, I do, and then no, I don't, as King is an ever-present buddy, as is nature itself. Oh, the wonders of nature, its awe that I've never paid much attention to in the past hustle-bustle noisy modern-day life of speedy highways, offices, busy stores, drive-ins, speed bumps, and the comforts of home, being entertained by other two-legged busy bodies doing what they do 24/7.

Even in this short period of solitude, I've learned the inspiring values of these times being outside society and the constant noise of machines, the voices on plastic screens, and the continual pull into distractions of technology and entertainment.

Once a week trip to town is good enough for me.

One day as I was rocking on the porch, a book in one hand and the cup in the other, I visualized myself smelling a sweet cinnamon roll on top of the Empire state building and then scaling the outside walls to get some.

Isn't that what ants do?

Consider the ants the Bible tells us. Yes, one day, those ants caught my eye as they crawled, or do they run up the seven-foot-high post and navigate to the hummingbird feeder for some sweet stuff. There's a long trail of them going to that sumptuous liquid and back down the post, to some sort of hiding place, and then back again. On the way, they bump into each other, stopping or pausing a bit, or is it only to say to their fellow ant, "Hi, Joe. Good to see you again." "Hi, Pete."

Those guys are just fantastic to watch. How do they do it? Do they thank me for putting it there?

In the beginning, that serpent spoke to Eve. Had that beginning design enabled Adam and Eve the ability to understand the animal kingdom. Did the animal world communicate with them? Did lions approach Adam asking to have his ears rubbed? Oh, I got off the subject again.

These ants seem to send a scout out to find those treats, smelling something far off somewhere, and then go find it. The word spreads back to the den, and wow, soon the entire ranch is on the way climbing seven-feet-vertically-high without falling backward. Then along the beam, even on the underside, and down the string to just far enough inside the opening. They get their bellies full, then down the same trail to the den, and again, they work at it all day long.

How do they smell that sweet stuff seven feet up?

And those hummingbirds, how marvelous are they zooming to the feeder smelling the nectar and then suddenly the wings change to hovering mode, the spear ready to dip into the small opening as the wings just slightly change to forward. They put the wings in reverse, hover like a helicopter, the wings slightly changing to forward again. The tiny bird moves to the next flowered opening, repeating the process until satisfied, then zooming off at a speed so fast it's hard for my eyes to follow the little bird as it flies off to a tree limb to rest upon.

Speaking of wings, how about those Monarch Butterflies that travel thousands of miles propelled by beautiful colorful wings of just a few inches? No road maps to guide them home. Are they doing it by smell, or perhaps remembering the trip north? Or, do they have their GPS designed specifically for them. Hmm! They're using their map integrated into that tiny head of theirs to find their way back to where they came from. Why did God create these as insects? Yes, they're born as a tiny worm-like creature nurturing their way out of that skin to flying more miles per day than we can run.

And how about those eagles? I watched one the other day circling an area of the lake a few hundred feet above the water. Gliding in a circular pattern, the spiked wings slightly changing, moving him up a bit or down a bit, his head pointed toward the surface of the waters. It slowly descends, and it seems like in a split second, he was zooming to the surface of the water, the wings pointed up, his legs were down, claws spread apart, and whoosh, the paws break the waters, and he ascends with a trout attached to his feet. Wow. What eyesight he must have to see a fish swimming below the surface, the coordination of the timing and swiftness of his claws to grab that twenty-inch fish before that fish recognized the approaching danger.

I've seen how fast those trout can change course when I'd like to catch one, yet those eagles can do it.

Only four very distinct bits of creation. Throw humans into the mix along with all other creatures, from alligators to camels to bears, whales, and goldfish; all living, breathing and navigating life under their unique design and GPS. Oh, how marvelous it is. Beyond awesome. Beyond our finite understandings.

Instinct. Yes, just plain instinct enables these creatures to amuse us and terrify too. They make scientists wonder, spending years inspecting their nature, concluding they're all merely a different formulation of cells evolving from previous not so wondrous ones.

We humans can't physically do anything remotely resembling what the animal world is naturally able to do. What good would it be for us humans to have the eyes of an eagle, the wings of a butterfly or the sense of smell of those ants, or have ears of the elephants? Oh, that'd be interesting.

The scientists, with numerous degrees and years of investigations under their belts, can't explain it either. All they have are various suppositions, theories, imaginations they have intoned as possible. Like in the beginning, nothing and then that zero of nothing caused a big bang and whoosh, all because one cell of nothingness divided or crashed into nothing. Then dividing again and again and again, somehow forming together into a body, some of the cells clung together into hard brittle bones. And others somehow formed muscles that knew how to surround those bones and arteries as pipelines for red-colored fluid cells which knew to stay within the arteries, or else a leak would drain them all out.

All that only took billions of years, eventually forming our fingers, toes, nose, and eyes and on and on they imagine. All evolving from nothing, the oxygen in the air from nothing, the sun, and earth from nothing, starting from a blank screen we see before the computer is turned on, which they now call a dark hole in space. Nothing but imaginings.

No, God the creator of all cannot be put under a microscope, although viewing through that microscope evidences this marvelous creation, and that's as close as we'll ever get.

Oh Father, how wondrous this is.

In that previous life of constant busyness and trouble beckoning at the door, I never could get still and quiet, finding a place of placid tranquility. A place where I was untroubled by the ever-present busyness of modern life. A place of calm, serenity, and stillness. I lacked the discipline back home, and now with only the sounds and sights of nature surrounding me, that darkened glass has been made clear, as I've learned as the scriptures tell us to Be Still and Know that I Am God.

No, I am not lonesome.

Eighteen

Waking up chilled, Sam rushes to get the fireplace going. He lets King out and is back, rubbing his hands together close to the new flames off the bark of the dismembered tree. He lights a match over the Coleman stove in the kitchen and the cast iron stove for more heat. While the coffee is brewing, he leans forward over the sink, looking out the window, seeing that snow accumulation is not much different from what it was a couple of days ago when the predictions aroused anxiety.

More comfortable as the cabin warms and his throat has felt the taste of coffee, Sam fixes a bowl of oatmeal sprinkled with a bit of brown sugar and takes them to the side table in front of the fireplace. He leans back on the couch and opens the scriptures for his morning read as the sun rises and shines its warmth through the window.

Starting in Jeremiah 28, He is struck by some verses in the 29th, bowing his head low in great appreciation, "Thank you, Lord. Thank You." *I receive them as historical exampled events that have been repeated and repeated throughout our human history."*

Sam leans back on the couch, summarizing, *A personal well-liked king comes into power, guaranteeing food and safety from enemies to satisfy the concerns of the people. Slowly the increased rules of the king demand complete obedience and worship. For selfish safety, security, and wanting peace, the people acquiesce to those commands, while prophets slide along, deceiving and dividing the people into opposing groups disrupting the peace, which demands additional controls and forceful obedience by the king. For their personal safety, of course. The Jews wanting peace, behaved obediently for seventy years, living as exiles. God then speaks to the hearts of the people,* "Take heed, let not your prophets and your diviners deceive you, for they prophesy falsely to you . . .. Then shall ye call upon me, and ye shall go and pray unto me, and I will hearken unto you. And ye shall seek me and find me when ye shall search for me with all your heart."

With all your heart? Sam wonders, *This heart of ours wants many things, so how do we put everything else aside, everything so that we can search with a single purpose? I searched on Google, the remote control, and my drafting software back home, usually finding an answer. Scientists do it with microscopes. Columbus did it on a ship. The early explorers did it on their feet or the back of a horse.*

An hour later, Sam reminisces, *not once this morning as I moved around, had the injured leg sent any signals of pain or discomfort to my mind,* "so here goes."

Sam dresses for a mid-morning outside in the fresh air and snow. He heads to the barn. He checks the oil, fills it with gas, pushes and pushes the choke and pulls the cord, pulls it again and again, and it starts, stumbling and missing, it stops. Sam increases the throttle, pulls the line, and it rumbles and then purrs. He maneuvers the blower to the open area in front of the barn door, lowers the blades, and soon the snow is thrown out the shoot as he steers it straight ahead toward the garden area following the trail left by tires, and into the pine-covered road and out to the street. He makes a few passes along the street in front of the mailbox and then turns to make the return trip knowing that it'll take another trip out and another back to widen the driveway enough for decent passage.

"Man, I feel good. Thank you, Lord." He skips going around the gazebo, and widens the path to the porch, back to the barn, and puts the snowblower back in its spot.

"Hey King, did you find anything this morning? Huh? No rabbits. Come on in, as this afternoon I'm staying in and read." Sam picks a paperback book that had previously caught his attention. Laying the book down on the side table, he places a few more logs in the fireplace and then grabs one of the decorative pillows for his head and a quilt covering for his legs. *Ah, comfort.* He starts reading.

King jumps up on the couch next to Sam, leaning up close licking the face of his owner. "Ah yes, you want loving. But King, do you ever think about tomorrow? About, what you want to do? Do you remember finding that deer?" Sam asks while rubbing behind his ears and down the neck.

"Huh? Do you have any concept of time?"

Turning back to the book, he reads the credits, scans the table of contents, and introduces thinking that this book is not that old compared to the others, yet grandpa must have thought it worthwhile. In the preface, Sam is struck by the authors' comments about how his wife had helped in so many ways while raising eight children and answering the phone. Sam leans back against the head pillow; *Angelia, you helped me with your comments and suggestions about my interior designs.*

Raising his head, King jumps off the couch, running to the front door barking signals to Sam that something is happening outside. Repositioning the bookmark to the current page, Sam turns to look out the window as the barking of King continues while scratching on the front door. Sam opens the half door seeing a shining white SUV pulling a trailer stop alongside the porch. Harry steps out of the back door. The passenger door opens, and Sam sees Meredith making her way to the front of the car.

Harry loudly hollers out, "Hey, Mr. Guardyall."

Surprised, Sam opens the bottom section, as King runs out and puts his paws on Harry's chest. "Greetings, Harry. What a great surprise, but what? Are the roads clear? Meredith, nice to see you again."

"No problem," Harry informs him. "Mr. Guardyall, I talked Meredith and her mother to help clear your road for you, but I see you've already taken care of most of it."

As the doctor slowly gets out of the car, Sam greets her, "Dr, Ingersall, good to see you again."

"Afternoon, Mr. Guardyall. Hope you don't mind. We're not disturbing anything, are we?"

"No, no, no. Come on in. It's a delight to see you again."

Dr, Ingersall tells Sam, "Meredith and Harry suggested, ah, said you'd probably be snowbound in here, and they desired to take care of the snow for you since your leg is still healing. Then we were shocked to see some of it had already been cleared. You didn't do it on your own, did you?"

"Yes, sure did. This morning."

"But what about that leg?"

"Ah, it's fine, Doctor. Thanks to you."

"Let me have a look at it. The kids are going to get rid of the rest of the snow."

As the doctor and Sam enter the cabin, Harry and Meredith unload a snow blower and shovels to touch up and finish the job of clearing away the snow around the gazebo area and to widen the entrance road. Harry guides the snowblower while Meredith handles the shovel removing the snow off the paths to and inside the gazebo and then at the porch.

Inside the cabin, the doctor pauses, scanning the room; the open ceiling, the fireplace, the desk, the half-pulled curtain exposing the double bed with the quilt, blankets, and sheets thrown in the shape of a triangle to the halfway mark, along with clothes drying on the line. She turns to take in the bookcase, the details of the kitchen area. She exclaims to Sam, "Meredith did a splendid job of describing your cabin, but seeing it in person is delightful. Mr. Guardyall, this has that comfortable, homey atmosphere. I'm envious."

"This is it."

"Okay, here, let me look at that leg of yours."

Sitting on the couch, Sam pulls the footstool close for his foot to rest upon and then rolls up his pants leg. She removes the gauze bandage exposing the stitch marks. "See that; you've torn a few." Her finger points to the bloody trail. She stands, opens the door, goes to the car, and returns with a black leather bag.

"Mr. Guardyall, you can't do anything you want and expect it to heal. Men!"

"It felt fine, and look. It's only a few spots."

She opens a small damp sponge wiping away exposed dried blood over and around the stitch marks, pats the area dry, and then places a few stitch bandages over the places appearing to have separated. She wraps the gauze around his leg.

"There. Now give it a few more days to heal." She closes the bag, places it by the front door, and returns to sit on the desk chair, as Sam's eyes followed her every move.

"Thank you. Now, can I get you a cup of coffee or tea, something warm?" Sam asks.

"Coffee will be fine. Thanks. Black." She answers, looking out the window seeing her daughter shoveling. While Sam is preparing the coffee, she picks up the typed pages lying next to the Remington and starts to read My Cabin Life 11.

Sam approaches, handing her the cup of coffee. Francinea says, "oh, sorry, this memoir you've written is wonderful. You don't mind if I read it all, do you? And this drawing of the cabin is good too. But your grammar."

"Ah, so you're an English critic."

"No, sorry, but I can't help noticing errors. As a doctor, I was trained to be precise, or the patient may suffer."

"Well," Samuel then says, "Those notes are just some of the revelations, or shall I say some…ah, some simple messages that have come to this mind of mine. The drawing? Best I could do without the tools and computer programs." He pauses, looking at her as she turns the page to read the rest. Catching himself admiring this woman from top to bottom, he rebukes his mind with the thought, *No, this cannot be, Angelia, I'm sorry. God forgive me. I can't.*

Breaking his thoughts, Sam says, "Doctor, shall we dispense with the formality, call me Sam."

"Okay, Sam, and yes, I'm Francinea. We might as well."

"Your name has a musical ring to it. Sounds French."

"Thank you. This My Cabin Life, you call it. I'm impressed. Your imagination is active and alive. I'd like to read the others."

"That inspiration to write of my revelations came from my grandfather, who left me with hundreds of notes. And my grandmother too, with the pictures of their life in this cabin, and how they survived here. She also left menus and a journal of their daily work together as a team."

"Don't you have any desire to update the cabin with electricity?"

"Sure, but I can't. Yeah, it'd be great to be able to turn on lights to see at night and to throw those dirty clothes in a machine, but I can't, and no, I won't either."

"You can't?" Francinea asks.

"Yes, those folks of the Forest Service are watching. They want this cabin as theirs, to show it off as a relic. So, if I did anything like connect to the grid, they'd take it over."

"What right do they have to do that?"

"Yes, I wondered about that too. When the Agency declared the forest land around this cabin a national forest, they agreed to let my grandparents stay in the cabin as long as it remained as originally built." Sam tells her and adds the bit about the visit by the agent.

"Yeah, the medical field is feeling the same pressure."

"You see that picture hanging over the fireplace. That picture appeared alive to me one day and saved me from my drunkenness after my wife's death. Now, I'm free."

"It's a beautiful painting."

Sam continues telling Francinea of the depression he went through, being drawn to alcohol to put the bitterness aside, and how he was permanently delivered and is now free from it all. He summarizes his thoughts to her with, "This God of ours is merciful to the nth degree. You know how far that is? It's endless, like the perimeter of a circle surrounding us, no starting point, no ending to showering us with the fullness of grace. All we have to do is recognize and accept it."

"That's precious. Jerome was a wonderful husband and father. Yes, he sacrificed his personal life to bless others by journaling into areas that we'd never get to see otherwise."

"Meredith told me some of it. He did some work for National Geographic, right?"

"Yes. That's one of many."

"Francinea, if you don't mind my saying so, but you've got a lot to be thankful for. Meredith is one of the most mature high school students I've ever run across. You've done a terrific job."

"Thank you. She got that from my mother."

"More coffee?"

"Why, yes, thanks." As Sam slowly rises, he purposefully limps to the kitchen favoring the right leg, carefully balancing the near-empty cups. Francinea asks, "Is it hurting again? Did I wrap it too tight?"

Sam pours additional coffee in each cup, ignoring her questions, and limps back to the couch.

"Sam, is the bandage too tight? You were limping."

"Nah, it's fine."

"You limped because it hurt. I'm the doctor!"

"Yeah, and I'm the patient messing with you." He snaps his finger across the top of the cup as if he was throwing drops of coffee at her.

Francinea lightly dips the spoon into the coffee thrusting the liquid at Sam.

Sam wipes the drops off his forehead with the sleeve of the sweatshirt, knowing the seriousness of their conversation has relaxed.

"Are you a reader? Do you like to read?" Sam asks.

"Yes, but it's not history like all those books you've got."

"What do you read then?"

"Mysteries mostly."

"Did you ever accompany your husband on any of his trips?"

At that moment, the door opens as Meredith and Harry walk in along with King, who, while shaking the snow off, runs directly for slurps of water. Meredith has a giant snowball cupped in her right hand, looking at her mother, her arm raised and ready to throw.

"Don't you dare," Francinea declares.

Meredith aims the packed snow at Sam. Sam raises both hands, catching it, and throws it right back at Meredith, who tries to grab it, but fumbles and the packed snow falls on the floor, breaking into pieces.

"Meredith! We're guests here. Now clean it up."

Sam says to Meredith, "So, you want a snowball fight. Let's go. You're on!" Sam throws his jacket over his shoulders, his arms into the sleeves, picks his gloves, opens the door, and runs off the porch and into the fresh snow. He packs down a handful as the two teens run off in different directions. A throw from Sam misses Harry reaching down for a handful, packing it as another one from Sam hits his leg. Meredith escapes to the other end of the porch. She gathers snow and throws it in Sam's direction, who has moved close to the Gazebo.

"Two against one is the way you play this game. Okay, have at it." Sam hollers as he aims toward Harry, who moves his head, just as one from Meredith brushes by Sam's arm. Francinea opens the door to watch. Sam throws one at her feet. "Come on. It'll be me and you against the kids."

Hesitantly, she looks toward her daughter, turns to see Harry hiding around the corner. She goes back inside and comes out in her coat and scrambles in the direction of Sam as two snowballs whiz by her. She reaches for some of the white stuff and throws it at her daughter, and then another, as one from Meredith hits her boot. Then at Harry, who has advanced closer with several in his hands aiming one at Sam. He throws one at Francinea and another at Sam, who is throwing them at Harry on his left while seeing Meredith on his right inching closer, throwing a large one hitting her mother directly on the top of her head as she tried to duck.

"Ooooh!" Francinea exclaims. "You're in for it now."

Meredith reaches down for more snow as one from Francinea hits her hand. "Mom!" She declares.

"You started this, so take this," as she hits Meredith on the head as she was bending over.

On and on, this game goes, with Meredith getting the worst of it. Francinea is ganging up on her daughter, who finally runs toward the pier getting out of range. Gathering a bunch of packed snow to use,

Meredith sneaks toward her mother, who is hiding behind the Gazebo, peaking out ready to let her daughter have it. Meredith moves closer while Sam and Harry have it out, when they both stop, seeing Meredith approaching her mother. Together at the same time, Sam and Harry throw toward Meredith, just as Francinea appears, throwing one at her daughter. "Take that." She yells as all three hit Meredith.

Francinea runs and tackles her daughter taking her down into the snow. They both roll away, start laughing, then relax, and soon moving their arms to make snow angels.

Watching the two ladies waving their legs and arms, Sam catches himself desiring more of this lady who has graced his path. He reaches out to help her get up.

Harry helps Meredith up.

"Let's go in, and I'll fix some hot chocolate." Sam declares, breathing in deeply.

"The wet boots can be left here," Samuel points to the left of the door as he slips out of his. He holds the door open for Francinea as she takes her boots off. The wet coats are hung on the available hooks next to the door.

Francinea grabs her daughter by the elbow, "just wait, you're going to be getting it big time," as they move to the fireplace to warm their chilled hands over the flames.

"Ah, you enjoyed it, didn't you," Meredith tells her mother. "About time."

Harry bends over to put two more wood pieces on the fire when Meredith slides her cold hands around his neck. "Oooh." He takes a slice of wood and lightly swipes her across her thighs.

Francinea turns and walks to the kitchen area where Sam has a pot of water warming on the cast iron stove. He's put pouches of hot chocolate on the butcher-block table. "Sam, what can I do?" she asks as her shoulder lightly touches his arm getting his attention.

"Ah, in there is a tray we can use," pointing to a curtain below the counter and to the right of the sink. "And there are some marshmallows in the closet over there." He points toward the full-length drapery.

Sam reaches up to the open shelf above the sink pulling four large white cups down setting them on the table.

"That's quite a collection of food. Your grandmother did that?' Francinea says as she returns with a bag of marshmallows.

"Sure did."

"When did she die?"

"A year before grandpa."

"This cabin is amazing, Sam, but ah, where do you do your laundry?"

He points to the sink. Looking at the big silver kitchen sink, she asks, "Do you ever go to town to do it?"

"Nah, I've been managing. Sometimes lazy, then getting caught up. It'll take a couple hours, but what else is there to do."

Francinea asks, "Adjusting to this . . . How did you do it?"

"The same way you have. One day at a time. My dog, the books, fishing, and strolls, and the typewriter have kept me busy between these visits by the wonderful people here. And it's my pleasure to have you here today. Thanks for coming."

"I've enjoyed it. If anyone had told me I'd be throwing snowballs today, I'd look at them as being crazy. But it was fun to let go for a change. I'm relaxed, can you believe that?" She says, looking directly in the face of Sam.

Sam dips his finger in the water flipping a few drops at her. "Here, the water is ready," watching her recognizing the gotcha moment.

Francinea empties the chocolate powder packet into one of the cups as Sam follows with the hot water. She stirs the mix and tops it off with a few small marshmallows. Samuel carries the tray of cups, following her to the couch in front of the fireplace.

"Thank you, Mr. Guardyall." Meredith takes a cup from the tray, as does Harry, sitting to the left of her. Francinea comfortably settles in next to her daughter as Sam pulls the matching single cushioned chair closer to the fireplace and the couch.

"Ah, this is wonderful. Mom, thanks for agreeing to this today."

Francinea turns to look at Sam, "I am fascinated with this cabin and those books. What have you read so far?"

"I started out studying Greek. As a kid, I was fascinated with Greek Architecture and those columns, but to be able to read and speak the language is far above any desire I thought I might have, so it's back on the shelf. More and more, I'm enjoying the quiet moments letting my mind roam and wonder."

"Let us have it, Mr. Guardyall," Meredith says.

"Just the other day as my leg was healing and I couldn't use it much, I sat where you are and stared into that fire when that imagination went into high gear." He recounts some of the random thoughts he had. "Fire. Have you ever sat and watched the flames of a fire like this and then wonder how it came about? We sit around campfires staring into the fire while keeping a safe distance away, fearing its terror. We've learned to use it to warm our food and bodies. Like so many natural elements, fire can be a force of evil or a benefit for good. We are the determining factor—our choice, evil, or goodness. Adam had the same choice, and here we are.

"That sun that rises every day keeping us from freezing is a ball of fire, but why is it not just a tiny bit closer? Why not a self-warming planet? That would've been nice, eliminating winters and extreme cold, no icebergs, just a warm, comfortable day every day. Is that the way it was in that garden paradise Adam and Eve inhabited at first? I know, I've visualized that garden as being much more of a local type area. They were kicked out for their disobedience. I had imagined it was just down the street a bit, or over the hill, where they could still look back through the newly installed fence wishing they had not done that." He pauses while scanning their expressions.

"Since then, this earth of ours has been changing. We've been changing, the animals have changed, and diseases are running rampant. We can't rely on favorable weather any time, all year, every year. Thunderstorms and lightning with excessive rains can disrupt the vegetable growing, drown a harvest, destroy homes and yeah, cancel a ball game. Tornadoes and hurricanes have plagued us ever since, along with volcanoes and pellets of ice thrown at us from above. Shouldn't all this be a reminder of our disobedience? Nope, we complain when it gets too hot, too cold, or the rains come when we want to go to the beach."

"See, mom, I told you he should be teaching."

"Hmmm? Yep, sure sounds like he'd be a great teacher." Francinea answers.

Continuing, Sam adds, "Throughout our entire human existence, humanity has had to learn to adapt to the climate of this earth or get sucked into the evilness of fire, lightning, volcanoes, tornadoes, and other weather conditions. Overall, we've done an impressive job of it too, and you'll go home tonight to a thermostat-controlled temperature. Now when I hear of a tornado or hurricane terrifying thousands, I sarcastically say, Adam, you turned the world upside down." Sam pauses and then asks, "Are these aspects of nature here to remind us just as that rainbow is a reminder?"

"You didn't ask for it, but here's some more." He pauses. Glances at Francinea. *Is she? Well anyway . . . this is me, and she needs to know . . . I can't keep this nature of mine hidden, uh, like. Ugg. Take control, Sam. Let it out.*

"We've come a long way in understanding how things work. But when we get into the spiritual nature of things, our spiritual leaders go round and round in circles, disagreeing with each other and causing divisions within the church, letting the secular scientists win as they agree that nothing caused everything. If we'd get rid of our cars and trucks, we'd eliminate the warming."

Sam pauses looking at each, "Francinea, have I bored you?"

"Ah ...No. Not at all."

"I've been discussing goodness and evil. Just as this earth and atmosphere have good beneficial features for us, there's the evil side too. We're the same with mostly good features guiding us, but then that other side erupts, throwing insults and balls of fire at others. We don't hear that inner voice instructing us, as we're so busy listening to all the other voices.

Francinea interrupts, "Talking with patients, I often ask what they think they should do to help change the physical disorders affecting them, and usually, they know. But they want to hear it from a professional. And so, I get paid to tell them what they already know." Francinea continues, "I've seen the insides of our bodies, but because I've done it for so long, it's become just a job to do, and I haven't thought about the inner workings for a long time. So, Sam, I thank you for waking me up."

"You did a superb job fixing my injury. Thanks." Sam tells her, "And, I had to pay you too. But back to this fire." Sam points into the flames in the fireplace. "Fire would not be fire long without having something to burn. Strike a match, and it will go out unless the blaze reaches something combustible. You've got to add wood to the fire continually, or it will burn itself out. So, how does that sun continue to burn? Wouldn't it have burned up already? What keeps it going?"

Meredith interrupts, "Why aren't we taught to think, to wonder like this in school, or even the churches?"

"Good question. I don't know unless the teachers haven't done any of it either. Perhaps afraid to, or it's just not part of the educational materials. Now, the churches that baffle me.

"To me, your questioning magnifies your belief," adds Francinea, and then sighing, looking toward her daughter and back to Sam, "Sam, I hate to end this, but it'll be dark soon, and we should go. And, yes, you should be teaching somewhere."

"No, I've got no desire to teach, and then have to be a scorekeeper too," Sam replies.

"Think about it anyway, Sam. It's been a wonderful afternoon. Thank you."

"Ah, there is still time. I'm enjoying your company more than you can imagine. Stay for a while. I could put together a pot of chili for us." Sam beckons.

Meredith looks at her mom, who is debating within, and then over to Harry; she asks, "Harry, you don't have to get home, do you?"

"No, I can call dad and let him know."

Francinea looks around, seeing approving expressions, says, "sure... How can we help?"

"I've got to send King out first to get a squirrel or two," Sam explains to their surprised faces, and then, "just kidding. How about some fish instead? It'll take hours for chili to blend. Do you like goldfish?"

"Goldfish?" Meredith screams, then recognizing his expression.

"Fish sounds good," Francinea adds.

Harry then adds, "I want two-dozen goldfish."

Sam goes into the closet to get a bag of Pepperidge Farm Goldfish snacks handing the sack to Meredith, "Here you go. That's all for you two. Your mother and I will have Northern Pike."

Opening the icebox, Sam removes four individually wrapped slices of fresh-caught fish, placing them on the butcher-block table. He opens the iron door to his stove, putting two pieces of wood on top of the diminishing flames.

Harry settles down on the couch, reading the book Sam had placed next to the typewriter.

"Meredith," Francinea directs her thoughts to her daughter, comfortably seated in the chair at the butcher-block table. "Think about this. Here we are in a cabin over a hundred years old. A fire warms it, and we are about to eat some fish prepared and cooked over an old stove that's heated by fire. In a way, I feel like I've been transported back to the days of Lincoln."

Sam adds, "Yes, you got that right. I've been discovering what their daily lives may have been like. We are only told of what those historical figures said and did politically, neglecting their daily hardships in history. And yet many of them were able to acquire tremendous wisdom."

Francinea addresses Meredith again, "A week ago, I never would have imagined anything like this afternoon. We have it so good, so easy. We shouldn't complain about anything."

Meredith answers, "yes, mom. I'll remind you of that."

The fish is seasoned and cooked. Vegetables were selected and warmed in a pot over the stove. All four seated around the butcher-block table, slowly finishing the dinner intermingled with conversations on the light side, one of the comments being, "Have you ever eaten a real goldfish?"

Sam starts softly singing, "If I knew you were coming, I'd have baked a cake . . . baked a cake . . ."

"Wow, I hadn't heard that for a long time," Francinea tells him. "That was, ah, back in the fifties? Now, Meredith and I will clean up, so you and Harry, go sit by the fireplace." Francinea exclaims, picking up his and her plates and silverware, placing them in the large sink as Meredith handles the rest, and starts pushing the pump up and down to fill the large pot and put it on the stove to warm the water.

"This is not as hard as we thought it would be, is it Meredith?" Francinea reflects as she hangs the frying pan on a hook.

Mr. Guardyall, can we do this again?" Meredith asks as she approaches the fireplace.

"You sure can. Anytime," Sam answers, looking up to the young lady now standing in front of the fireplace. Sam looks back to the kitchen as Francinea folds a towel and places it on the rack on the side of the table. She looks at Sam and walks toward the fireplace. "Again, Sam, I must say, this has been a surprisingly wonderful day. Thank you. But we must be going."

Sam replies, "Thank you! A surprise visit like this is welcome any day. Thank You. Harry and Meredith. Thanks for your hard work on the snow, and I'll be prepared for the next snowball fight." He then looks directly at Francinea, holding his arms outward, and pulls her in for a hug.

"Thank You, thanks for coming out today." He whispers in her ear.

Nineteen

"Ah, good morning, Lord," Sam tells the air as he throws off the quilt and blankets. He slides into his slippers and steps into the bathroom, telling King, "me first, buddy."

"King, let's see what the outside looks like," Sam says as he opens the Dutch door to feel the fresh cold air. "Out you go!" *Ah, to have the fur that he has.*

Sam places several logs on the grate over to the fireplace and strikes a long match holding it under crumbled pieces of paper until a flame ignites a part of the kindling and loose bark. Coffee time, but first, he steps into the bedroom, opens a drawer to grab a long-sleeve sweatshirt, a pair of jeans, and wool socks. *Now I'm ready.* "Good morning Lord, thank you. I welcome this day."

The stove is warming the kitchen area as Sam is sitting at the butcher-block table with a bowl of cereal, a dish of mixed fruit, and that cup of coffee with the Bible opened to Ecclesiastes. Sam reads and re-reads and reads more and more, wanting that sullenness to leave. "All is vanity? What's the use?" Sam questions. *According to this, all that I do is nothing but vanity. Is this the meaning Solomon begs? Ultimately yes, at the end, when my life here is finished, will I remember? Will I gratify my soul as I did when I adored my designs, singing my praises that others licked up, expanding my pride? And so, I more and more loved the money they paid me. Compared to being face to face with the Almighty, all that stuff boils down to plain and simple vanity. We can't imagine that, can we? Standing in front of the great I AM that initiated light to penetrate the darkness, the eternal one who imagined and put together the process of thermal dynamics. Here we are on a planet within this vast universe governed by those natural laws.*

In this world, I'd be in awe, thrilled on the one hand and be shaking in my boots too, to be able to shake the hand, get an autograph, snapping a selfie of me standing next to a sports celebrity, a Hollywood star, a famous person, or the president.

Our spiritual nature yearns for the heavenly, while that other nature runs from it.

Refreshing some of the verses, Sam thinks, *now here's one for me*: "it is better to hear the rebuke of the wise than for a man to hear the songs of fools."

"Did you hear that, King? Yep, sometimes your bark is a rebuke."

Summarizing what he's read as pure wisdom from one of the wisest. *All this then is meaningless in the eternal end. Our existence then depends on that one tribute we must all decide during our brief lifetime; that God is worthy to be praised, God is to be feared, His commandments to behold, and singing His praises while we are here on His earth is all in all. All else is vanity. All that secular accumulation of goods is vanity. Is that the entire message left us by Solomon?*

"Wow." Looking down at his dog lying near the legs of the chair, Sam asks, "How did a guy way back then, a few hundred years before calendars changed from BC to AD, get such wisdom? No books to read. No libraries to go to. Not even a Google cloud to search."

"King, you don't have such problems, do you? "Come on, let's go for a walk in the snow."

Sam has his insulated jacket, leather gloves, and boots on, standing at the door as King barks and barks waiting for Sam to open the door. Sam partially opens the door as the nose of King peeks out in anticipation, and then Sam closes the door. King backs away, looking up at Sam, and barks some more as he paws the door. Sam does it again and again. Each time King is ready to run out. King sits, tail wagging looking up, letting out barks that are getting higher pitched. Then the dog turns in circles at Sam's feet, bumping him off balance into the edge of the door, his elbow knocking the latch loose.

"Okay, okay, I've had my fun, let's go."

Standing on the edge of the covered porch, he notices spots of snow partially covering the rocker seats, so he reaches for the broom to sweep the flakes off the chairs, and then picks up the small mat in front of the door, shaking it and moving it off to the side. Looking out further, he estimates *it's eight to ten inches deep.*

King is off and around the gazebo sniffing and sniffing the ground, getting his nose wet and white, sticking his nose into the shady depressed areas.

"What have we here? Ah, no, King, those are ours from that snowball fight. Come on, let's explore the path. Sam starts the walk to the lake, pausing on the way, he stops and looks out over the clear blue waters meeting the snow-blanketed forest, the colors so vibrant in their shades of light to dark green blanketed by white. "Thank You, Lord, for these eyes to see."

King takes the lead along the bank and into the woods. Sam peers into the trees on each side, looking for any sign of life, rabbit or squirrels, paw prints of wolves, larger prints of bears, or deeper, sharper indications of jumping deer. *Where did all you guys go?* He stops as the sign stares at him. King has already turned the corner, going deeper and further into the tree-covered path and out of sight. Sam whistles and whistles again, shouting out, "King, King, come here, boy."

Turning around, Sam decides that this morning would be a good time to do a little fishing, as he served up the fish he had. Sam chooses two poles and the tackle box from the barn. At the pier, Sam starts pushing the rowboat off the beach when King comes running.

"Come on, King, we're going to get some fish. Jump." Sam loosens the rope from the post, stepping into the boat, and pushes away from the pier. He digs the oars in deep, pushing against the water, and the boat slowly moves into the deep, heading toward the flowing stream. He lowers the anchor, grabs a rod, and casts the fly bait out to the stream flowing into the lake. King is at the front of the boat, barking into the air while shifting his weight from side to side, rocking the boat. "King, stop it! Be still."

Sam feels pressure on the rod as it bends. Carefully, he turns the knob of the reel while lowering the rod near the water, then raising the rod, and lowering it while reeling in more line thinking, *Hmm? This feels like a big one.* The rod is straight up, and Sam reaches out for the line seeing the outline of a fish thrashing below the surface. He pulls it in as the fish revolts being pulled out of the water as King jumps and barks at the fish.

"Another trout." Sam pulls a line through the fish's gills and drops it into the water beside the boat. He casts again.

The fishing continues for an hour catching five more when Sam hears a voice shouting out and waving at him from the shore. "Hey, Sam. Samuel," the man shouts out again.

"Hang on. I'll be right in." Sam howlers back. The man holds his hands up to his ears. He grabs the oars and starts rowing toward the shore left of the inlet. King barks and barks, his nose pointed off the edge of the small boat. Nearing shore, Sam speaks loudly, "What's up, Gene?"

"Ah, we can't find the key to the door to put your ice away."

"The key is where it always is," Sam shouts.

"It's not there," Gene says in a raised voice.

"I'll be right up." Sam rows to the pier as Gene walks along the shore, helps pull the rowboat in, and tying it around a post. King jumps out to sniff at the man's feet and legs. Sam holds the fish up, "got me some."

"Looks good, Sam. Sorry to bother you, but we've never had a problem delivering your ice when you're not around."

"I'm sorry too. The key must be there. Let's go see."

Norman is on the porch, "Hello, Mr. Guardyall, you got a few beauties there."

"Hi, Norman, Good to see you again."

Sam pulls the door's handle discovering the resistance, and then looks at the usual hiding place under a corner of the doormat, and then at another spot, then at another. "Now, I don't know what happened because I did not lock it. I know I didn't and have not removed the key either. Why would I?"

Gene exclaims, "Sorry, Sam."

Sam looks at the area around the door, the porch in front, and to the shuttered windows on each side, exclaiming, "Yeah, it has to happen when the shutters are over the windows. Why? Why now? Lord, I need your help."

"Sam, how can we help? Anything? We can come back. We got a few more deliveries we have to make, and it'll give you time to figure out what to do."

"Yeah, I guess."

"It'll be a few hours."

Still stunned at his carelessness, Sam focuses on researching the area as the two get in and start the truck to drive off when a thought comes.

"Hey, wait a moment. Hold up!" Sam hollers, running alongside the passenger side, knocking on the fender. Gene breaks, and Norman rolls down the window.

"Norman, you've got a cell phone there. Would you call the sheriff for me and tell him about this situation? They have a spare key. Ask if they could bring it out. I can't drive in and get it as the key to the truck is also inside."

"Sure. I'll call, and you can tell them." Norman pushes several times on the phone, waiting, and then "Hello, this is Norman from Whitecraft Ice, we need a favor. Here, I'll turn it over to Mr. Guardyall."

He hands the cell phone to Sam, who relates what happened, and then the agent informs Sam their hands are full right now and they couldn't possibly get out. Sam tells that to Norman.

"After our deliveries, I'll drive into town, get the key, and come back," Gene informs Sam.

"Ah, thank you. You're a life savior. Sorry, but I don't know what happened."

Gene replies, "We'll be back with the key, Sam. Go get some more fish. Can we get anything else while we're in town? We'd offer you to ride along, but as you can see, there's no room."

"Thanks. I'll be here." Sam answers as they drive off, splashing into a higher snowbank along the drive.

Resting in the rocker on the porch, Sam thinks back to the day's activities. The fishing, getting the rods and box from the garage, doing the fishing, rowing the boat. He refreshes all that he remembers of the morning, even the part of sweeping the snow off the porch. Then at the sight of the fish lying on the porch, he gets up, grabs the stringer, and heads back to the pier where he drops the stringer with the trout in the water and ties it to a post and back into the boat again to pass the time. "Come on, King, we'll go catch some more."

As he starts to push off, a thought comes to him. "Dang it, I goofed again. King, you've done it before, and you can do it again. King, let's go." Sam climbs out of the boat, and they head back to the cabin.

"King, here, smell this," Sam points to the lock on the Dutch door. King stands on his back legs, his nose to the lock, the insides, around the outside, and back to the opening.

"Got it, now find the key." King backs away, on all fours sniffing around the edges of the door, along the floor in front, to the doormat, around the edges of the mat, and as he gets to the inside edge, he stops and intently smells, the tail pointing straight back.

"King, it's not there. We looked at it." Sam picks up the mat anyway and turns it over as King concentrates on the underside and then moves a bit to the floorboards and stops at a point, an open area between two boards, his head and nose now sniffing both sides of that spot of deck boards.

"What are you telling me?" Sam asks.

Then the vision of him brushing the snow this morning comes sliding across his mind. *Yep, I did it while sweeping the snow away. Yeah, I moved the mat and unknowingly swept the key, and it fell between the boards. Stupid!* He kneels intently, looking into the darkness below the boards. *If it is down there, I can't get it without tearing up these boards, and I'm not doing that.*

"Thanks, King." Sam bends and rubs the ears, down his neck, and his sides. "You're my finder."

But, Sam muses *it still does not solve the mystery of why the door is locked,* "Anyway, King, let's do some more fishing."

He throws the fly out as far as he can, starts the reeling process repeating it again and again, slowly bringing in the fly bait. *A couple more would be good,* he surmises. The rod bends, the tip bends into the surface of the water. "I've got one." The trout is reeled in and thrashing around in the boat as King smells it and steps on it as the trout splashes the bits of water. It's put on a stringer and back into the water with one other. Suddenly, a vision comes flashing across his mind, and then another pull of the rod, and Sam happily reels in another one. "Hey buddy, it's time to call this quits today."

Onshore, Sam has the stringer of three more fish covering them in snow. Relaxed in the rocker petting the dog at his side, admiring the blanket of snow, the still waters of the lake, the tree branch tips bending down from the weight. "Thank You, Lord, for today." He tells the air.

He heads for the barn and grabs two bundles of wood, a few pieces of kindling carrying them to the gazebo area where he starts a campfire. He turns the cushions over. The kindling fires up. He watches the flames catch the bark and then slowly the wood itself. "Ah, King, up here." He signals with his hand patting the open spot on the bench.

"For Gene and Norman being good and friendly, helping me out of my foolishness, Thank You, Lord." He reflects: *In Indianapolis, I turned down a friend who asked for a bit of my time. And another time, I foolishly pushed another acquaintance away asking for help, and another.* "Oh, Lord, forgive me. I've done others wrong, and here I am being helped by acquaintances. I don't deserve it."

As the fire warms, Sam unzips his jacket to let the warmth reach his sweatshirt. He leans back, peering into the distant snow-capped mountains, the blue waters, and the tree tips bent from the snow and then back to the flames of the fire. Back and forth, his eyes go as his mind is reviewing the happenings of the day. *Now here I am locked out of my own home because of some stupidity. But Lord, I don't know how or why that happened. If it hadn't been for the ice delivery today,*

I would have found the door locked and no one to help when I got back in from fishing. "Thank You, Lord."

King jumps up, starts the barking, and runs off to greet the truck coming around the bend and stopping by the front porch.

"Good."

"Mr. Guardyall." Norman hollers.

"Thank You!"

"Here it is."

Taking the key from Norman's hand, Sam steps up on the porch to insert it in the lock. Thank You. Thank you."

Mr. Whitecraft is at the back of the truck, reaching in for a block of ice as Norman turns to get the forks from his dad to carry in the ice. Norman goes back to get the second block as Sam moves the frozen food to make room in the upper half.

Finished, Mr. Whitecraft looks around the cabin, "It's just like your grandfather left it. Beautiful Sam, I'm envious."

"Thanks, and double thanks for your help today. I don't know what I'd done when I discovered the door locked when I quit fishing. You saved the day."

"Ah, you're welcome. Your grandparents and I had some great talks sitting right there in front of the fireplace. Times that a person never forgets."

"Yeah, I gave you one of those today."

"Ah, forget it, glad we were sent to help. Sam, from what I've heard from some of my students, I want to discuss something with you. Harry and Meredith have suggested that they'd like to have you come and share your thoughts and knowledge of history."

"Ah, Gene, I'm…. I just ramble on and on."

"That's what they liked about it. And, they said the most important part of your rambling, as you call it, is that it gets them thinking too. That's very important in this age of continual amusement. Kids aren't taught how to reason things out. Consider it, will you? Seriously."

"I wouldn't know where to begin."

"Good. That's a start. I'll okay it with the principal, and then we'll get together and work out a starting point, focusing on a subject. Thanks, I know Harry and Meredith will be excited."

"Oh, I don't know." And Sam pauses a bit. *In the past, my ramblings have been about my encounter with the spirit of God since I've been at this cabin.* "Okay, let me put it this way. I will not be muzzled in what I can or cannot say, and you can tell the principal that I may or may not bring up this marvelous creation. I might even mention that the crucifixion and resurrection of Jesus is part of recorded history, if that's okay. I'll do it. I'd be happy to."

Gene lowers his head, thinking about those demands. "This day and age we're in when any religious question gets raised in a public setting like schools are outlawed, I don't know. The issue is not pushed out here, so I don't know."

"Gene, that's it. If the principal agrees, yes, then we'll get together. It's your class. Go talk to your boss and get back to me." Sam then adds, "Changing the subject. I know how that door got locked." He relates the incident in the morning playing with King, getting knocked by him, forcing me against the latch when my forearm knocked it loose.

"And then, when sweeping the snow away from the door, I swept that spare key between those boards."

"Sam, I suppose you won't do that again, will you?"

"Stupid, wasn't it. Paul tells us to beware of dogs and have no confidence in the flesh."

"Sam, glad we could help. I'll get with you sometime next week."

"Ah, thank you for your gracious willingness to help me today. God Bless you. Thanks again. You're welcomed here anytime."

Twenty

"King, come on over here." Sam reaches in his pocket for some chunks of goodies. King smells and grabs the treat, and in one chew, it's gone. He bites another one held in front of his nose, wanting more. "That's it, now lay down and rest. I've got some reading and then typing to do." Sam opens his Bible to the beginning of Isaiah for his morning read.

After several minutes Sam summarizes in his mind: *how horrible the prime creation of God has acted throughout history. Turning toward idols, lusting after each other, living as if the natural laws of the Creator are mired in a darkened mirror. Even though we have all the tools of learning and wisdom at our fingertips, we have acted in the same way as the ancients. We go our own way, we war against each other, we are quick to argue, and at the same time, we are fearful of offending. Our idols are the stars of notoriety, those that strut on red carpets, and those that play games between chalk lines. Money,. Lots of it is our goal.*

He looks up for a glance out the window seeing water dripping from the roof. At the typewriter, he inserts a blank sheet rolling it up an inch

My Cabin Life 12

Ah, the other day, I did something foolish. It was just something different. I did it, thinking it would be fun, entertaining, something that'll start the day lightheartedly. And what happened? I got locked out of the cabin. Did not know I was locked out until several hours later as King and I went fishing. Yep, I caught some beautiful Brown Trout, enjoying the good fortune during the beautiful chilly morning, a few days after a snowstorm hit, leaving us almost a foot of fresh first of winter snow. Breaking my enjoyment, the ice truck came. Gene yelled at me from the shore that the cabin is locked, and the key is not in its usual hiding place.

Can't be. Thinking that Gene must be wrong. I hurried through the snow to the cabin, and yes, I discovered it myself, the key was missing. What happened? I had not the slightest idea. It had never happened before, and why now, and how? Perplexed, agitated, and humiliated there in front of Gene and his son doing their chores. All I could do was scratch my head, apologize for something, express my sorrows for them being a witness to a mishap of some sort, a misunderstanding, a mystery.

Humiliated. Me, humiliated? My pride was hurt. No. Why I'm Samuel Guardyall, I've got everything under control I always tell folks who ask how're things going out there?

But they saved the day, telling me he was glad they had been sent to help at that specific time when I needed it. He offered to drive into town to get the spare key left at the sheriffs' office after finishing their other deliveries. During their absence, I went back to fishing. When, during one of those times of managing the rod and reel, I got a revelation. I saw what I had done while sweeping away some snow. A picture it was, what today's technology would possibly call a you-tube video streaming across my mind. Yes, the spirit of the Father God, creator of everything, manager of it all had captured the event on a type of film that could be used if necessary, to show me what happened with the key, just in case. God knows me. God recorded it. I saw it. I knew.

But there was another mystery, the one about how the door got locked. I thought and thought hard, reasoning about how it could have happened. Nothing there but imaginings. Again, I asked, Lord, I need your help.

And, after they had returned with a spare key and we were inside the cabin discussing Gene's request that I come and teach his history class, another video sped across my mind or soul, whatever those theologians call it, and I knew how the door got locked. The picture I saw was when I was messing with King. I partially opened the door enough for him to think he was being let out, and then I closed it on him. I was teasing him. I did that several times. I was having fun. King got agitated and jumped up on me and pushed me off balance. His tail whipped my butt, and I lunged forward, hitting the door latch, loosening it with my forearm.

When King and I left, I pulled the door shut like always, thinking all is well. But this time, the inside latch went down, locking the door.

So, folks, there it is. I goofed, and God, knowing all, knowing that I was going to be foolish, sends someone to help, and that ever-present ministering spirit records events as they are happening to inform me later when I request help.

As the secular Christian that I once was, an event like this would have been dismissed, explained away, and not even thought about as a divine inter-working of the spirit. But now I know, the darkened glass was made clear, my eyes saw the recorded video, and I knew.

Thanks to the ever-present El Shaddai.

"Okay, King, the snow is melting. What shall we do? Haven't been to town in a while, so let's venture out. We both need some food?"

Arriving in town after the noonday rush, Sam stops at the diner.

"Hello Sam, how are you? You doing all right?" Joanna asks as he settles down in a booth.

"Yeah, sure, I'm making it. Glad to see the snow melting. What's the forecast?"

"It'll be nice for a few more weeks, and then the sky falls in. Hey, have you heard that Mary, the librarian, was killed in a car wreck?"

"No. When? How? Sorry to hear that."

"The funeral is later today behind the native church. We're going to close for the rest of the day."

"You're closing?"

When she leaves for the kitchen, he ponders. *The diner is closing so they can attend a funeral? He then thinks back to the days of his decision and the hours spent wondering whether it would be a good idea to move here. How will the local people treat a stranger coming from a big city? What sort of people choose to live way off in a small town next to a national forest? Are they friendly?*

Joanna soon brings his coffee, and before she leaves, Sam asks, "You're closing to attend the funeral?"

"Mary and I were cousins."

"Oh, I'm sorry. How'd it happen?"

"A drunken bum," Joanna hatefully replies. "And he survived. That's so wrong."

"Joanna, I'll be praying for you and the family."

"Don't pray for the idiot, except he is put away for a long-long time."

"I hear you. Is there anything I can do?"

"Nah. Well . . . hey . . . Yes, you're welcome to come. Oh, you see those two sitting over there. The guy, he's the high school principal, and she's the something called the social director. He asked about you."

"Huh, he asked about me?"

"Yeah, why are they interested in you?"

"Ah, it could be that Gene Whitecraft asked me to address his class."

"That explains it. All I told him is that I've seen you a few times in the diner and you seem like a nice guy from back east somewhere taking over the cabin. Then he wanted to know about the cabin. Should I let them know you're here?"

"Joanna, what do you know about them?"

"This is his first year as principal, so he's still a mystery. Came from Denver."

"Oh, I think it better if I did not talk to them now."

"Up to you. I'm being called." Her jaws move again as she leaves the booth.

Curious about those two, Sam ponders, *What did Gene tell them? Should I go over and introduce myself? What then would I tell them?*

The questions keep coming when a thought crosses his mind, *"I am with you always."*

Joanna brings his sandwich and a refill of the coffee. "Sam, I'd be honored if you would come to the funeral."

"I will. What time?"

"It starts at four."

"Sure, and I'll be praying for you and the family that your grief is brief, knowing that Mary is now living our dream to come, and you'll see her again."

"Thank you."

Finishing the meal, Sam pays Joanna at the register. "You do know God is with you always."

"Thanks. Sam, I'll see you there."

As Sam turns to leave and begins to push the door open, the words come back, so he turns and meanders over to the table where the principal and the lady are taking their time with whatever it is.

Approaching the table, Sam hesitates, facing them as they look up. "I'd like to introduce myself. I'm Samuel Guardyall. Joanna said you had asked about me, so I thought I'd come over and we could get acquainted."

The gentleman slides to the edge of the booth, stands, and extends his hand, "I'm Michael Broomsted, and this is Susanana Homer. Mr. Guardyall, it's good to meet you. Gene Whitecraft, our history teacher, approached me the other day with an idea he had. Oh, won't you sit down and join us. Please."

"Sure, thanks."

Susanna leans forward over the table while her hand reaches into her purse, and she places a cell phone on the table. A green light on its side starts blinking.

"Anyway, Mr. Guardyall, Gene has briefed me on this cabin life you're living and how some of his students had approached him wanting you to talk about your take on some parts of history."

"Yes, he did ask me if I'd be interested."

"What would you talk about?"

"Ah, Mr. Broomsted, Gene told me that if he got the okay from you, then he'd get back to me, and we'd discuss the parts of history he desired me to concentrate on; probably something to do with civics. But he hasn't done that yet."

"We're still working on it. The request has been passed through proper channels, whom I expect to hear from over the next few days. Mr. Guardyall, as administrators of public schools, the safety and protection of the children is our main concern, along with providing them with an educational background. What interests do you have in the education of our students?"

Pondering the question, Sam replies. "I'm just a guy who has the privilege of living my daily life somewhat like our forefathers lived without any of the modern conveniences enjoyed today, except I can plug into this current life by driving here for a cup of coffee. And yet, somehow, they gathered their knowledge and wisdom under oil lamps and were able to come together in unity and formulate the greatest government contract in the history of this world. It's that constitution of ours, which enabled the average person the freedom to invent, build, and pursue their dreams without governmental interference. And now here we are two-hundred years later comfortably conversing inside a brick and mortar building fitted with button-controlled warmth."

Pointing to the cell phone, Sam continues, "who needs an encyclopedia when that tiny device can answer any question by someone in a comfortable office suite, perhaps in India, or some other locality thousands of miles away using the memory bank in a cloud."

"So? What are you getting at?" the principal replied as Susanna appears puzzled.

"Do the kids think about that? Do the kids wonder how our founders were able to gather such wisdom under those circumstances?"

"I'm sure our teachers cover that." The principal states. "Gene told me also that you had some stipulations you'd want, like the freedom to say anything, possibly bringing up religion."

"Is there something objectionable with that? One of our supreme court Justices said, 'the principle of free thought is not free thought for those who agree with us but freedom for the thought we hate.' Should not all ideas be part of our children's education?"

"We're in different circumstances now, Sam."

"Yes, we are, but no, we're not. Considering that there are twenty-some students in his senior history class, I would assume there are students with emerging talents in various disciplines after high school. Perhaps chemistry, medicine, engineering, mechanics, carpentry, possibly working as police or firefighters, a national sports profession, and teaching too. So, wouldn't you agree that each of these subjects has a historical background?

"We are all interconnected with the past." Samuel continues, considering that it's been a bit over two centuries since our first fourth of July celebration, which means that your father's grandfather's parents were probably alive during the writing of that Declaration of Independence. By the way, it says, 'all men are created equal, that their creator endows them with certain unalienable rights.' Sam emphasized the word creator. "Yes, endowed by their creator.

"Most of those wise men agreed together and wrote those words using quill pens and, yes, they were Bible believers too. Don't students have the right to understand what and why those men seriously believed those ideas were the basics of life?

"I leave you with those thoughts, and you may do with it as you please." Sam slides off the chair, stands, and adds, "and yes, the birth of Jesus was a part of history too, and the world has not been the same since."

Sam offers his hand to each of them, "Mr. Broomsted and Ms. Homer, blessings to you. You have a grave responsibility, the formulation of educational materials. Now you have heard it directly from the horse. I'm only interested in providing the kids with a perspective of their own unique God provided gift residing within each of them, the curiosity to ask what, when, where, who and why, and then the right to get answers."

Sam pauses, then adds, "I'll be waiting to hear from Gene, but whichever way the decision is decided, my prayers will be answered."

"Thank you, Mr. Guardyall, for coming over and talking with us. We'll let Mr. Whitecraft know soon enough."

"Good day to each of you, and now you have a recording to play before the proper channels. I am only a man transferred from a busy secular urban life to a quiet rural life next to a wilderness of beauty where the majesties of creation are still conveniently evident."

Twenty-One

"Sam, what are you doing here? Is something wrong with your leg again?" Francinea asks, seeing Sam sitting in her office waiting room.

"No, it's fine." Sam answers. He pauses, sighs standing up with his hands holding his Ben Hogan cap.

"What's up, Sam? Did something happen?"

"No. Everything is fine." Looking her straight in the eyes, "Francinea, I came here to ask you if I could take you to dinner. Would you go to dinner with me?"

Surprised, Francinea asks, "Huh? You want to take me to dinner, just the two of us?" She pauses, takes a deep breath comprehending the surprise visit and nature of his question. "Are you asking me out? Would this be a … a date?"

"Yes, I'm asking. I've thought about this since the other day, and yes, I'd like that, you and me. Have you been to that restaurant in Johnsonville?"

"Sam." Francinea stares, then sighs, looking past him toward the office window seeing the clerk smiling and nodding her head. "I don't know, I'm sorry, but this sounds like a date. I haven't had that thought for a long time. Sam, I'm happy here. Enjoying it. Got a wonderful daughter, a developing practice. Now, I had a wonderful time at your place, but just the two of us together. I don't know. That sounds like a teenage date, like ah, gee. I don't know. You caught me off guard."

"Yeah, I'm sorry. It's okay. I understand. So, let's remember the other day as friendly, fun times. Perhaps another time." Sam turns, reaching for the doorknob.

She carefully watches Sam as he was about to leave. "No, hold on a minute. Sam, I'd, ah, Yes. But we got to make some rules."

"Are you sure?"

"Yes, I'd like to have dinner with you. Ah, and oh, that truck of yours. Let me pick you up at your place."

"Hallelujah!" Sam exclaims, and then explains why he'd prefer picking her up and then they could take her car. "Is Saturday evening okay? Say at seven."

"Sure, seven it is. But Sam, umm, No, ah, we'll talk about that later."

"Francinea, nothing formal, okay. Just a casual dinner. I'm not going to dress up in a suit and tie, so let's keep it . . . ah … simple, a relaxed time."

Back in his truck, he rubs the ears and down the neck of King, thinking of the coming new event in his life. "Get a hold of yourself."

Okay now, he begins to reason. *If God did not sanction this, would He have prevented it, or am I being led down a dark alley by my desire? Francinea could have refused, but she finally agreed, so is God in this? Is this one of my fleshly desires, and I'm placing that desire above that which the Almighty has planned for me? Oh, the questions, not knowing without a doubt that this relationship I seem to desire is part of His divine plan for my life, or not. Is my faith weak? Why am I thinking along these lines? Am I wanting to replace Angelia?*

"King. Let's get out of here. Go home. No, got to go to the funeral."

Later after the native funeral, he's barely out of town when he starts singing, "Glory, glory, hallelujah," repeating the chorus over and over again.

Turning into his driveway, he stops to retrieve the mail of numerous advertisements, which he adds to others in a trash bag behind the seat. Inside the cabin, he lights three oil lamps, adds wood to the fireplace embers, and the stove as King devours what was left in the bowl, licking it clean.

"You want more, don't you? Give me a minute. I want something too." Sam refills the bowl and prepares the pot for coffee. He reaches into the icebox for a chicken breast and a package of mixed vegetables. He places his hand over the stove sensing its warmth as he puts the iron frying pan on the plate to let it warm while he prepares the chicken with his favorite seasonings. The coffee pot starts whistling.

"Ah, okay, time to read." He tells the air as he places the empty dish, knife, fork, and spoon in the sink. Sitting comfortably in front of the fireplace, his legs on the footstool, and a blanket around his shoulders. He opens the book to the earmarked page of volume three of the 'Story of Civilization' by Will Durant. He reads the passage about the supposed contradictions of the four gospel books, and then he comes to Mr. Durant's summary. He reads it repeatedly, and his thought processes go streaming like a locomotive on the first trip over the rails across the Mississippi into the west. Pushing the book away, he throws the blanket off and heads to the typewriter. *I've got to write these thoughts as fast as they come.*

Inserting a fresh sheet of paper, Sam starts.

My Cabin Life 13

Anyway, I'm back to the reading program, now delving into Will Durant and The Story of Civilization. Picking up from where I left off about the so imagined conflicting accounts of the authors of the first four books of the New Testament, Mr. Durant summarized their accounts as being a miracle far more incredible than those recorded miracles that Jesus performed. Yes, it was a supernatural miracle that four different simple men, writing for thirty to sixty years, would have separately, each in their own way invented such a unique personality; so powerful, so appealing with such a lofty ethic and inspiring vision of our human brotherhood. Those writers recorded some miracles performed by Jesus inhabiting a human body. And after centuries, such accounts of the life, crucifixion, and resurrection of this engaging human-divine personality spread across the globe. It changed people and the entire course of history. Even the Jewish historian Josephus wrote about Jesus calling Him the Messiah.

History was recorded. Truth is truth. Reality is real. It cannot be changed. Imagination is imagination, continually changing. And heresy is inventing imagined truth.

Why then is there still such discord among men? Simple, this sin-filled world appeals to our fallen nature. Those thoughts of Adam that the knowledge of something else, something different than what they've been used to, something called evil, would be a blessing. It couldn't be so bad, could it?

Going back some, I remember seeing in five-inch bold type headlines, "GOD IS DEAD." Boy, that newspaper sold lots and lots of copies. The broadcast news went bonkers, magazine sales went up and people tuned in to see if it was true. Had our scientists found indisputable evidence that indeed God had died, and His remains had been discovered in that remote desert of Roswell New Mexico. Oh, how they invent stories for profit.

So now those experts tell us we are left on our own to live and enjoy it. There's nothing more; dirt-to-dirt and ashes-to-ashes. Yes, the esteemed scientists claim, we've evolved a little bit higher than chimpanzees swinging from tree to tree, so swing away everyone and have a good time. There's nothing more they continually tell us.

Now, when that headline appeared, the average person across the fruited plains tossed it aside and continued going to church, continued reading the Bible. Some of those self-identified as so much more educated and enlightened than the rest of us had their mission presented in bold underlined type. They came together and cemented the theory of atheistic secular humanism, and here we are today. The media, the entertainers, the professors of the sciences, the politicians and bureaucrats going where the money flows, and many of our churches following where the money grows.

Change the tax codes, they say, as we can't have pastors speak the truth about corrupted politicians and fools singing the praises of scientists. We still, softly at first, went to see the movies turning morality upside down. The experts tell us what right do you have to impose your morality on others.

Hey buddy, we did not invent that morality.

Those are not our commandments. We just try to obey them.

Oh, Sodom, your sting has come.

Come, quick Lord, Come. Society is about to bust.

But hang on there for a bit, okay. Ah, thank you. As of today, my feelings led the way, and I asked Francinea out on a date. Hmm? I am attracted to her. But then, I wondered if this was the right thing to do. Questions again. I guess I'll find out in due time if God is in this or if it's only my feelings. It is one dinner date or does the rapture come first, and I miss a date.

Saturday evening comes with excited anticipation.

Driving through Prairieville's main street, Sam, following the directions of Francinea, turns right on the fourth street after the main stoplight, turns right at the next stop sign, and follows the rural winding road of homes on small acreages, backing up to the forest. Sam is looking for the red-bricked home with four white columns supporting the porched roof, number 404 on the mailbox.

"Please park on the right side of the driveway," Francinea had told him. Driving up the driveway, he admires the home setting on a few acres of tall spruce and pines surrounding the home, with a small pond visible behind the garage. Small trees with shrubs line the driveway, the open porch extending the length and around the side, one large picture window with two smaller windows evenly spaced to the left of the six-paneled front door.

 Sam nervously rings the doorbell.

"Good evening, Sam, Come on in," Francinea greets.

"Thanks. What a beautiful setting!"

"Thank you. Meredith picked it."

"And you too, without your white coat. Wow!" Sam states as the words flow out, admiring her deep red long sleeve dress with white lace loosely hinged around her neck, flowing to her knees, the lace accentuating large red buttons inches apart, all of it highlighting the curvature of her body.

 Meredith appears from around the corner with a big smile, "Good evening Mr. Guardyall. Nice to see you again."

"Hi Meredith, I love your home. The setting is beautiful. How many acres do you have here?"

Meredith replies, "Four and a part. Mom said something about going to the new restaurant in Johnsonville."

"Yes, at first, I thought it'd be okay, but then I heard about Cattlemen's Steak House. So, if your mom agrees, that's it."

"Yes, yes, go there. You'll like it." Meredith responds with a high five salute to Sam.

Francinea hugs her daughter, "That essay is due Monday, so get with it."

"Yes, mom! I know. And you remember you're under a curfew too."

"Have fun." Meredith cheers them on, watching as Sam holds the coat for Francinea as she puts her arms through each sleeve and pulls the sides close. She reaches back to push her hair over the collar.

Meredith whispers in his ear, "Thank You."

"Thanks, Sam," Francinea turns to her right, opening the door to the garage and handing Sam the keys, "You're driving."

Carefully, Sam backs out of the garage, passing his truck and down the driveway turning back toward town.

"Francinea, this road is quite remarkable, must have been a logging trail at first the way it follows the curvature of the land."

"Yes, the realtor indicated it was when he first took me to see the house. I like it. So why did you change your mind on restaurants?"

Sam describes the restaurant, the initial shock of seeing so many waiting outside, going through the trellis, having his photo taken, being told to stand still as the mat recorded his weight, and being provided a menu with his picture and name on it. Summarizing, he says, "The food was good, but the idea of being given a special menu based on my BMI turned me off."

"Huh? Did you say you were photographed and weighed? Why do people continue going there?"

"I don't know. I was told it was free desserts."

Francinea turns in her seat, adjusting the seat belt to get a better side view of Sam, "No, that's the tip of it; that's the excuse."

"The excuse, what are you getting at?" Sam asks.

"Underneath, it's unconscious conditioning over the years pushing our sense of personal responsibility onto someone else, so then we can blame them for our goofs."

Taking his eyes briefly off the road, Sam turns to peer into her delightful eyes, "I remember while studying Roman architecture, there was a notation that the contractor building the arches had to stand under it while the scaffolding was removed. Now that was accepting responsibility."

"Sam, Meredith told me that the other day, she felt like she was sitting at the feet of an old grandfather being intrigued at his stories."

"An **old** grandfather?" Sam asks.

"Yes, she wanted more, like a kid sitting in the library listening to someone making the story come to life."

"Thanks. She's a talented young lady. You've done a great job with her."

Reaching Johnsonville's outskirts, Sam slows and turns right at the first stoplight, and there it is. An impressive horizontal wooden ranch type building with canopy covered wood decks. Several couples are chatting together under the roof. A statue of a cowboy on a bucking horse is centered on a grassy island. The parking lot is full.

"Here we are. We may be waiting a bit."

"We could go to that diner," Francinea suggests.

"No. I'd rather not."

"Your call."

He sees a lone spot around the side, carefully maneuvering her SUV into the slot.

Opening the door to the restaurant, they are greeted and escorted to a comfortable booth. Sam helps her out of the coat, placing it on the hook at the end of the booth. He watches her slide across the soft cushion.

"Outside, I was thinking we'd be waiting in line," Sam says while hanging his emblazoned leather jacket with the "Colts" symbol across the back, along with his cap.

Looking over the menu of drinks, Sam states, "I'm ready for a glass of wine. How about you?"

"Yes, sure." Francinea pauses, looks around at the other tables, the customers, waiters, then to the young couple sitting behind Sam, then back to him. "You choose the wine as Jerome, and I were never wine lovers."

Sam decides, taking his eyes away from the two-page folder of appetizers to noticing an approaching waiter. He's dressed in blue jeans, a long-sleeve plaid shirt, a red tie, a sleeveless blue-jean vest, a white cowboy hat tilted to the rear, and a black towel hanging off the waistband. The waiter stops at another booth on the way.

"Angelia and I got used to one along the line of Red, California, Merlot. Ah, no. I vowed earlier that I'd never again be tempted by alcohol. Agh! So, coffee for me. And you Francinea?"

The waiter approaches, "Are you ready?" he asks, kneeling at the edge of the booth with his tablet and felt tip pen.

"Coffee for you, sir, and hot tea for the lady." Here's our menu. The special tonight is the ten-ounce tenderloin, baked potato with steamed and grilled broccoli. I'll get your drinks."

Scanning the menu, Sam tells his date, "I got a question when he comes back."

Sam decides and puts the menu off to the side, looking up at the beautiful lady sitting across from him, "Francinea, we've both been through tragedies and have handled them somewhat in the same way, by moving out and away from our former life. But I was given the opportunity, whereas you chose to relocate on your own. How did you decide on this area?"

"Sam, ah, we've got to get something straight right from the start, okay? I'd rather we'd remain friends, nothing else. We've only spent a little bit of time together, but I can feel it already. But I can't. I will not get interested in anything more, no romance, no other desires. Okay? We're both adults; let's just keep this on a friendly basis. We can do that, right? And I'll pay for mine too!"

Noticing her seriousness, he's stunned at her blunt statement. Remembering the initial hesitation on her part and the thoughts he had. Sam replies, "Yes, I've been pondering this too. I do, and I don't. But, then, I don't. Huh, did that make any sense?" Sam pauses. He looks down at his hands and his fingers rubbing the tabletop, feeling a blush coming. "What say we push all that aside and relax about this?"

"I'm sorry, Sam, but I had to bring it up. Now, that's out of the way, back to your question. Meredith and I sat down together looking at maps and the brochures we sent off for."

The waiter sets the drinks down as Sam gives him their steak choices. "The lady wants it medium well, and I'll take mine medium rare."

"Yes, sir. Thank you."

"I got a question."

"Sure, go ahead."

"The prices are in even dollars. We're not going to be charged that extra ninety-nine cents when we get the bill, are we?"

"Huh? No, of course not. It's eighteen, and that's it."

Sam replies, "Okay, thank you."

"Anything else?" the waiter asks.

"No, that's all. Thanks."

"What was that about?" Francinea asks after the waiter is out of sight.

"Ah, it's just a pet peeve of mine. At the gas stations, the advertisements, everywhere. The price always ends with a nine. I guess nine-ninety-nine sounds better than ten dollars. At the gas stations, it's one-eighty-nine with a very small nine at the end. Are you going to drive two miles because the new station just opening has the price at one-ninety?

"Well, you're right, but that's just the way it is. We're used to it." Francinea answers.

"Ah, where were we? Oh yeah, you were telling me how you got here."

"Yeah, Meredith and I looked at maps and decided we wanted a smaller out of the way type atmosphere, so we explored upper Wisconsin as well as western Minnesota and Idaho, and New Hampshire too. But I also had to find an opening for work."

"You didn't mention Colorado."

"You're right. I didn't. At first, Colorado never came up, and looking back; I don't know why."

"What changed?"

"A friend at the hospital suggested it. She had read of an opening in a small Colorado town and suggested I should at least check into it, and here we are."

"Amazing! Isn't it? Part of that mystery."

"It is. Meredith and I have had several chats about how this all came about after we settled in and began to count our blessings at being directed here. It's a beautiful area. It's been terrific for both of us, even though she left some good friends behind whom she misses. And now I'm sitting across from a man I've briefly met who's had a similar experience, and I'm wondering why."

"Here I am, seeing the similarities too and wondering." Sam pauses looking at her, expecting a response or something. "Through all I've been through, I now look back and wonder why I didn't treat every day as precious from the first moment I woke up. Is it because we're so busy?"

Francinea asks, "Was it all houses you designed or did you get into other projects?"

"Mostly homes the last several years as the town was growing fast, developing new neighborhoods as people moved out of the city."

"I like the name, Samuel. It sounds so authentic and rich versus Sam. You don't mind if I call you Samuel, do you?"

Sam pauses a second, then says, "ah, forget it."

Francinea straightens in the booth leaning back while replying, "Forget it? You'd rather be called Sam?"

"No, No. No, I was about to say, just don't call me late for dinner."

"Oh, that." Then she adds, "One of the things I'll never forget hearing from my mother. Don't give your children common names. Give them something uncommon and different, sort of unique. And then tell them they're anything but common, they're one of a kind, special. That's one of the reasons I gave Meredith her name, three syllables and hard to shorten. I've told her many times she's not common, so I also add this, so, don't act like it. I emphasized, don't follow along with what everyone else is doing. Mom did the same to me."

"I like that. Your name, I could easily shorten it to Fran, but Francinea has a musical tone to it, and I've liked the sound of it the first time I heard it. Is it French?"

"Francine is, but mom added the a."

Samuel then asks about her mother. Was she still living, or how and when she passed on, and he adds that both his parents are gone, when, and how.

Francinea informs Sam of the type of cancer her mother had and nothing medical science could do about it. "It was a quick passing, one that was expected, and we all had time to prepare and accept the inevitable."

"You've been through so much. How did you manage? The sudden death of your husband, how did you find out about it?" Sam then wonders if he should be so curious. "Oops, I'm sorry. I shouldn't have brought it up."

"It's okay, Samuel. The news was broadcasting the killings of an investigative military exposition in Iraq. I knew Jerome was part of a crew that was doing that kind of work. He texted me about it. Was that his assignment, I wondered? Was Jerome one of them? How? Why? For three days, we were in misery. Normally, I'd hear from Jerome every day, but nothing. The silence was confirming what I feared."

"I can't imagine not knowing, the wondering. I wouldn't have been able to sleep."

Francinea continues, "It was. I'd toss and turn with the cell phone still in my hand, begging for a good night's sleep and begging for a call. I wondered how another news crew could get in there to film the massacre and not get their heads chopped off? I called all the stations, but no one could or would confirm anything. I was mad. Called them names I shouldn't have, but in my condition, I didn't care. I wanted to know!" She pauses and bows her head, wiping a few tears away, then raises her head, looking at Sam and says, "Sorry."

"I'm sorry for bringing it up. It still hurts," Sam consoles.

"We didn't find out for sure until four days later when a contingent of military brass came to the house." She pauses, trying to hold back her emotion. "I'm sorry you're listening and seeing me like this."

"Hey, I'm honored to have been trusted with your deepest hurt."

"Here you go, folks. Please cut into the steaks to see if it's the way you like it. Would you like a refill on the coffee and tea?"

"I'm fine on both accounts," Sam answers after taking the knife to his inch-thick filet.

"Thank you, mine is perfect," Francinea nods.

Sam reaches across the table for her hands. Finishing the prayer, he adds, "And, Lord, I thank you for this gathering of two of your servants here this evening. Bless our time together and all that we do now and in the future. Amen."

"Thank You, Samuel. Now, tell me about yourself, your wife and all."

"Oh, where do I start?"

Francinea states, "Your wife, am I right that she was a surgical nurse? How did you meet?"

"We met at a golf outing. The company I was designing for was sponsoring a charitable event for the Children's Hospital. She was beginning her nursing career and had volunteered to help. She was standing at a table, interacting and taking the tickets from us and handing out the gifts. From then on, I wanted to know this beauty. After we finished playing, I saw her again, approached her, and we started talking. Six months later, we were engaged."

"You work fast. How soon was your son born?"

"That was four years later. She desired to wait as our careers were hard on our home life. She would get the evening shift, being one of the latest hired. She wanted to wait for the seniority to come."

"How did you occupy yourself in the evenings then?"

"Mostly, I'd stay in the office. As a new architect, there was a lot I had to learn about the business side of it, so I committed to that."

"Meredith told me your son died of epilepsy," Francinea says while taking a bite of the steak. She waits for Sam to finish chewing his, and then he mixes a chunk of butter and sprinkling more sea salt on the potato.

Sam finishes chewing the potato. "Yeah, right from the beginning, we knew something was wrong, not quite right. Before his first birthday, he'd be sitting in the high chair and suddenly start shaking. Not often, but still troublesome. It was soon diagnosed, and medicine recommended."

"What kind?"

"I don't remember what they were."

"Did they perform any brain scans?"

"Not that I recall."

"There are so many medications now; it's hard to know which is best."

"Years later, our schedules were about the same, allowing me to drop her off on the way to the office, and I'd pick her up on the way home. We did that most of the time, but that day I opted out. I needed to stay longer, which forced her to drive. And then that accident causing her to die instantly. The guilt took over, and I drowned myself in booze."

"I'm sorry."

"I begged for an answer, anything. So, I turned away, away from church and all my Christian friends. I turned to booze.

Sam pauses, wanting to change the subject from tragedy to a lighter side. "Now, when I get to heaven, I want to find Adam and have a good talk with him. 'Hey buddy, why did you do that?' You know God could have told them the same thing we were told as kids. Don't do anything like that again, or you'll be out of this garden, and on your own, giving them another chance. We always want a second and third chance, don't we?"

"I didn't drink as you did. I went through depressions. Our church helped a great deal. Someone was always bringing over food and spending time with us. Meredith, wow, she was amazing. It was like, ah, she was the mom, comforting me." She pauses again to take another bite of her steak. "Yeah, I want to have a good chat with Eve too, so you get Adam, and I'll get Eve when we get there." Francinea smiles at the thought.

Pausing while watching her delicately wiping her lips with the cloth napkin while he forks in a big chunk of the potato, Sam then asks, "How's the steak?"

"The steak is fantastic. I'll have to bring Meredith here for her birthday. Samuel, what's been the hardest adjustment moving into that cabin?"

"Ah, now that touches on the personal. I'd say cleaning. Washing the clothes and me too."

"Yes, that's got to be difficult."

"The physical part of this universe. . ."

Francinea interrupts. "Hey, look behind you. Isn't that, Harry?"

Turning around, Sam does indeed recognize him as Harry. "Yes, it is. Hey, Harry." Sam raises his voice and waves his arm to get the kids' attention.

Harry looks in the voice's direction and sees Sam and then Francinea. He leaves the basket on the table. "Hi. Meredith called and said you might be here."

Sam stands and reaches out to shake his hand, "How long have you been working here?"

"This is my third weekend."

"Do you like it?" Francinea asks

"Yeah, it's good. I'm enjoying it."

"Good!" Sam tells the teen. "The food is terrific."

Harry looks back at the booth, "It's great to see you, but I better get back to it."

"How'd the game go last night?" Sam asks.

"We won 34-27."

"So, what's your record so far this year?"

"We've won all four."

"That's fantastic. Good going."

"They want the table. I'm glad you called, but I need to get the table ready."

"Good to see you, Harry. I guess I'll see you in church." Francinea says as Harry strolls away to return to his duties. For a few moments, they watch him putting the dishes, silverware, glasses, and dirty napkins in the basket, wiping and placing the condiments in place, wiping down the table and the seats—Harry waves as he heads to the kitchen.

"You didn't know he was working here?" Sam asks.

"No, I didn't. Meredith didn't say anything about it."

"How's your practice doing now? Are you enjoying it?"

"Yes, my patient base is expanding."

"How did you get into the medical field?"

"My mom. As a teen, she volunteered for the Red Cross to help our men suffering from battle wounds. Her stories fascinated me, and the interest in medicine grabbed hold. So, here I am."

"I was the same way with architecture. As a kid, I'd lay on the floor with a pad of paper, a pencil, and sketch anything, animals, birds, skylines, and then houses. I won a prize in a contest the Ford motor company was sponsoring among eighth-graders to design a car of the future. And like you said, here I am." Sam pauses, "And now, I'm writing about my experience of living closer to nature, and seeing its wonders up close, and the intelligence behind it all."

"The one I read was terrific, and I wanted to reread it. Are they all like that?"

"Someday, I'll get to the library and make copies." Pausing, he glances at his empty cup of coffee and feels his full stomach. "It's getting late. But then, oh, I want to stay here with you until they close and shove us out. I've enjoyed it. Thanks for this wonderful evening. You are delightful company."

Francinea starts to slide toward the aisle. "We could stop at . . ." Francinea pauses and takes a deep breath, slowly exhales.

"You were about to say something?"

"Nah, forget it, let's go."

Francinea stands, and Sam helps her with the coat, and then he puts his cap and jacket on. Walking to the car in the cooler air, she gently places her hand inside his elbow, which he pulls close to his body and reaches his left hand over to hers. As he does that, Francinea suddenly withdraws her hand, which causes him to turn and look. *Why did she do that?* Sam wonders as he opens the car door for her. He warms the engine and begins to back out and into the main road.

Breaking the silence, Francinea says, 'Sam, I'm sorry, but we can't do this anymore. Take me home and forget about me."

Sam looks at her. *What brought this on. Did I say something I shouldn't have? Huh? Why? I thought we both enjoyed it.*

"Did I say something that hurt you? What's going on?"

"Sam, watch where you're going," as a tire hits a curb.

"Francinea, tell me. What happened there?"

"Just take me home, and I don't want to talk about it either."

While keeping his eyes on the road, his mind runs in circles. *She liked the name Samuel, and now she's calling me Sam again. What did I do? God, what's going on?* Leaning back in the seat, Sam glances at the strange lady somberly staring out the side window, bundled up in her coat, the collars up partially covering her face. His focus shifts to the road and back to her, wondering what happened. Renewing the conversations and exchanges, he sees no clue. Desiring to respect her wishes, he notices the speedometer. He slows down to sixty.

"We got to get this in the open. Francinea, I care for you, yes, more than that. There, I said it. So please, let's talk about it."

"No, I can't. Get me home."

"What did I do?"

She continues staring out the window, the collar of her coat pulled up over her ear.

Reaching the driveway, Sam pushes the button opening the garage door and carefully parks the SUV. Turning off the engine, he leans back in the seat, wanting to talk.

Francinea grabs the keys, opens the car door, and says, "Goodbye, Sam! Don't call or come by." She quickly steps around the front of the car and enters the house leaving him alone in the garage.

Twenty-Two

Monday morning comes early when King licks his cheeks.

"Eh, No. No." Sam softly pushes his pet aside, rolls over, and grabs the pillow to move over his ear and cheek. "King! Stop it! Go! Go!" The dog backs off, runs, and jumps against the door, barking, again and again. King runs and jumps back on Sam, landing near his waist, his nose now pushing and licking Sam's neck.

"Oh, . . . sometimes . . . Okay! I'm getting up."

Reaching for the handle, Sam opens the bottom door, "There," as King dashes into the brisk morning breeze as swifts of the air rush through the open door and onto his pajama covered legs.

Sam throws a few logs in the fireplace and then rubs his hands together over the emerging flames.

"Sorry, Lord."

Comfortably sipping coffee between spoons of oatmeal, Sam stares at the knee-high flames in the fireplace. He reflects on yesterday's memoir. *It was too, well, not well written.* Sam reads it over again, crumples the paper, and throws it into the flames. Bowing his head, he begins to pray. "Okay, Lord, that's it. I leave it all in your hands."

Later, Sam is resting in front of the fireplace, reading Durant's book, while periodically brushing down King's side circled next to him on the couch. Looking down at his peaceful, without a care in the world pet, his head lying on top of his hind leg pulled up to meet the front paws, Sam begins to wonder. *Why didn't you get mad at me for treating you the way I did this morning? Huh? You could have taken a chunk out of my ear instead of licking it. Hmmm? Boy, I'm glad you haven't been given the emotions of us humans. Whew, I'd get rid of you in a second."* Huh? Do you want to get rid of me?" Sam asks his pet. "Yeah, I wanted to kick you for disturbing my sleep."

Hmm? Animals don't seem to have that double nature that we do. One minute we're as happy and content as can be, and then wow, something triggers a raw emotion, and the roaring lion comes out before we can count to one. And that all goes back to you, Adam, you bum. But then I'd probably had done the same thing with a beautiful and marvelously made woman standing by my side enticing me to devour that beautiful fruit across the red line. What if it was a demonized dog. Would it be dogs that now give us the heebie-jeebies like snakes do, and have a poisonous bite to boot? Was it only that serpent that could entice Adam and Eve, or could other animals speak?

"Someday Lord, I'll get those answers," Sam speaks to the air, and then he starts punching the keys of the typewriter wishing to summarize some thoughts while going over the reasoning of Durant. King jumps up to the window sill, barking.

Sam opens the door, "Gene, it's good to see you again. I've been wondering when I'd hear from you. Come on in." Sam welcomes the teacher and iceman as King races out the door.

"Sam, I had to come and give you the bad news. Mr. Broomsted denied our request. I'm sorry, Sam. I was hoping he'd okay it, but…"

"Yes, I half expected it anyway, after my brief conversation with them in the diner."

"You talked to him?"

"Yep, sure did. Joanna pointed him and a Mrs. Homer out to me last week. Joanna said he asked about me, so I went over and introduced myself, sat down, and we chatted a bit."

"Oh, that Mrs. Homer. That sort of explains it."

"He told me he had to put the request in front of some board for approval, the proper channels, he called it."

"That's the procedure, but they've been lenient in the past."

"Lenient to what standards and to whose benefit? This sounds like the schools are headed downhill like a snowball, getting more protective of their interests with each turn. I told them straight up Gene, about how I'd address history to the class, that I would not be muzzled in what I could say. And that Mrs. Homer was recording everything I said."

"I'm sorry, Sam, but this is the 21st century, not the 19th."

"The saddest part of now is that our children are not receiving a truthful historical education."

"Anyway, Sam, I do have another idea. We seek parental approval for inviting their student to a neutral location after school hours. Right here in this cabin. I'm formulating a letter that I'd send home with each student for approval."

"Here? But it's too small."

"No, it's not Sam. Three rows of folding chairs of seven each or four rows of six might do." Gene speculates, spacing it off.

"Perhaps. But still kind of tight." Sam replies, visualizing the chairs placed in rows. "Gene, I'd be careful about that. The board may still see it as a school-sanctioned event since a public employee originated it. Let me initiate the letter and send it to the parents."

"Oh! Yes, Sam. Good. Thanks. I like it, and the kids would love coming out here."

"Okay, the letter. I'll need your help. Do you have time?"

Gene takes a hard look at the Remington. "Wow, this is antique!"

Sam inserts a blank sheet. Gene starts dictating as Sam pushes the keys.

Greetings. This letter presents an optional opportunity for ....

"Leave space for me to write the student's name." Gene then continues dictating.

"It's not a requirement for completion of the class, on a volunteer basis. No grades will be given."

Sam interrupts, "Gene, Slow down. I can't type that fast."

Gene slowly dictates, watching Sam press the keys.

I desire to present your student an opportunity to personally view one of the oldest log cabins still standing in America. And to hear some historical oldies, some pertinent facts of American history which are glossed over. How those early Americans lived on a day-to-day basis, how they managed, and what propelled them. They'll be hearing it from the great-grandson of the person who built the cabin.

We, Samuel Guardyall and I, Gene Whitecraft, solicit your agreement and permission. This opportunity is voluntary and not part of a school-sanctioned activity, nor is it required to complete class studies.

"That's it. There, we emphasized the voluntary basis," Gene says.

Sam rolls the paper out of the typewriter handing it to Gene to double-check.

"Good. Now sign it above your name. I'll sign it, have copies made, and mail it to each student. I don't expect them all to come, possibly half."

"Hey, it's your game, Gene, and I'll do my best. How much time will I have?"

"An hour or so. They will get a kick out of it. We'll get together once more, going over the final details. See you then. I've got to get back to school."

Sam examines the area between the kitchen table and the couch, imagining 20 teens assembled there. He contemplates moving the couch to one side, the desk next to the fireplace. *Will they be comfortable for an hour? Will they be taking notes? How will they react? What will be on their minds? Gene indicated his class has 3 more girls than boys. Hmm, I may be inviting a hornet's nest into my home. Will any of the parents wish to come? The time element. Drinks? Snacks? Deserts? Why do I allow myself to get involved in such an undertaking? I'm not a teacher, nor a preacher, nor do I wish to become a policeman or undertaker.*

"Okay, Lord, this is your ballgame. Lead the way and speak through me. And, on another note, Lord, this yearning I have for Francinea. I'm bewildered as to what happened. It's bugging me. You know what's going on, but I sure would like to know, so how about it?"

Pondering what he'll tell the kids while making a fresh pot of coffee, Sam's thoughts get broken by King barking out the window. "What's up now, buddy?" Sam asks. He opens the door as his pet scrambles out into the cold. Sam pushes the top door out to see King tearing off into the woods after a buck and two does. Sam steps out toward one of the rockers breathing the fresh cool air, his eyes on the area where the deer and King disappeared between the close-knit trees.

Yes, a nice easy walk through the woods. He goes in and slides into his hiking boots, dons the leather jacket, the knitted cap, and grabs a pair of gloves.

The thoughts of Francinea shutting him out keep coming up as he strolls through the woods. He returns to the cabin and sits down at the desk to write his thoughts.

My Cabin Life 14

Why? What happened? This thing that happened between Francinea and I, after such a delightful time together is puzzling me to no end. It's been lonely days thrown outside her marvelous graciousness. I must admit, I'm at a loss. My heart was opened by Francinea. Don't know what to do. It can't be only about what she said. There's more. Got to be. Oh, Angelia, I miss you. I miss that continual knowing deep within of your love for me and mine for you. And now, I seem to have fallen for another. Can that be? Why now? Is this the same stress Francinea is facing? Lost a loved one and now facing a new love, perhaps thinking that it'll destroy the image of the first love. Will it? Does it have to?

Okay, I must go see her. Can't wait. I'll be a total wreck without knowing, still wondering. But I can't intrude, push myself upon her. I've turned it over to the Lord. Is this His lead now, or do I wait? Ah, wouldn't it be easier if I'd see one of those white puffy clouds turn into a face speaking my name, getting my undivided attention, "Samuel, this is what you must do."

Adam heard the voice of God in the garden and then hid away. Moses saw a burning bush. Now Noah must have heard the physical voice of God telling him to build an ark, the purpose of building such a thing, the specific dimensions, even the kind of wood to be used and how it was to be sealed.

Gads! What a job laid out before him. What a guy! Hmm? Did Noah enter his tent that evening? "Honey, guess what? I've been instructed by God to build a huge boat so when the rains come, we will survive." Hmm? What did she think about that? Was she with him hearing God speak? How about his sons, what did they initially think, do, or say?

Nowadays, the kids would want to put dad in a straitjacket. 'You're crazy man, we don't have the resources for that, and you think two of every kind of animal will come-a-running to you. Elephants? Dad, you need help. You should see a counselor. That's the craziest idea ever.'

But Noah proceeded, and they all helped to gather that wood, cutting each by hand. Huh, what kind of saw was available back then? And they nailed those hardwood pieces together and sealing all the seams. Measuring tools? Hah. Did he have number two pencils to make marks using a yardstick and right angles where the wood was to be cut? Skill Saws? 16-penny nails? Glue? Varnish? Stain? During the construction process, did Noah ever have doubts wondering if he was going crazy, or that voice he heard was the Almighty Creator God who was so upset with the way His prime creation was behaving that He was going to start all over again, and Noah and his family was it.

Because of that devotion and faith, Noah was the beginning of a new beginning.

Then after the rains quit, God spoke to Noah again, and the waters began the receding process. It was time to leave the ark after nearly a year of wondering when is this going to end after a dove came back. Wow, what a storage cabinet he must have had storing food for over a year, plus having to feed all those animals. Oooh, it must have stunk in there.

"Lord, don't you think that's enough? Come on now, be realistic, we're tired of all this rocking, and I'm in the mood for an apple pie."

The water receded. The ark rested, the land began to dry. Now, there are all these mountains, some still erupting, and the continents have separated. Fully anew, as there were no animals to hunt, no vegetables ready to be picked, no trees bearing fruit. Under normal circumstances, that would've taken years.

A fresh clean start.

Wow! And to think we so easily get upset when, well, whatever interrupts our easy life.

Now that beautiful rainbow reminds us that our Almighty Inventor God set a sign, a reminder in the skies that never ever again will this earth be destroyed by water. And what does society do? We've turned that rainbow into a symbol of our own Sodom.

The recollection suddenly came to me that a few days before the snow there was a stormy rainy day when a double rainbow appeared over the lake, rainbows of colors, no blacks, no whites, a blending mixture of red, yellow, and blue producing seven colors. There's that number seven again. After six days of creation, God rested on the seventh. The importance of number seven repeats throughout the scriptures until the final blowing of seven trumpets.

Three primary colors blended together to produce the rainbow. The three natures of God created the three natures of us; body, soul, and spirit. God created the three elements of time; yesterday, today, and tomorrow, and the physical earth, the heavenly bodies, and heaven itself. After three days Jesus rose from the dead.

Noah was moved to untilled land to start a new life. Adam and Eve were moved out of a garden to start a new life. Those who built that tower were dispersed to start a new life. Jesus was captured in a garden and moved to a cross, was crucified, buried, and rose again to provide a new life for all of us. I was dead in my sins, starting a new life. I moved to this cabin to start anew.

The wonders of it all.

So now this is what I must continually do since yesterday is gone, my work tomorrow will be based on what I do today, so today must be spent preparing for tomorrow, six days straight and then a day of rest.

Shouldn't we rest? Shouldn't our churches demand us to rest on the Sabbath? I mean, take a day off from everything; no work, no shopping, no entertainment, nothing but physical, emotional rest for our souls on the seventh day of each week. The Amish seem to do that. If nothing else as we don't seem to be commanded to anymore, but to do it in fear, remembrance, and honor to our Jehovah Almighty God?

In fear and remembrance. Remembrance yes, but fear God? Huh? Shouldn't that rainbow be a sign to us, yeah that this earth could be wiped clean again and we'd be drowned skeletons? But no, God has decreed, Jesus has come, so all our sins have been wiped clean.

So, live it up folks, we've got nothing to worry about, no more floods.

That was my attitude not long ago.

Help me, Lord, to remember and fear.

Enough of my ramblings today. Time to relax and read, but where's King? Looking out the window, King is not on the porch. He's not been thumping on the door wanting in.

"Where is he?"

Dressed for the weather, Sam is on the porch with the whistle looking, blowing, and waiting, blowing, and waiting. Again, and again. *This has never happened before.* "King!" he shouts into the forest with all the breath in his lungs. Reaching the path toward the national forest, he continues shouting out the name of his pet, whistling again and again. But nothing. No dog coming a running.

Sam follows the path to the sign looking through the trees. He slowly makes the way around the bend up the slow incline when he reaches the sight of the road. Nothing. All is still. No, could not be; he counters the thought of the buck or a bear taking on King.

Through the trees, he's reached the road seeing a few cars, a truck rumble past on the way to somewhere, unconcerned about a missing dog. Continuing the slow, deliberate hunt peering through the lower branches twenty-feet above the ground, Sam reaches the mailbox. He inspects the sides of the road for evidence. *Possibly a deer got run over as King chased it out of the yard.*

"Lord, I need your help." He lifts his voice to the heavens.

Starting to search along the other side of the road, he shifts his focus back and forth from the ditch next to the asphalt to inside the forest. Inspecting a good half-mile, Sam crosses the road repeating the gaze, the process continuing back to his entrance. Along the far end of the fruit stand, he finds the body of a possum. *Keep going.*

"King!" he shouts out between the blasts of the whistle. The cars continue past at high speed, a few honking as he meanders along the ditch looking and wondering, another half-mile. "King! King!" At a curve in the road leading away from the forest, Sam crosses and begins the five-minute trek back to his entrance road. Nothing but weeds and discarded trash.

Sam retrieves the mail from the mailbox and proceeds down the path to the cabin, perplexed at what had happened to his dog. *He's never stayed out this long before. At my whistle, he usually comes running.* Nearing the bend in the road, Sam's attention gets diverted to low whimpering groans. He stops, looks ahead in the direction of the sounds, and seeing the sight. He runs ahead.

King is lying on his side in the middle of the path. Sam kneels alongside the dog, looking over the limp body when King raises his head with his jaw wide open; tongue limped over the teeth.

"Oh my God, what happened to you?"

Sam takes off, running to the cabin. He gets the key to the truck and throws the dogs' favorite pillow in the back.

"Now, King, this may hurt." Sam reaches from the backside under the large dog's body, trying to hold his head from drooping and from putting direct pressure on his hind legs. "Gads, you're heavy." Struggling with the process, King rebels, kicks, whines, barks, his body shaking. King attempts to bite the arm holding him, but Sam holds tight, managing the dog onto the truck's bed, sliding him onto the soft pillow.

"There. Now we'll get you fixed up."

Driving to town to find the vet, the thoughts of what happened. *How did he get halfway down the drive? What's broken? A leg, his backbone, what? Will the vet want to put him down? The office open? You know how vets are. Come on people drive faster, oh the heck with it, I'm passing. Got an injured passenger.* Sam turns on his lights, bumps his horn. *Sorry lady, but I gotta go. Two more miles, that's it. What's up with everybody today?*

Twenty-Three

Here we are. "Thank you, Lord." Sam opens the office door noticing the waiting room is empty, no one in the office. Sam knocks three times on the sill, then seeing a bell, he rings it several times, and again louder.

 "Can I help you?" a young lady asks as she enters the office.

"My dog! He's injured. In the bed of the truck. I need help."

"Okay. How big is it?" She asks, as a man dressed in all green enters the small office.

"A German Shepherd."

"Oh", the man says, then instructs the lady to get the stretcher, and to Sam, "let's go have a look. I'm Doctor Mason."

"Samuel Guardyall. I don't know what happened. He took off after a couple of deer and never came back. Went looking and found him lying in the driveway."

"Mr. Guardyall, we'll find out soon enough."

 Reaching the truck, Sam lowers the gate, and King raises his head to look.

Sam informs the doctor, "We can slide the pillow closer where we should be able to get him onto the stretcher.

"Did you notice any blood?" The doctor asks. "Mr. Guardyall, how did you get him in this truck without him muzzled?" the doctor asks.

"Not easy. No, no blood." Sam answers as the office lady and another appear pushing the table out the door, through the sidewalk entrance, and alongside the truck, when Sam hears, "Mr. Guardyall, is it King?"

"Meredith? You work here?"

"Yes. Started an internship. Is King hurt? How did it happen?"

"Slide that muzzle on," The doctor informs Meredith.

"Okay, ladies, let's get him inside. Ready?" Dr. Mason puts his hand under the center edge of the pillow as the others reach in, one on either side of the doctor, their hands grasping the edges. "Okay, pull."

"Mr. Guardyall, you're welcome to come in the back with us or stay in the waiting room."

"Thanks. Yes, I want to see." As Meredith helps guide the stretcher through the waiting room and into the back office, Sam asks, "Internship, huh. Good for you. How's your mom?"

"Okay, I guess. Working all the time."

The vet takes a heart reading while the aide adjusts the loose muzzle over Kings' nose and mouth, bringing the strap tight behind the ears. Slowly and softly, his hands rub over the side ribs, the front legs, his underbelly again, down the back and around the hind legs.

"Mr. Guardyall, I'm going to sedate your dog and take a few x-rays, so please go back into the waiting room. I'll call you when I know."

Waiting in the entrance room, Sam picks up one of the magazines, scanning the table of contents, turning the pages, passing the time. He finds an article titled, "German Shepherd, not man's best friend." *Ha. What's this guy got up his sleeve?* Sam scans the lines finding the author's conclusion at the bottom of the third paragraph, "No, man's best friend is his wife, but the Shepherd comes close." Reading more, the author reasons that a man cannot have, or better not have sex with his dog, and that's the difference. "Gads," Sam tells the paper. *Even a magazine about animals has to bring sex into an article about dogs. Why?*

Opening the door, the aide tells Sam he can come in. Inside, the doctor is wrapping gauze around the leg. "Your dog has a fractured left leg and a badly bruised backbone right above the tail. He's sedated, and it'd be best if we keep him a couple of days to monitor how he reacts after the sedation wears off. The splint should take care of the fracture healing process, but the backbone is my major concern right now. We also gave him an antibiotic."

"Thanks. You're the doctor. Can I see him tomorrow?"

"Of course, anytime you wish. The sedative will wear off in an hour or so if you'd like to come back then. We close at five. Oh, Meredith told me you took over that cabin in the forest. I should have recognized the name right away, but . . ."

"Yes, I did. When can I take him home?"

"Thursday or Friday. Now, he's going to need mostly rest. The hardest part is the constant monitoring, as he'll try to bite off the bandages. And his need of relieving himself. Try to keep him occupied with something, a toy, or something he can chew on. You'll need a leash and walk with him when those times come. It may take a few months for it to heal completely, and I'd prefer to check on him the first couple of weeks."

"Thank you, doc., How about if I leave him with you until Monday?"

"That'd be fine too. It might be better as we can watch him closer and nourish his wound longer. Sure, Monday."

"We'll send you the details, recommended treatments, and the bill. Good luck, Mr. Guardyall. You've got a beautiful dog. He'll be chasing those deer again."

"Doc, do you mind if I talk with Meredith for a moment?"

Meredith and Sam exit into the waiting room, where Sam opens the conversation to ask about her mother. "What's she been up to? Did she say anything at all about the dinner, any remarks about it, about me?"

Meredith answers, telling Sam that no, all she said when she entered the house that evening was that she saw Harry and the steak was fantastic and then went directly into the bedroom. "I haven't seen her much at all since Saturday. She gets up before me. Calls later to tell me to fix my dinner and study hard, as she's taking an extra shift at the hospital. What happened? This is not like mom. What happened, Mr. Guardyall?"

"I can't speak for her, but for myself; I had a great time and thought we were progressing along nicely when on the way out, I tried to hold her hand while going to the car. She suddenly shifted gears and, well, told me not to call as she did not want to see me anymore. This hurts. Please don't tell her any of this, will you? You can let her know about King, but that's it. Okay?"

"I'm sorry, Mr. Guardyall, I suspected something was wrong."

In the truck, Sam reviews the short conversation with Meredith chastising himself for sharing it all with the daughter of the woman he's become fond of. *Gads. I've reversed it all. It's teens who should be opening up to adults.*

Thursday afternoon, Sam quickly finds a seat in the diner. He is settled back in the booth, slowly sipping the coffee while reading a book from the library and making notes about the upcoming gathering in his cabin. He reads a bit and scribbles a note. Reads and writes. He leans back, looking toward the ceiling, thinking, trying not to let his thoughts wander back to understanding how his pet got hurt. *The doctor indicated it looked like a side hit by a vehicle, and then the dog attempted to run home when the leg gave out, the pain was too much, and he ended up lying where I found him.*

For the third time, Sam forces his mind away from King and back to his confusion about the history class's meeting. "Ah, I'm not making much progress." He softly tells the air. He closes the book, puts the pencil back in his pocket, and takes a final sip of coffee when Joanna returns with the coffee pot.

"No more, thanks. I need to go."

"Okay, then. Oh, and thanks for coming to the funeral." She turns to leave, then stops. She sets the coffee pot on the table and sits down opposite Sam. "Sam, you remember Betty? She and her lesbian partner joined you once a while back. She asked about you the other day. Asked if I had heard anything about a meeting you're planning at your cabin with her students."

"Huh? Betty asked about it?"

"Yep, sure did. She teaches American History. Said you were working in secret, sending letters to parents, and keeping it from her and the school. You better be careful, Sam."

"Betty doesn't teach that class. Gene Whitecraft says he teaches American History."

"Yes, Betty teaches it. She's been telling me that for years."

"Joanna, the schools not big enough for two classes."

"How else would she know about it?"

"Hey, I'm new here. Only seen Betty once."

"It's none of my business, but this is a small town, and I've known Betty for some time now. People talk."

"Yes, they do. Now I have to go! Thanks, Joanna." He pays for the sandwich and coffee and leaves the diner.

Leaning back, his hands pushing against the steering wheel, Sam's head is spinning. *Okay, school is out. Will Gene still be in school or home? I trusted him. He said he's the teacher, and now I hear Betty is the teacher. Both of them can't teach the same class.* Driving down Main Street, past the YMCA, the library, he turns to his right, down the street a few blocks, and pulls into the small high school parking lot. Walking to the front door, he finds it locked. He scans the three cars in the lot, looking for a sign of Gene. Back in the truck, Sam heads back to Main Street, looking at all the cars as he slowly passes the library, the Y, the hardware store, and the Laundromat. He goes around the courthouse square, intently looking at every vehicle. He turns back to the main street, passes the diner, the Ford dealership, and heads out of town. Sam makes a U-turn for another view. *"No cell phone! I need one. Augh."*

Slowly, Sam pulls to the right into the town square, then to the left, and another left when suddenly he notices Gene and another man entering the Library. "Thank You, Lord." He pulls into the lot.

"Hey, Gene, we gotta talk."

"Hi, Sam. Ah, this is Walter. He teaches math."

"Hi, Walter. Samuel Guardyall."

"Great to meet you. Gene has told me some of that venture you're living. I'm impressed."

"Gene, we need to talk about this. Got to do it fast as only a few more days to make any changes in the plans."

"It's all in the works, Sam, everything."

"We may have to make some changes, as I've had some second thoughts."

"What's on your mind?"

"I'd rather it was just the two of us. Sorry, Walter."

"Walter's a friend. It's okay."

"Sorry, Perhaps later at your house."

"Sam, it's okay. Walter knows what we are doing and is all for it, thinks it's a great idea. So, please, feel free."

Sam looks back and forth from Gene to Walter to their hands, wanting a sign of some sort to continue or walk away from Gene, whom he had put his trust, who has now become suspect. "Okay," Sam concedes. "It's Betty Wilson. Doesn't she teach American History? Shouldn't she have been part of this too?"

"Oh. It's Betty you're worried about."

"Not only that, but you told me you're the American History teacher, and now I find out your subject is civics, governmental history."

Walter enters the conversation, "Sam, this Betty you're talking about is a substitute teacher. That's all. Yes, she's filled in for Gene and for me, too."

"Walter is right, Sam, she's only a substitute, but she leaves that part out."

"Huh? Oh my. But how did she find out about it?"

"Probably from a student," Gene answers. "My class covers both parts, civics as part of American history. I told you that. I cover it all. Where are you getting these half-truths?"

"Oh, wow. I'm sorry, Gene. Forgive me. I was suspecting you."

Gene smiles, saying, "Of course, Sam." He pauses and adds, "Ah, ha, you've been listening to Joanna. Sam, she hears smidgens and passes it on. That's all."

Feeling embarrassed, he looks at his fingers clasped together, "What a fool I've been. Sorry, Gene, forgive me."

"No problem, Sam. The meeting is set up. We've received replies and questions from some of the parents asking if they could attend also. There would be fifteen students attending and three mothers. That's what we have so far, and I doubt there will be many more. Have you done much preparing what you'd tell them?"

"Oh, yes. That's all I've been thinking about these last few days. Now, my dog got hit by a car, is in the Vet hospital until Monday. But now, it's bothering me thinking that Betty could cause problems. You're not putting yourself in danger, are you?"

"No, no. I ran it by the principal, and he gave me the go-ahead. This is a small town, not one of those big cities back east, and we'll not have any complaints from parents either."

"Great. But Betty."

"There's nothing she could do except show up. We'll be fine. You told me yourself that you felt that God was in this, and He'd lead you in what and how to address these students."

Walter adds, "Sam, Gene and I have been teaching in this school for thirty-some years. Some of our former students are now parents of the students we're teaching. And this Betty is, well, ah. She's looking for recognition."

"Relax, Sam," Gene says. "I sense how you feel. You're in uncharted waters here in a new town and now being thrust right in the middle of something you've never done before. God is directing this. I know it."

Sam says, "I'm sorry, Gene. The last few days have not been good to me."

"You told us about your dog, but is there something else too?"

"I'll be fine. Ready to go Saturday afternoon. Thanks, I appreciate it. I'll see you Saturday." Turning to Walter, Sam asks if he'll be coming out too?

"If you don't mind, I'll try."

"Good. See you both then," Sam concludes.

"Time to see King. I can't wait."

Sam arrives at the veterinarian's office, and he's permitted access to the back room where King and a few other animals are in cages that have a soft-blanketed area in a corner.

While Meredith leads Sam to his pet, she tells him how his pet reacted when waking up, "Doctor Mason had to administer additional sedatives as the initial dose wasn't enough. And he's still a bit drowsy."

Sam looks at his not fully conscious pet lying on the pillow. "But he's going to be fine, right?"

"Yes, he will. I'm sorry this happened, knowing how much King means to you." Meredith softly sympathizes, looking up at him.

"Thank you. It's the waiting game that's tough on an old codger like me. Meredith, you're sweet, and you'll do fine. You'll be a terrific doctor."

"Thanks. Harry and I plan on attending your historical briefing on Saturday, so we'll see you then."

"Any chance your mother would come?"

"I don't know."

"Tell her I miss her, will you? Now, I must go. So, thanks for everything."

Sam starts to open the door to the waiting room when the doctor stops him, "Mr. Guardyall, I want to discuss a possibility with you."

"Sure, Doc."

"When King gets well, I'd love to use him as a mate to my Shepherd. I'd give you one of the pups."

"That's an interesting thought. I might like that."

"Good, we'll discuss it more later, okay?"

"Thanks, doc. I'll see you again when I pick him up Monday."

Sam passes through the outside door, following the sidewalk to his pick-up. Turning the key in the ignition, shifting to reverse, he starts to back out, stops to let a car pass. He then notices the familiar SUV pause at the front entrance, then continues toward the rear and turns into an alleyway and out of sight. *That was Francinea. Yeah, it was her car, I'm sure of it. What is going on with her? Got to get this over with. Now!*

He pulls back into the spot. S*he'll be back as she has probably come to pick up her daughter, as it's almost quitting time.* Getting another thought, Sam backs out and finds a spot out of sight, and hurries back into the waiting room where he can see out the window to view the parking lot.

Soon, he sees that familiar car stop by the entrance door and notices Francinea sitting behind the wheel. Sam opens the office door and quickly struts to alongside her door, "Francinea, we've got to talk."

She slowly rolls down the window. "Sam. There's nothing to talk about. It's over. I'm sorry."

"No, it's not. If it was over, you'd have parked when you first pulled into the lot. But you saw my truck and took off. No, it's not over. It won't be over until we talk it through. This suspense is killing me. It hurts."

"I'm sorry. Oh, come on. Get inside out of the cold."

Sam settles down in the passenger seat and turns to get a direct view of her expressions. "Francinea, I thought we had something going between us. I know I did and still do, and I can't let this continue without expressing to you, so you'd know. Francinea. I wasn't looking for someone to care for. I was doing fine, but then you came into my life touching my heart, and here we are."

"Sam, forgive me. I'm sorry I hurt you. But it can't be. It's better if we end it. Period." Francinea tells him, exhibiting the same empty expression as in the garage.

Sam quietly looks down and then out the window at nothing. His mind in turmoil focused on nothing, wondering, yet hoping that what he told her would reach her heart, not knowing what to say next.

"But why?" he finally asks, staring out the windshield.

He feels her fingers lightly touching his hand. Not wanting to be rebuked again, Sam ignores the caress by continuing to look away. He soon feels both of her hands softly on his left hand.

"Samuel, forgive me, I'm sorry, but I'm having a difficult time with this."

"I know. We've both lost our first love. We moved on and away but losing still hurts. I cried out, wanting Angelia back, also thinking that by embracing something new, I'd disappoint all those wonderful times still in my memory bank."

Sam pauses, breathing deeply, and adds, "Francinea, can we, oh I don't know, but, ah, possibly continue to be friends? Right now, that's all I want, to know that you care enough and to leave the rest to our Father God."

"Samuel, I do. You're more than a decent man whom I respect. I couldn't believe the thoughts I had. The shame of that hit me hard."

"Shame?"

"Yes, okay," She breathes deeply. "Ah, when I suggested we stop at your place to get the papers to make copies, I wanted to, well … okay, I'll say it plain as day. Ah, I desired to give myself to you. To get you in bed."

"Oh, that. Wow! That's it? Thank you, Lord."

"That's it?"

"Oh my. Yeah! Hey, I'm no saint. Do you think those thoughts did not come to me, either? Knowing those impulses, I might have gone along with it, but the spirit of God used you to stop something like that from happening."

Samuel slides his left arm around her head and shoulder, slightly pulling her close. She shifts to lean into him. He feels her body giving in and relaxing in his embrace. He enjoys the moment, wanting it to continue as his hand gently moves along her back from side to side.

She tears up and pulls herself away to look at Sam. "We're not teens anymore, Samuel. We're adults. We know what is happening, but the fears are still there. I don't want to be disappointed again. Not ever again. It's hard to put into words."

"Yes, I have fears and doubts too. When moving here, all I wanted was a change and to get away from memories. Yes, it was an escape. I've worked hard to adjust. I'm enjoying the solitude with King alongside. And, I have adjusted and enjoyed the pleasure of being my own man, and then you came into my life. You caught my eye that first day."

Pausing and breathing deeply, Sam adds, "Now, there you've heard it, and I've heard your heart too. So, Francinea, I'll back off and give both of us more time."

"Thank you." Francinea softly and sweetly reaches out for his hands. She places a soft, quick kiss on his lips as her hands softly touch his cheeks. "Take care."

Sam opens the door, steps out, turns, and leans in far enough to touch her hands. "I'll see you sometime, even if I have to split my leg open again."

She chuckles. He closes the door, turns to walk to his car, notices, and waves toward Meredith, closing the entrance to the office when she raises her voice, "Bye, Mr. Guardyall."

Hmm, was Meredith looking out the window seeing us in the car together, and then waited till we finished?

Twenty-Four

Friday morning comes, and Sam did not want to wait till Monday to get King back. Entering the Vet's back room, he is jumped on and licked by King released from the pen.

"Mr. Guardyall, please consider my offer. Bring him back in two weeks, and we'll check how everything's healing."

"I will. Thanks, Doc."

"Up you go! Inside today." King jumps three-legged up to the passenger seat while making his woof sounds, woof, woof, and louder and louder barks, as Sam slides into the driver's seat when King licks his cheek.

Sam starts the engine, shifts into reverse, and backs out of the space, stops, and turns onto the main street heading for the cabin. Entering the tree-lined road, King paws the window wanting out, turns his head back toward the road, to the partially open window, to the master next to him, King lets out exclamations of joy.

"Okay, buddy, here you are again. Stop, look, and listen when crossing the road."

Inside the cabin, King drags the hurt leg toward the water bowl and food dish, lapping up the water, devouring some bites, and between each one, looks at Sam, who's tossing a bowl of his favorite salad ingredients. He brings the salad, some crackers, and a cup of coffee to the desk. He leans back, looks out the window, letting his mind wander a bit thinking of the Saturday event. Sam scribbles down a thought and adds it to those previous notes on the upcoming meeting with the students.

At the bookcase, he reads the titles to find one that may touch on the thoughts going through his mind. He scans the contents, turns to a page, and brings it over to the desk to read and make notes. He selects a different book. Six books are now lying open on the desk. He's searching, reading, taking notes, peering out the window, reflecting, scratching his head, scribbling another note, and throwing a sheet in the fire.

Ah, it's all good, but to organize these into a comprehensive presentation befuddles me. Ah, it's time for a break."

"King, let's go for a short walk. We both need the exercise." Preparing for the brisk cold air, he dons the jacket, cap, gloves, and boots. He looks down at his pet. *Now, why don't you need a coat and mittens? Huh?* He fastens the leash to the collar, and King hobbles three-legged to the gazebo area. Having watched King stumbling on his injured leg, Sam sits to rest his dog.

Leaning back against the cushion, he peers over the rippled waters of the lake, above the trees lining the shore, the upward rolling green forested hills into the snow-capped mountains scene. A ribbon of clouds pencils a line in the background skies as the changing shapes of the cottony clouds slowly shift from bunches of white silhouettes dancing through the blue sky, mingling with companions to lose their uniqueness, and then breaking apart again into lonely smoke puffs. Looking back to the waters' ripples and back to the clouds, the two areas in his vision are alive and moving. The rest like a painted picture.

"Ah, dag gone it, King," Sam yells as his pet pulls on the leash bringing Sam back to the here and now.

Beginning to feel a chill, Sam announces to his pet, "Okay, back inside we go."

My Cabin Life 15

Sitting in the Gazebo just now, thoughts were circling, so here I am putting them on paper to read and meditate on later.

I don't see the air moving. I see the results.

And wow, what a good thing that is. If my eyes were like a microscope, instead of feeling the cool breeze across my cheeks, I'd see those minute molecules of nitrogen and oxygen pelting my face, and I'd be swatting those like gnats or spraying them with a chemical.

Up and beyond those clouds to the sun, the stars, and galaxies farther off than I can imagine, all of which are constantly in motion following natural laws. Those natural laws are invisible also; only their sustaining effects are seen and felt.

Oh, what a sight that must have been for those astronauts looking out the window to view the heavens and this earth set in place by Jehovah God, who is in-comprehendible to us animals. We're just like those ants. They can't comprehend a human with the power to watch every move, to feed it, or to step on 'em.

That area above this earth is not merely air. It's alive, it keeps us alive, and somewhere, out or up or within there somewhere is where Angelia is, where my mother is, where the redeemed are, where the heavenly gold and silver mansions are, where the angelic beings are preparing a place for me. And I suppose it's good that I can't see or feel into that realm either, as I'd probably ignore it or swat it as a nuisance.

Now we've got the invisible computerized connections from point A to point Z, not even stopping at point C or K, only at its target a thousand miles away through space. No copper wires. Nope, those unseen waves go through the air, avoiding and not mixing with other waves, nor colliding with the molecules making up the air. How does it do that?'

Will the future enable a relative in Chicago to view and converse through the air in real-time with a cousin vacationing somewhere? Oh, we can already do that. Will the future provide the ability to follow another by tracing his body print, seeing him sitting in a crowded stadium in Timbuktu, then zooming in to see him and his companions and hear what they are saying? Why not?

Another one of those possible marvels of technology for an elderly gentleman having a hard time understanding words spoken. The background noise interferes with those words, even with expensive devices stuck in his ears. He wishes he could read closed captioning on his glasses read from the lips of his friend. Why not?

Here I am in one of those old log cabins, unable to use any of that stuff. However, I'm still full of life and vigor enjoying the security of knowing that some being out there somewhere with evil intentions cannot pull a wire disconnecting me from my Lord.

Pulling the paper out of the roller, he inserts his notes in a folder, thinking; *oh, if I just had a computer and printer to copy an essay and drawing, I want to hand out. Tough. Can't do it here.*

He pushes himself away from the desk, strolls to the kitchen area, grabs the coffee pot with a glove to refill the cup, and then returns to the desk to formulate the outline of his presentation to the students.

He leans his head back, looking at the ceiling beams, and starts singing. "When peace like a river attendeth my way…"

"Wake up. You have less than a day to be prepared," Sam tells himself. *I'll be standing in front of twenty-some teens and maybe a few parents and telling them something about the genius of the American founding. What can I tell them? I'm only an architect from the city learning to live this way. Why did I agree to this? Can I cancel it? How, at this late date? Do I say anything at all about sexual relations? Abortion? They both have a long history. What about questions?*

"Oh Lord, now I wish to lay me down to sleep. I wish to escape from this, so I need your help. Oh, yes, how badly I need it. But, ah, yeah, Even though I walk through the valley of the shadow of death… Hmm? Yes, Lord, I see that; it's just a shadow; it has no substance, no power, just a shadow of fear, and your light eliminates that shadow, and, yes, Lord, you are with me. Thank You."

Sam looks at his pet sleeping on the pillow. "King, help me to remember that. Yeah, put a paw on my knee when I drift away." *Oh, if only he would know to do that.*

My Cabin Life 16

Here I am a day away from an engagement I agreed upon with Gene Whitecraft, the Civics/American History teacher of high school students. In one sense, it's driving me up and out the ceiling, and it also thrills me that he proposed the idea to me, wanting me to share some of the challenges of living off the grid as my grandparents and those generations before them had done.

They had no choice, but I do. I can chuck it all, let the forest service have the cabin, and move back into society. Those thoughts arise every so often when I'm faced with a difficulty I'm not familiar with. Gads, I had to learn how to pump water from a well, when kids back then probably were experts at the age of three.

Oh, how many times I wished I had the easiness of modern technology.

I could do that with this meeting too, go see Gene and cancel it all, disappointing him and those students who are looking forward to it. And there it is, the word that rings my bell; disappointment.

Language is a gift to us humans. Do animals have the ability to communicate their wants, fears, and inspirations to their comrades? Now King can communicate much to me, it's his bark, that woof, sometimes one alone, and then the two or three together mixed in with body language. Those numerous barks that rise in tone seemingly expressing, 'now is the time, right now, not later, but now'. He can lay his head in my lap and I sense his love and care for me. He can lick my face expressing that too. But to talk with words. Nah. If we had not been given the gift of language, we'd be relegated to a somewhat similar station as King.

Language then is one of our most important attributes. Ever since the beginning, we must be taught the meanings of words as we grow in age, using words to express our thoughts, the ideas we wish to communicate to others. We don't have to think about how we say words, what parts of the body to move either slightly or tightly. No, we automatically do it as it's computerized into our system. Oh, how amazing this is.

But the choice of words and how we express them is what we do have to think about. Hmm? What do I want to say to these students? What word or combination would be best to express it? And to complicate it more, certain words bring up emotions that are amplified in our body language, which also leads to misunderstandings. And many times, we get it wrong; sometimes intentionally deceptive.

Misunderstandings. So, everyone must agree upon the meanings of the words we express. If I say I want a banana, but your understanding of a banana is a rounded green pepper type item, and you bring me one of those, I'm gonna want to knock your block off, you dummy. But then you'll call me an idiot and wish to knock my block off. Hence, the beginnings of conflicts and war.

So, there must be something that sets the meanings of each word, an agreement we all look to for understandings. That must be our commonly accepted English dictionary. Simple for us now. Noah Webster began compiling definitions in a single work way back in the early 1800s. But then, to the words we speak, we add another dimension that further complicates our understandings of each other; body language. There is no one book to look to for definitions, so we have set up a system of courts and Judges to examine each side and rule according to established law. Moses was told in what numbers to set judges. The lowest denominator was judges of tens? Why such a little number? Ten families needed a judge?

There must be common standards in everything; otherwise, chaos develops. Sports have rules monitored by officials that must be obeyed, so when an in-fraction is noted, a penalty is given. In baseball, with nine players on the field, ten counting the batter, and possibly three more base runners, there are six judges. On and on, one could go listing the many organizational rules throughout society and the world. Some overlap, and there are loopholes in some. An official or judge must decide when disputes arise.

What about life itself? Why are we here? How should we live? Is there something after death, or is this it, that's all, nothing more, dead as a doorknob, nothing more. Nope, the way we are designed indicates a designer and a final judge above us all, invisible to all, the one who instituted the rules and those standards we must go by and judged by those common standards.

There is a book that answers those questions better than anything else man has come up with. This Bible, composed of 66 separate short books or essays from 40 different writers over hundreds of years being put together in one volume. The one I have next to me is it. A book, translated into every language, has been the best-selling book ever put on paper. It's the most complete, the final best-ever explanation of the wonders of this world, our purpose, and our relationship to this universe that we live in. It informs us of the Creator and His relationship to us and ours to Him. The Bible tells the good and yes, even the bad relationships, along with instructions on how we humans should live and get along with our neighbors.

Can't we all agree on that?

Simple, when we get down to basics. But then, some don't want simplicity, as then their power and prestige are restrained.

We use our easily misunderstood words to describe it all. We are either a male or a female, a he or a she, and not an it. We wouldn't call God an 'it' as the word 'it' refers to an inanimate object, and God is life itself.

In that prayer, Jesus taught us to say, "Our father who art in heaven. . ..￼" Again, it's a reference to the male gender as we understand things. Do we then think of the creator as a father, like, "Hey dad, can I use the car tonight?" By doing this are we lowering our thoughts of God into our finite human realm? Even Solomon used a male pronoun to refer to our creator as in, "He leadeth me beside the still waters...", which He (God the Father) has done for me. There are no pronouns to describe the Creator, so we refer to the great I Am as a He, as a Father who gave us life, nurtures us, instructs, and corrects too.

Yes, this place has allowed me to get quiet, as I have here a placid, serene, tranquil place, where I can and have been still long enough. Yes, I've been beholding, perceiving, discerning, and comprehending some of the majesties in the visible heavens, of this earth, of nature and this body my soul occupies.

The heavens declare the glories of God.

Okay, there it is. Some of this then I hope to expound to these students. American history is secondary to the basics. What are they expecting, a good time, entertainment? What are they interested in? Why are they giving up a Saturday afternoon of leisure? Do they desire to have more favor from their teacher by attending this meeting? Do they expect to get a better grade, or is it to see the insides of an old cabin? Most of them, from what I've heard, have already seen the cabin. Are they truly interested? Ah, to be able to pierce their brains to see their real motivations. Do they even know what their motivation is? Is it socializing, hanging out in a different place, and using this as an opportunity to get out of the house?

Twenty-Five

Samuel takes a breather on the porch after a morning of cleaning, straightening, organizing for the afternoon meeting, and preparing the snacks. He's put plates, plastic cups, silverware handy on the butcher block table. On the stove, Sam has a pot of coffee warming. In the icebox, he's stacked canned drinks in the top section.

It's a chilly, breezy day with clear blue skies, only bunches of snow remaining, the tops of trees cheerfully waving back and forth as the waters rush toward shore.

Sam is reflecting on the meeting. King, at his side, is licking the bandages and periodically told to stop. One last look around, Sam realizes he needs more wood beside the fireplace. He places several bundles onto the wheelbarrow at the barn for the short trip to the front door. He lays them on the porch and heads back for another load. He carries twenty pieces inside to place next to the fireplace that's warming the insides.

Sipping the coffee and rocking back and forth on the porch with a book, he impatiently waits while rubbing the ears of King.

"Finally," Sam exclaims to the air as a vehicle rumbles around the corner into his sight.

Gene parks his truck near the barn as King struts toward him as far as the leash allows. "Afternoon, Sam. How are you?"

"Good. I've been waiting, wanting to get this meeting over. I've never addressed a group of teens before. At times, I've wanted to cancel it, but here you are."

"Sam, You'll do fine. We'll have possibly sixteen students, three to four parents, yes, and Betty is possible. Meredith, yes, and her mother, well, maybe." Gene tells Sam as they carry the folding chairs into the cabin and place them in rows facing the fireplace.

Harry is the first of the youngsters to arrive and assumes the responsibility for attending to King by keeping the leash tight. Another car pulls in, and another, and another. Boys and girls get out and enter the cabin. Some are accompanied by a parent finding a place to park the car. Slowly the cabin is filling up, and they're milling around, talking, looking around the insides. Two teens are at the bookcase, scanning the titles and paging through a book. A few looking over the kitchen area, the cast iron stove, the pot rack above the thick butcher block table. The fireplace and the spinning wheel have captured four. Sam had moved that antique in front of the closed curtain so they can see it. A couple of teens are silently seated on the couch, which Sam moved in front of the bedroom curtain. A few are looking at the desk and the old typewriter.

Sam has been introduced to the sixteen students. Peter is there with his camera hanging around his neck, talking with two other students. Although freshmen, Peter and Jounger, were invited as special guests of Sam. Three mothers have opted to stay, now chatting with Gene.

"Jounger could not make it," Peter informs Sam.

Next to the table, chatting half-heartedly with one of the mothers, Sam ponders the kids interacting and the feat before him. *All these students are here to hear… Me?*

"Sam, this is great. Are you ready? Walter's not coming." Gene breaks into the conversation of Sam and one of the mothers.

The door opens, and Meredith, with her mother, enters. Sam moves to the door to greet them with a quick hug. "It's good to see you, Meredith, how you doing?"

"Good," She replies and takes a few steps over to Harry.

"I'm glad you came, Francinea. I've missed you." He whispers in her ear and brushes her cheek with his lips. He relaxes the hug and steps back to view her reaction.

"I've missed you too, Sam," she softly replies.

The door opens, and Sheriff Olsen withdraws his nightstick and raises it to eye level. "Mr. Guardyall, do you have a permit for this meeting?" he asks in a raised commanding voice, getting the attention of everyone, who stop whatever they're doing to focus on the sheriff.

"Huh? A permit?" Sam questions thinking *we don't need a permit. What's he talking about? There's no law against this. I thought we were friends.* Sam looks at Gene for acknowledgment seeing him smiling.

"Yes," the sheriff replies. "The county requires a permit for any meeting or gathering of more than six individuals, and you exceed that. So did you get one?"

"We don't need a permit. We would have known about that. You got to be kidding, sheriff," Sam states.

The sheriff slides the nightstick inside the belt while changing his stern-looking features to a big smile, "Yes, I am. Joking around Samuel, having fun." The sheriff then adds. "Relax, everyone. I was messing with you." He announces to the students. "Sam, I heard about this, and so, here I am. Thought I'd make a good entrance. This brings back lots of memories of your grandparents."

Sam moves closer, "I could bust you one for startling me like that." He tells Sheriff Olsen. "But welcome. I'm glad you came, as you may have to use that stick of yours on Gene."

Gene makes his way to the front of the fireplace. "Let's start, shall we." He announces in a raised voice. "Please find a chair. Get comfortable. The lecture is about to begin."

"I want to thank you for coming and sacrificing a Saturday afternoon of whatever to attend this meeting. I'm happy to see you all here. We had a scary entry by our familiar sheriff, and I want all of you to welcome him for doing that to us with a big boooo!"

All the kids smile and repeat several boos and a few thumbs down as they look back for the reaction from the sheriff.

"Welcome, Sheriff Olsen," Gene says. "And now I wish to thank you for your dedication to our safety and especially to your unconventional ways of doing it. We all appreciate it. Thank you. You are one in a million. I just remembered a quote by Daniel Webster, "The purpose of government is to make it easy for the people to do good, and difficult for them to do evil."

"Now, let's give him a round of applause."

Gene waits for the applause to cease.

"Okay, let's get on with it. You've had a chance to look around this cabin built somewhere in the mid-1800s. The cabin was here before the area surrounding it was declared a national forest. When the feds made that determination, they agreed to let Sam's grandparents stay, as long as nothing is changed; it must remain as it has always been, outside the electrical grid, none of the modern conveniences we take for granted in town. Samuel does not even have a phone line. A cell phone is useless too, as those require electricity to charge the batteries. His water comes from a deep well, which must be pumped up by hand. I'm sure you've noticed it's a little chilly in here compared to your comforts at home, as the heat in this cabin is this fireplace, along with that stove in the kitchen area. He's told me that sixty degrees feel warm, and when he wakes up, the temperature inside has dropped into the fifty's or the forty's, and winter is just beginning. He said that splashing cold water on his face in the morning gets his attention.

"Students, would you choose to live like this? Samuel did.

"The cabin was willed to Samuel by his late grandfather, who was born right here ninety-five years ago, in front of this fireplace. Some of us have had the privilege of hearing his grandfather address my history classes years ago, and some may remember him telling stories in the library. You can see by the books he collected and studied that he was a history buff. Not only did he know the names and dates, but he also went deeper and learned the inner motivations of the people in power throughout American history and the history of this world.

"Samuel, you are blessed to be part of the Joshua Guardyall heritage.

"So, ladies and gentlemen, Mr. Guardyall has agreed to lead us into neglected and forgotten parts of our great American history. Samuel, it's all yours."

Everyone applauds as Gene makes way for Sam to take his spot next to the fireplace. The audience of twenty squeezed together on folding chairs four rows deep.

"Thank you, Gene, and perhaps after a few lines, you may wish you had not asked me to do this. I tend to ramble on and may repeat myself. This would be a great afternoon to be strolling through the woods, and perhaps you'd rather be roller-skating or something. And that too, is part of our nature, preferring the enjoyable to the studious. But you're here, so buckle up and pay attention.

"Over the past few days, I've been fuming on what to tell you. I created an outline, but I decided to throw it away and let it flow. The words seem to flow like a thunderstorm after a bit, and then I wonder why I'm doing it, as fishing is slow and easy. You may feel the same way. Is it part of our human nature? Some people are gifted in this area, and some in other areas, and that's one of those mysteries we would wish to have explained in a three-ring binder.

"So, buckle up as now you're in for a ride on a roller coaster into somewhere.

"Hmm? I just said buckle up. We've all got to buckle up when we pull out of the garage. As we navigate this roller coaster into history, if you tend to nod off and slide off the chair, the sheriff may want to inspect these chairs for safety belts."

A few chuckles break the silence.

"Safety. That's what it's all about. Sometimes we don't take our personal safety seriously, and the government steps in to protect us. And sometimes they do it to show us they've got the power.

Samuel looks back at the sheriff sitting in the back next to Gene and Francinea. "Our taxes make it possible for the sheriff to have a job. Does he thank us for that? No! He pulls us over for not being buckled in? He gives us a ticket and then goes to get a donut.

"Touche! I'm joking, sheriff.

"Well, enough of that. Now, I may repeat myself several times. That's how Hitler was able to get the German people to believe they were the superior race, and the Jew's enemies, by repeating a lie over and over again until they accepted Hitler as a friend. So, if you recognize a repetition, okay, it may be on purpose.

"I now give you an option to leave if you wish, as what I say may offend some, but I will not shy away from telling it as it is. We're not part of a random happening without meaning. If that were so, then you'd be following the program computerized into those trillions of cells forming your body.

"No, a master designer created this world, the animals and us, humans, too. You can go back as far as you want, to the beginning of recorded history, as this human mind has always desired to know the meaning of things. If this universe was outside of any meaning, then wouldn't it fall in line that our intelligent human life would have no desire to understand anything. Our minds would be programmed as just another fox seeking something to devour. We'd be automotive, like a robot behaving as it was programmed. But we humans have been given the ability to wonder, to imagine, to choose between available options, and the majesty of this creation is part of my discussion." Sam pauses, looking for facial expressions.

"If that will disturb you, then you can choose to leave. This is your chance." Samuel pauses, looking around to all, and noticing the quietness.

"Good, now you're in for it.

"You're part of an American history class concentrating on the civics part of the great American experiment. Hmm? Why has it been called an experiment? Let's take a moment and go back years before our founders told Britain to take a hike. The pilgrims arrived at the worst time of the calendar when that first winter decimated them with diseases, and about half died. The following spring, they worked the land as a group, growing crops and sharing the harvest. They worked together as a community and shared it all as a community, all receiving the same amounts. All things ought to be shared equally, was their thinking at the time. Hmm? Community. Where do you think the word Communism comes from?

"We still hear the idea that commune living is the best way for society. Plato passed down that concept. Even though it never did work, the rulers throughout history thought the peasants needed more prodding, a modification here and there, and then it would work. But it never has.

"William Bradford, the governor of the Plymouth colony, held a meeting about the idleness of able body men, and the decision came that each family would choose and be provided a piece of land to work as they desired, using their abilities and then reaping that harvest. Some did well, others not so well, and the ones that had abundance voluntarily shared it. Those ideas go back to the days of Moses. And soon, we will celebrate that experiment when our Thanksgiving comes.

"I've been fortunate to have developed a successful architectural career back in Indiana. Looking back, it seemed that I was born with a pencil in my hand. As far back as I remember, I would escape to my room to sketch something I was looking at or something I saw in my imagination. Even though my mother kicked my father out because of his addiction to alcohol and abuse, I was able to focus enough to succeed. Over the years, that skill developed, and I acquired a degree in architecture. I concentrated on designing new houses, offices, and apartment complexes.

"During those years of busy schedules, I went to church an hour a week, sometimes for a mid-week service. I enjoyed and professionally benefited from the fellowship of others at those meetings. God was out there somewhere, and Jesus was a hero. I accepted that, and that's all Christianity meant to me. Inside I was pursuing success above everything else, and it took devastation to penetrate my hardness.

Sam pauses, breathes deeply, sighs, and then continues. "I'll tell you more of that later, but let's explore our differences, and there are many you well know.

"Every one of us is a unique personality gifted by the creator with a talent or a particular interest in some field of endeavor. It may be music, art, design, mechanics, chemistry, a dozen different fields, or just plain water polo. One could break the field of mechanics down into perhaps fifty parts, and medicine; how many areas are there in the field of medicine?

"As students, perhaps some of you may be aware of that special gift already, some may be still searching, and perhaps some may not even care. Yet one of these days, something will catch on, you'll see something, and you'll dig into it more and more, and that will be it. And then you may wonder; why didn't I discover this years ago. Do you think Abraham Lincoln knew his talents as a great orator when he was only a teen? How did he learn such wisdom?

Suddenly King starts barking and tightening the loosely held leash by Harry. Everyone turns to look as the door opens, and Betty stops, steps back, looking down at the big dog barking before her.

Getting up from his seat at the butcher-block table. Harry pulls back on the leash to restrain the aggressiveness of the dog.

Gene softly greets Betty.

"Sorry, I'm late," Betty tells him.

"Betty, have a seat. We've just got started," Gene says. "Students, I'm sure you recognize Ms. Betty Wilson, the substitute teacher you're all familiar with." He opens a chair for her and places it next to one of the mothers sitting in the last row.

"Okay, let me continue," Sam gets their attention. "Betty, I have given them all the option to leave. If during this afternoon, the mention of and a discussion of a heavenly creator would make them uncomfortable, but they all stayed on. I assume you came to witness this, so welcome and be free to ask questions.

"I had asked if they ever wondered whether Lincoln knew of his skill of becoming a great orator when he was their age. As a youngster, George Washington had an appetite for math, trigonometry, for surveying, along with enjoying the theater, novels, and music. He was later influenced by his older brother in military service. You may know how that turned out.

"How about Thomas Edison, the curious inventor who loved to tinker and eventually discovered the light bulb that has blessed the entire world. His biography indicates that even as a kid of five or six, he was inquisitive about everything. He wanted to discover things for himself. Desiring to solve the mystery of hatching eggs, he went into the barn to sit on some chicken eggs to see if they'd hatch. I don't know how that turned out. His formal education stopped early as the teachers had a hard time with his constant questions. His mother undertook his education at home, possibly using *Orbis Pictus,* a picture book by John Comenius, born in 1592, who believed that learning, emotional, and spiritual growth were all woven together. That book is still in use today, more than four hundred years later.

"At the age of eleven, Edison had read detailed history books such as *The Decline and Fall of the Roman Empire.* He had also built a rough chemistry lab in his cellar.

"Could you do that now? Would your parents be scared you might blow something up? You're only eleven, come on now, put that stuff away. Didn't they have other kids to play with? To toss a ball around, or choosing sides and playing a game, hanging out, riding a skateboard, or skipping on the sidewalk. Nope, these ancients did not have the distractions that modern life has besieged us with, nor the regulations against a chemistry lab in the basement.

"But the point is, Hmm? I don't know what the point is, except modern educational standards may be failing its purpose. For me, I wonder how Edison, and those of his generation over a century ago acquired so much knowledge and understandings of how things work without the technology of our digital age, that is so easily available to us now. You don't need to go to the library, as it's available on any computer twenty-four hours a day. It's a blessing and saves us a bunch of time.

"But there's another side to technology, the abundance of fun things to do that eats up much of your available time because, well, it's more enjoyable to play games than work, study, or critical thinking.

"How many of you have read *The Decline and Fall of the Roman Empire* originally published in 1776? A show of hands. Hmm? How about Shakespeare? Voltaire? Plato? Francis Bacon? Al Gore?"

Sam pauses a moment. "Ah, I saw a few smiles there. Hmm? Books by those antique authors are there in the bookcase. Yeah, my grandfather had collected them. Yes, Mr. Gore too. Now I've started a reading program intending to delve into those ancient histories and old philosophies. Some may be misleading and have missed some truth, but it's good for an open mind to read them too.

"Ah, come back in ten years, I might have finished then.

"Has your teacher ever told you that it is the mark of an educated mind to be able to entertain a thought without accepting it? No? Those are the words of Aristotle from four hundred years before Christ. Huh? Twenty-four hundred years before the internet? Here's another one of his, 'For the things we have to learn before we can do them, we learn by doing them.' You learned to ride a bike by getting on and doing it. Did Aristotle pass the time away by shooting hoops? How about Solomon? His wisdom is recorded in the book of Proverbs. Yeah, how did he acquire such wisdom way back in the stone ages of three-thousand years ago? No TV. No Internet. No cell phones.

"Are those classics not required readings? Do we look upon them as Neanderthals because they did not have cell phones, or as monkeys still evolving into humans not yet figuring things out? No, we don't read them because there is so much going on all day long that distracts us, and we don't even think about it. We call it a blessing, yes, a blessing to have a cell phone in your pocket, a computer, and a fifty-inch screen in the living room.

"How easy it is for us moderns to discredit the ancients as they did not have cheerleaders jumping up and down encouraging the fans to root, root, root for our team.

One of the students raises his hand.

"Ah, a question. Go ahead, young man, what is it?"

"Are you saying that we should not have a TV, or a computer, or even cheerleaders?"

"Okay, James, what do you think I'm implying?"

"It's not good for us. We shouldn't have football teams, no sports at all, and then we wouldn't need cheerleaders."

"Yeah." Another boy adds his two cents. "It sounds as though you want us to go back and live just like they did. Isn't that what you're doing?"

Samuel looks around the room for more questions, more input, wondering, thinking, *well, that sure raised an interest.*

"If that's what you think I'm saying, then that's what you think," Samuel answers. "You questioned what I'm saying, and that's good, so now we can have a conversation together, and perhaps, we'll get somewhere.

"That's how the great statesmen wrote our constitution: questions, lots of questions, lots of debates, and more discussions. They stayed together. It took a few years of focusing on that one purpose in mind; that of finding some common agreement. Yes, we can and should agree that we can disagree and still live peacefully together.

"No, I am not suggesting that you should shun technology as I have done. No, but I bet you could find a quiet place to marvel at the wonders of this created nature that surrounds us, wondering how we got to this point in history. Every week take a few hours away from the technology to quietly meditate. Couldn't we all do that? Would that make a difference in our society? God rested after six days, so why don't we rest just one day a week in this age of plenty?"

Breathing in deeply, he looks around the room for reactions. *Humm? Have I entered forbidden territory by suggesting that our technology should be put somewhat aside?*

"So, let me continue.

"Go back in history when the only books available were those original parchment manuscripts that had to be hand-copied by scribes in monasteries using a quill pen continually being dipped in ink. That took days upon days of meticulous copying one letter at a time. Where did the original manuscripts come from, and when?

"Let's go way back to our originals, Adam and Eve. They were communicating from that first day. The scriptures tell us that Adam named the animals. Did he draw pictures of the animals and label them to be passed them down to Cain, Abel, Seth, and the rest of their kids not mentioned, and they passed those names down to the next folks to come along. Did Adam then correct the kids? No, that one is a lion, and that one other there is a zebra.

The first humans were provided a divine gift from the beginning: no parents and no schools to teach them, no government to regulate. So how did they learn anything? They learned the way Aristotle wrote:

by imagining, starting somehow, somewhere, correcting mistakes, and then proceeding.

"When did someone, somewhere, sometime start the process of taking spoken words, forming an alphabet, and matching the letters to a sound to write a dictionary? When you were a toddler, how did you learn the stove was hot, the snow was cold and wet? Some of it by experience, and some by words and demonstrations. Thus, it has always been throughout human history. Someone had to start the process of writing words or drawing pictures on something that could be passed on to another in a written form rather than mere words, which can be misunderstood.

"History is intriguing. There's a lot we can learn about ourselves and how we got here by studying the bygone days. We have the idea that people back in history were so backward in their understandings; barbarians, we like to call them, of inferior intellect, illiterate, just plain dummies. But in actuality, the human being of yesteryear had the same internal mechanisms as we do today. Our makeup, our body, our minds have not changed since the beginning when Eve begat her sons. They were born naked, just as we are, just as Jesus was.

"Hmm? Did Eve wonder what was happening to her as she started the weight gaining process? No doctors to see. No nurses to tell her to push, push. 'Oh, the pain, give me a pill,' she yells at Adam, and then a baby appears. 'Huh, what is this? Adam, where are you?'

"Wow. Ladies, imagine you in that situation."

Sam pauses to look around his cabin full of students and a few mothers. *Where am I going with this rambling?*

"I feel that I've been rambling. My secretary butted in on me once when she told me I was going off the deep end, without an oar." Sam then chuckles and adds, "But, King has never told me to stop. You want me to stop?"

Gene quickly buts in, "No, Sam it's good. Keep going. But, ah, try to concentrate more on the civics part of American history. What you say, students? Clap if you want him to continue."

A student in the first row starts clapping and then stands to clap louder. The rest follow.

Twenty-Six

"Okay. Thank you. So, button-up. Ah, Where was I? Back to today, in this cabin, I wonder how future generations will look upon this 21st century. Scientists and futurologists are speculating about that right now. A hundred years from now, if that divine intervention does not come first, humans will still be born naked, and the process of early education will be the same as it has always been. But mom and pop may be replaced by robots, computerized to tell the kiddies to clean their room, and then they can have a cookie. It seems to be heading that way. What kind of work will there be for us as robots take over the physical part of manufacturing, cutting your grass, cooking dinner, and driving you to see a movie? Would those robots be programmed to play football as we watched and cheered?

"Yes, my daily life is like it was 150 years ago. But I do have an advantage; I can get into that pick-up, drive a short distance, and plug into the 21st century. After a few hours of that, I'm ready and eager to return to this cabin, pick up a book, read right here in front of this fireplace, or outside in the gazebo, or by the stream, letting my mind somewhat connect with nature. And I may sing an old hymn.

"I am so blessed. I thank God every day as I wake up being where I am instead of living somewhere else. I have it so good, and yet at times, my temper is aroused when King disturbs my sleep when he needs to go out.

"Why don't you have a doggie door for him?" a student in the front row asks.

"I can't, the authorities insist, the cabin must remain the same as it always was.

"Well, anyway. When you see on the news scenes about the German Nazi police with rifles strung around their body, herding the Jews into railroad cars, do you imagine what's going on inside the heads of either group? The police are just people like you and me. The Jews are people like all of us. Millions of individual human beings created in the image of God. One group was indoctrinated to believe and further their stance as the master race. The other group has been taught their heritage as being blood relatives of the chosen people. Each of them believing and following the dictates of those in authority over them.

"Can you picture yourself as a policeman watching a mother helping her child get into the four-foot-high bed of the railroad car?

"Hmm? That's just a small part of our human history, and I wonder why the Almighty hasn't just thrown us all to the wolves to have at it, as He must be fed up with our behavior toward each other. Yep, time for another flood.

"Ah, enough of that. In this bookcase, I found a song and service book printed in 1942 with hymns galore, a book provided to our Army and Navy boys fighting for their lives. It's been said that there are no atheists in foxholes. Would our current military pass out a Christian hymnbook to the soldiers? I think you know the answer to that, which shows how much we've rejected the past.

"I use this old typewriter to make ink marks on paper. Hmm? The typewriter. It was an invention that started way back in the fifteenth-century by a German named Johann Gutenberg. His history indicates that he was desperate to find a way to make some money, so he began to investigate a way to modernize the printing process from letters and images cut out of blocks of wood. They were then swiped with ink and hand stamped on parchment, one block of letters, one word at a time. They wore out quickly. The wood chipped, and another block had to be hand-carved while they waited. So curious, Gutenberg went to work and eventually developed those letters, dots, and commas made of metal. He placed them together to form words and sentences, each separated by metal spaces. And then put on a frame attached to a roller, which moved through a machine to print the same page over and over again.

"That was page one. Then he started putting together the pieces for page two. His first large project was two-hundred copies of the Bible. That sold like crazy. Ordinary people could now read it themselves. How long did that printing process take? Did he order a pizza, as he was too busy changing the metal pieces to go out?

"Now we press a button, and in seconds the printed piece comes out of a plastic printer. We, the enlightened folks of the 21st century of technology penetrating every area of our lives, think that previous generations' ability was backward. You hear it from the academics, the media, the scientists, and the elites all the time that the idea of a simple man named Noah was able to build a boat longer than a football field, big enough to hold two of every kind of animal to survive a world-wide downpour and earthly eruptions lasting forty days and nights is nonsense, just a fairy tale.

"Hmm? He had to be simple as that was something like four thousand years ago. Those experts say it never happened, it was impossible, nothing but a fairy tale. How could a man build such a ship with only hand tools? No way. Couldn't be done.

Betty speaks loudly, "You actually believe that stuff?"

"What's that Betty?"

"You think that there was a flood that wiped out all life and destroyed everything."

"Yes, I do. Why do you think it could not possibly happen? In West Virginia in 1945, weather data indicateded that a storm poured rain at the rate of 13.8" in one hour. That would be over 300 inches in one day. Do you think God, the creator of everything, cannot create a big enough storm to flood the entire earth? Hmm? And now we see a rainbow reminding us that it will not happen again.

"You don't or won't believe it's possible?" Sam asks as Betty searches for a rebuke.

Emphatically Betty says, "Ah, it's fairy tales to indoctrinate people in religion."

"A fairy tale? A method to indoctrinate? Is there evidence, absolute scientific proof that it did not or could not have happened? Scientists are now discovering pieces of evidence in the rocks. But now we want a video too. Ah, even if Noah had taken pictures with a Polaroid, they'd claim it was photo-shopped. CS Lewis described this kind of thinking as chronological snobbery. He stated, 'the uncritical acceptance of the intellectual climate of our own age and the assumption that whatever has gone out of date is on that count discredited.'

"Think about that. Out of date, and thus it must be discredited. How far out of date must something be; 2000 years, 500 years, or last year?

"No, Betty, I don't have a photographed picture of Noah standing in front of the ark as two lions enter. But it's written in the most read book ever printed. I believe it, and I've got that right, just as you have the right to dismiss it any way you wish.

"Another question?"

"Okay, good, I'll continue. Is Aristotle to be discredited as an uneducated cannibal? Would that kind of thinking also include the brainpower of Edison and Gutenberg, Isaac Newton, or Einstein, who said, 'Look deep into nature, and then you will understand everything better.' Or, how about the philosophy of Francis Bacon? Should we discredit the Wisdom of Solomon as out of date? And how did those great philosophers such as Plato, Locke, and Voltaire get their understandings of human nature and government corruption without the Internet, without sharing everything on Facebook? How did they do it?

"We think we're so smart. Plato was a socialist. Locke was known for his embodiment of Enlightenment values and ideals. Voltaire was imprisoned for attacking the government authorities. We often hear this quote from Einstein, which is often used against politicians. 'Insanity, doing the same thing over and over again, expecting different results.'

"Oh, but they did not have computers or televisions, so forget it.

Pausing a moment, Sam takes a pencil from his shirt pocket. "You may have wondered why there was a pencil on every chair. Pick it up. Feel it. Look at it. Turn it around. Can anyone tell me how that simple instrument is made? You take it for granted, don't you? Did you ever wonder about it? How does the graphite get inside the wood? Where did the eraser come from, and what makes it an eraser? Why are there six sides? Why is it yellow? Where did the materials come from? Do you even think about it? I doubt it. No, it's one of those wonders we don't wonder about anymore.

"Could that be one of our modern-day symptoms, that we are so busy enjoying the technology that we don't wonder how and we don't question why. We don't care, it is what it is, and we've got more important things to watch.

"Now, look at the pencil again. What can it do? By itself, nothing. You use it to make marks on a piece of paper. Is that all? That simple pencil transfers what's on your mind to paper, and then it can erase those thoughts. No one will know you wrote that nasty thing about your teacher when it's erased.

"My words have been going into your ears. What if I said each of you is an idiot for being here? Those words would bring up emotions, right? The sheriff is here." Sam points to him. "Hey buddy, you should be out there protecting us from rabble-rousers, instead of relaxing here. Oops, sorry. I didn't mean to say that. Erase what I just said. Nope, he can't do that. I said it. He heard it. You heard it. What we write down can be erased. I can use that white-out. Typed notes can be thrown in the fire. Books can be burned, and or they can be saved as keepsakes, and that's a blessing.

"I was inspired a while back to sketch the insides of this cabin. Without the use of a computer drafting program and just using that pencil and oh, how many times I had to use that eraser. Anyway, if you'd like a copy to take home, there's some over here at the desk.

"Where was I? Oh, yes. What we say to another cannot be thrown in the fire. The one that heard it might want to throw you in the fire. Those words have entered you and have become part of you. Can you erase them from your mind?

"But there is one way to erase a hurt by another. It's called forgiveness. That's your eraser. Forgiveness erases that emotional hurt that's lodged away within you. It alone brings healing. But again, our human nature is such that if another hurt comes from the one we previously forgave, the old hurt, filed away in your memory bank, comes streaming back, amplifying the hurt requiring more forgiveness.

"Jesus has done that on the cross for each of us. He's ready to use His eraser.

"The design of our human brain cannot be duplicated. But how about computers, some may ask. How about it? Can a computer dream, imagine, reason, or invent? The computer can only do what it's programmed to do, but we humans are programmed to think for ourselves. That's the God-likeness of us humans, and only us. Yes, there are limits to what technology can do, but humans' inspirational designer has no limits.

"This mind of ours was created to process and retain an unbelievable amount of data. So wow! What kind of mind was able to put into motion this vast universe; an ant with six legs, to a horse with four. Yeah, the ant has six legs to support a tiny body compared to only four legs supporting a two-thousand-pound horse. Do those two extra legs enable the ant to crawl up a tree and not fall? That creative mind envisioned a simple dandelion, to having a tree grow a coconut, to placing the stars of the big dipper pointing North, along with freshwater lakes and salty oceans, sand, granite, and dirt.

"That's why there are so many who have dedicated their lives to debunking the story of creation as they think it must be impossible for one intellect to have done it all. Is that why some of the ancients had many gods they worshiped, a sun god, an earth god, a good god, and an evil one too? But we want proof. We want to see this creator, while animals don't care one bit. Yes, we want to touch, smell, hear, see, and taste the creator, and then we might obey. Ha! Perhaps. We hear that Madonna is coming to a stage, and we'll scramble to get there first. The Romans, in the days of Jesus, scrambled to beat the life out of Him.

"Have you heard of Louis Agassiz? One of the greatest scientists of the nineteenth century, born in 1807. Maybe not, but you have heard of Charles Darwin, right? He was born around the same time. Darwin extolled the idea of evolution, theorizing that humans evolved from lower forms of animals, a chimpanzee, an ape, or something, which evolved from whatever. Agassi debunked those imaginations with more proof than Darwin could muster. So why do the academics and media praise and accept Darwin's theories? You seldom hear Agassiz mentioned, who stated that 'each species of plants and animals are the thought of God.' Now, they both had some flawed conclusions from their many studies, but boy, oh boy, everything about evolution from nothing is hollered out as established science.

"Look at your hand now. Hold it up. Look at it. You see five fingers, one of them much shorter and separated from the others by a squarish palm. Why is that? Now pick up that pencil. How did you do it? Your thumb held one side while your index and third finger held the other side. What if we were designed without a thumb, just those four fingers? Now pick up the pencil holding the thumb away. Hmm? And what if those hard fingernails were on the bottom of the fingers? We use those hard nails for scratching, scraping, peeling away soft surfaces, which the skin cannot do. Those hard nails enabled Adam to peel an orange. Did he and Eve trim their nails? How long did they get? Did Eve paint her nails?

"Usefulness is why and how things are designed and created, and that pencil is only half as useful without the eraser. Your hand is extremely useful as it is, and it's merely one part of this physical body designed by the intellectual magnificence of the master designer we call God.

"Ah, a question. Yes, what is it?"

Jack asks, "Since you're saying that everything created is useful, then why do we have mosquitoes?"

"Hmm. I've often wondered the same thing as those pesky little disease-carrying bugs seek to get our blood and then infecting us. Yes, ouch, how many of them have I've smacked?

"Good question Jack. I don't know why, but let's reason together. In the beginning, when everything created was good and peaceful, mosquitoes could not have transferred diseases, as there were no diseases in that garden paradise. Was the mosquito's sting as irritating then as it is now? Perhaps they did not stick their stinger into Adam or Eve but into rabbits and squirrels. Then Adam and Eve disobeyed and were kicked out of that paradise, which ended the designed peaceful disease-free existence. Has it become an irritation down through the ages because diseases changed the makeup of the mosquitoes?

"That's all I can surmise.

"Yes, we wonder about bees and skunks too. And those thorns on beautiful roses. Why are they there? Since the fall of man, could these changes be there to remind us? Now, every time I pick a rose trying to avoid the thorns, I am reminded of that initial disobedience. If you want to believe in evolution, then yes, believe some aspects started after Adam and Eve's disobedience.

"It's been told to us that the master designer repented that He made man providing him with the ability to choose because, over time, every imagination of the thoughts of their hearts was evil. But God did not completely start over by using a different pile of dust.

"I imagine that God being God could have started over, but no, God found Noah favorable, saved him and his family, but wiped out everything else. Noah's descendants got a second chance. Eventually, over time that did not work out either, as building a tower to go into the heavens sounded like a good idea. They were then dispersed and given a third chance. Finally, another plan was instituted, sending another option for mankind; sacrificing part of Himself, Jesus to die for us, providing us a personal choice to become a new creature, having all those words and deeds we regret erased. We become new creatures in spirit when we accept that.

"Let's take the field of medicine. After years of hard study having passed a serious exam, the student is honored with a license to practice medicine. I've always wondered why it's called a practice, as that word means one is not yet proficient and needs more instructions and to practice more. Words. Does our military call it practicing war? Our politicians don't label their profession as practicing representing the voters. Oooh, tell a newsman he's practicing broadcasting the news, so he needs more training. Tell that to your teacher. Words.

"Surely God would communicate precisely what He means eliminating any areas of confusion, right? A toad is a toad. An Eagle is an Eagle. A sin is a sin. A man is a man, and a woman is a woman assigned at conception and evident at birth. No confusion, there right?

"Hmm, there is a question from the back. What is it?

A boy speaks up. "What about those that now say they're a different gender than their body indicates?"

"Hmm, good question. Ah, your name is?

"Daniel."

"Okay, Daniel, what do you think?"

"Ah, he hates being a boy. He's always played with dolls instead of cars and trucks. He insists his genes got mixed up at birth."

"You defined it already."

"Huh? I did?"

"Yes, you said he hates being a boy. Hate is an emotion, right? What do feelings have to do with biology? A friend back home shared with me that his father told him that when he was born, they wanted a girl. His feelings were hurt, so he started to wear girl's clothes, thinking he would then please his parents. Later, he saw the foolishness of that, dismissing the hurt feelings he had at first. Those feelings lingered on until his actions overcame those hurt emotions.

"Where do our feelings come from? Is there something scientific about our emotions? Does love never change into hate? Desire never changes to; oh, no, I don't want that? Are feelings an emotional certainty that does not ever change? Not ever? Hate, love, anger, disgust are feelings, and they are subjective to our upbringing and surroundings. A boy says he feels like he's a girl, but do his feelings change the objective truth of biology and that he's got a boy's chromosomes.

"Does that answer your question?"

Betty emphatically speaks out, "But still, the person going through this wants to be a girl instead of a boy. Does he not have the right to think and behave like that?"

Looking directly at Betty, Sam says, "Rights? Did I say anything about his rights? We've all been given the right to think anything we want. It's our nature. It's a divine attribute we've been given. This boy thinks or wishes he were a girl? Sure, he does have the right to think that way. But does his thinking change his biology?

Standing, Betty loudly exclaims, "Yeah, what about love. A person has the right to love someone. So, how about that? Yeah, a man has the right to love another man if he wants to. They should be able to do that without all the screams against it. It's as if you're writing the rules we all have to live by."

"Betty, there's a right to do something, and then there's a right and a wrong, a yes or a no, a positive or a negative. One right is based on choices. The other is based on laws, standards, the concept of righteousness, or sin handed down to us. We've got the right to obey or disobey, got the ability to kill, steal, or lie and then pay the…."

Betty interrupts, "So, it's the likes of you and your kind who determine what is right and wrong, and we had better accept it."

"Betty, please let me continue. No, me and my kind, as you say, have accepted the concept, a standard ideology, that those morals of life were instituted by our creator. Me and my kind look to that as our compass. We didn't make it up. Where do you and your kind look to for answers, guidance, and submission? Huh? Feelings or standards? Where does your standard originate?

Interrupting, Betty states, "So we can't get married, is that it and then you'll be happy." Betty responds.

"Betty, as a society, we've got to agree on standards to live by, or we're doomed to a struggle that'll never end, all those different standards dividing us into multitudes. You have yours, and I have mine, and you want me to change, and I want you to change each of us thinking I've got that right, so leave me alone. That's been the struggle from the beginning, and it will not end till we all stand aside, accepting those universal standards provided us by the Almighty God who does not change.

"You can live with whoever you want, and nobody would interrupt? Yes, you can commit your life to another, live in the same house, and do whatever you want behind those closed doors, and nobody would come and disturb you. There are no laws against it. So, go do it. If I come and knock on your door, you can refuse to let me in, and I'd go away leaving on your doorknob some thoughts for you to think about. And you could do the same with me. You'd throw mine in the trash, and I'd throw yours in the trash. We've got those rights.

"What is marriage anyway? When did the concept of a man and a woman coming together as one, which is called marriage, start? Like everything else, we have to jump back in history to find that out. The Father God, the creator of us, initiated it when the first woman was created out of the rib of the first man. Two physical bodies distinctly created to enlarge the human population. The sperm of the male impregnating the egg of the female creates the fetus of a baby. Marriage is defined as a male and a female bound together as one to have children to nurture and train, so, when they grow into adulthood, they leave mama and papa to bind together with another, united together as one for the same purpose.

"Betty, if this world only consisted of two males or two females binding together, the human race would eventually end.

"Over time, society has muddied this basic concept into confusion. Now love is being reduced to an emotionally changing subjective concept of plain self-satisfaction. Oh, I don't love you anymore. I want a divorce. I want out. I love someone else now. Marriage is not subjective to our changing emotions. It's a commitment, a vow until death while nurturing those little ones in that blessed close relationship called family.

"We can submit to standards of a higher than human realm which does not change or submit to a chosen or appointed human realm, which will change over and over again. This generation likes this idea, and the next generation may accept another concept. The universal unifies. The others are divisive. As I said earlier, the creator has designed, and we've witnessed it throughout human history. There's a male eagle and a female eagle. They look the same, but can a male eagle lay eggs? Has a male monkey ever changed into a female monkey? Wow, there's a subject for those evolutionists to investigate.

"I know this is a subject that has captured everyone's attention lately, and it appears it will continue. But God is divine, the same yesterday, today, and tomorrow as there's no variance in standards with the master designer, who created those universal natural laws that repeat again and again, along with providing universal behavior laws. If we all followed those Divine principles, there would be no wars, no disputes.

Sam breathes in deeply, looking around the room.

"Okay, I feel a need to take a break, so let's do that, a ten to fifteen-minute break to relax. Look the cabin over, take a short walk, but the bell will ring in fifteen minutes.

"Thanks for your attention so far.

"Oooh wait, it just came back to me, something I wanted to present to each of you. Not a requirement, it's a voluntary challenge. You don't have to do it. You can forget about it. I know each of you could do it if you set your mind to it. It wouldn't be that hard, but for sure, there would be temptations. You can do it if you put your mind to it. A challenge from me, and I want to know how it turned out. Did you start and not finish? Did you make it all the way through? Did you learn anything from completing the challenge? Okay? Are you up to it? Will you even be tempted to accept this challenge?"

Sam continues to ask these roaming questions when one speaks out.

"What is it?"

"Yeah, what's the challenge," another student asks.

"Are you going to tell us? Or keep us wondering"

"Oh, you want to know. Good." Sam answers and silently look across each row.

Harry raises his voice, "Mr. Guardyall, you've been beating around the bush."

"Yes, I have. It got your attention, right? Okay, here it is. Are you ready? But your friends may ask, why are you doing that? Huh? Yeah, why? How many will accept the challenge, not this weekend but next weekend? Will you do it?

"Well, do what?" One of the students sitting in the front row asks.

Another one emphatically states, "tell us, what is it?"

Viewing their anticipation, Sam pauses some more and then, "So, here it is. Here's the challenge. For two full days, starting when you wake up Saturday morning, untill you wake up Monday morning; no TV, no computer, no cell phone. No calls, no texting, no games on computers, absolutely nothing involving those three pieces of equipment. Your TV, Computer, Cellphone. None of that for forty-eight hours.

Sam pauses to look around the room, seeing them turning their heads to look at their friends. Sam notices Daniel's open mouth, plus a few more appearing stunned.

"That's it. Okay. I challenge you to do it. And I'd bet a good day of fishing to anyone who completes it and writes an essay on what was learned, or not.

"I'll be anxiously waiting. Okay, Gene, now it's time for that break."

Twenty-Seven

Gene steps outside to the edge of the porch, looking for the students. He sees a few in the gazebo and a lone boy throwing rocks into the water, and yells, "Yo," waving his arm and blowing the whistle.

Slowly the students gather together inside the cabin joining the three mothers who remained inside visiting.

Raising his voice, Gene calls out, "Okay, folks, it's time again. Let's go."

Gene waits for the students to get seated and quieted down.

"Another lecture is to begin. What did you think of what's been said so far? Did he get you thinking? Have any of you been pondering that challenge he presented to you? Were there any areas Sam brought up that did not sit right with you? We can talk about it more Monday in class, but anyway, if you don't give Sam your full attention, you're the one who'll miss out, so heads up. Or should I say, buckle up?"

"Now, Sam, it's all yours."

As Sam approaches the front, the applause dies down.

"All right," Sam starts. "Gene has asked if I would concentrate more on the government angle to our lives, so here goes. Open your ears and hearts.

"What is it that we expect from our government, and what does the government expect from us? Throughout history, what role did the government play in people's lives? Was it only safety and or security? Police and Fire departments and the military for protection? Since the industrial revolution days, our government has provided us with water and systems for waste, the electrical wire grid, and pipes for gas to heat our homes. They provided us with highways with yellow lines down the center and speed bumps throughout neighborhoods. How do governments pay for these services?

"That's easy. Taxes on everything. Everything!

"Why do we need rulers over us telling us what to do, how to do it, where and when to do it, and with whom we can do it?

"Consider the ants the bible tells us. They don't have rulers or kings telling them what to do and when. No, they just go do it. Have you ever seen a herd of cows gathered in a circle watching two of them butt heads again and again? Have you ever seen two rows of horses thirty yards apart facing each other, pawing the ground, ready to advance to kick butts over the rights to that pasture?

"Nope, the animal world does not need authorities over them, but we do. That's been a continual struggle of humans since those first two decided to go against a rule. Did they think it was just a suggestion?

"History tells us that tribes of people had a leader whom the people trusted to lead, advise, instruct, and keep them safe. They were the elders, those with the most experience, knowledge, and wisdom gained because they had lived the longest. Moses was instructed to make rulers over tens, the fifties, hundreds, and thousands. You see the pattern, smaller groups integrating with larger groups.

"The philosopher of the eighteenth-century, Montesquieu penned there were three types of governments, a Republic, a Monarchy, and Despotism. The despot is one who rules by absolute authority, by whims, and by force. The Monarch is a King who is bound by certain established national laws. America has been called a democratic republic.

"What do those two words mean? The people elect those to represent them in the various levels of government. America was divided somewhat like Moses was instructed; rural areas, towns, and cities were collected together into counties. Each of those counties gathered together to form states, bound together into our federal government. The national government was divided into three different branches, the legislative, judicial, and executive. We've got one president, fifty state governors, numerous county supervisors, and thousands of city or town mayors. Each of these agreed to look up; first to the county, then the State and the collective states looking to that one document to guide us all.

"That constitution was debated and debated, back and forth over a few years, and then they finally agreed and put it to paper a couple of hundred years ago.

"Why is this concept so important? Hmm? The average person living in or near a town is closer to and more familiar with how their elected official has been performing the responsibilities granted to him. This is the most relevant part of our system; the local citizens can replace those abusing the system, knowing firsthand how he carries out those local responsibilities.

"Do you know the mayor of Prairieville or just his/her name?

"By law, the president is limited to two terms of four years. Governors and mayors are limited. Why are the elected members of congress not limited to a certain number of terms?

"Have you ever attended a town-hall meeting? Have your parents? I never did. I had no idea what they would be voting on until it became law affecting me.

"Multiply the actions of the mayor and city leaders of this small town to other towns, counties, states, and federal, and wow, we've got problems galore. It becomes unmanageable, and usually, the rural areas don't like being regulated by the same methods of governing the large metropolitan areas. There is a difference in those needs.

"So, what is the solution?

"There is only one, each of us obeying the commandments of the Creator to live peaceably, respecting, and honoring each other, putting others first. No stealing what is not yours, no storytelling on others. That's just a couple of the restrictions we must place upon ourselves.

"Our inherited nature is such that I want you to adapt to my way, and you want me to give in to your ways, so we butt heads or peacefully debate. So, let's go to watch the horses butt heads because it's more fun, and we'll talk about our differences later. Our worst behavior is the reason for more regulations and additional changes in existing laws hoping to restrict and change that behavior. To keep us from running over children playing in the streets is why we have speed bumps.

"As a human, we either willfully change or refuse to change ourselves because, well…I'm not the problem, you are. And it's been that way since the first two brothers had a fight.

"That's why we need judges over us.

"We change our minds all the time, which varies our behavior making it more difficult for others to understand us. When it comes to our finite reasoning about the creator of all, do we think God changes too?

Disturbing King as the leash is pulled when Harry raises his hand.

"Ah, it seems Harry has a question."

"Yes. You said earlier that God repented that He made man. Is that not changing His mind?" Harry asks.

"Good question. Thank you, Harry. A good question it is. Let's see. Harry, I believe you have a strong desire to play football, right? It's a desire to be the best, play hard and beat the other team, and that desire won't change as long as you play the game. You practice and spend lots of time physically working-out to be the best.

"Do your methods of playing the game ever change? Like ah. . . you rush harder than you used to, or change positions to get a better view and or better opportunity to muscle your way in to take down the quarterback? If the coach wanted you to play a different position, say the running back, would that change your desire?

"In the past, I wanted to play golf; lots of it. It was a desire of mine to play well all the time, to par every hole, but as I got older, my methods of playing the game changed from wanting to hit the ball as hard and far as I could to just get that white ball in the short grass. But I still wanted to par every hole.

"In this world, we change our methods in this game of life all the time. But the desire of God that His prime creation would live righteously according to that original plan has not ever changed, but those methods of dealing with our unruly behavior are adjusted from time to time. That's the best I can come up with. Harry, thank you for that question.

"From the beginning, Adam and then Eve were expected to obey that one command, and all would be well forever and ever enjoying the plenteous harvest. They were peacefully enjoying it with the lions, the alligators, and snakes mingling alongside them. They were in a beautiful garden to walk through every day and to live for hundreds of years. How magnificent that must have been. How long did they live in that beautiful garden until they acted upon a lie? Was it only a day or two, a month, fifty years, or more? Did they get bored looking for excitement?

"Since that act of disobedience, mankind has had to struggle for survival, wars against enemies, defenses against animals and nature, working hard for our daily needs; what the evolutionists call survival of the fittest. Yes, since that time, there has been some micro-evolution taking place in the animal world and ours too. This human body of ours now has dozens of different races. And our expected lifetime has changed.

"Your survival as a student and later in the marketplace depends on the effort you put forth versus the efforts of a competitor wanting the same opportunity, the same job you desire. It's a competition, the best wins. You've always got to do your best to enjoy the benefits.

"All of that is just basic stuff, but we must periodically remind ourselves of that too. Otherwise, we tend to push it behind the present circumstances forgetting history.

"Okay, let's step ahead to the subject of medicine. Those ancient's way back four-hundred years BC initiated something that is still in use today. That Hippocratic oath all doctors must take. It is full of, I will respect, I will apply, I will remember, I will not, I will prevent, and then it ends with: "If I do not violate this oath . . .." The boy scouts make a promise, 'on my honor, I will do my best'. The girl scouts take an oath. When you get married, you'll make a vow of honor and respect to death do you part. Attorneys and judges take an oath to abide by the constitution and established law. When called upon as a witness in a trial you take an oath to tell the truth. Our elected representatives pledge an oath, and they have been doing that with their hand on the Bible in front of millions of viewers.

"Does it make a difference in how they perform their duties, or is it just words that must be said?

"Hmm. An idea just flashed across my consciousness. Since the pledge of allegiance to the flag was banned from being done in schools, then how about this? As a student, should you take an oath, make a promise, a vow to study hard, to hold in high respect your teachers and administrators, your coaches, to learn and apply the principles being taught, to respect and honor the other students, your parents, and refrain from la-di-la-da.

"You can finish it.

"Yes, why not? This is your assignment from me. You are now assigned to create an oath, a pledge for all students to take every year, and then explain why it would be beneficial.

"Got it? Create an Oath all students should or must take and explain why. Turn them into Mr. Whitecraft on Monday.

"Hmm? Is God leading you to make a vow to promise to respect and honor your teachers because that relationship needs a godly blessing?

"Wow! Imagine this. You may start something here in rural Colorado that expands statewide, then nationally, and fifty years from now, kids may be wondering who started this and why.

Samuel pauses as he breathes in deeply while lowering his head. He takes another deep breath looking up at his audience. Another deep breath and he begins again.

"Back in 1895, a German chemist witnessed an unusual happening in his lab that inspired him to investigate, and six-weeks later, he was able to capture a picture of the bones in his wife's hand. Before that, medicine was a sense of touch to determine the maladies of the body. X-ray machines were developed along with CT scanners.

"Have you ever heard of Ignaz Philipp Semmelweis, born way back in, ah … I think it was 1818. He summarized that their bare hands were likely transmitting unseen microbe type diseases to the newborn babies. So he advised the nurses and physicians to wash their hands with a chlorinated lime solution before tending to patients, especially when aiding in a child's birth. Yep, after instituting this policy, the mortality rate dropped dramatically. Yet, some of the authorities dismissed it as quackery, and he ended up in a mental ward dying at the young age of forty-seven.

"These new machines discover more of how this body is put together along with seeing the inside ailments that cause us problems. Microscopes can peer into the minute unseen particles that the universe is built upon, but they still can't find what has been called 'the god particle' even with those huge telescopes peering into outer space.

"No, if God was visible to our eyes, then the mystery would be solved, and we would stop seeking. Solomon tells us: 'happy is the man who finds wisdom.'. Yes, finds. We find things by seeking after it. Seek, and you shall find. But one seek usually is not enough. Keep going on and on and you'll find what your curiosity is seeking. And, it may not be what you expected.

"The Wright brothers, who never finished high school, sought a way for man to fly like a bird by taking one step at a time. They put together a machine that finally flew through the air for one minute. And now we don't even think about how. We board that bird with hundreds to go wherever.

"This mind of ours is a physical thingy within our head, but what a thing it is. Scientists have looked at it in numerous ways; x-rays and MRI's, along with dissecting it, but do they know how it works? Sure, neurons or electrical charges cause stimuli, which cause certain parts of that matter to send signals to other parts of the body. The eyes see something annoying me, and that sends a signal to raise my arm and use my open hand to swat that fly. How does this brain cause me to talk using my vocal cords, tongue, and lips to form sounds that are interpreted by you as words, sentences, and meanings? Do my lips say words without my thinking about it? No. I decided to say no, and the word came out of my mouth. I had a thought. The mind read that thought and sent the signal to my lips.

Sam pauses, moving his lips up and down without making a sound. He looks at the students for reactions.

"Hey, I, … me, . . . my soul inside this body decided to move my lips silently, and the order going to my brain and back again instructed the lips to move and the vocal cords to remain silent.

Raising his voice, Sam then says, "Whooie! Booie!", and then pauses to look around the room. "Hmm? Now you've got inquisitive looks on your faces. I said that to see the reactions. That whole process of visualizing your facial expressions and interpreting them is wonderment all by itself. Interacting with others is a complicated and often mystifying adventure. You look at one another sometimes wondering what they're thinking, or why they reacted the way they did to what you said or did, which prompted you to say or act determined by how you interpreted their actions or words. Did you understand what I just said?

"I'm not sure I fully comprehend it all either.

"But physically, how does our mind do what it does? By itself, it's only a physical part of this body. Could this body continue to live if the brain shut down? Would we be able to talk? I've known people with the dreaded disease called Alzheimer's when their memory bank fades away, the emotions sometimes run wild, but the rest of the body still functions. They can eat, walk around, tap you on the shoulder, but their mind does not record it. They may remember you but can't recall your name or much else. Are those lost memories still there but somehow locked up somewhere in the cavities of the brain? Why? How? Could that memory bank be re-opened? If you're interested in medicine or chemistry, perhaps you'll be the one that seeks and finds the formula to re-open those memories and or to keep them from being lost.

"This body can survive without fingers, arms or legs, and some inside organs, the brain can partially shut down, but without the intake of oxygen and flow of blood, this body dies.

"From the beginning, our life outside the womb begins with that first breath of air. Air is an invisible element. We don't see it unless it's put under a microscope large enough to see the atoms of nitrogen, oxygen, argon, and minute quantities of carbon dioxide. And if we had an even more powerful scope, could we see inside the nucleus and electrons forming the atom or atoms which form together to make the basic elements of nitrogen with one atom, helium and oxygen with two, or is that it; nothing smaller than that. Those are mere building blocks for everything. How many of those atoms does this body have? How many stars in the universe? As humans, are we living at the center of the universe, in the middle of outer and inner space? We can now view outer and inner space with those powerful scopes, and the quest for finding God continues.

"Then, there is another invisible force called energy. Scientists have proposed that electrons spin around the nucleus at the speed of light, a tremendous amount of energy locked up in that minute atom, and so we've discovered that splitting the atom and we get a boom. That energy is released, resulting in atomic and nuclear bombs capable of wiping out entire cities. The atom won't split apart by itself, no it needs that outside force to unleash the energy locked up inside. What kind of strong material forms the outside layer of the atom to keep those electrons from escaping and exploding?

"That tennis ball needs my outside force to throw it out for King to fetch.

"But where does energy come from?

"Just as a stone in this driveway of mine will not move unless an outside force comes upon it, so our physical mind will not send signals to my vocal cords unless a force outside the mind signals it. I breathe in and out all day long without thinking about it. The heart continues to beat without my thinking about it.

"But to communicate with you, I have to think about it. I have to use a part of the brain inside this body. Did you notice that? I said I have to use it. I'm using this physical body. Hmm? You are using your body. The you, using that body is the real you, called your soul, which is a spiritual being using your physical body as a means of moving about on this earth. When you communicate with another, your soul is reading your life experiences of what you desire to say, and then those electrons shoot from the brain to cause your lips to move. When you say you remember something, your soul reads the book of experiences recorded in your brain.

"Our soul is in the driver's seat, shifting gears, causing your body to accelerate and brake, turn and curve around corners. You, yes, your decision-making attribute can abuse that body in numerous ways, causing pain and discomfort. Or, you can make profitable decisions enabling that body to live longer and healthier than others. What are those decisions based upon?

"When the body dies, the soul, that invisible spiritual you will live on, either in a glorious palace as the good book says, or some other spiritual realm outside the physical. We don't visibly see the soul move out when this physical body dies, so we question it, wondering if what those scientists and atheists, who are telling us we came from nothing and will return to nothing are right, because we don't want to go to that lake of fire. When you think that your time is about up, will you still be wondering, or will there be a smile on your face signaling, yes, bring it on?

"Hmm?

"Being out here alone has enabled me to wonder and marvel about this unseen world surrounding us. Sometimes I ask stupid questions. I've wondered about that too. Many accused Columbus of taking a stupid journey, and many thought the Wright brothers were off their rocker.

Sam steps back, breathes in deeply, scanning the students, wondering if he's boring them, pondering where to go from here. It appears the interest is still there. A girl in front has been taking notes throughout the afternoon, as has a few others. *Are they just scribbling? Overall, they've been quiet and respectful*. One of the boys in the back has been looking down at the cell phone, looking up at Sam, back and forth continually, while the boy on the next seat leans over to watch.

"Anyone wishing to take a short break? Yes, let's do that. Stand and stretch for a few minutes."

Twenty-Eight

Ten minutes later, Sam stands and calls out: "Times up. Let me continue." The teens separate and take their seats.

"You've been great." Sam starts. "After classes are over, what do you do to enjoy the rest of the afternoon, or the evening after dinner? Huh? What? Have you ever wondered what Lincoln did as a kid for pleasure, for his personal enjoyment? Was it a mere stroll to a nearby lake or pond sitting there with a bamboo pole in his hand? Did he play catch with the kids down the block? Did Thomas Jefferson play games between his studies? What did Einstein do as a teen? It's recorded that at the age of five, Mozart could read and write music. They say he entertained people on the keyboard at the age of just five. What are five-year-old's doing nowadays? What did you enjoy doing at that age?

"Music is another boundless subject with a history going way back. The harp is first mentioned in the book of Genesis, and the trumpet and cymbals are also prominent Biblical instruments of four-thousand years ago. What inspired ancient man to develop some string that would make a sound when pulled tight and vibrated? Those ancients discovered that the sound intensified when the string vibrated over a hollow core. How did they discover such wonders? And here we are now with pianos, organs, violins, guitars, and hundreds of different instruments using strings to send music to our ears.

"The first trumpet? Where did it come from? Somewhere back in history, someone could have blown into a discarded ram's horn, discovering that the pitch could be changed by the way he blew into the small end. Think a minute about how these bits of nature have been used by mankind as a blessing to our lives. Perhaps originally discarded pieces of nature decaying away, and then someone is inspired to pick it up, look at it, turn it around, pluck it, blow into it, and hear a sound they never heard before. Did the first one to blow into a Ram's horn take it back to the tent to tell his wife, "here, listen to this," and she replied, "wow, honey, but what have you for dinner? The kids are hungry."

"So, if music inspires you, go for it. Give it all you got. It brings pleasure to us all. I often wish I had a piano here, but I never learned how to play. If you got a voice for song, sing. Get yourself into the forest and sing to the animals. Write your own songs. You may be the next Mozart. If you can play the trumpet, you may be called upon for that first sound of the last trumpets.

"I've discussed some of ancient history and how we accept those things as if they'd always been. Yes, we don't think much about how ancient man developed clothing for our bodies. We pick them from a rack in the store, put them on, and go about our daily business. But someone had to come up with the idea sometime earlier in history. How did those after Adam and Eve dress? Sheepskins? Buffalo hides, or a bunch of rabbit skins tied together? How did they discover that killing and removing the skin would provide comfort for the body? How far back did someone discover how to weave cotton into a sweater? The first taste of that plant's white fluffy substance was horrible, but it sure felt nice in the hand.

"That first day here, I saw this spinning wheel my grandmother used for making garments and blankets out of threads of material supplied by nature. Someone way back in history may have knelt in the dirt looking hard at the little silkworm spewing out a long fiber. They started gathering pieces together while imagining a scarf of silk wrapped around their neck.

"Then how and when did humans learn to clean those dirty garments? Who invented soap? How far back was it discovered? Did a mother wonder how she could re-use that woolen or cotton cloth her baby was messing up? Who invented buttons for shirts with sleeves and a collar? Neckties? Belts? How much of that is necessary, and the rest purely custom?

"Everything has a history. We need and consume every day without thinking about the food we eat and how often. Why do we consider three meals a day the standard? Did the apostle Paul eat three times a day on those long journeys of his? If we miss a meal, do we try to make up for it? Were there obese people in those olden days? Who says we must consume the basic food types to get a balanced meal? In that restaurant in Johnsonville, they provide you a menu based on your age, height, and weight. So, the experts have determined what kinds of food and how much you should eat to maintain a healthy body, something God planned from the beginning by providing His creation with various foods that grow plus animals to devour.

"Then, from the moment of the fall, we have continually gotten more confused, especially in the last one-hundred-years.

"Who discovered that removing the shell of a hard pecan had a delicious nut inside? Were two guys watching a squirrel bite that hard shell apart and then chew the nut inside? And then dig a hole to bury another to get in the off-season. "Hey bro, let's try that."

"The egg of a chicken. Perhaps a chicken never sat on one egg, and a lady picked it up, wondered, or it accidentally broke and was then cooked over fire sunny side up. Hmm? Tastes good to me.

"Ah, we so easily dismiss all that as not in my lifetime stuff and continue on our merry way. Convenience is what technology has done, and with it, our bodies have conveniently expanded from a thirty-inch waist to thirty-eight or more. Is it convenience plus gluttony, or just plain chronic hungriness to feed the addiction?

"There are several places in the Bible telling us to fast, yep, no food at all for a day or two or three. Moses is recorded as going without bread or water for forty days. Wow! forty days and nights. I've done a three-day fast since I've been here. It wasn't easy. I tried to get King to do it, but he refused, and I was tempted to get on my knees and put my tongue into his bowl.

"Yes, you could graduate from school going through life seeking your fortune and had never been taught nor learned about the profound effect the founding fathers had on this country, enabling the American experiment to develop into the superpower it has become. Easily you could do that. I was doing that. I had my head in the sand, my ears were plugged, and eyes shut, not seeing the slow but consistent deceitful ways of the invisible evil ones undermining our inherent freedoms. How will you know which side of the line to stand on? There is truth, and there are very apparent lies and not so easily detected falsehoods. You will have to choose one.

"Now that's an interesting word; falsehood. Why do you think untruths, deceits are called falsehoods? Those fabrications are the hood over the otherwise easily seen truth. Hmm? Deceit always has a shield. It has a beautifully designed hood disguising the truth, just as that serpent, using his forked tongue, spoke to Eve. There was an element of truth shielded, and all she heard or wanted to hear was that the fruit was good to eat, and perhaps they were tired of parsley and wanted something else. So surely, they would not die. And knowing more about evil, they would become like God. "Hmm? What is evil anyway?" They never experienced evil before. "What is that? Yeah, let's try it."

"That was the hood covering the truth. Can we see through the hood? Does modern technology itself have many hoods? Are we so addicted to technology that we can't and don't recognize the hoods of deceit?

"I get a kick out of those who do not believe this place we inhabit was a part of creation by a master designer. No, they say; we are nothing but a chance happening over millions or billions or mega-trillion of years ago by some big bang that caused one molecule formed from nothing, splitting or crashing into another formed from nothing, and nothing caused them to split. On and on, the divisions of nothing eventually sticking together in different configurations caused by nothing. After billions of years, the stuck together bodies formed into huge stars, galaxies, moons, and planets, which enabled rocks, dirt, and water to form groups of atoms on this one lonely planet from nothing, making an atmosphere conducive to life, all of it caused by nothing.

"And, so it goes they intone, but they can't explain how life came from no life, how a rock started to breathe.

"You read and hear it every day from folks dropping the line of so many billions of years ago the feathers of a goose spread out to become wings. Oh, over billions of years, the rough skin of a turtle turned into a hard shell to protect it from falling tree branches.

"Everything that is living must have food to survive, so both food and life must have evolved along the same timeline, or the living thing would die. So, food must have been first. Did we come from monkeys or chimpanzees? When, where, why, and how? So, once upon a time, a monkey may not have liked being just a monkey, because well, nothing else was happening, and the contest of who could swing the farthest was getting old.

"Can't prove any of it, can they? How did the eye become a physical element that could transmit a colorful vision interpreted by the brain? How did that happen? How did our nose develop the ability to smell chocolate, and how did chocolate get its aroma? How did the ear develop to hear strings making music, and the brain to interpret all that? How did the male and female parts of nature begin? How did the male sperm learn to penetrate the female egg? Was it just bumping into each other, and one said, hey, let's do something together.

"Only speculation because they cannot or will not let themselves imagine nor accept a being so magnificent, so intelligent, so awesome in that unseen spiritual realm to create and develop a process to shine into the nothingness along with creating laws governing this new physical realm.

"You're looking at the computer screen before you turn it on; it's black, it's nothing, just a blank screen. Was that how it was before the Almighty created light? You press a button, and that energy makes the screen come alive with the background you chose. You see the pictures or diagrams of your favorite places to go, waiting for you to point to it by pressing the button on the mouse. Who created those icons? How did they get there? What makes it tick? If it's overloaded or the device is old, you may see a tiny blue circle going round and round.

"That computer is made up of different configurations of the basics of a one and a zero, millions or billions of those two basics in different bunches create the pictures, the software, the games within that cell phone and computer. Someone or the entire office of programmers figured out how to do it. That computer did not fall into place over millions of years by random happenings of those two digits, the electrical current of a positive and negative, a yes or a no, it's on or it's off. Nope, a designer made it appear alive and do what it does when you press buttons. And there are certain rules you must follow and be mindful of to use it correctly.

"The same with this universe, a master designer did it, and we must take it to heart and apply those rules for us to live correctly as the designer programmed, or we just go round and round in circles.

"We want to solve our mysteries, but some will never be scientifically solved, and we don't like that.

"When in time did it all began? There it is, the one element that's missing in our deliberations, the concept of time. Time moves. The clocks tick. The sun and moon rise and disappear from view. The calendar changes. But the almighty is beyond time, before time, therefore no beginnings, no endings, only now. We can't comprehend that, as we are immersed in this time element with a beginning and an ending. Time was a brand-new element from the first ray of light, just as this physical realm was a brand-new element inside the spiritual.

"So how magnificent, how wondrous this creator must be, and what do we do? We're too dag gone busy to notice or pay tribute to this God Almighty, the Jehovah God of the Universe."

Samuel pauses, looks around from the kids in front to those in back, to the few mothers, to Gene, and the sheriff standing in the rear. Sam breathes in and adds, "I think that's about it from me today, except for a personal testimony.

"Because of the devastation I went through after my wife was killed in a car wreck, and trying to forget it all, I became a drunk. I was going through a wilderness, seeing nothing but weariness; I had no hope, no purpose to life. I was dead spiritually. A zombie holding dear a bottle of beer. Then one day, as I was biding time with a sack of beer nearby, watching men tackle each other.

Sam turns to point to the framed picture.

"This picture right here above the fireplace got my full attention. My dear wife loved it and had it hung above our television. My eyes focused on it. It was like seeing it for the first time. I envisioned a manifestation of the boundless love of the almighty that woke me up and took the darkness away, bringing light into my soul.

"I saw the truth, and it set me free. The drinking stopped, and I went back to work, telling my secretary what happened. She then said that she had been praying for me. A few days later, she brought me the envelope containing the news that this cabin was mine. I was stunned to silence. Huh? What? Then, I slowly warmed to the thought and excitement as I contemplated the change.

"It was a fraction of time between being an out of control drunk to a new spiritually alive person receiving the good news. And then this opportunity. I came to this cabin not knowing what to expect except a drastic change in living conditions, as "He leadeth me beside the still waters." I called it my log cabin escape hatch.

"Being alone most of the time, I began to see the wonders of nature, a wilderness full of life and mystique, and with that, the wonders of the beginnings and sustainability of life. The heavens declare these things for us, and nature shows us the Alpha and Omega of that handiwork. Yes, no longer was I bowing down to the TV as my Shepherd nor the twenty-four-hour news as my guide. With my new sight, I saw the ants and butterflies, the weeds, the big trees with hard trunks and soft leaves somehow breathing the air while being provided with nutrients from the water within the dirt.

"Jesus became more than a figure to admire, but the manifestation of the Father's love for His creation. One day, Jesus was enjoying the heavens. The next day a seed was supernaturally implanted inside the womb of Mary, and after the usual amount of time, Jesus was born naked becoming one of us, like the millions before. His mother cleaned his body, nurtured him, and showed him how to walk and talk, knowing that there was something very special about this baby.

"After antagonizing the authorities, Jesus was brutally beaten, whipped, and tortured to death on a cross; then wrapped as a corpse and put in a cave tomb. Three days later, the stone rolled away, and that human body was supernaturally endowed with life again, walking with and teaching his disciples, who initially had a hard time believing what they were seeing and hearing.

"My spirit was once numb, and a new life was given to me. You know what numb is like? The body is alive, but there are no feelings, a physical body without sense.

"Okay, this was not supposed to be an evangelical meeting, but a meeting about history, but I can't help it, I don't want to help it. I want to let the spirit flow through me. So, if there is anyone here who'd want to know more, or to decide you'd like this same relationship I've found, then I'll make myself available… now… or later. Your choice. You'd be welcome here anytime.

"No doubt, I've been redundant in some parts, but isn't that the way we learn, by hearing or seeing the same over and over again? That's how you learned the A B C's, how to walk and talk, and that eight added to four equals thirteen.

"Oops, hmm? I saw some eyebrows raise there. Yeah, you recognized the mistake right away. Your ability to recognize deceit and those falsehoods will increase as the reality of truth gets cemented into your consciousness.

A girl in the front speaks up, "Mr. Guardyall, are you saying that we can't walk the Christian walk unless we do something way-out, something like this?"

"Ah, good question. Your name is?"

"Samantha."

"That puts me in a spot Samantha, and I suppose you want a simple answer, a yes or no. So here goes; there is no simple answer. No, I'm not saying you must live as I do without all the conveniences of modern life to walk the straight and narrow. What I do believe is what Paul wrote in the scriptures, that we are to come out from among the unbelievers and separate ourselves from them. My escape to here made it easier to do that. We have been put in this world, but we are not to be part of it. Now, how to do that is the part that gets theologians, our leaders, and each of us tied in knots.

"Ah, there are so many ways we could act and behave differently than the unbelievers. My generation and those before me blended in too. So this goes back a long way. But how different would our culture have developed if those before us had done that? The Amish have separated themselves, and we easily recognize them.

"So, how should or could we separate ourselves from the unbelievers? Think about that. The evil one is alive and deeply involved in this mixed-up world, easily deceiving us, so it's difficult to recognize a fellow believer as you walk the mall or the halls of your school. Yes, you may see a cross hanging around someone's neck. Do you dress differently? Do you talk differently? Do you perform differently? Or, have we been deceived so well that perhaps we don't want to be looked upon as being different?

"Thanks for your question, Samantha.

"My grandfather left a note about when the stores and restaurants in America started to open on Sundays; the churches at first fought the idea, but it did not take the congregations long to adjust and welcome the convenience of shopping and dining out on Sundays. Sunday is the first day of our week. Throughout the Old Testament, the seventh-day Sabbath was always the day of rest, just as God rested after formatting creation for six days.

"Gads, if the inventor and creator of this world desired to rest after a week's work, shouldn't we? It's that fourth commandment, 'Remember the Sabbath day to keep it Holy.' The Almighty desired and commanded all to rest on the Sabbath, which according to Jewish law, starts at sundown on Friday evening. The Saturday Sabbath was observed up until the fourth century when Constantine, who supposedly had converted to Christianity, conceded to the pagans, who worshiped a sun god on the first day of the week. That's where the name Sunday comes from. The early church also considered that the coming of Christ abolished many of the Jewish traditions. And here we are today, blending in with societal changes acting as if one hour per week in a church service is enough. The divisions into hundreds of denominations has also been a stumbling block to many, as has the disagreements between Protestants and Catholics.

"With the technology you now have available, compared to when the founders of America sat together debating together to devise and form our constitution, you are now able to ask that plastic machine any question and get answers in seconds. Many of those numerous replies will be reliable. But then there are the biased answers also, as the confusion, the deceit, the propaganda has gotten much worse because of that technology bringing us news from hundreds of localities, from people being paid millions to point out what they believe you should know.

"Aristotle said 'it is the mark of an educated mind to be able to entertain a thought without accepting it.' You can do that. You must be able to do that. It also takes a questioning mind to do it, so raise your curiosity factor using the five W's about everything, then use that technology to get correct and truthful answers. Now you may feel dumb by asking questions, but if you don't get it you may look dumber because you did not get it."

Sam pauses, looking around the room. His eyes go from student to student, to the mothers. He breathes deeply, looking over at Harry with King on the floor next to him, to the sheriff, to Francinea, to Betty and Gene in the back.

Sam lowers his head and then raises it, looking to the ceiling rafters, then raises his arms. "Hallelujah, Thank You, Lord."

"Gene, it's all yours. I've done my whistling. And, thank you for your undivided attention."

There's a big round of applause for Sam as he steps to his right, beckoning Gene to take over.

Gene slowly walks to the front allowing the applause to die down while he approaches the spot in front of the fireplace. "Now, let's all give Mr. Guardyall another great round of applause."

"Thank You, Samuel. For me, it was more than I'd hoped for. You sure got me thinking. As for myself, I've experienced the same forgiveness. Okay, class, don't forget about your assignment. I'll be ready and anxiously waiting to see your suggested student oaths on Monday. That's it and thank you for coming. Oh, and also, anyone who chooses the challenge, I'd like a report on how that turned out. Then I can provide Sam with those and see his reactions.

"Now, let's enjoy some snacks and a drink available on that beautiful block table. Any questions, Sam said he'd make himself available."

"That's it. And again, thank you for coming."

Twenty-Nine

Sam is at the butcher-block table, joining Francinea and Meredith, separating the paper plates and slicing into the large square vanilla-chocolate cake. Harry, still holding King close with the leash, is on the way to taking King outside. He stops to thank Sam for the inspiration. Harry then suggested to Sam that he'd contact the youth director at church. Sheriff Olsen congratulated Sam, briefly telling of the similarities to his grandfather. The students and two of the mothers are somewhat falling in line chatting together, waiting to thank Sam. A few have gathered in front of the fireplace and the bookcase. Peter is snapping pictures.

One of the mothers approaches Sam, her daughter standing nearby, chatting with a friend. "Mr. Guardyall, my daughter insisted that I come along too. I resisted at first, but I'm so glad I came. She's been evangelizing me lately, as I've grown stale about the church over the past few years. Your talk has…well…woke me up, and I'll be meditating on it more and more. My husband is an alcoholic. He, ah, would you mind if I brought him out sometime?"

"No, of course not. Your husband may want to see the cabin. So, sure suggest that, and we'll sit and chat and see where the Lord leads. Some are leaving a note at the mailbox, and then I get back to 'em setting up a time. And, I don't mind spontaneous visits either, but I might be out fishing or exploring the forest.

"Thank you. I may take you up on that. Thanks again. It's what I needed to hear, and now wish I had it recorded."

"Hey, thank God. I'm just a messenger. Glad you came." Looking over her shoulder, recognizing the daughter as the one taking notes throughout the talk, Sam asks, "Your daughter likes to write, doesn't she?"

"Yes, she does. She's always got a pen and a notebook handy, even while watching TV."

"I saw that as I was talking. She has a special talent there. Encourage it and keep a good supply of paper handy. Thanks for coming. And blessings to you."

The cake and drinks are distributed. Meredith moves toward Harry after returning inside. He's still holding the leash of King while tending to the fireplace along with two other boys starring into the burning embers. Two students stop to thank Sam for the opportunity to see inside the cabin. Another shakes his hand and heads out the door. As the students notice a familiar vehicle make its way around the drive, they excuse themselves to get their ride home.

"Mrs. Ingersall," Gene addresses Francinea. "Your daughter has become one of my favorite students. She is doing great. You've done a terrific job with her, especially since that horrible thing that happened to your husband. Meredith told me about it."

"Thank you. She's a big encouragement to me."

"Sam, I must be going too," Gene tells Sam. "Thank you again for doing this, and I'm looking forward to what reactions I'll get. Oh, I noticed that Betty was recording it all, so I'm sure I'll hear something. You've got the gift, Sam. Use it. And that idea about the student oath was brilliant. I'll let you know how that turns out. Thanks again."

"Yes, please do. I'd be interested in what they come up with. You did the work. All I did was open my mouth. Take care. Hey, next Saturday, come out, and we'll do some fishing."

"I'd like that. And oh, by the way, my son will bring some ice Monday, and pick up the chairs then."

"Thanks."

Francinea moves in close to Sam, reaching for his hand, and looking up into his eyes, she softly says, "Samuel, again I'm so sorry about the fuss I made. Please, forgive me. Your speech was terrific, and Gene is right. You've got a gift. I am proud to have heard it."

Recognizing her mixed anxiety and endearment, Sam tells her, "Thanks. That other part is over and done with, and. yes, erased." He puts his arms around her pulling her close for a hearty embrace. Her arms slowly go around his waist. Sam feels her head leaning on his shoulder, then senses her head and body relax and rest. Sam relaxes, softly saying, "Thank you, Lord."

Pulling back from the embrace, she looks up into his eyes, asking if he'd come to the house for dinner Sunday.

Meredith approaches, "Mom, Harry, and I are going to Johnsonville for dinner if that's okay."

"Sure, honey. Go and have a good time. Which one you going to?"

Meredith looks to Harry, who replies, "I've wanted to try that Home Town restaurant."

"The food is good, Sam says. "But don't you have to work tonight?"

"No, I asked for the night off."

Reaching to shake his hand, Sam adds, "Harry, thanks for watching King for me. He takes to you quite well. Thank you. And thanks for that question. I'll be pondering that one some more. Meredith, you're always a great help. God bless you."

As the two teens close the door leaving Sam and Francinea alone in the cabin, Sam looks back to her, "Eh, how about we go back to Cattlemen's? I'm ready for a good steak."

"Sure. But Sam again, you do understand why I'm so skittish about our relationship."

"Yes, I do. I'm with you on that. We've both gone through the same kind of horror. We've got our fears about something new. I do too. I'm adjusting quite well to this life and don't know if I ever want to change that. But, I still enjoy your company. Can we leave it at that?"

"I want to, Samuel. But as before, I wanted you, and that's the part that scares me. We're adults. We can handle it, can't we?"

"Now, Francinea, do you think that I didn't have the same thoughts as you expressed? Ha. Those bulls were running around my head like starved lions. But hey, I'm not going to put myself at the mercy of Niagara Falls, so we must put those temptations aside, knowing it's only our flesh, those fleshy desires for a half-hour of enjoyment. Jehovah God is with us, is in us, and sees us all the way, and I won't forget that. That's one red line I will not cross. Let's go and enjoy conversational fellowship and another good steak as ah— yes, as brother and sister in the Lord."

"Oh, brother and sister? Hey, I like that. My older brother. Hmm? Treat me nice now, or I'm gonna tell."

"Oh! Yeah, sis. I got some things to tell about you, remember."

"Oh, you're going to be mean again. I can play that game." Francinea then pokes Sam in the belly, pushing him off-balance. "Let's go, bro."

"I'm driving your car, sis, so hush, or you'll sit in the bed of the pick-up."

Thirty

It's late Sunday evening after a wonderful dinner with Francinea, Meredith, and Harry. Sam's got a lantern burning next to the typewriter.

"Ah, I got to write this down. King, sit!"

My Cabin Life 17

This past Saturday's meeting turned out great. At first, I felt intimidated at the idea of teaching or sharing with these students some aspects of our history as Americans. But once I got going, those words just seemed to flow as the thoughts breezed across my consciousness, recalling what I've previously read or studied. The thoughts came and turned into words.

Is this how St. Paul spread the good news? He saw it happening. He was an antagonistic witness. He was against it all. He persecuted those that believed. And then he was called by name: "Saul. Saul, Why are you doing that. I need you to speak forth and spread the news as far and wide as I lead."

No maps. No three-by-five note cards in his pocket. He traveled far along the dirty, musty trails, to towns and villages he'd never been to before.

Was he following the movement of the sun to keep from going in circles? No drive-thru restaurants along the way. No hotels. No rest areas. No porta-johns. What size was his suitcase, or did he wear a backpack? Barefoot? Sandals? Rode a camel? Had he thought to bring ten bottles of water as he walked through the aired land?

Nope, none of that. The Spirit of God Almighty guided him. Through the Mediterranean choppy waters, he rode along in one of those old sailboats. Months on the seas, and then crashing near an Island. He survived and was directed across the Mediterranean sea to Rome.

Is that what guided me in my talk? Oh, Thank You, Lord, as I certainly was on an unknown path, and You, the Spirit of the Almighty, guided me, a word, or phrase, one at a time. In this new path I'm doing by living in this old cabin, I can't see the future. I don't know what tomorrow holds for me. I'm only familiar with the now, feeling my fingers touching these keys.

Hope and the recent past are all I've got. Tomorrow, perhaps I get – my hopes, desires, and wants.

Sam pauses, breathes deeply in thought as his mind wanders back to Francinea. *"Looking out the window now, I see moon rays highlighting the tops of distant trees and those uncountable stars helping to shed light across the dark paths."*

"Oh, the joy of the forest compared to the city where man-made midnight lights hinder our views of heavenly lights. And now Lord, I need your light to illuminate tomorrow's path for Francinea and me." Yes, the path I want is hindered by those city lights Francinea needs for her work and all.

He breathes deeply and turns back to the typewriter.

I've hoped that Francinea and I would reconcile our differences and unite together in loving fellowship. I've missed her. And by her attending the meeting encouraged that hope. After my rambling, we had dinner together again, enjoying the fellowship and food. And again in her home this evening. While looking at her across the table, I imagined. I desired her company every day. Yes, I want it. I hoped that I would find an opening to ask her to come and join me in marriage and life in this cabin. She seemed to like the cabin. Said she was envious.

That would be fantastic. A partner in this venture. I wouldn't be driven so often to go to the diner just for human fellowship. Oh, how many times, I've used the excuse of needing some supplies so I could listen to Joanna or visit Sheriff Olsen and chat a bit.

Lonely life this is. Yes, King removes some of it, but what kind of conversation can I have with King? He does let me hold his paw when I'm praying.

But, would she? She's got a nice home. She's got a fantastic job and loves it. Meredith is great. But Meredith may be leaving for college, which would leave Francinea living alone. Would she then want a companion to come home to, or would she spend more and more time serving others' medical needs? She does communicate with others during the day, whereas I do not. There's no chance of her giving up the comfort of a beautiful home to live in an old, ill-equipped cabin. She'd come home from work, and instead of relaxing in pj's, she'd be wrapping blankets around her shoulders and snuggling up next to the fireplace. Oh, if she ever wanted to bake a cake, it'd be a new learning process. Would she be up for any of that?

Is it my selfish desire to ask her to give all that up for me? Nope, can't do it.

Then the thought came that I could sell the cabin, or just use it as a get-away periodically. Then the thought returned that I had vowed unto the Lord that I would adjust and learn to like and enjoy it. But I made that vow at that particular time under those circumstances known then. These are different circumstances, so is that vow still relevant? I don't want to move. I wouldn't be able to sit by the stream. No watching the ducks. No strolls through the woods. No hundreds of books to choose from. Instead, that TV would be staring at me.

So here I am—one perplexing moment after another. Lord, You know it all, so dang it, why can't I know tomorrow, as supposedly we're all made in Your image. But all I see is a tinted window reflecting me typing these notes.

As the good book says, "Do not fear. Have faith." Actions speak louder than words, and that's all I've been doing here.

Okay, Saturday, when I again enjoy Francineas' company, I will not be afraid to ask right there on my knees. Let her decide. Faith outlasts hopes. Faith transforms fear. Action defines words thought. Faith without works is dead, waiting to be activated. My action. Her reaction.

Oh, I've got to quit this rambling away like a kid trying to enjoy a discarded toy.

Lord, I leave it to you. You know what's best for both of us. I only guess.

"Hey, King, Time to hit the sack. Oh! You better go out first. So go! But be careful."

Thirty-One

As his feet touch the chilly floor this Friday morning, Sam exclaims, "Yes!" almost three weeks after the students' meeting.

"Hey, King! What happened? I beat you getting up."

King raises his head and then rolls to life, swinging his tail.

"Okay, buddy, I've had my turn, so out you go." Sam follows the dog to the door. King stops to lick up some water, and as Sam opens the door, King runs toward the gazebo.

"Oooh, it's cold out here," Sam tells the outside air as he notices the 22^0 temperature. *It's freezing in here too.* At the fireplace, Sam lights a crumbled piece of paper under some twigs watching them quickly catch, and then some bark of the logs he's carefully placed on top. He lights the logs in the kitchen stove to help the inside warmth, and sets his coffee pot full of clear water on the Coleman stove. He glances out the window and then turns to rub his hands together over the warmth of the stove. *Well, today is stay inside, read and start writing that book.*

After two cups of coffee and a bowl of oatmeal with sliced bananas and raisins sprinkled on top. Sam is comfortably seated on the couch in front of the fireplace, starting to read *"The Essential C.S. Lewis."*

King is slouching on his near-by pillow. It's a clear day two weeks to Thanksgiving. Over the forested hills, the whiteness of snow continues creeping down the sides of the mountains.

Suddenly King jumps from his pillow, barking and running to the door.

"Yeah, I heard it too," Sam tells the pet. He puts the book down, looks out the window, and sees Gene getting out of his car.

"Come on in, Gene. Great to see you," Sam says as he holds the door open.

"Good afternoon, Sam. It's my lunch break, so I thought this would be a good time to give you copies of what the kids have written for you."

"Great, I've been wondering. Coffee?"

"Yes. Thanks." Gene follows Sam to the butcher block table. "Sam, you're gonna love these." He places a folder on the table. So, what'cha you been up to? Anything new and exciting?"

"Ah . . . Oh . . . nothing new under the sun," Sam softly says, almost revealing a promise not to. He places the coffee cup in front of Gene.

"So, how many took me up on the challenge?"

"Four."

Sam picks up the folder, opens it, and sees four pages of handwriting. "They penned these. Why not computer initiated?"

"That was their idea. They said they wanted them to look old. Something like what you're doing here."

"What's your take?"

"All I can say is—astounding. My methods of teaching are changing since this. I'll never again put the emphasis on dates, events, and names for them to memorize. I'll be asking questions like you did. I can't thank you enough."

"And the student oath, how did that go?"

"Oh! I gave a copy to the principal, and he just looked at me with that stunned look as his jaw dropped open. I'm not gonna say anymore.

You read it, Sam. I had to bring these out for you to digest. This is their own. I did not correct or suggested anything. I sat in the back of the classroom as the students debated on the wording of the oath. It took three hours to agree."

"Appreciate it, Gene. Yes, you better come back, or I'm gonna bust into that classroom with the sheriff. But not this weekend as the scouts are coming out."

Sam, sitting on the couch by the fireplace, opens the folder to read the notes from those who took him up on the challenge.

Mr. Guardyall, you owe me a day of fishing.

Saturday morning, after breakfast, and a few chores around the house, normally I would read the comments others make on FB and twitter. I reached to turn the cell on, and I stopped dead. No. My brother called for me to play games on the tablet. No. I went out in the back yard and pulled weeds. Mom saw that and froze, looking, wondering if something was wrong. I went to a friend's house, and we walked thru the woods to watch the Mill workers, then to where the trees were being cut. After dinner, Mom wanted me to watch this movie. No. I picked up a book. Sunday was the same. A No here, a No there, and more No's all day long.

I did it. Thanks for the challenge. I, me, was in control, and it felt good. Thank you.

Jack Johnson

I did it, accepted your challenge.

Sat morn, instead of grabbing the tele and an hour of scans, and then the laptop for games, I got this old box of Lego off the closet shelf. Three hours of one piece after another to make a castle on the floor of the BR. No blocks left. Went to store and got a 2000 piece set. I Used my allowance.

Mom knocked on my door, "what you doing?" I told her about your challenge.

"Are you serious ?"

Yes. today and tomaro, no tv, computer, tablet, or cell.

"Good, I got chores for you. when you finish.. That's beautiful."

Sunday, I finished it. When can we go fishing? And, Mom's taking me to the hobby shop to get pieces of round wood to make a Log cabin. Anything can be done when the mind is put to use instead of following along.

Thank You.

Olaf Bensen

Our suggested Student Oath originated by the students in the class of Mr. Gene Whitecraft.

I ____________________, a student here at Prairieville, Colorado High School do promise and swear that:

1. I will do my best at all times while in or near the school campus for any event.

2. I will respect the principal, teachers, coaches, support personnel, and all others under their authority.

3. I will respect all students.

4. I will respect and do my assignments.

5. I will refrain from abusive talk.

6. I will listen first.

7. I will answer when asked.

8. This I will do to the best of my ability desiring that my abilities expand under this time here at Prairieville High School.

Signed on ___ /__ /____

_________ _____________ A Student of Prairieville High

\# ______-____-____

Witnessed by _______________

"Wow!" Sam surmises. "And all I did was make a suggestion."

Sam looks down at his pet, fast asleep on the cushion. "King," Sam says. "Soon you're gonna have another body to bark at. For me, it can't come soon enough. But, when?"

Epilogue

Later that day, around seven, Sam is comfortably seated in front of the fireplace reading.

"King, what are you barking at now?" Sam asks his pet, and he then hears the knock on the door. He gets up from the couch and goes to open the door.

"Francinea! What a great surprise," Sam greets her with a hug.

"Good evening, Samuel. I hope I'm not disturbing you, but here I am, wanting to experience this during a cold evening again," She says as she relaxes in his hug after the quick kiss. "And I got great news for you."

"Ah, you will never disturb me, even with great news. So, what's the news? But first, make yourself comfortable, and I'll get you that hot chocolate you love." Sam steps toward the table, takes a cup from the shelf, drops the pouch in, and adds the hot water. Then stirs and adds a few small marshmallows.

Francinea is sitting at the desk. Her eyes move back and forth all around the cabin and to his laundered items hanging on the line. She reads the oath the students had formulated.

"Wow, this is great," she says as Samuel approached with the Hot Chocolate. "But the news is greater. I had to come and tell you. We were sitting at the dining room table when Harry got on his knees and proposed to Meredith. So how's that?" She then describes Meredith's reactions and hers, too, witnessing it all. "I was amazed. I still am. A mom and daughter accepting proposals on the same day."

Sam is about to sit in the cushioned chair but stopped to face her on the desk chair. "No, kidding. I thought he would, but not until after graduation. Have they set a date?"

"Right after graduation."

"Hmm?" Sam says. "What about their college plans?"

"They're pondering that. Meredith indicated that if Harry gets that scholarship, she'll apply to the same school. And she said if he doesn't get it, then he'll find a carpenter's job where she goes. That's where it's at now."

"How do you feel about it?"

"Hey, I'm all for it. Whatever they decide, I'll back 'em one-hundred percent." Francinea tongues in and swallows a marshmallow, and sips the hot chocolate.

"Wow! This was Sunday, and I'm just hearing about it?"

"Well, on Tuesday, late afternoon, Meredith and I took a walk in the woods behind the house just talking and sharing things of the heart. And, well, I then told her about our engagement. She jumped with joy, hugged me, and it felt great to get it off my chest. We agreed to keep it a secret.

"She then said that she and Harry do not want to tell anybody yet. But today, I had to stop and tell you. If you see Harry, don't say anything, because he doesn't know of ours yet.

"Wow!" Sam says. "Why is she keeping our engagement a secret from Harry?"

"She feels the same way as I did about telling her of our engagement–that'd it spoil his excitement. She and Harry are going for a long walk in the woods tomorrow, and she'll let him know then. There's something about being alone together in the woods. You feel free to share everything.

"Yeah, I couldn't agree more. With Angelia, we'd talk about anything and everything when we were sitting around a camp-fire on those once-a-year trips. Brought us closer together. And soon, we'll be able to do just that." He pauses, noticing the paper she was holding. "You read that student oath?"

"Yes, it's fantastic. Ah, yes, You suggested that in your talk." She breathes deeply and exhales with a long sigh. "Samuel, you haven't told anyone, have you?"

"No. I haven't. I wanted to shout it out. Gene came by with the oath, and I almost did. But why are you so hesitant about announcing our engagement to our friends?"

"I want to, but then hearing Meredith's side. I'm glad I didn't. "

"You're right. So now what? What have you been thinking?"

"Lots of things, But what's your thoughts now?" Francinea replies.

"You first," Sam states.

"No. You!"

Sam reaches in his pocket for a coin. "Okay, heads or tails?" he says as he puts the silver nickel on his thumb.

She quickly reaches out to take the coin.

"Okay!" Samuel says. "Here's what came to me just now. Thanksgiving, We can either have it here or at your home and invite our friends over after dinner for pies and such. The sheriff and his wife, Gene, and George with their wives to join us later that afternoon so that we can tell them."

He looks into her eyes and adds, "That would be a Thanksgiving here in 2019 we'd never forget."

"Gads," Francinea replies. "You read my mind." She breathes deeply and then adds: "Except, I want my medical partner to come, too. And then I can tell him, I'll be leaving."

"Leaving? You didn't say anything about quitting your practice. You know you don't have to. You enjoy that too much to quit. And I hope it's not something I suggested. Is it?"

"Sure, you did. You implied that if I didn't quit working, I'd never learn how to bake a cake in that oven of yours."

"I never told — oh, you've read my cabin life notes."

"Touché! Gotcha. That's for that one you pulled on me."

Sam reaches over to pull her off the chair and onto his lap and into his arms. She leans her head back, puts her hands on his cheeks, and plants a kiss.

"Samuel, Yes! Thanksgiving would be a terrific time to tell everybody."

"Kneel with me and let's thank the Lord for this," Samuel says.

They kneel on the carpet in front of the fireplace, holding hands, and she starts praying. Sam is quietly praying as she does. He finishes with, "Oh, Lord, how marvelous are your ways of bringing us together. Now help me, Lord, to be the man I need to be for the safekeeping, for the support of this new love of my life. Thank You. And lead us day by day. Amen and amen."

Sam then starts singing while peering into her eyes. "And through it all. Through it all, my eyes . . . are on you. It is well . . .with my soul. It is well . . . with my soul."

"Oh, Samuel. Stop it, or I'll want to spend the night."

"Hmm? Yes, why not. I'll sleep nice and warm right here on the couch, and you over there in the bed with the curtain drawn. Then you'll feel how it is to wake up in this cabin."

"It's tempting, but Meredith will be wondering. I've been thinking about when to set our date. I'd rather wait until warmer weather, and then I'll have those warm months to adjust to this life before winter. So, let's wait. The same place, time, and date as Meredith and Harry."

"Yes, I like that. It'll be a mom and daughter ceremony. Yes! Do you think Meredith would go for that?"

"She already suggested that on our walk. Okay, that's it then. We will let everyone know Thanksgiving."

"June can't come fast enough," Sam replies, and then passionately brings her close and kisses his bride to be. They relax in the embrace breathing the comfort and warmth of their close-knit bodies.

"Oh, Samuel. I love you, and I promise I'll do my best to adjust to this lifestyle. You've done it, and with your help, I can, too."

"Tomorrow's Saturday, right? Let's do something," Sam says as she relaxes from the hug. "Oh, almost forgot. George is bringing a few scouts out at noon for another camp-out. You're welcome to come for the campfire chat."

"Nah, that's all boy stuff. I gotta go, so good night, and God's blessings. Sunday evening at church?" She gets up off his lap after a peck on his cheek.

He opens the door. "Good night, soon to be *my* Francinea. I love you. Sunday evening, then?"

They hug and kiss, exchange love notes, and she drives off with King running and barking alongside the car.

I sketched my cabin using only a pencil, eraser, and cardboard for straight line angles. The rest is freehand sketch.

Samuel Guardyall.

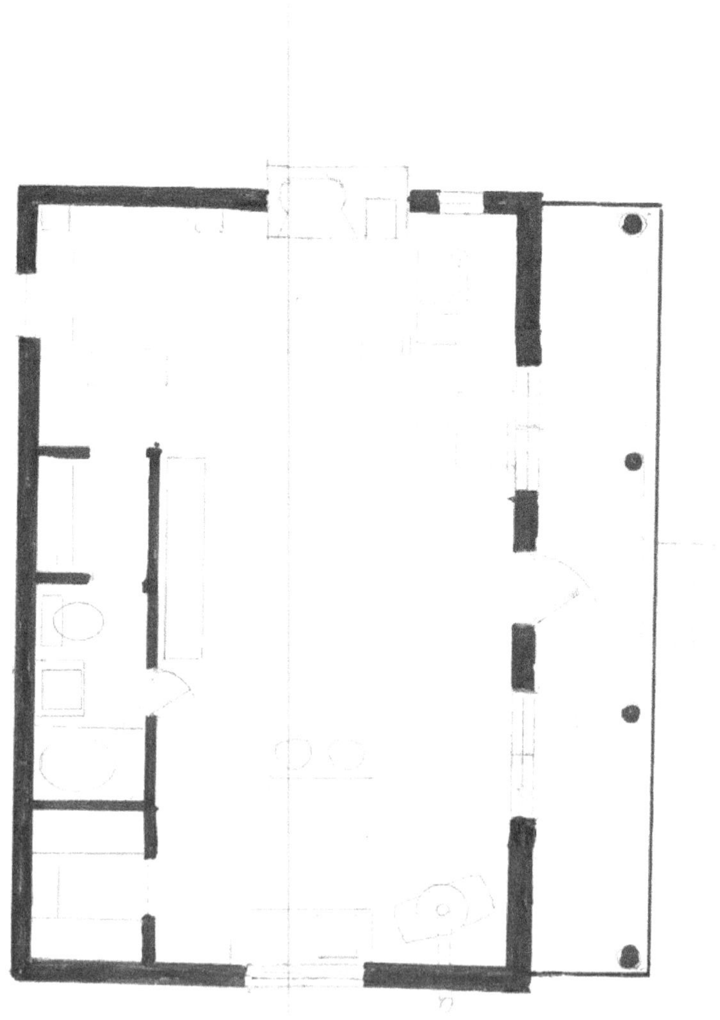

Arnold was born and raised in Chicago, the home of the Bears and the Cubs, oh, and the White Sox. Fantastic museums, one of the many is the Museum of Science and Industry, which has a U-505 German Submarine to tour. There's the famous Navy Pier, Lake Shore Drive, Buckingham Fountain, elevated trains, and subways to get to Wrigley Field.

During his Army service as a morse code operator in a Long Range Recon Patrol in Germany, he vacationed in the Alps of Switzerland and visited his mother's uncle in Stockholm on the Baltic Sea. He saw the walls dividing Berlin. Toured the Nuremberg Stadium where Hitler made speeches.

On the trip back to the states for discharge, Arnold stated that tears slid down his cheeks when the ship passed the Statue of Liberty. A year later, he spent the summer as an exchange student living with a German family while working in a local factory spot welding drawers for computer cards.

Arnold started public writing in 2005, posting political and inspirational comments on his web page about the happenings of the day. He also blogged on a well-read political news site. Those posts are published in one volume titled "Rummagings."

That's history.

Post-retirement, Arnold chose to part-time drive a school bus of all things. Try that sometime. The best part has been the fellowship with the other drivers, aides, and support personnel. Wow, what a fantastic, diverse, talented group coming from varied vocations, working together as a team to transport the next generation of parents, celebrities, elected officials, judges, doctors, teachers, nurses, police and fire personnel, plumbers, carpenters, and authors.

Arnold thanks them all for their daily lighthearted fun, educational fellowship, support, and encouragement in his writings.

My web site. *One Day at a Time.* "https://arnoldkropp.com/"

e-mail me at "arkropp1234@gmail.com"